SHERLOCK HOLMES

THE AMERICAN YEARS

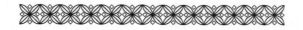

SHERLOCK HOLMES

THE AMERICAN YEARS

edited by

MICHAEL KURLAND

MINOTAUR BOOKS
NEW YORK

SHERLOCK HOLMES: THE HIDDEN YEARS. Copyright © 2010 by Michael Kurland. Foreword copyright © 2010 by Leslie S. Klinger. All rights reserved. Printed in the United States of America. For information, address St. Martin's Press, 175 Fifth Avenue, New York, N.Y. 10010.

"Inga Sigerson Weds" copyright © 2009 by Richard A. Lupoff; "My Silk Umbrella" copyright © 2009 by Darryl Brock; "The Old Senator" copyright © 2009 by Steve Hockensmith; "The American Adventure" copyright © 2009 by Gary Lovisi; "The Sacred White Elephant of Mandalay" copyright © 2009 by Michael Mallory; "The Curse of Edwin Booth" copyright © 2009 by Carole Buggé; "The Case of the Reluctant Assassin" copyright © 2009 by Peter Tremayne; "Cutting for Sign." Copyright © 2009 by Rhys Bowen; "The English Señor" copyright © 2009 by Marta Randall; "The Stagecoach Detective: A Tale of the Golden West" copyright © 2009 by Linda Robertson.

Book design by Jonathan Bennett

Library of Congress Cataloging-in-Publication Data

Sherlock Holmes : the American years / Michael Kurland, editor.—1st ed.
        p. cm.
    ISBN 978-0-312-37846-2
    1. Holmes, Sherlock (Fictitious character)—Fiction.   2. Private investigators—Fiction.   3. English—United States—Fiction.
4. Detective and mystery stories, English.   5. Detective and mystery stories, American.   I. Kurland, Michael.
    PR1309.H55S46 2010
    823'.087208—dc22

                                                            2009039821

First Edition: February 2010

10   9   8   7   6   5   4   3   2   1

To Love with Linda

CONTENTS

vii

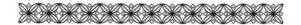

FOREWORD

Students of the life of Sherlock Holmes quickly discern that there are few certainties. We accept the convention of using the names "Sherlock Holmes" and "John H. Watson" for the Great Detective and the Good Doctor, knowing full well that the real identities of these individuals were concealed behind aliases with the connivance of Sir Arthur Conan Doyle. We can deduce that Holmes's year of birth was likely 1854, Watson's a few years earlier. We know with reasonable assurance that the partnership of the two commenced in 1881; that in 1891, Holmes disappeared at the Reichenbach Falls, only to return in 1894; and that in late 1903 or 1904, Holmes retired. In his twenty-three years of active practice (according to his own accounts), he handled well over 500 cases of note, although records of only 56 have been made public. Two postretirement cases are chronicled, one in 1907 or 1908, and one commencing in 1912 and ending on the eve of the Great War in 1914.

The world's first consulting detective has left us little information about his ancestry and youth. His parents were "country squires," his grandmother the sister of Vernet, the French artist. He has a brother, Mycroft, seven years his elder. He spent two years at college, then took rooms in Montague Street in London, where he endured months of inaction. He frequented the British Museum, handled small matters for largely unmemorable clients (although "The Musgrave Ritual," which belongs to this period, is surely one of Holmes's greatest triumphs, solving a disappearance/murder and restoring a long-lost national treasure in one stroke), and dreamed of greatness. One may long to know more of the Tarleton murders, Vamberry, the wine merchant, the old Russian woman, the singular affair of the aluminum crutch, or Ricoletti of the club foot and his abominable wife, but the annals of Dr. Watson are silent on these matters.

Of course the United States and Americans are frequently mentioned in the recorded tales of Holmes's life and work. One scholar counts fifteen cases involving American characters or scenes. American villains appear on English shores in *A Study in Scarlet*, "The Five Orange Pips," "The Dancing Men," "The Red Circle," "The Three Garridebs," and *The Valley of Fear*. Holmes is engaged by an American client in "Thor Bridge" and comes to the aid of two Americans in "The Noble Bachelor," much to the consternation of his English client. "It is always a joy to meet an American," Holmes exclaims in that case, "for I am one of those who believe that the folly of a monarch and the blundering of a minister in far-gone years will not prevent our children from being some day citizens of the same world-wide country under a flag which shall be a quartering of the Union Jack with the Stars and Stripes." In "The Dancing Men," probably in 1898, he claims at least one American friend, Wilson Hargreave of the New York Police Bureau, suggesting an earlier unreported visit to the United States. It is definite that Holmes visited America in 1912, in the guise of an Irish American named Altamont, beginning with a stay in Chicago, then moving to Buffalo.

Interest in the United States was nearly universal. During the Victorian era, the United States expanded remarkably, acquiring Texas, California, and other southwestern territories from Mexico, and the northwestern lands that became the states of Idaho, Washington, and Oregon from England. An enormous system of roads, canals, and railroads was developed, and German and Irish immigrants, as well as Chinese laborers, poured into the country before the Civil War. Then came the polarization of the country over the issue of slavery (abolished by England in 1833), and the resultant Civil War took a terrible toll on both sides. The South counted on English support, expecting that cotton exports would be the determining factor. England delayed, and although it recognized the Union and the Confederacy as belligerents, the hoped-for diplomatic recognition of the South as an independent nation never occurred.

Many English families, with relatives in both the North and the South, had mixed sympathies. Following the war, relations with the United States normalized, and as the American economy boomed, England benefited from transatlantic trade. In the decade following the war, eastern and southern European immigrants began to enter the United States in record numbers. Eastern cities continued to grow explosively, but many immigrants joined the great American westward migration. Travel to America, although tedious, became relatively commonplace. Arthur Conan Doyle, for example, made numerous trips to the United States to visit friends (such as Rudyard Kipling, who settled in Vermont), promote his books, and speak to the American public on a variety of topics. Yet it was still viewed as a sufficiently exotic land for Conan Doyle to see a market for three books reporting on his American visits, the last published in 1924.

Despite the intercourse between America and England, misconceptions and myths about America persisted in English minds and made their way into the Sherlockian canon. For example, *A Study in Scarlet* is a tale of evil Mormons forcing Lucy Ferrier into polygamy. This reflects the contemporary fears of white slavery, spread in W. Jarman's popular sensationalized memoir *U.S.A., Uncle Sam's Abcess; or, Hell upon Earth for U.S., Uncle Sam* (Exeter: privately printed, 1884) and the Rev. C. P. Lyford's sober-seeming *The Mormon Problem* (New York: Phillips & Hunt, 1886). The geography of *A Study in Scarlet* is distorted as well, with American mountains and deserts placed where none exist. "The Five Orange Pips" reflects a misunderstanding about the continued existence of the Ku Klux Klan in America as late as the 1890s. America is also viewed as a haven for criminals, including Abe Slaney ("The Dancing Men"), the quintessential Chicago gangster presaging Al Capone; counterfeiter "Killer" Evans ("The Three Garridebs"); and mafioso Giuseppe Gorgiano ("The Red Circle"), who relocates to America from Italy.

In Vincent Starrett's seminal collection of Holmesian essays, *221B: Studies in Sherlock Holmes* (New York: The Macmillan Company, 1940), Christopher Morley famously pondered, "Was Sherlock Holmes An American?" Although Morley's examination of the question is inconclusive, he suggests that Holmes's mother may have been American. Holmes may have traveled in the United States between college and Montague Street, Morley points out, and he would have been interested in the opening of Johns Hopkins University in Baltimore in 1876 and the Centennial Exposition in Philadelphia. Other scholars concur with the idea that Holmes visited America, although the trip "proven" is usually, by amazing coincidence, to the scholar's hometown! More seriously, in an article entitled "The Early American Holmes" (*Baker Street Journal* 29, no. 4 [Dec. 1979]), Wayne Melander gives an absorbing account of his suppositions with respect to a visit by Holmes to the United States in 1876. Melander contends that the trip extended as far west as Denver and included excursions to Baltimore, Philadelphia, Chicago, Kansas, Boston, and the Vermissa Valley (see *The Valley of Fear* for the location of the latter).

No less than Franklin Delano Roosevelt asserted that Holmes was an American. In a letter dated December 18, 1944, to Edgar W. Smith, then head of the Baker Street Irregulars, Roosevelt wrote:

On further study I am inclined to revise my former estimate that Holmes was a foundling. Actually he was born an American and brought up by his father or a foster father in the underground world, thus learning all the tricks of the trade in the highly developed American art of crime.

At an early age he felt the urge to do something for mankind. He was too well known in top circles in this country and, therefore, chose to operate in England. His attributes were primarily American, not English. I feel that further study of this postulant [sic] will bring good results to history.

On March 19, 1945, Roosevelt again wrote to Smith:

I am delighted to know that my postulate with reference to Holmes's criminal background in America brought such heated discussion and debate. It only goes to show that interest in the whole field of Sherlockiana is perennial.

Although new material has been published shedding light on many aspects of the life of Dr. Watson's friend Conan Doyle, much remains hidden about the histories of Watson and Holmes, their families, and their American connections. Until more definitive evidence is discovered, students of the Great Detective and the Good Doctor must be satisfied with speculations such as those in this collection.

—LESLIE S. KLINGER

INTRODUCTION

Once again I am called upon to justify our poor efforts to emulate the Master. In one sense no justification is possible; the four novels and fifty-six short stories have created a world much beloved by those of us forced to dwell in this one and visit Sherlock Holmes and his domain only through the pages of a book, or watch pale approximations of the stories acted out for us on the stage or screen. Some think that to expand on the works of the Master is to profane his memory.

But in another sense, no justification is necessary. Only four novels? A scant fifty-six short stories? How can we be expected to subsist on such meager fare? The canon must be expanded. There must be a never-ending supply of Holmes stories just as there must be air and water. And they must be the finest Holmes stories that we can create. Not the true quill of the Master perhaps, but still nourishing to a parched and hungry soul.

Every year or so it is incumbent upon us to entreat the finest authors of our time to dwell for a while in the land of Holmes and return and report their findings.

Gathered and transcribed within the pages of this book are the contents of a box crammed full of adventures. There are reminiscences and memoirs from across the vast expanse of North America: cities, villages, countryside, states, and territories; settled townships, badlands, and raw frontier. Whether written with pen and ink on foolscap and preserved in the vaults of the Chicago Stockman's Bank or laboriously printed on ironed butcher paper with the stub of a thick lead pencil and wrapped in oilcloth to lie unread in an ironbound wooden trunk full of rusted farrier's tools, they are alike in recording the American exploits of a young Englishman named Sherlock Holmes.

In his native United Kingdom, Holmes was to achieve a measure of fame as a successful consulting detective who pioneered many of the forensic techniques still in use today.

Exactly when Holmes came to the United States can only be conjectured, but it was certainly within a year or two of his leaving Midlothian University (or possibly, as some would have it, Cambridge—this is in dispute, as is whether he received a degree or merely left to pursue his own interests). And the precise date of his return to London is unknown, but it was certainly within a year of his meeting with Dr. John Watson, who was to become his erstwhile collaborator and amanuensis.

That he spent some years across the Atlantic is without doubt;

his knowledge of the language, manners, and customs of the United States doth witness it. So it was reasonable to assume that a search of the diaries and memoirs of the 1870s and early 1880s might reveal some glimpse of such a memorable man. And so it has proved.

If I may digress for a moment from the world we have created back into the world we gratefully leave behind:

Creating new stories set in the world of Sherlock Holmes is an entertaining exercise for a writer, albeit one full of peril. I am now torn between writing, "The entertainment is easy to understand, but the peril?" and, "The peril is easy to understand, but the entertainment?" Perhaps I should back off and take each separately.

The entertainment: The fiction writer is a creator of worlds. This sounds like unlimited freedom and power—deus ex scrivener, as it were. But unlike God—as far as we know, anyway—this creator has a gaggle of people looking over his shoulder and critiquing every stream and meadow, every fish and fisherman, every plot device and character trait. "That Bishop Lumley whom you introduce on page twelve," says the chubby little woman with the piercing eye and the wart in an unlikely place, "he don't behave like no bishop I've ever been acquainted with, and I've made a study of bishops." Or as the man with the twisted lip and the old leather flying helmet with oversized goggles points out, "You have Dick Dennison piloting a Ventrix autogyro to the North Pole in September, 1927, when everybody knows the Ventrix autogyro didn't go into production until April of 1929."

It's the "everybody knows" that the writer finds most aggravating. Why, I'll venture that if I were to stop the next twenty passersby outside the main entrance to Saks Fifth Avenue, not more than ten or twelve would know the exact date of the release of the Ventrix autogyro.

But Conan Doyle has done all the hard work of world creation for us. In the world of Sherlock Holmes, Doyle has given us a ready-made, fully earthed-out countryside full of bright objects and colorful people. As *The Economist* magazine put it in its October 4, 2007, issue,

> The Sherlock Holmes stories continue to exercise extraordinary power. The writing is never more than efficient but the setting remains perennial: the comfortable, carpeted, fire-lit Baker Street sitting room shared by Holmes and Watson, the paradoxically womblike world of a Victorian bachelor set above an anarchic underworld full of violence and immorality.

We may carp with the magazine's estimation of the writing, but all will, I think, agree to the extraordinary power that it continues to exercise.

—MICHAEL KURLAND
In the 112th Year of the Master
September 2008

SHERLOCK HOLMES

THE AMERICAN YEARS

Why did Sherlock Holmes first go to America? Why
else, Mr. Lupoff tells us, but to attend a wedding? But
complications ensued . . .

INGA SIGERSON WEDS
by
RICHARD A. LUPOFF

*A single loud report. Shards falling, colliding,
tumbling, red, green, purple, yellow, glittering,
reflecting flickering gaslight, crashing to the parquet,
all against the sounds of the orchestra playing, four
hundred voices in anthem raised . . .*

I was womaning the counter, waiting on
customers, accepting payments, and wrap-
ping baked goods, when the postman's bell
was heard in the courtyard. I refuse to refer to
myself as "manning" anything. Such usage de-
means the female gender and implies that I am
in some manner inferior to and subservient to
the male.

Mr. Tolliver leaned his bicycle against the
postern and, after taking a moment to sort
through his sack of mail, came forward and

1

handed me a small bundle of missives. He smiled through his gray mustache. "Mum all right, Miss Holmes?"

"She would rather work," I replied, "but the doctor insists that she rest during these final weeks. Once the new arrival is here, he says, she will have work enough to do."

"Aye. And Dad, what has he to say?"

"He is in league with Doctor Millward. As am I. Mother insists on cooking for us all, but at least she has consented to yield her duties in the shop."

"You take care of your mother, Miss Elisabeth. She is a dear lady."

I handed Mr. Tolliver a complimentary crumpet and he retrieved his bicycle and pedaled away.

The shop was busy this day. It was all that young Sherlock could do with mixing batters, keeping the ovens in order, and placing fresh goods on display. Dad alternated caring for Mum and napping so he would have his strength to tend to the heavy baking duties overnight. And of course Mycroft sat in the nook that passed for an office, working as he ever did over the bakery's books and studying formulas for new products.

Mycroft also handled our correspondence, such as it was, ordering supplies and paying bills. Ours was a reasonably successful family business, but a most demanding one in this busy section of London. Competition was keen as well.

By the time the shop was closed for the day, darkness had fallen over London and gas lamps were casting soft shadows outside our dwelling. Gas had also been installed indoors despite the grumbles of older residents who insisted that the new lighting was unnatural and unpleasant compared to traditional oil lamps.

Father had risen from a nap. Mum had made a rich soup of orange pumpkin and had roasted us a piece of beef with potatoes and greens. There were, of course, baked goods from our own shop. Mycroft was as usual prompt to reach his place at the family table. It seems that Mycroft spends his entire life in a stationary posture, save for his rare and unexplained "expeditions." At irregular intervals he will rise ponderously, don headpiece, take walking stick in hand, and disappear for an hour or a day.

On one occasion that I recall he was gone for an entire year. My parents had given him up for lost when he strode into the shop, greeted a number of our regular customers familiarly, and returned to his accustomed place without a word of explanation. My elder brother is as portly as my younger is scrawny; could they but exchange a few stone of avoirdupois I believe they would both be better off.

But this night it fell to me to summon Sherlock, who had retreated to his room to practice his fiddle playing.

I do not know which is more distressing, the sounds of scraping and screeching that he calls music or the unpleasant odors of the experiments he conducts from time to time. Why my parents had gifted me with this bothersome stringbean of a younger brother is beyond human comprehension. I hoped only that the next addition to the Holmes household would be a pleasanter companion. The Fates willing, a girl!

Of course, this pregnancy is a late and unanticipated one. Still, Mother gives every evidence of pleasure at the prospect of having another Holmes about the house. Father worries about expenses. Mycroft appears oblivious.

As for the execrable Sherlock, I suppose that he is accustomed to the privileges associated with being the youngest member of the family. When mention is made of the fact that he will lose this distinction, his expression resembles that of a person who has bitten into a fruit, thinking it an orange, only to discover that it is a lemon.

To be honest I will confess that my little brother is not entirely brainless. On one occasion I recall, he asked me to assist him in his so-called laboratory. He explained that he was developing a technique to transmit energy by means of sound waves. He had arranged an experiment in which he mounted a metallic object in a brace, surrounded by sound-absorbing batting. He stood nearby, scraping hideous sounds from his fiddle. He played notes higher and higher in pitch until, to my astonishment, the metal object began to vibrate violently.

"Now, sister, I want you to stand on the other side of the apparatus and match that note on your flute."

I complied, with similar results.

"And now," Sherlock proclaimed, "for the peas of resistance. We shall stand on either side of the apparatus and, upon my signal, both sound the keynote."

I did not correct his solecism but merely shook my head in exasperated compliance.

Sherlock placed his fiddle beneath his chin, laid bow across strings, and favored me with a nod and a wink. The grotesquerie of his bony visage thus distorted far exceeds my mean verbal powers. Indeed, the awfulness of it must be imagined rather than described.

We both sounded the crucial note, he upon his fiddle and I upon my flute. Within seconds the metal object began to vibrate violently, then to glow with red heat, and finally to liquefy and fall in a silvery rain upon the floor.

At this moment, Mother entered the room. "Elisabeth, Sherlock, dears, has either of you seen my precious silver spoon from Her Majesty's Silver Jubilee?"

Alas, there it lay, a formless puddle of molten metal upon the floor of Sherlock's laboratory.

The meal proceeded pleasantly enough, each family member in turn describing his or her day, as is our long-standing custom. Talk had turned to affairs of the world as they filtered into our household through the conversation of our customers when Mycroft announced that he had found a missive addressed to our parents in the day's arrivals.

Mycroft is by far the most brilliant man I have ever encountered. I cannot imagine him spending his life in our family bakery, but for the time being he performs invaluable service. He can also be the most exasperating of men, surpassing even the annoying Sherlock. Wiping his chin free of a drop of grease, he muttered and patted himself here and there, searching for the missive.

At last he found it. He drew it from an inner pocket and handed it to Father.

It was an envelope carefully addressed to *Mr. and Mrs. Reginald Beasley Holmes, Holmes Family Bakery, Old Romilly Street, London, England.* The stamps were of an unfamiliar hue and design, denominated in something called "cents." A return address in the city of New York in the United States of America provided the solution to the mystery of the odd stamps.

There followed an act that could have been performed as a

comic turn at a Cheapside music hall. Father patted himself on the chest, blinking all the time. "I cannot find my spectacles," he announced at last, handing the envelope to Mother.

Mother shook her head. "I must tend to my kitchen duties. Perhaps one of the children will read this letter to us all."

Somehow the duty fell to my lot. Somehow, it seems, in this household it always does.

I opened the envelope. It was unusually stiff and of a finer grade of paper than most ordinary correspondence. From the envelope I extracted a card. In embossed lettering it read as follows:

> MR. AND MRS. JORGEN SIGERSON
> REQUEST THE PLEASURE OF YOUR COMPANY
> AT THE WEDDING OF THEIR DAUGHTER,
> MISS INGA ELISABETH SIGERSON
> TO MR. JONATHAN VAN HOPKINS
> IN THE CITY OF NEW YORK
> ON SUNDAY, THE TWENTIETH OF JUNE, 1875

I had read the card aloud. Upon hearing it Mother clapped her hands. "My dear brother's child is to be married! It seems but yesterday that she was an infant."

"I knew it," I exclaimed. "I knew that a wonderful event was about to befall my cousin Inga."

"A joyous occasion indeed, but of course we shall send our regrets," Father stated. "The twentieth of June is mere weeks ahead. There is no way that Mum could possibly undertake an ocean voyage, nor would I, under the circumstances, even consider traveling to America while she remained at home."

Mother reached for the envelope and I extended it toward her. As I did so a slip of paper fell from it, barely missing the vegetable bowl and landing in front of the bony Sherlock. He snatched it up and refused to surrender it until Father commanded him to do so. Even so, I had to tug at the slip before he would release it.

The note was written in the familiar hand of my cousin. *Dearest Elisabeth,* I read silently, *My Jonathan is the most wonderful man. He is a skilled printer and editor and we plan to move to the West once married. Please, please, cousin dearest, do find a way to come to my wedding. I shall be heartbroken if you do not. I want you there as my maiden of honor.* The note was signed, in my cousin's customary manner, with a cartoon drawing of the two of us, our arms linked familiarly.

Although we have never met, I believe that we have had a psychic link throughout our lives. My mother and Inga's father were twins. Mother remained here in England while her brother emigrated to the United States, where he married an American woman, Miss Tanner. We two cousins were born on the same day and, as far as we have been able to determine, at the same moment. My cousin was named Inga Elisabeth and I was named Elisabeth Inga.

The invitation to my dear cousin's nuptials was confirmation of a knowledge that I had carried for weeks.

Gathering my courage, I announced that, in view of my parents' inability to do so, I would represent the English branch of the family at Inga's wedding.

Father shook his head. "Out of the question, Elisabeth. We shall obtain a suitable gift for your cousin and dispatch it by transatlantic transport. You will not travel to America, certainly not alone."

Mother fingered the strings that held her apron in place, tying and untying them in distress. "Inga is my brother's only child, Reginald. She is Elisabeth's only cousin. It would be sad if she could not be present on this occasion."

"No," Father insisted, "a young woman traveling alone under these conditions would be most improper."

"Perhaps her brother could go with her, then. Mycroft is a responsible young man. Surely he would be a suitable chaperone for Elisabeth, and I have no doubt that my brother and sister-in-law would welcome him into their home."

I will confess that even in this moment I found it amusing to think of Mycroft boarding a ship and traveling to America. Mycroft, whose daily movements seldom vary in route from bedroom to office, from office to dinner table, from dinner table to parlor, and from parlor to bedroom.

With a single word Mycroft rejected our mum's suggestion, nor was any further discussion useful.

Following dinner and coffee we retired to the parlor for our customary family hour. Some evenings Mother will read aloud from a popular work of fiction. Others, I play familiar airs on my flute, on occasion accompanied by Sherlock's execrable fiddle-scratching. Rarely, Mycroft deigns to entertain us with a recitation. He has committed to memory the complete *Dialogues* of Plato, Plutarch's *Lives*, the scientific works of the great Mr. Charles Darwin, and the Reverend Dodgson's *Alice's Adventures in Wonderland*, a favorite of my own.

But this evening there was but a single topic of conversation. It was the wedding of my cousin.

Mother and Father having ruled out their own presence at the nuptials, Father having forbidden me to travel alone, and My-

croft having refused to contemplate the journey, there
but one possible solution to the puzzle. I swallowed m,
proposed that Sherlock accompany me.

I half hoped that he would reject the idea. To be honest, I more
than half hoped as much. But my dear younger sibling took this
occasion to torment me by giving his assent. Of course he did so
with a demonstration of reluctance bordering upon martyrdom.

Mother seemed ready to give her blessing to this plan when
Father raised the question of money. Fare for two persons traveling from England to America and back would come to a substantial amount. It might be possible to run the bakeshop without
Sherlock and myself for a time. But there were simply not sufficient funds in the till to provide passage for Sherlock and myself.

Father rose from his chair and stated, "We will send a suitable
gift, perhaps a gravy boat or salver, to the happy couple."

"Not yet." Mycroft's words, spoken in the same rich voice that
he used for his learned recitations, brought Father to a halt.

"Not yet?" Father echoed.

"Sir," Mycroft replied, "do not be so quick to give up on our
family's being represented at the wedding. Remember that Inga is
my cousin as well, and I would wish to see my sister and her cousin
together on the happy day."

Father reached for his spectacles, unfolded their arms, and
placed them on his face to get a better look at his elder son. "I
trust you do not plan to rob a bank, Mycroft, an behalf of Elisabeth and Sherlock." Father seldom makes jokes, but I believe he
thought he had just done so.

"Please trust me, father. I make no promise, but I venture that
Elisabeth and Sherlock will be at Inga's wedding." He reached into

his vest pocket and extracted a turnip. After consulting it he shook his head. "Too late this evening," he said. "Give me twenty-four hours, Father. I ask no more."

The next morning found our bakeshop fully stocked as usual, the product of Father's industry. I took my place at the counter; Sherlock, his in the area reserved for handling goods; and Mycroft, at his desk, tending to his administrative duties. Nothing further was spoken of last night's family conference.

At noontime Mycroft rose, took hat and walking stick, and strode from the shop. He disappeared into the pedestrian traffic on Old Romilly Street. He did not appear again until the family had gathered at the dinner table.

Mother had roasted a chicken and small potatoes, and there were hot and cold greens and of course dinner rolls and butter. She assumed her place at the head of the table; Father, at the foot; Sherlock and I, facing each other across the cloth and dishes. Father had just taken carving implements in hand and reached for the brown-crusted bird when Mycroft entered the room. He rubbed his hands together, smiled at each family member in turn, and took his place.

He spoke at length during the meal, but his sole topic was the excellence of Mother's cooking and Father's baking. "We are not the possessors of financial wealth," he stated, "but we are a fortunate family to have a comfortable home, a successful business, one another's company, and the finest cuisine, in my humble judgment, in all the realm."

He may have exaggerated but none at the table chose to dispute him. Not even Sherlock.

Following our meal the family assembled in the parlor, at

which time Mycroft actually stood rather than sitting, and made his announcement.

"All is arranged," he said. "I met this afternoon with certain persons, and it is done."

"You have tickets for us?" Sherlock asked. His voice is less discordant and irritating than his playing upon the fiddle, but not much so.

"Tickets? No, Sherlock. You will not need tickets."

"Oh, a riddle, is it, Mycroft?" Sherlock ground his teeth audibly.

"If you wish, stripling. Or if you would rather, I will simply explain matters in words comprehensible even to so mean an intellect as yours."

"Please," I put in. "Mycroft, do not lower yourself to the child's level." Even though, I thought, the scrawny beanpole is already the tallest member of our household. "Just tell us what you have done."

"Very well." Mycroft did lower himself now into his chair. Mother had served coffee and sweet pastries from the shop and Mycroft placed an apricot confection upon his tongue. He chewed and swallowed with evident pleasure. "As you may know," he said, "the *Great Eastern* departs from London on the twenty-fourth of May. She crosses the Atlantic in eleven days, arriving in New York on the fourth of June. I believe that will provide ample time for you and Cousin Inga to work with Aunt Tanner upon the trousseau."

"Yes, yes, Mycroft. But how can Sherlock," I shuddered at the thought, "and I travel on the *Great Eastern* when we have no tickets and no money with which to buy them?"

"Dinner music and entertainment is provided aboard the *Great*

Eastern by the orchestra of Mr. Clement Ziegfried. You are an accomplished flautist, dear sister, while young Sherlock," and Mycroft shuddered visibly, "does on occasion manage to scrape a recognizable melody from his instrument. I have arranged for you both to become members of Mr. Ziegfried's orchestra. Passage and meals will be provided, and a modest stipend will be paid."

There was a silence in the room, broken at last by Mycroft himself, "There is one minor consideration, however."

Sherlock grinned.

I waited.

"A small cabin will be made available for your use, but you will have to share it. In the interest of propriety you will be expected to travel as brothers."

I moaned.

Sherlock laughed.

"Why not as sisters, then?" I asked.

Mycroft grinned. He has a most adorable, winning grin, has my elder brother. "A splendid thought, Elisabeth. Most amusing." He paused to sip at his coffee. "Alas, it is already arranged that the Holmes Brothers, Sherlock and Ellery, are to perform with the Ziegfried orchestra."

Eleven days, I thought. The voyage would take eleven days. That would mean eleven days of passing for a male and eleven nights of sharing a stuffy ship's cabin with the noisome Sherlock. I shuddered.

And so it was settled. I persuaded my good friend Clarissa Macdougald, who lives two houses from us and with whom I attended school for many years, to take my place in the shop. Her brother would substitute for Sherlock. Father approved the arrangement. I take pride in my skill with needle and scissors, learned from Mother. The two of us altered male clothing to fit my needs and to conceal my gender.

Sherlock and I arose long before dawn on the twenty-fourth of May and made our way by rail from London to Southampton. Once in that southerly city it would have been impossible not to find our destination.

To me the *Great Eastern* was a great and famous ship, but to Sherlock, of course, she provided an occasion to deliver a learned lecture.

"The *Great Eastern* is undoubtedly the greatest nautical achievement since Noah's ark." Oh, that nasal voice! "Her designer, the genius Isambard Kingdom Brunel, perished at an early age, doubtless due at least in part to the stress of his enterprise. The ship's bottom was ripped by a hitherto unknown underwater mountain on one of her early voyages, and only Mr. Brunel's brilliant design of a double hull saved her from sinking. She was designed to carry as many as four thousand passengers but, alas, has never been a commercial success."

Thank you, dear brother. I restrained myself from throttling the weedish know-it-all.

Even so, and despite my having seen many images of the nautical behemoth, my first sight of her took my breath.

Sherlock and I were clothed in similar garments. We wore tweed suiting, elasticized knee breeches and long stockings, plain cravats, caps on our heads, and brogans on our feet. I found the male garb uncomfortable and impractical. I yearned for a proper frock and flowered spring hat, even an outfit of blouse and jumper. But if this unpleasant costume was the price of my being accepted as Ellery rather than Elisabeth, it was a price I was willing to pay.

While Sherlock was in fact my junior by some five years, whiskers were already beginning to make themselves visible upon his upper lip, while my own countenance, of course, was unblemished by such excrescences. Thus, it had been decided that Sherlock Holmes would pass as the older of the musical siblings while Ellery Holmes would be the younger. A further insult to me, I felt.

Sherlock and I each carried a gripsack containing toiletries and changes of costume, and a separate case containing our respective musical instruments. We had been warned that the ship's orchestra were expected to appear in proper dinner costumes, and with Mother's deft management and my own long hours of sewing, Sherlock and I had so furnished ourselves. We made, I am sure, a picturesque pair.

We were met at the head of the *Great Eastern*'s gangplank by a ship's officer, who directed us to our quarters. There we met Mr. Clement Ziegfried, our maestro. He was a harried-looking person. He wore his dark hair quite long, as was, I believe, not uncommon among members of the musical fraternity, and a luxuriously drooping mustache that seemed too heavy for his small face and thin neck.

He smiled and shook Sherlock's hand and my own. He said, "Holmes Major and Minor, yes, welcome. I see you have brought your instruments with you. Good! You are of course unfamiliar with my orchestra's repertoire." He paused and consulted a turnip that he pulled from a brocade waistcoat. "We have rehearsal in twenty-two and one-third minutes in the grand salon. Place your belongings in your cabin and present yourselves promptly, if you please!" He spoke with a peculiar accent, obviously Continental.

He turned on his heel and strode away.

He was a very strange little man.

Because the *Great Eastern* was so huge—longer than two football fields laid end to end—and had space for so many passengers, room was not at a premium. I had expected to have to live in cramped quarters with dozens of smelly males. Instead, Sherlock and I were housed in a comfortable cabin of our own. Each of us would of course have a bunk of her or his own. And having lived for twenty-two years as Mycroft's younger sister and for seventeen as Sherlock's older, I was not shy about enduring the mundane presence of a male.

We deposited our gripsacks in our cabin, found a crewman on deck, and were directed to the grand salon. This was a spacious chamber, clearly a souvenir of the *Great Eastern*'s glory days. The walls were decorated with friezes of classical scenes. Satyrs and caryatids stood in classical poses, supporting the high, domed ceiling of the salon. That ceiling was of stained glass, a magnificent design that would have done proud any architectural showplace in the land.

The musicians assembled upon a small dais. Sherlock and I were apparently the last to arrive. Maestro Ziegfried stood before us, half hidden by a black music stand, turnip in hand. The watch buzzed audibly. Maestro silenced it by pressing a lever and returned it to his pocket. He surveyed the assembled musicians and nodded his satisfaction.

"Gentlemans," he announced, "we have three new musicians with us for this journey. I will introduce them to you." He lifted a baton and tapped it on his music stand.

"Mr. Holmes Major."

Sherlock bowed slightly, holding his fiddle at the height of his shoulder.

"Mr. Holmes Minor."

I emulated my brother, showing my flute to my fellow musicians.

"Mr. Albert Saxe."

A portly musician standing in the second row bowed slightly, holding a glittering cornet in the air. He wore a mustache and beard. How he could maneuver his cornet through that hirsute decoration was a puzzle to me.

Speaking in his oddly accented manner, Maestro Ziegfried announced that each of us would find sheet music before us. "You will take six minutes and twenty-three seconds to acquaint yourselves with the notes. Then we rehearse."

What an odd man he was! Still, one followed his directions. My parents had replied telegraphically to my Cousin Inga's wedding invitation, expressing their regrets. I had dispatched a personal message as well, telling Inga that Sherlock and I would arrive on the *Great Eastern* and that we anticipated the occasion of her nuptials with the greatest joy.

And, of course, that I would be happy, thrilled, honored, and delighted to participate as maiden of honor. I was certain, also, that her fiancé, Mr. Van Hopkins, would prove a splendid individual whom I would be pleased to accept as a cousin-in-law, were there such a position in the rules of family relationships.

With a blast of her whistle the *Great Eastern* pulled away from her dock and moved into the channel toward Portsmouth, rounded land, and headed in a westerly direction. By the time we passed Penzance the orchestra was warmed up. Maestro Ziegfried was a stern leader. There was no concertmaster; he coached and prodded the musicians himself, shaking his head with joy or anger or passion at each passage until his long hair flew around his head like the wings of an angry black bird.

When rehearsal ended, Maestro laid his baton upon his music stand and pulled his turnip from his pocket. He pressed a lever and the watch's engraved metal cover sprang open. He studied the watch's face, then nodded and announced, "Gentlemans, you will assemble here ready to perform in one hour, fifty-six minutes, and eleven seconds."

He jammed his watch in his pocket, turned on his heel, and took his departure.

Although I had stood for Mother to prepare my suit of dinner clothes, I had never worn this strange black-and-white costume for any extended period of time, nor attempted to perform even the meanest of tasks in it. How strange and uncomfortable it was, with its stiff wing collar, miniature black cravat, satin lapels, and itchy woolen trousers. What in the world is the matter with the male gender that they choose to get themselves up in such impractical outfits!

The *Great Eastern*'s passengers had already begun filtering into the grand salon when the orchestra assembled, strictly on time per our maestro's eccentric directions. I found myself seated beside another flautist, a gentleman with round, rose-colored cheeks. I could not tell whether he was prematurely white-haired, amazingly well-preserved, or perhaps was simply the possessor of Scandinavian blood and blond hair so pale as to resemble snow.

My brother Sherlock, I saw, was immersed in a section of violins, violas, and violoncellos. *Good*, I thought, *there are enough of*

17

them to drown him out. Or may he have the sense to hold his bow a fraction off the strings and avoid making any noise at all!

Waiters were serving beverages and food to the passengers. The *Great Eastern* is so huge that a virtual barnyard of cattle and poultry is kept on her deck, providing fresh provisions during her voyages.

Maestro had planned a program that mixed recent works by the great composers of Europe with popular tunes suitable for performance in the music halls of England and America. For some selections only parts of the orchestra were required to perform. Maestro called upon the string section for a new quartet by the young Bohemian musical folklorist Dvořák. This was followed by a full orchestral rendering of an American tune by Luke Schoolcraft. Clearly influenced by what I believe is called "darky music," this jolly piece, titled "Oh! Dat Watermelon!" was indeed a rouser.

Between numbers, when I was not busy shuffling the sheets upon my music stand, I scanned the tables of well-dressed diners. For all that the *Great Eastern* had proved a commercial failure as a passenger liner, she had been turned to a number of other uses with far greater success. That she had been refitted for her original purpose was a melancholy matter. Word was that she was to be sold and turned into some sort of commercial showboat, a floating advertisement hoarding, and moored in a resort town, perhaps Brighton or Torquay. This, the greatest ship in the world, which had been visited by Her Majesty herself, and by His Highness the Prince of Wales, on several occasions!

Still Captain Halpin and his officers maintained the appearance of grand sea sailors. Their uniforms were elaborate, as neatly tailored and sharply pressed as those of any naval officer, their buttons sparkling, their decorations looking like the awards granted to the victors of great marine engagements. The captain himself was a portly man, bearded and mustachioed in the manner made popular by the Prince of Wales. He was seen from time to time striding the *Great Eastern*'s deck in company of his wife and three lovely daughters and their great dog, Harold. How I envied those three girls their freedom to be themselves and not play-act at being boys!

The other diners in the salon were an assortment of well-dressed and well-groomed ladies and gentlemen. A few of them, I surmised, might be emigrants intending to make new lives for themselves in the Western Hemisphere. Canada and Newfoundland sounded attractive to me, especially the former. The United States with its red Indians, its many thousands of black former slaves, and its Irish gangs must be a dangerous and exciting nation. Soon enough I should find out for myself!

One man I noticed carrying on a particularly animated conversation. He chopped the air with hands in time to the music and jerked his head up and down in agreement with himself at every moment. He was apparently without companion, but was seated at a table with several couples who gave every appearance of discomfort with his expostulations. When he paused for breath he drew back his lips to reveal teeth that reflected the salon's gaslights, causing me to wonder if he had not had them drilled by the new electrical apparatus of Mr. George Green, and filled with a metal amalgam.

My attention was drawn back by the tapping of Maestro's baton upon his music stand. We were to perform a suite of flute duets by Wolfgang Mozart. The rosy-cheeked flautist at my side smiled encouragingly and we set out upon a sea of the loveliest melodies ever composed.

It pleases me to state that we started and ended together, the performance was not a disaster, and most of our listeners actually lowered their implements and hushed their conversations while we played. Maestro Ziegfried smiled and gestured to us to rise and take a bow at the conclusion of the suite, and the room applauded most generously. My fellow flautist shook my hand and gave me his name, Jenkins. He had, of course, already learned mine.

That night I sat up in my bunk composing a letter to Mother and Father. I would post it when the *Great Eastern* reached New York. I was bursting with happiness. I was in the world at large. I had performed musically to acclaim. Even the presence in the other bunk of the annoying Sherlock could not dampen my cheery spirits.

As the voyage proceeded, our days on shipboard were not unpleasant. Our meals were excellent in quality and generous in portion. When not rehearsing or performing, we musicians were free to roam the *Great Eastern*'s extensive decks, to borrow volumes from her library, even to explore her gigantic engine rooms. These were extensive. She carried volumes of coal with which to fire the huge boilers that powered her twin paddle wheels and her screw propeller. The ship even bore tall masts, but her sails were seldom unfurled.

From time to time I would encounter my friend Mr. Jenkins. We even shared a glass of wine on occasion, discussing the great ship, Maestro Ziegfried, and various members of the orchestra. Mr. Jenkins seemed to have tidbits of gossip, most of it not unpleasant, about each of our fellow musicians, with the exception of the cornetist, Mr. Saxe. When I asked if Mr. Jenkins knew anything of this gentleman he quickly changed the subject.

Our musical repertoire was varied, with each evening's performance including both orchestral and solo performances. Maestro Ziegfried proved an expert pianist, interpreting compositions by Joseph Haydn, Frédéric Chopin, and several of the Bachs, most notably my favorite, the underrated Carl Philipp Emanuel.

During Maestro's solo performances I was able to observe the audience. Time and again my attention was drawn to the man with the metallic teeth.

His behavior changed but little each evening. He would arrive at the appointed hour and take his place, the sole unaccompanied male sharing a table with three couples. At the beginning of the meal his mien was respectable, but he inevitably consumed copious alcoholic beverages. As he did so he became increasingly animated and, apparently, belligerent. On an evening near the end of our voyage, two days before we were due to make landfall at New York, his six companions rose in a body and departed from the table, leaving him to fume amidst empty bottles and soiled napkins.

Early the next afternoon Sherlock and I strolled on the *Great Eastern*'s deck. The starboard side was reserved for the ship's seagoing cattle ranch, as I had come to think of it. The port side was the promenade deck, so lengthy and broad that it had come to be known as Oxford Street.

Sherlock was speculating upon the availability of scientific instruments in the savage streets of New York. I listened patiently, or half listened, pretending a greater interest in his monologue that in truth I felt. The *Great Eastern* must have been breasting a warm Atlantic current, perhaps the fabled Gulf Stream, for the air was warm and so moist that it seemed almost to hold a heavy mist. Figures appeared and disappeared as they approached or distanced themselves in what I finally came to think of as a displaced London fog.

A well-dressed couple approached us. The gentleman bowed politely. "Mr. Holmes and Mr. Holmes, is it not?"

My brother and I conceded that we were indeed the Holmses.

"You are not really named Major and Minor, however?" Apparently these people were Americans, returning to their homeland. Had they been British they would have been familiar with the customary identification of elder and younger brothers.

"My name is Sherlock Holmes," my beanpolish sibling explained. "My little brother is Ellery."

"Boatwright. Bertram and Bonnie Boatwright, of Back Bay, Boston," the gentleman said.

There followed much tipping of hats and shaking of hands. I had to remind myself that I was one of three males in the presence of but one female. I would have liked to identify myself by my gender; I could imagine how Bonnie Boatwright must yearn for the companionship of a fellow woman, but I determined to maintain my disguise.

The Boatwrights invited Sherlock and myself to join them in their stroll along "Oxford Street." Both of these Bostonians were kind enough to compliment me at length upon my rendering of the Mozart flute duets with Mr. Jenkins. No mention was made of Sherlock's violin performances. It was well, I thought, that Maestro had not singled my brother out for any solo.

The prow of our great ship split the waters gracefully. A thin spray on occasion rose above the ship's railing, reminding one and all that we were not in truth at home, but many hundreds of miles from the nearest land.

At length our conversation, which had consisted for the most part of what is sometimes known as small talk, turned to the Boatwrights' dinner companion.

"It is a good thing that we are Americans," Mr. Boatwright announced. "That fellow—what is his name, darling?"

"Beaufort. John Gaunt Beaufort, or so he fancies himself."

"Thank you, my dear. Beaufort. Yes. As I was saying, it is a good thing that we are Americans, and your English politics with your dukes and princes and suchlike don't mean much to us."

"And why is that?" piped Sherlock in his irritating voice.

"Why, young fellow, this Beaufort pipsqueak seems to think he's the king of England."

There was a shocked silence.

Then Sherlock and I exclaimed simultaneously, "What?"

"Yes, that's what he says."

Mrs. Boatwright nodded agreement with her husband. "Yes, he claims to be the rightful king of England."

"Surely he means that as a jest," I put in.

"I think not. Have you seen his conduct? He became so agitated that he knocked over a bottle of wine and ruined my poor darling's frock."

"He is serious, then?"

"Very."

"Upon what does he base his claim?"

"He says that he is the legitimate heir of the Plantagenets. That each monarch since Henry the Seventh has been a usurper and a fraud. That upon the death of Richard the Third the crown should rightfully have passed to Margaret Pole, Eighth Countess of Salisbury. That her beheading in 1541 was an unforgivable crime and that only the recognition of this fellow, this—what was his name again, darling?"

"John Gaunt Beaufort," Bonnie Boatwright dutifully supplied.

"Yes, this Beaufort fellow claims that the crown is rightfully his and that once he is recognized as rightful monarch of Great Britain and her empire, he will take the name Richard the Fourth." He shook his head in disbelief. "Kept muttering about houses. Do you think he's a real estate developer?"

Bonnie Boatwright said, "No, dear."

Bertram Boatwright ignored her. "Don't know why a real estate developer would complain about kings, eh, Holmeses?"

I felt compelled at this point to give the poor overlooked Mrs. Boatwright her due respect. Calling upon the authority of my faux manhood I interrupted. "Mrs. Boatwright, what was your point regarding real estate?"

Her gratitude at even this small recognition of her worth was manifest. She said, "Beaufort's reference to houses was directed at the dynasties of the British monarchy. At least, such was my education, even in Boston. He mutters about the Angevins, the Lancasters, and the Yorks. He is quite opposed to those who came later. To the Tudors, the Stuarts, and the Hanovers."

Bertram Boatwright said, "Quite right, my dear, quite right." Then he shook his head. "My manners, my manners," he exclaimed, patting himself on the chest. From an inner pocket he drew an elaborate cigar case of yellow metal and green stone—I guessed, gold and jade—and opened it. "Will you have a smoke, Mr. Holmes? I prefer the torpedo myself, but you may prefer a smaller and milder product. Perhaps this panatela."

He extended the cigar case to Sherlock and to me. It contained a variety of smokes. We each extracted a cigar from it.

"The finest Havana," Bertram Boatwright announced. He drew a packet of lucifers from another pocket and struck one to light.

Sherlock bit the tip from his panatela, bent toward the flaring lucifer that Mr. Boatwright held for him, and drew a flame into the cigar.

This, I thought, will be the supreme test of my masquerade. I imitated my brother and managed to get the cigar going. I had expected to collapse upon the deck in a coughing fit, but instead I found the flavor of the smoke not unpleasant.

We soon parted from the Boatwrights and returned to our cabin. Sherlock sat upon his bunk, making arcane computations in a notebook while I penned another missive to our parents in London.

I made it my business to arrive early that evening at the grand salon. Our voyage was drawing to a close. We expected to make land on the second day following, and a peculiar air had descended upon the ship. It was an amalgam of melancholy and excitement; the former, I suppose, deriving from the imminent dissolution of the little aquatic community that had formed on our ship; the latter, as women and men thought of the homes that awaited them or of the adventures they might experience in an exotic and undeveloped nation.

Mr. Beaufort made his entrance as usual. I thought that the night before he had drunk almost to the point of unconsciousness, and I rather expected him either to miss tonight's meal altogether or to arrive shaken and contrite. No such symptoms, however, were visible.

The Boatwrights of Boston and the other couples who shared their table arrived in turn. They exchanged greetings with one another and even ventured a polite nod to the self-styled monarch who favored them with his company.

Maestro's selections of music for the evening were subdued for the most part, although the performance climaxed with a chamber arrangement of Peter Illich Tchaikovsky's *Pathétique* symphony—not the lugubrious piece that its title implied, but in fact a rousing composition.

Mr. Beaufort—I still thought of him as "the man with the metal teeth"—managed to avoid any outbursts, and retired even before coffee and brandy had been served.

The next day was to be our last full day at sea. The *Great Eastern* had performed admirably and I was saddened to think that this would, in all likelihood, be her last oceanic crossing save one. That, of course, would be her return journey to England. I stayed up late composing another missive to my parents, then lay in my bunk, imagining the wedding to which I was journeying.

If I was in truth to serve as my cousin's maiden of honor I would of course need a suitable costume. Knowing my Cousin Inga from a lifetime of correspondence, I was aware that she and I are of similar proportions. Inga would have served as a draper's model in my stead, and a lovely gown would await me. Of this I was certain.

I passed from wakefulness into the land of sleep without being aware of the transition, and dreamed pleasantly of the experiences that lay ahead of me in the company of the wonderful cousin whom I had known all my life through the medium of correspondence but whom I had yet to meet *in propria persona.*

The morning of our planned arrival in New York dawned hot, with a brilliant sun, a lovely blue sky, and even a great white albatross circling above our ship, the traditional symbol of good luck to all nautical enterprises. I breakfasted in company of my brother and several other members of Maestro Ziegfried's ensemble.

It was, perhaps, an indication of nervousness on my part that I was able to take only a cup of fragrant Indian tea and a half slice of toast lightly coated with orange marmalade for my meal. Need I describe the quantity of scrambled eggs, the slab of broiled ham, the potatoes and biscuits with warm honey that Sherlock consumed, accompanied by a series of cups of rich, steaming hot chocolate *mit Schlagsahne.*

My traveling gear was small and so I was able to pack everything into my gripsack quickly enough. I spent the next hour strolling on Oxford Street. At one point I had the misfortune to cross paths with the terrible Mr. Beaufort. Clearly, he recognized me, certainly because of my appearance each night with the *Great Eastern*'s orchestra.

He tipped his hat and offered me one of his metallic smiles. In that moment I felt a chill as I feared that he had penetrated my disguise and recognized me as a member of the female sex. Should this be the case, a most unpleasant conversation might all too easily ensue.

But he merely bowed slightly as we passed, walking in opposite directions. "Mr. Holmes," he hissed.

"Mr. Beaufort," I returned.

I walked on as rapidly as I could, hoping that he would not turn and follow me. Fortunately, he did not.

The hours seemed to drag that day, and yet I was taken by surprise when I realized that night had fallen and it was time for me to repair to my cabin and don my evening outfit.

As is traditional, the last evening of the voyage was observed with a gala dinner. Captain Halpin and his officers were present, each wearing a splendid uniform. The captain's lady and their three daughters were gowned in the most charming fashion. The passengers who filled the salon were similarly garbed in their finest.

The meal featured cold lobster, roasted squab, lamb chops with fresh mint sauce, baby peas, and carven potatoes. Champagne flowed freely. The repast ended with coffee and brandy and portions of trifle.

Toasts were offered to Her Majesty, to Mr. Disraeli, to the American president, Mr. Grant, and to Vice President Wilson. A special toast was offered, to the memory of the great Isambard Kingdom Brunel. A resolution of thanks to Captain Halpin and his officers and crew was proposed and adopted by acclamation by the passengers.

Maestro Ziegfried's orchestra performed a series of numbers alternately stirring and amusing. Our American passengers were clearly pleased to hear the jaunty "Carve Dat Possum," by Messers. Lucas and Hershey. A great cheer greeted the *Water Music* of George Frideric Handel. The maestro had chosen to end the program with a salute to the United States of America and to our own blessed isle. Alas, the Americans have no accepted national song. Many of them, I have been led to understand, enjoy singing a set of lyrics by the poet F. S. Key, set to the tune of "The Anacreontic

Song," but those very words are deemed to be anti-British. Instead, there was an instrumental rendering of their so-called "Battle Hymn of the Republic," Mrs. Howe's reminder of their own Civil War.

At last came the great moment, the orchestral rendering of our own glorious anthem. For this occasion the maestro elected to add his pianistic talents to those of the rest of the orchestra, whilst conducting, as the expression has it, "from the keyboard." All present, further, were invited to give voice to the patriotic words.

Throughout the evening I had cast an occasional glance at Mr. John Gaunt Beaufort, the man of the gleaming teeth. He had drunk a great deal, this much was obvious, but to this moment had behaved himself in an acceptable manner.

All rose.

Maestro raised his hand in signal and the first notes rang out stirringly.

I could see Mr. Beaufort leave his party and stumble drunkenly toward the front of the grand salon. He climbed clumsily onto the vacant conductor's podium and began to wave his arms as if conducting the orchestra.

Four hundred voices rang out:

> *God save our gracious Queen,*
> *Long live our noble Queen,*
> *God save the Queen.*

Mr. Beaufort reached inside his evening jacket and drew an old-style, two-barreled pistol. He pointed it upward and fired. *There was a single loud report. Shards falling, colliding, tumbling, red, green, purple, yellow, glittering, reflecting flickering gaslight, crashing to the parquet, all against the sounds of the orchestra playing, four hundred voices in anthem raised . . .*

Half the orchestra ceased playing. Half the room ceased to sing. The other half, perhaps unaware of what had transpired, perhaps too stunned by the suddenness of Beaufort's act, played or sang on:

> *Send her victorious,*
> *Happy and glorious,*
> *Long to reign over us.*

Beaufort lowered his pistol, pointed it before him. He shouted, "*Deo, regi, patriæ!* Bow before your rightful monarch, Richard the Fourth, Rex Anglorum!"

Mr. Albert Saxe, our cornetist, stood forward, his massive chest expanded like the breast of a pouter pigeon. He spread his arms, the salon's lights glinting from his silver cornet. "Shoot," he commanded, "if you must. I am your target. Aim well!"

But the delay had given Sherlock time to raise his fiddle and bow, and I, my flute. At his grotesque signal I breathed into the air-hole of my instrument, and he drew his bow across the strings of his. The two sounds converged upon Mr. John Gaunt Beaufort. He screamed in pain and tossed his pistol into the air. As it crashed to the parquet he tumbled from the conductor's dais and rolled on the floor, clutching his jaw in agony as smoke rose from his mouth.

In moments he had been seized by crewmen and hustled from the room to end the voyage in irons, as he well deserved.

An hour later I sat upon my bunk, trembling. I had decided to end my charade a day early and was garbed in comfortable female costume. Sherlock had doffed his performer's finery and donned his tweeds.

There was a knock upon the door. Sherlock rose and answered it. Standing in the doorway we beheld the rose-cheeked Mr. Jenkins, my fellow flautist. He nodded, smiling, and said, "Mr. Holmes, and"—he hesitated but for a moment—"may I presume, Miss Holmes. Would you be so kind as to accompany me."

Mr. Jenkins offered no explanation, but there was something in his manner that persuaded my brother and myself to comply.

Without further speech we accompanied Mr. Jenkins to a suite guarded by two armed ship's officers. At Mr. Jenkins's knock the door was opened and we were ushered into the presence of two bearded, portly gentlemen. They were remarkably similar in appearance. One was Captain Robert Halpin, master of the *Great Eastern*. The other was Mr. Albert Saxe, the talented cornetist.

Mr. Jenkins addressed the latter personage. "Your Highness, may I present Mr. Sherlock Holmes and Miss Holmes."

"Elisabeth, please," I corrected.

Sherlock and I were in the presence of none other than the prince of Wales, the heir apparent to Victoria's throne. Sharing the suite were Mrs. Halpin and the three Misses Halpin, and a woman whom I recognized as a leading beauty of London stage.

The prince shook Sherlock's hand heartily, then reached and embraced me in his great arms. I was bereft of words.

"How can I thank you both," His Highness said. "My equerry, whom you know as Mr. Jenkins, was kind enough to tell me who you both are. Your courage and resourcefulness are quite amazing."

SHERLOCK HOLMES: THE AMERICAN YEARS

Not one to hold his tongue at a moment like this, Sherlock asked, "Who was that drunken fool, Your Highness?"

The prince uttered half a laugh, then became more serious. "Apparently he is a Plantagenet pretender."

"A criminal!" Sherlock expostulated.

"Perhaps," said the prince. "Or more likely a madman. It is not for me to say. Everything will be sorted out in due course, I am certain." He issued a sigh. "I wish I could reward you both suitably but at the moment I am traveling incognito and any ceremony would be unsuitable. But when we return to England, rest assured, you shall hear from me."

Sherlock scrabbled in his tweed jacket for pencil and paper. "Here, Your Highness, I'll give you the address."

The prince waved his hand. "No need. No need, young man. I well know your older brother."

MY SILK UMBRELLA
A Mark Twain Story
by

DARRYL BROCK

London

18 May 1897

My home country's so thick with sleuth-hounds nowadays that a body can scarcely open a door without some would-be Pinkerton chucklehead—the breed *must* be chuckleheaded to keep spawning like it does—tumbling out from a rigged-up hideaway. *This* budding sleuth was cut from his own design, though, and since I first encountered him, on this very day, twenty-two years ago, he's become notorious, puffed everywhere like a dime-show marvel, a walking, snorting, detecting legend if you judge from what all the puffers claim, especially Dr. John H. Watson, that tireless puffing engine.

This balloon of a detective specimen—Holmes—was still an unknown article then, and as a result of our bumping together, an encounter I equate to a plague of aching molars, I somehow became one of his first paying customers. Not that I volunteered for this unlikely distinction, or paid him directly, or even *knew* about it till nearly the end of the dismal episode.

18 May 1875....

My recollections of that day are nigh perfect. It was on a spring Tuesday with nature all tailored out in her new clothes that fortune threw us together at a base ball match in Hartford, where I'd moved my family the previous year. Dawn had delivered a coating of frost, and the morning papers prophesied rain showers—not that it was easy locating weather tables amongst the columns bristling with tawdry revelations from Grant's latest corruptions—but my darling Livy managed the task, and she insisted I pack along my prize umbrella.

I had no worthy excuse for dodging work, except that the promise of today's match was too potent. Our hometown nine, the Dark Blues, had shaken off last year's bottom finish and somehow catapulted themselves to a 12-0 start in the National Association. Coming to face them were Boston's champ Red Stockings, themselves with a gaudy record of 16-0. The matchup was a sockdologer—and I was burning to see it.

I set out along lanes canopied by cherry and peach blossoms. Golden shafts pierced the cloud-swollen sky, and I felt the air heating up. The day was built for pleasure, aburst with vital juices, redolent of sweet lost loves. Though my umbrella was superfluous, I twirled it to add dash to the figure I cut in my linen duster and new green spectacles. I nodded to passersby who greeted me, most invoking my nom de plume, calling, "Top of the morning, Mark."

Downtown was tarted up like a parlor-house madam, festooned with bunting and overhung with whip pennants and banners proclaiming the Dark Blues' invincibility. I joined the crowds on Willys Avenue heading toward the ball grounds near Dutch Point. At several places I had a prickly sensation of being watched—more than usual, that is—and took the trouble to ensure that my billfold resided in its customary pocket. Once I spun around but found nothing to provoke suspicion beyond some noisy street-boys, whose numbers grew thick outside the grounds. I watched a squad of fly-cops try to keep young invaders from gaining entry over, under, or between the planks of the tall fence. They also labored to pacify those who had not purchased tickets ahead, and now found the sales office closed.

"But it's a glorified game of rounders!" I heard a decidedly English voice protest, and turned to see a tall, thin young man in London-cut tweeds engaged in negotiations with a shady-looking hawker. "Why the deuce is your price so dear?"

He would prove to be Holmes.

Inside the gates I moved to the Pavilion, a new covered stand built for the occasion. Tickets for it, originally 75 cents, had been trading upwards of five dollars, and the dullest saphead could see that these seats had been criminally oversold. Now they were fairly bursting. With gyrations to make a snake blush, I worked my way to my allotted space near the top. From there I could see the 50-cent "bleaching boards" that flanked the Pavilion likewise packed with raw humanity, and beyond them, behind ropes stretching around the outfields, men standing shoulder to shoulder in the 25-cent "bullpens." With a seasoned eye I put the throng at ten thousand—surely the biggest ever for a New England sporting event.

Who was pocketing all the gate money?

As if galvanized by the thought, my lefthand neighbor, an over-stuffed banker by the name of Ashcroft, introduced himself—or rather, *re*introduced himself, claiming we'd met the previous winter—and presented his prune-faced wife, seated on his other side. She gave me a sour stare through an ivory lorgnette, her general demeanor lifted from a chromo ad for galloping dyspepsia. Noting Ashcroft's jowls quivering with each utterance, I *did* recall him: I'd been trapped with him in a club room and sorely regretted the experience. Politically, he regarded high tariffs as proofs of God's workings. Personally, he was a raging dullard.

The red-legged Bostons trotted on to the field; then came the Hartfords, natty in their navy blues. I leaned back contentedly, ignited a cigar (only my fifth of the day; I was heeding Livy's dictum to cut back), and inhaled an elixir of tobacco, pungent mustard, and the Pavilion's fresh-planed pine. The grass of the outfield radiated emerald green. Vendors' cries—*Soda water here! New York ginger snaps!*—sounded in my ears.

How perfect, I thought, tracking wrens in the rafters above me, how *dear* to be playing hooky like the rawest of schoolboys. Like my own Tom Sawyer, whose adventures I'd nearly finished writing—*should be at home working on it that very instant*—but instead of squeezing out Tom's story up in my study, here I was free, *being* Tom. Work on the boy's novel had thrust me deep into the territory of my own youth. Today's sporting affair, though conducted by top-paid professionals, quickened memories of town-ball games in Hannibal played in drowsy summer afternoons during those too-brief years before my pap died and I'd apprenticed as a type-setter, my boyhood effectively ended.

"Sorry," a voice said, as I was jostled and felt a hand briefly grip my shoulder. I looked up and saw the Englishman I'd glimpsed outside the gate; he must have accommodated the hawker. Squeezing in on my right side, he looked no more cheerful than I about the tight circumstances. "Yours?" With a bony finger he indicated the umbrella, perched at the bench's rear edge. I thanked him and moved it to safety.

Staring idly at urchins trying to scale the weathered boards bordering the grounds, I felt an idea stirring. The whitewashing scene wherein Tom is enslaved for the day by his Aunt Polly lacked ginger; infernally *tame* it was, and its repair had eluded me. In exchange for entry to only a single match, couldn't those street-boys be employed to paint the fence in a matter of hours? The lads would gladly pour out their labor; any wretch missing out would expire of mortification! The answer came: *Aunt Polly's fence=30 yards long and 9 feet high. Day's end=three bright coats.* With a chortle I pulled a stub pencil from my pocket and scribbled on the back of a scorecard the capper line that popped into mind: *If he hadn't run out of whitewash, he would have bankrupted every boy in the village.* Delighted, I tucked the scorecard in my vest pocket and told myself to come to the ball grounds more often. Here, by glory, useful work could actually get *done.*

As I'd made my notes, I grew aware of the young Englishman's curious scrutiny. Now I took a moment to study *him.* I put him at perhaps fifteen years my junior, in his early to mid-twenties. His clothes were of current European mode, but somewhat ill-pressed. Up close he was even thinner than he'd first appeared.

The pallor of his sharp features—sufficiently hatchet-edged to rival my own hawkish visage—suggested that he spent his days indoors. His slate-gray eyes seemed to hold a languid alertness, hinting at a keen brain but perhaps one not easily aroused.

I was fixing to introduce myself when the crowd commenced to holler, "Play BALL!"

"Is there some cause for delay?" asked the gaunt Englishman.

Cheers broke out when the first Dark Blue batter swatted the ball over second base, but died out when a Boston infielder raced back to make a prize catch.

Ashcroft opined gloomily that if the Bostons were to field like *that*, our gooses were halfway in the oven.

"Your batsman spooned it up," the Englishman countered crisply. "He'd do better with a horizontal stroke."

"Goose-egged in the first inning!" groaned Ashcroft after the next two Dark Blues went out.

"*Innings*," said the Englishman.

During the visitors' ups, daisy-cutters between basemen, a mis-played sky-ball, and a carnival of base running gave Boston a three-run lead.

"Pool-sellers favor them at 100 to 70," Ashcroft said with ponderous condescension, as if financiers alone appreciated such knotty matters. "At this rate—"

"Am I to understand," the Englishman interjected, "that wagering is openly conducted?"

Color spread over Ashcroft's neck and jowls. "Do you find fault with it, sir?"

"To the extent that it encourages the criminal classes," the Englishman replied, "I do indeed."

"*Here?*" Ashcroft said. "What criminal classes?"

"Pray look for yourself." The Englishman pointed to boys scurrying from the Pavilion to the bullpen. Casting furtive sideways glances, they performed some nature of exchange with one of the men there, all done very quickly, then moved back toward the Pavilion. "It requires small shrewdness to theorize that they are pickpockets fencing ill-gotten gains." His tone said that only a simpleton would dispute it. "Gambling can do naught but increase such misdeeds."

Ashcroft had no ready answer. He and his wife had been rendered tight-faced and straight-backed by the stranger's impertinence. I watched the boys for a minute; it was impossible to say they were guilty—or innocent, either. They did cast wary glances all about them, but in their place I would too if I lacked an entry ticket. Not wishing matters to grow hotter between my seatmates, I stuck out my hand. "Clemens is the name."

"Holmes." He clasped my hand briefly, then gave me a start by asking for a sample of ash from my cigar. "For my collection," he explained. "This will make 102 separate varieties of tobacco ash." With that he produced a vial and scraped in the desired amount, leaving me to ruminate: *Ash collection?* I was fond of boasting I'd run afoul of every human type during my piloting days, but this Holmes might be a new one for *my* collection.

A dismal succession of Dark Blues went down in order, leaving Ashcroft in a humor to tear his hair, and prompting Holmes to say, "If they attempted cover-drives instead of deep midwickets, they could exploit those gaps." He pointed to right field. "Incidentally," he added, "is it a sixer if the ball flies over the fence?"

While I pondered these mysteries Ashcroft muttered something about sending foreigners home. I confess that I too was growing a bit irked. It rankled to have my boyhood game called up for judgment and found lacking.

"Terrible luck!" Ashcroft moaned when yet another Boston hit safely.

"Tut," countered Holmes. "Luck is a product of strategy. Your club shows extremely little of it, attacking or defending."

Before Ashcroft could summon an answer, our attention was caught by voices rising from the field.

"What is it?" asked Holmes.

"A rhubarb," I said, as if any saphead would know *that*, and was pleased at his puzzlement.

"This certainly isn't cricket," said Holmes at length.

That was too much for Ashcroft, who launched a salvo of elevated rhetoric I wouldn't have thought was in him. "You are correct, young man!" he snapped. "Base ball is *not* cricket. It is rough and contentious, a *democratic* pastime. It requires team play, yes, but individual pluck as well. It is rambunctious in its vitality. It is not weighed down with ornament and tradition, like your cricket, but alive and vital! It is *our* game! A true portrait, sir, of our national character!"

Well, I considered it first-rank argumentation, and was generally inclined to agree. But Ashcroft was mistaken if he thought he'd scored a home shot. Holmes took his time in sizing up his opponent with those gray eyes of his, and said, "Your 'true portrait' would be a good deal more absorbing with elements of *success*, not mere energy." He added a *sir*, not outrightly mocking but in the neighborhood. "And your national game"—he gestured toward the diamond, where the dispute continued—"would be improved by more perfect agreement on its rules."

The crowd's agitation exploded into hisses, groans, and boos.

Holmes made a palms-up gesture. *See?*

The Dark Blue captain had produced a rule book. "Read it out loud!" some wag yelled; another added, "Pass it around and let us *all* read!" A swell with waxed mustachios and a collapsible top hat turned and pointed at me. "Let Mark read it! Don't HE know somethin' about words?" It stirred a laugh, and heads turned my way.

"You are well known." Holmes's leaden eyes regarded me.

"I'm a bit of a scribbler," I admitted modestly.

"That man indicated as much," he said dryly. "The stains on your fingers and cuff previously suggested it to me as well."

I looked down. Sure enough, faded black smudges were visible on my right cuff, and my fingers bore traces of ink from notebook entries that morning.

"I might also surmise that you began as a compositor," said Holmes.

I have to admit that it rattled me. How'd he know of my years setting type?

"A trifling observation," he said, noting my puzzlement. "Those calluses on your left thumb—old, strongly ridged—could result from nothing else but gripping heavy composition boxes."

I nodded, thinking his feat clever but not *so* remarkable. On the other hand, nobody else had ever done it.

"Incidentally," he went on, "what are your accents? I can distinguish forty-two London dialects, but I confess that many here in America are as yet beyond me—and yours, Mr. Clemens, is unique."

I told him it was Missouri at base, Pike County with some Negro dialects tossed in, and overlayered with a sight of traveling. "And

41

yours, Holmes?" I considered myself no slouch either when it came to sounding out a man's pedigree. "I reckon you've spent some years in rural territory yourself—more so than in London." I waited while he smiled with an attitude of *not bad*, then I sprang my capper on him. "Reared in Lincolnshire, were you? Among the squire set?"

"Why, close by!" he exclaimed. "Near the Yorkshire Wolds, actually, not far distant from Lincolnshire. Splendid work, Clemens!" He couldn't have looked more surprised if I was a monkey busting out with gospel hymns. He confessed that he'd spent his growing-up years in the countryside before attending university, which he'd recently left. Before returning to settle in London, he'd taken it on himself to see parts of the world. "You enjoyed your time in England, you said?"

The crowd's rumble became anticipatory as the players took up their positions again.

"I had the bulliest stays." I held back from saying I was hailed in London as "the greatest satirist since Swift and Voltaire" but I did recount how I'd come by my fine umbrella: namely, when a London reporter asked why I carried a cheap cotton model, I said it was the only kind Englishmen wouldn't steal—and it was reprinted to nationwide laughter. At a banquet soon after, I was presented the one I carried today.

"My brother sent me a clipping at university about it," Holmes said. "I imagine it's in my files, under *Americans*."

It didn't sound wholly complimentary but I let it pass, and presented the umbrella for his inspection. After a short look he handed it back.

"Well, what do you think of it?"

"Perfectly satisfactory."

Hurrying boys pushed through the cramped space behind us. Knots of them had sped here and there throughout the afternoon, taking new routes to evade pursuing cops. I realized that I'd had a feeling of being watched again, and made sure my billfold was safe. Holmes stared after the boys in apparent fascination.

"Satisfactory?" I said with some spirit. "Not a champion model?"

Seeing that he'd ruffled my feathers, he extended a bony hand for the umbrella and gave it closer inspection. "Manufactured by James Smith & Sons. Very good. They are top-drawer in the field. I'm familiar with their New Oxford Street establishment— indeed, I made a study there." He hefted the umbrella. "Fine silk canopy. Not the alpaca or oiled canvas used by lesser makers." His hand slid along the shank and extended the spreaders. "But note here, Clemens, how these steel ribs are of recent Hanway design. Not handcrafted whalebone." He touched a fingernail to one of the amber tips with a dismissive click, closed the spreaders, and extended the handle to me. "Pistol grip design, most common now, this one plain bone. No carved ivory or ebony figure as on Smith & Son's finest models."

I boiled with resentment. The nerve of him branding my trophy second-class!

"Sorry," he said, "but you *did* ask." Then, as if to divert me, he brought up the topic of the new typing machines and inquired if I knew of them. My spirits lifting a notch, I told him I *owned* one, and that with regular practice on two fingers, I'd boosted myself up to beating out "The Boy Stood on the Burning Deck" at eighteen words per minute. Why was he interested?

His thick brows drew together. "I perceive possibilities in their use for crime."

I looked at him; his face was perfectly sober and intent. Was the man gripped by a lunatic vision of wrongdoers everywhere? "You said you 'made a study' at Smith & Sons," I reminded him. "Toward what enterprise? Do you plan to enter the umbrella trade?"

That brought a short laugh. "Not quite."

"What, then?"

"Consulting detective."

I chewed on it for some moments, letting it hang there in the air between us, thinking how he'd wanted to know my home dialect, been eager to get my cigar's ashes. "You scout out clues?" I said. "In *advance* of crimes?" I'd read Poe, of course, even enjoyed some of him, and extracted an inkling of how the deductive mind could work. Not that I had one. Nor, as far as I could fathom, did the tin-plated heroes in illustrated magazines packed with farfetched feats of city detectives, railway detectives, prairie detectives—maybe even squirrel detectives. Seeing how rich a vein it was, I'd done some prospecting on a detective yarn of my own, calling back my old jumping-frog character and titling the yarn *Simon Wheeler, Amateur Detective.* Tried it as a story and a play, and in each it was a thundering failure, which did not render my heart fonder of the detective species.

"How can one recognize and evaluate clues without systematic knowledge?" Holmes was saying. "And so, yes, a crucial element might be discovered in the intricacies of umbrella manufacture." He waggled a forefinger like a schoolmaster. "And in subjects more arcane."

A Boston hitter rocketed a ball into center field, and the **4** vanished from Boston's peg on the green telegraphic board beyond the left-field foul flag, and was replaced by a 5. Beneath it, Hartford's 0 hung sadly.

"Do you truly believe," I said, "that crimes can be solved mainly by applying brainpower?"

"I *know* it," he said with exasperating smugness. "When all other possibilities are eliminated through a process of keenly applied deduction, the one remaining must be the truth, however improbable." It came rattling out of him like a Sunday-school verse.

"*Could* be the truth," I amended. "Could be pure bunkum, too. Look, if this was as simple as you claim, Holmes, every sneak thief and back-alley mugger would be snared in no time—the big crooks, too. Didn't the Pinkertons take a stab at the James gang just this past winter?" I jabbed a finger of my own, sure I had him in a corner. "The papers told how they tossed a bomb into his mother's house and blew off her hand—but they didn't get Jesse."

"I would venture to remind you that it all depends on who is employing the deduction," he said. "Police may *see* but as a general rule they fail to *observe*. And deduction in criminal cases is rarely simple—in fact, it is complex and demanding, but ultimately it is reliable." He'd gotten excited—at least for him—his nostrils flaring slightly the way I'd once seen an Arabian gelding's. "As Flaubert said, *'L'homme c'est rien—l'oeuvre c'est tout.'* The man is nothing, the work is everything."

"Yes, he wrote that to George Sand." I felt considerable glee at Holmes's look of startlement. Now I set myself to trump him to flinders, having taken to memory some of Flaubert's phrases reprinted in London papers. "I believe it goes, *'L'homme* **N'EST** *rien, l'oeuvre tout.'*

45

His frown at my drawling French deepened into a scowl as he perceived my accuracy. Again I'd astonished him, and this time he was not charmed. It didn't take a gallery of scholars to see that he wasn't used to being corrected—and that it suited him about like a case of hives.

"But despite *you* being a mere man," I added for spice, "I gather you claim this singular capacity to observe and deduce?"

"Now you fault me for immodesty," he retorted. "I do not count modesty as a virtue. To the logician things should be seen exactly as they are. To underestimate oneself is as much a departure from truth as to exaggerate one's powers."

"In my line of wares," I told him, "truth is often a laughing matter, and things rarely form up in anything like a straight logical chain. Won't you agree that life doesn't operate according to—"

Fittingly, *my* logic was lost in an explosion of yells as the Hartfords finally began to show their mettle. A Dark Blue hitter smacked a long ball that sent two runners home. Rattled, the Boston pitcher called time-out.

"See?" I pointed to the diamond and proceeded to float new arguments. Who'd have predicted—putting cash on logical deduction alone—this shift in fortune? Wasn't the human lot precisely like that? At the mercy of unforeseen, chaotic bursts of providence? How could uncovering "clues" restore order when there wasn't any particular order to *start* with?

He gave me a withering look, as if my propositions were too ignorant to consider. Undaunted, I piled on more. Detective stories had tidy resolutions, I pointed out, everything tucked in and pat by the end. But this sporting contest testified as much as anything to the folly of taking such an approach seriously. How could "logic" be applied in order to produce "truth" here, when most of base ball defied rationality?

Holmes nodded absently, and I judged he was showing the white flag. His eyes had an introspective, faraway look. He seemed intent not on me nor on the players but on the movements of itinerant boys. Was his single-rut mind fixated on child outlaws?

Several batters later, a Hartford sailed the ball into an apple tree just inside the fence, knotting the score, 5–5. How we loved it! "Hurrah!" I yelled, subordinating my rebel-yell instincts to local custom. "HooRAW!" Ashcroft whooped and pounded my shoulder with beefy fists. I couldn't recollect such giddy spirits at a ball game since that long-distant day when Tom Blankenship, my model for Huck Finn, clubbed a ball through Widow Holliday's kitchen window and smashed a bottle of painkiller on her sill. The widow's old yellow cat, Last Judgment, sampled the stuff and lit out to settle grudges with every dog in the township.

It was when we settled again after the last out and I checked for the umbrella that I found it was gone. I bounced up again as if visited by angry hornets and stared at the plank bench.

"Something amiss?" said Ashcroft.

"Could you get up?"

"Beg pardon?"

I tried to peer around his outsized hips. "Obliged if you'd elevate yourself."

When he grudgingly accommodated me, I concluded with sinking heart that the umbrella had not lodged beneath him but must be somewhere in the gloom below the Pavilion benches. How to descend? I surveyed the slope below me: jammed so tight that no hint of aisles existed. Getting to the bottom would be pure hell—and perish all thought of returning.

Holmes tapped my elbow. "I should inform you that one of those ragged lads barged through here again just as you were involved in—" he paused to find the word—"cheering."

"The boy snatched it?"

"I would have stopped him in that event," Holmes said. "I turned and saw him after he had pushed past. His hands were empty but I would stake a guinea that he dislodged the umbrella—and I'd venture it was deliberately done."

I labored to puzzle through it. The Englishman's penchant for finding felons at every turn was suspect, but he'd offered a plausible explanation for the umbrella's disappearance. If true, the culprit himself or a confederate would be retrieving it at that moment. What to do?

"Here, could you…" I dropped to my knees and folded nearly double, working to get my face beneath the bench. Ashcroft grumbled and resisted my efforts with his ham-pillar legs. Seated beyond him, Mrs. Ashcroft, whose panniered dress took up a good three feet of bench and fit her like a circus tent—she couldn't have gone within eight points of the wind in it—began expressing herself in a voice carrying all the honeyed sweetness of a #6 bastard file. Added note: *Give Aunt Polly steel spectacles, nigh-crippling rheumatism, and pinch her face!*

From a torturous corkscrew position I was rewarded with a narrow view of the Pavilion's netherworld. Squinting down at bottles, cartons, tins, wrappers and heaven knew what, I thought I saw a handle protruding from a heap of sodden newspapers half-submerged in a puddle. Rainwater, I hoped, not tobacco juice—

or worse. When my eyes adjusted, I saw that it was only a broken-off buggy whip.

I angled my head sidewise for a wider view. Two dark figures lurked near the frontward seats. They lacked collars and proper headwear—the smaller of the two wore a jockey's cap of the style affected by ballists—and they lacked tickets, certainly. I might have admired their pluck if not for the fact of the smaller one clutching my umbrella under his arm.

"You, boys!" I called.

They spun and stared at my sidewise countenance suspended below the benches like a holiday bulb. The smaller looked down guiltily at the umbrella, spoke urgently to the other, tugged the jockey cap lower to hide his face, and poised for flight.

"I ain't the cops," I said assuringly. "Come over here."

The larger boy yanked the umbrella from the smaller, and with wary steps moved a bit closer.

"That's mine," I told him. "I'm obliged to you for rescuing it." We studied each other. I could see that he was a gap-toothed, freckled, filthy specimen. After some deliberation, he seemed to reach a conclusion about me and thumbed his grubby nose.

"Why, pickle your devilish hide!" It came out louder than I'd intended, and I heard Mrs. Ashcroft's shocked gasp. With a motion worthy of Barnum's India Rubber Man, I reached back and fished out my billfold, jostling Ashcroft as I did so. "Boys?" My voice oozing with trust, I said, "That umbrella you're holding? It's a paying proposition to bring it up to me."

"How much?"

I waved a banknote. "A whole dollar."

"Let's see yer bill," the boy said. "Drop it down."

"*That* old cat won't fight." I snorted at his impertinence. "Hurry that umbrella up here, and the cash is yours."

The boy consulted his smaller mate, who shook his head; they seemed to argue. "How can we know you'll pay?" demanded the bigger one, twisting the umbrella in his grimy hands. The other hung back, his face shadowed.

"I *told* you so."

"*He sed, she sed*," the boy intoned mockingly.

"It's a keepsake!" I took a long breath to quell my anger. "It's valuable—but only to me. I'm square as a dry-goods box. I'll give you the money."

The boy cocked his head. "Give it first."

"Confound your polysyllabled insolence!" Recoiling, I knocked my head against the edge of the bench and swore with some spirit.

"If you PLEASE!" said Ashcroft.

I stared down at my umbrella, seeing in my mind's eye the applauding London banqueters, and with a regretful sigh I released the dollar. Curious how the stripling scoundrel, with his ragged knickers, *looked* enough like my boyhood Hannibal companions—indeed, something in his thin frame, reddish hair, and freckled features whispered to my memory of myself—but this boy conducted his affairs like the meanest Yankee trader. The bill fell into his clutching hand and disappeared.

By now others were bending down to see the cause of the disturbance. Holmes's sharp features appeared a row above me. Had he moved to find room or was he standing on his hands? The boys conferred below, the smaller tugging at the umbrella before once more retreating to the shadows.

"What's the trouble?" I demanded.

A burst of booing lifted away most of the other faces.

"Come up here and collect your cash!"

The boy lifted his head. "Want more," he said succinctly.

"Why, you sawed-off, infernal, perfidious—" My endearments were overwhelmed by new eruptions of crowd displeasure. "It's too many for me," I told him when it subsided, "as to exactly *why* you crave a prince's ransom to return my possession!"

" 'Cuz of the risk," he answered. "We get pinched for no tickets, they'll clap us in the calaboose." At this the smaller boy made another failing try at the umbrella.

"Okay, two dollars." The sawed-off swindler would see me reduced to bacon and beans. I reached for my billfold but did not find another small-denomination bill. "Holmes!" I said, knowing better than to ask that money-squeezing ass Ashcroft, "lend me a dollar—I'll beat this game yet!" I reached to him above the bench.

"You're taking the wrong approach," he said, but handed over a silver coin.

I lowered myself again as loudest-yet boos crescendoed from the crowd. The smaller boy saw his chance and this time succeeded in carrying off the umbrella toward the front of the Pavilion, where between spectators' rumps I caught a glimpse of crimson socks flashing across home plate.

"Come back!" I yelled, arms flailing.

"Do you *mind*?" Ashcroft's knee jabbed painfully into my ribs.

"We'd *all* like to *enjoy* the proceedings," Mrs. Ashcroft chimed in, her acid tones eating into my brain.

I reared up in protest, knocked my cranium in the same spot, and shouted, "Enjoy 'em over the part of me you see best!" This provoked sounds of outrage and what felt like the point of a bayonet jabbing my rear. I pivoted, thumping my poor head yet head again, and saw them glaring down at me, Mrs. Ashcroft's parasol held aloft in a two-handed grip. *I'll take their measure*, I vowed grimly, and looked down again to find that the bigger boy had recovered the umbrella.

"Here," I told him, and tossed the other dollar.

He scarcely looked at it, but peered around anxiously for his companion. "I want five."

"*WHAT IN THUNDER FOR?*" As I felt the parasol's retaliatory probe, a red haze clouded my wits. My feet kicked backward and met solid resistance, simultaneously barking my shins and bringing a rain of blows.

"That's *enough* from you!" said Ashcroft, and took hold of my ankles.

"Hands off!" I struggled furiously to free myself. "I'll flay you both!" Then, seeing the boy turn and flee: "NOT YOU!" He headed for the Pavilion's opposite side, umbrella in hand. "WAIT!" Clutching the bench, I saw him disappear outside into the crowd. "COME BACK! *STOP!*" I broke away from Ashcroft, thrust myself upright, and plunged down the Pavilion stand, angry spectators boiling in my wake. "Vile ruffian!" yelped a woman whose picture hat I'd knocked askew.

By the time I thumped to the ground, there remained no trace of the boys. The constabulary, of course, had witnessed nothing. While the game careened through its late innings I lingered dumbly at the foot of the Pavilion, bitter lamentations—*Carry me home to die*, and the like—coursing though my head. I vaguely knew that Boston was winning, but my fancy was caught by the rhubarbs that continued to erupt, the nines swarming on the diamond in shifting formations of reds and blues. Hadn't old-time jousting tournaments provoked such contentious pageantry? In my daybooks I'd jotted notes for a tale of medieval England wherein a modern-day Yankee introduces lethal firearms and other nineteenth-century delights, provoking a cataclysmic conflict. Should I have him bring base ball to the Round Table? Divide the knights into rival nines? The notion of wiping them out at a single stroke captivated me, and I pulled out pencil and scorecard again. When I ceased jotting and looked up again, the teams had departed the field and the Pavilion was nearly empty. I stood amid a litter of spoiled food and oilpaper wrappers and cigar stumps and rumpled scorecards and newspapers, my heart low. But then, gradually, a miracle of restorative vision began to emerge. Soon I was busy hatching a scheme to regain my pilfered prize.

Its design had rounded into satisfying shape when movement behind the benches caught my eye. Somebody was there. The thieving brats? With pounding heart I circled around to peer beneath the structure, and caught out Holmes crouched beside a murky puddle, studying the ground through a magnifying lens. "Scouting for catfish?" I inquired with some sharpness.

He took a final look, straightened slowly, and regarded me with granite eyes; I reckoned he knew I'd lost tolerance for him. Fact was, by then I resented most *everything* about him: his cultured syllables, his youth, his height, his uniformly black hair (my own auburn thatch had flared gray at the temples), his haughty English demeanor, and—this most of all—his blasted cocksureness. The whole of it had me on the spit and was giving me a slow roast.

"You disdain my methods," he said. "Pray allow me to test *your*

53

observations. *Exempli gratia*, can you describe the youngsters' shoes?"

Of course that boosted my temperature a few more degrees. Their *shoes?* No images came to mind. "It was dim down here," I protested, "with all them bodies blocking out the light above." Holmes appraised me coolly and waited. "I fancy they wore common brogans."

He shook his head pityingly, as if I'd confirmed myself as a fraud. "Very well, then, what colors were their *shirts?*"

I tried to think but my wits were a hopeless muddle. "Well, not store clothes, that much I can swear. The larger boy's shirt was— why, gray, I fancy."

"Olive," he corrected, looking smug as pie.

"And your purpose?" I inquired. "To boost yourself at blind man's bluff?"

"Rather to boost, as you put it, my ability to observe." The tartness of his tone matched mine.

"Observe *what?*" I pointed to the spot he'd inspected. "Even if you managed to find the little bastards' footprints—what then?"

"Precisely the question," he replied. "*What then?* By observing where they stood, I was able to make certain discoveries."

I let out a harumph. "Such as?"

His thin lips tightened in a way that suggested a pleased reptile angling in on his next meal. "For the present, it would be untimely to disclose my methods and findings." He was lording it up to beat the band. "To do so might bear ill on this case."

"*Case?*" I echoed hotly. "There's no *case* here! You've hitched your nag to the wrong rig if you think I'll invest in your fool notions to get my umbrella back."

"It might profit you to learn," he said in icy tones. "that I intend to proffer my services only when *asked*."

"Well, I ain't asked," I snapped back. "And I've got *methods* of my own. Tell you what: I'll wager for any stakes you want that I'll have my umbrella back within three days—and I'll manage it without leaving my house to search! Who in perdition needs some self-labeled detective?"

That riled him! We locked glares, our visages honed to keenest edge. Passersby might have thought us a pair of roosters squared off.

"Assuming that you actually have one," Holmes said, "what is your plan?"

I considered not telling him, but pride impelled me to sketch it out.

Instead of folding his cards at the genius of my scheme, he said bluntly, "I doubt it will work."

"Put up or shut up," I shot back.

He rubbed his long chin and considered. "I'd thought to proceed with my journey," he said at length, "but I'll agree to stay your three days—more if needed—and succeed where you fail."

We shook on it. His hand was larger but pure natural cussedness rendered me his equal. I asked what he intended.

"Observation and deduction," he replied, as if naming the pillars of the universe. "And employing methods some might consider…" His eyes followed a lingering knot of street urchins clambering over the fence. "…irregular."

I held back from guffawing. "And the stakes?"

"When this matter concludes," he said. "you will know them quite well." He turned then and moved away with long, brisk, forward-leaning strides, his lean face coursing through the air like a clipper's prow.

In truth, I didn't expect to lay eyes on him again.

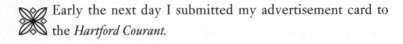 Early the next day I submitted my advertisement card to the *Hartford Courant.*

> TWO HUNDRED AND FIVE DOLLARS REWARD - *At the great base ball match on Tuesday, while I was engaged in hur-rahing, two boys walked off with an English-made brown silk UMBRELLA belonging to me and forgot to bring it back. I will pay $5 for the return of that umbrella in good condition to my house on Farmington Avenue. I do not want the boys (in an active state) but will pay two hundred dollars for their remains.*
>
> SAMUEL L. CLEMENS

The first day, I waited in tip-top spirits. The second, in some-what tempered spirits. The third, in a rising fever of agitation. The fourth and fifth, in a swamp of despair. It was on the evening of the sixth day that a ragged hostler showed up beneath my porte-cochère claiming he possessed vital information for me alone.

I took his inventory in a lightning glance: a horse-handler's typical slouch hat that shaded heavy brows, a bulbous nose, and muttonchop whiskers; his head tilted at a cunning slant, his pos-ture slightly stooped, one leg twisted. *From the war,* I thought.

"I'm not a-beggin', Guv'nor," he said. "Just an honest stable-man." His voice was gravelly and laced with phlegm, some of which he loosed just then on the fine imported gravel of my drive-way. His accents were vaguely Bowery but notes in them rang false. "Are you *this* Clemens?" he demanded, and from his coat pro-duced a soiled square of newspaper with my notice.

"Do you have the umbrella?" I countered, stepping closer to peer beneath his brim.

He took half a step backward.

"Well, Holmes, do you have it?"

It hit like a thunderbolt, crumpling him. He straightened slowly and tugged from his face the stage brows and sideburns and putty nose, chagrin like that of an errant schoolboy written on his revealed features. He pointed to his ill-kempt clothes, and when he spoke his voice gradually took on some of its customary assurance. "A close camaraderie exists among the hostlers," he said. "Become one of them and you can learn much of what there is to know. As a groom out of work, I discovered precisely what I sought."

"Then you *do* have the umbrella!" A rush of feeling came over me. "Grand news!"

"I have this for you," he said, and withdrew another paper, this one fresh and neatly folded.

LETTER OF CONSENT
The undersigned hereby agrees to:
- Purchase in London a Smith & Sons city umbrella model #17b, with violetwood toucan-head handle and silver lapband (£25.50 + packaging & freighting) at his earliest convenience.

- Upon its delivery, place an advert in the *Courant.* specifying a precise hour of a particular day.

- On that day, at the given time, deposit the umbrella in a suitable wrapper beneath the Ball Grounds' Grand Stand.

- Depart the premises and return no sooner than two hours afterward to that location, there to find and repossess his original umbrella.

(Signed) _____ This ___ day of _____ , 1875

I read it a second time, and then a third, my elation wilting away as my eyes strained to draw sense from of it. "Violetwood? Toucanhead?" I breathed. "Twenty-five pounds? That's nearly one hundred dollars! 'Repossess his original umbrella'...." I shook my head like a dog clearing water. "Is this your notion of a prank?"

"On the contrary," he replied, "it was *your* attempt at a prank that produced this. Once certain facts were in my possession, it became obvious that your published threat was not taken as levity by members of the underclasses—in particular, the girl who coveted your umbrella. And, more significantly, her father."

"Girl?" I echoed. "*What* girl! Are you addled?"

"Not in the least," he said calmly. "Had you heeded me after the ball match, you would have learned that I collected interesting details from a partial imprint of the smaller child's shoe. Three details, to be precise. First, I observed that the sole of this cheap McKay-type shoe was narrower than those made for most boys. Second, a perceptible arc in a pattern of nail holes suggested a girl's tapered rather than squared toe. Third, slightly greater depth at the rear suggested the possibility of a raised heel—again characteristic of manufacture for females."

Holmes paused to let these revelations sink in.

"Then, too, there was the manner in which she grasped the umbrella. You didn't note it, of course." His tone said that I was the *beau ideal* of dunces. "Yet it was instantly evident to me that, although frightened, she wanted something even more than she wanted to flee—she wanted *that umbrella.* That is why her brother—yes, he was the other one—tried to sway her with more money. But she was adamant. Your silk umbrella, as it happens, was the most wondrous prize ever to grace her vision—it might have come from *The Arabian Nights*—and once she held it, she naturally wanted it for herself. In the end, her brother—and later her father—indulged her."

Holmes favored me with his reptilian smile.

"By the time your notice appeared, I knew that I needed to enter the world of those rapscallion children. Who could provide the necessary information? The horse-handlers, of course, and so they did—as the result of hours and dollars I spent in the public houses where they congregate. Pursuing their instructions, I managed to ingratiate myself, again for a price, with a gang of young swells, who, once they believed that I would not bring the police, let me know that I was correct: the umbrella had been pinched by a brother-sister pair. Yet more cash outlays led me to their grimy domicile."

"If it's your squandered money you want," I told him, "nobody asked you—"

"I do not seek recompense," he interjected. "I was about to say that I arrived at that place barely in time to dissuade the outraged father—he'd been told of your notice—from his threats to give you a thrashing."

I didn't like the sound of *that* and so I ignored it. "If not for money," I demanded, "why'd you keep mixing into this?"

"The true reason?" He showed a hint of the snaky smile, but his eyes held some other expression I couldn't decipher. "To escape the humdrum of everyday life, I suppose," he said slowly. "These little problems help me to do so."

My umbrella a *little* problem! The soaring arrogance of the

man! "Once you knew the thieves' whereabouts," I said with a de-
fiant stare, "why didn't you go to the police?"

"And do their work for them?" he said. "The chief reason is that I
gave my word as a gentleman that I would not. Then, too, there was
the matter of your challenge." He nodded at the paper in my hand.
"Fortunately for your sake, I was able to recite *ex tempore* from Smith
& Son's list of umbrella models—and render several sketches. The
girl was fascinated, but loath to surrender the one in her possession,
naturally enough. At length we negotiated the result you hold—I
must say, the toucan-headed model *is* quite elegant—and the girl
was able to prevail upon her father to accept the arrangement. And
so here we are. Mystery solved. Umbrella within your reach."

I stared at the consent note. "It'll take a month to get the new
one here from London," I said sourly. "That price is unadulter-
ated banditry!"

"It's only half what you offered to pay for the thieves' remains."

"That was in fun! Nobody'd think I meant it!"

"Some did," he replied. "And were quite serious in their resentment. Thieves' honor, you might call it." He gave the paper a
significant glance.

"Suffering Moses," I muttered in my misery, and called for a
pen to sign his wretched note.

"If it happens that you prefer the new umbrella," he said, "you
could renege on your promise and not make the exchange."

I'd thought of it myself. The urchin would still have her ill-
gotten prize and I'd have a grander model. But Holmes's tone
said that no *gentleman* would stoop so low. Besides that, I wanted
my old model back. And I'd never particularly fancied toucans.

* * *

Well, it all happened twenty-two years ago, and this day, May 18, is the anniversary of that cursed ball match. Worn out from the rigors of our recent travels, I am back with my family in comfortable London for a while. This morning, after penning the final words of *Following the Equator*, I set out from our rooms near Tedford Square to celebrate its completion with a walk along the Chelsea Embankment. Gazing at the fog-streaked Thames put me in a reflective mood. I recalled how the umbrella episode played out just as Holmes had arranged it. When I left the new model under the Pavilion, I worried that I'd come back to find no replacement, and I'd be out both umbrellas. But my old one was waiting for me in prime condition, and with relief I hugged it to my breast. Once my indignation finally smoldered out, I was able to dine out on the story in handsome style—still do, to tell the truth.

All these years later, that old bumbershoot remains a practical and sentimental friend. It reminds me of my first conquering visits here and also of those tender years in Hartford, when my family was yet young. Here in its home climate it receives regular exercise, and nobody comments except to praise its mature vintage.

Several times in recent weeks, while strolling near Regent's Park, I've caught sight of Holmes through the side-windows of passing broughams. We're considerably older in appearance, but we recognize each other. I tilt the umbrella in his direction, and he smiles that thin smile, pounding it home that he hasn't forgotten.

The ironic capper is that just this month Smith & Sons introduced a new deluxe model at the top of their line of men's umbrellas. Its teak handle features an elegantly carved bust of Sherlock Holmes. While I'm not a likely candidate for purchase, I have to confess that the notion of crimping Holmes's head in my fist has a powerful pull. As for the likeness itself—I've studied it with some care through the show window at Smith & Sons—it rouses one like military music on parade! So grand and noble is it in conception that it puts to shame the general class of carved profiles! Why, in its royalty it rivals Caesar! Only the most ill-natured of ninnies would fail to agree that it's a thrilling wonder—and even more dizzying in its wonderment when compared to the original thing.

And once in Hartford, who knows in what further adventures Sherlock Holmes might find himself embroiled? Steve Hockensmith has a good idea.

THE OLD SENATOR
by
STEVE HOCKENSMITH

My dear Brother:
First off, let me quickly allay your fears. This missive does not convey the news you've no doubt been expecting and dreading. The Old Senator still lives. Feebly, painfully, at times bitterly and one could almost say begrudgingly, yet he lives.

I also do not write to ask you to leave Washington. Father insists that his infirmity should not impinge upon your preparations for assuming office. Much as you might like to be at his side, know this: The Old Senator takes great comfort in knowing that the Young Congressman is, even now, following in his footsteps.

He takes comfort, too, in constant company and the good wishes of his many admirers. Mr. Hayes and Mr. Grant have sent their regards, as have a host of old friends from the Party, and the Hookers and the Beechers (among others) are regular visitors. And, of course, one of us—Mother or Eliza or I—is ever at the Old Senator's side.

But alas, so to, I must tell you, is pain. Father struggles to breathe. He cannot take more than two steps unaided. He has no appetite, and what food he does eat only brings on new agonies and indignities. He is always tired yet cannot sleep deeply.

It is not enough to say that our father is dying. Much of him, I think, is already dead. It just remains for the last of the body to give way and for the spirit to depart.

Yet while that spirit remains—and fervently it does so, undiminished even as its vessel decays—the Old Senator is with us. And in that I have found a blessing, much as I wish to see his misery brought to an end. Even in the grip of his final sufferings, you see, our father has put an older hurt behind him.

It is that I wish to tell you about—as well as (to descend into the realm of the petty) a shocking bit of gossip that will no doubt filter out to you through the Hartwells or the Gilberts or some other old Hartford stalwarts. Take their whisperings with a grain of salt, Brother, and take my account as gold, for the Old Senator and I were *there*.

Naturally, you might expect Father not to be anywhere other than his bed, of late. But last week he was feeling well enough to take the air around the grounds twice a day, and Dr. Dahlinger came to think that an outing might actually do the Old Senator some good.

"Nothing taxing, mind," the doctor told us after finishing his near-daily call on Father. "A picnic. A speech. A recital. Something that will get him out of the house for a few hours without wearying him too much. It's not exercise the man needs. It's engagement."

"I know just the thing," Eliza announced, and she scurried out of the room.

She returned shortly with a creased copy of the *Courant* folded open to an article I recognized ... because I'd read it with great interest almost four weeks before. The headline: EMINENT THESPIAN TO TAKE HARTFORD STAGE.

After conquering New York City with his powerful Orsino, it seemed, the Russian/English actor Michael Sasanoff was taking his production of *Twelfth Night* on tour across the States. The second stop would be Hartford's own National Theater. The performance was now mere days away.

"Father should go," Eliza said. "Willy can take him."

As you've said so often, our sly sister would surely have made the best politician of us all, so cunning and tenacious can she be in pursuit of an objective—such as, for instance, total reconciliation between the Old Senator and his Prodigal Son.

Mother read the notice with the air of barely concealed disdain that has ever characterized our parents' attitude toward "the boards."

"Eliza," she said gravely when she was done, and she looked up at *me*, "I think it's a splendid idea."

And so it was decided that I should squire the Old Senator, of all people, to an evening of theater. (How quickly Father acquiesced to this plan I do not know, for Mother took it to him in the privacy of their chambers. Needless to say, it was a *fait accompli* before it was even broached, as the only member of the family who can match Eliza's powers of persuasion is the woman who birthed her.)

More than once, in the days that followed, I thanked God that it was *Twelfth Night* and not *Lear* the venerable Mr. Sasanoff would be gracing us with. A comedy the Old Senator and I could endure together. A tragedy about ungrateful, intractable children, on the other hand, would be sheer torture.

We hadn't spoken of the rift between us in months, Father and I. I had resigned from my troupe, come back to Hartford to be with him, and that seemed to suffice. Whether I would again pursue acting at the first opportunity—"first opportunity" meaning, of course, upon his death—he did not ask. Perhaps, I thought, he was afraid to hear my answer. Perhaps, I thought, he lacked the strength to debate it. Perhaps, I thought (incorrectly, I now know), he simply no longer cared.

If Father had asked about my plans, my reply might have surprised him, for I had no plans upon leaving Louisville, beyond being at his side. After I'd spent years fruitlessly trying to convince our parents that my future was in The Theater, The Theater seemed to be telling me I was quite mistaken: The only "future" I had with it, it appeared, was as an obscure utility player in stock companies in the hinterlands. Whether I would ever act again, I did not know.

The evening of the performance, Jason drove us to the theater in the rockaway. It would've warmed your heart to see the Old Senator come down the front steps, dressed again in a fresh-pressed black suit and not a wrinkled and stained nightgown. His movements were slow and stiff but steady, and his head stayed high even in those few moments he did stumble. Though Eliza and I hovered beside him, he even managed to pull himself up into the coach unaided.

Once I was settled in next to him, Father gave the roof two raps with his walking stick, and off we went. I looked out to see Eliza smiling at us as the rockaway rolled off—while Mother was wearing an expression so dour you'd have thought Father and I had just boarded the ferry across the River Styx.

We said little on the way to the theater. There was idle talk of the grandchildren; of the Rands and the Turnbulls and the other neighbors whose homes we were passing; of this or that triviality of the day (the bacon at breakfast had been terribly salty, etc.). But nothing was said of where we were going. I almost came to think Father had forgotten our plans for the evening entirely.

"Is it autumn so soon?" he said at one point, staring out at the fading leaves upon the trees lining the road.

"Yes," I said. "Hard to believe summer's over already."

Father sank back into his seat looking strangely uneasy, and in my heart I had to wonder: If he doesn't know the season, does he even know the year?

Yet it was a different man who stepped from the coach a quarter hour later. Father's back was straighter, his eyes clearer, his step livelier than in months. In the course of the twelve-step climb up the steps to the theater doors, we were hailed at least two dozen times, and Governor Andrews himself seemed to speak for all when he boomed out, "By gad—it's a pleasure to see the Old Senator among us!"

The reactions to me, of course, were more muted, where a reaction was visible at all. The huzzahs were reserved for Father. I was acknowledged only with the occasional nod . . . or smirk.

Ahhh, the wayward son returns with his tail between his legs, I could almost hear the Skeffingtons and the Wests and the rest of them thinking. *And still he struggles to warm the Old Senator to the theater.*

Of course, one of the friendliest receptions I could have expected would have been from the Clemenses, yet I was relieved not to see them there. As you know so well, it was Mr. Clemens who secured my first professional engagement in Boston and later underwrote my apprenticeship with Mr. DeBar's company in New Orleans. Relations have been strained between him and the Old Senator ever since.

What's more, I had my own selfish, cowardly reason for avoiding "Mr. Twain": I didn't want to admit what little success his money seemed to have bought. If not for *The Adventures of Tom Sawyer*, I fear I would have bankrupted the man.

All in all, it was a relief when we were safely settled in our seats (in one of the boxes, naturally—Mother would have it no other way). The theater was at its most radiant that night, every gaslight shining like a star, the proscenium aglow with promise, and for a moment I managed to lose myself in that keen excitement that reaches its crescendo just before the curtain rises and a new world opens up.

"So," Father said, "the stages you play out west…they're as impressive as our National?"

"No," I admitted. "Not nearly."

The Old Senator grunted, and just then—as if in sympathy with my spirits—the lights dimmed.

I wish I could say the play brightened my mood. Unfortunately, it embodied everything I find embarrassing about my calling. Mr. Sasanoff's Orsino was purely porcine—ham sliced thick and served with a generous side portion of tripe. The Great Thespian was not merely heavy-handed but heavy-booted, stomping around the stage with such an exaggerated swagger he trampled not just the floorboards but any trace of the Bard's nimble wit. His company, predictably, followed suit, turning in performances so broad it's a wonder they could all fit upon the same stage.

There was one notable exception, however, and it is here—with the entrance of the sour, glowering Malvolio—that things took an unexpected turn that continued on not just through the remainder of the play but through the remainder of the night and beyond. As Malvolios go, he was young—my own age, I would guess. Yet there was about his performance a striking combination of mesmerizing intensity and masterful restraint that would have seemed more fitting in a seasoned old campaigner like Mr. Sasanoff. If he played a few moments with a tad too much hand wringing and eye rolling, I placed the blame on his manager/star, not him, for a completely understated turn would've seemed as out of place as Edwin Booth in a Punch and Judy show.

I wasn't the only one who found the rest of the company's muggings unamusing. Father didn't so much as chuckle the once, and between acts, I asked him what he made of the proceedings.

"A bit juvenile, isn't it?" he said. "I mean . . . 'Sir Toby Belch'?"

I nodded glumly, knowing there was much more such juvenilia to come in the following acts.

"I like the villain, though," Father went on. "Malvolio." And here he reminded me that our dignified old *Père* has a droll humor of his own he's doled out far too infrequently in recent years. "A good Puritan, like our ancestors."

"Yes. The actor who's playing him—I think he's the best in the cast by far."

"Of course, you'd think so," Father said. "He's your mirror image."

The comment jolted me. Not because I perceived it to be a jab at my actorly egoism—though I suppose it was. In truth, though, I simply hadn't noticed the resemblance.

When Malvolio returned to the stage a few minutes later, I saw it. He was taller than I yet slighter of build, with a jaw that was more a pointed V than my blocky U. But in all other regards—gray eyes, hawkish nose, dark hair, long limbs—we were what the rubber-stamping bureaucrats in Washington would call carbon copies.

We even shared a name: The program listed him as *William* Escott. I spent the remainder of the play marveling that a talent such as his should bloom in so infertile a field as Mr. Sasanoff's troupe, and I couldn't hold back a "Bravo!" as he took his bows. The rest of the audience, however, saved their cheers for the star—Sasanoff, who was favored with such a wildly overenthusiastic ovation one would have thought Shakespeare himself had just taken the stage. It roiled in me a deep bitterness, I'll admit, that so many in that hall who judged me a fool for pursuing a career in theater couldn't see, when actually in one, the difference between brilliance and bluster.

The Old Senator's applause was half-hearted, to say the least. Not because he was so wearied by the evening's (supposed) entertainment. As the curtain fell for the final time, he was much refreshed . . . having slept through the entirety of the last act. Still, I thought it best not to subject him to the jostling hordes pouring toward the exits, and he and I remained in our seats waiting for the crowd to thin.

This would have been the perfect moment to act on the opportunity Eliza had provided, broaching our old quarrel—my career (or lack of same)—and putting the matter to rest somehow. Yet I didn't have the nerve. How could anyone justify a life on the stage when a travesty like Sasanoff's *Twelfth Night* had just unfolded upon it?

So we just sat there in silence until there was a rap upon the door, and who should come barging in like a herd of buffalo in evening clothes but Horace and Eleanor Turnbull! And, no—they hadn't wandered into the theater by mistake thinking it was hosting a debutante ball or a Presbyterian worship service or a witch burning or some other function they might find socially acceptable. The self-same Turnbulls who once had been so scandalized that I—a notorious and unrepentant *performer*—should take an interest in their daughter were now inside a theater, and the team of wild horses that had dragged them there was nowhere in sight.

Believe it or not, they were there willingly. And what's more, they were hosting a reception for Sasanoff and his actors at their home... and they were asking us to come!

"We would've sent an invitation," Mr. Turnbull said to Father, "but frankly..."

Frank he was not ready to be, though—he stopped himself with an awkward cough. But it was easy enough to follow his train of thought.

We assumed you were at death's door, Senator... and your disreputable son may as well have passed through it long ago, as far as we're concerned.

"I'm so sorry," I said, employing all my acting skill to conceal the gritting of my teeth. "But the hour is so late, and my father—"

71

"Accepts the invitation," the Old Senator rumbled. "I would very much like to meet this Sasanoff, and I'm sure my son would as well."

"Splendid!" Mrs. Turnbull brayed. "Why, having you there will make the affair seem almost respectable!"

The Turnbulls laughed—Mr. Turnbull rather sheepishly, I thought—then said hurried farewells and scurried off to see that all was in readiness for the reception.

"There was a time," Father mused, "when people like Horace and Eleanor Turnbull wouldn't set foot in a theater, let alone invite theater folk into their home."

I nodded, silent, not stating the obvious: There was a time—not so long ago—when *our* family had been like that as well.

The Old Senator gave his head a weary shake.

"Things change, I suppose," he said. "*People* change."

"Father...," I began, not sure what words were about to follow.

I don't think he heard me.

"Well, we mustn't dawdle," he said, and he pushed himself to his feet with a tremulous grunt. "The Turnbulls are depending on us to provide the illusion of decorum."

"Counting on *you*," I said.

This he surely heard—and merely chose to ignore.

Not half an hour later, we were in that overstuffed museum of porcelain and crystal and Quality, the Turnbulls' manor. As you might imagine, it was bittersweet being there: The last time I'd been allowed inside, it was to see Miss Mary Turnbull (now Mrs. David Crowell of Boston, I understand).

Yet I didn't linger over old slights. There was Father to think of, of course, with his shuffling gait and watery eyes ever searching for the next available chair. And what's more, wherever in the house we went, whoever might be stopping the Old Senator to pay homage, nearby I could pick out that most intoxicating of sounds: the vainglorious yet endearing chatter of actors talking about acting.

There were perhaps fifty guests milling about the foyer and dining and sitting rooms, and the ten members of Sasanoff's company were spread evenly among them. I'm sure you can imagine my acid amusement upon seeing the young scions of the Adams and Asbury families crowding around the ingénue who'd played Viola or the Fosters and Miltons chuckling at some bon mot tossed off by the portly player who'd embodied "Belch" not long before.

Actors, it seemed, were no longer the lepers they once were… provided they have English accents and patrons like the Turnbulls. Or perhaps, I thought to myself, it wasn't so much a matter of certain low-borns rising as the high-born falling. How many of the families represented at the reception had seen their fortunes go up in smoke, along with that of the Hartford Fire Insurance Company, which had supplied their once-massive wealth, in the great Chicago inferno eight years ago? How many were simply keeping up appearances after being wiped out in the latest financial panic, now only a few months behind us?

For all I knew, even the Turnbulls themselves might be but a step away from the poorhouse. Certainly, the reception lacked the panache of social events of old. There were no ice sculptures, no imported caviars or live lobsters, no musicians playing tasteful, sedate chamber pieces.

SHERLOCK HOLMES: THE AMERICAN YEARS

Still, second-hand or not, the red carpet had been rolled out for Sasanoff and his troupe, and I couldn't begrudge them their social acceptance. Being "theater folk," they were, in a way, *my* folk, and no matter how poor I'd found their production, I was pleased for them as comrades now.

Which exponentially compounds the irony of the fact that it was I, of all those present, who managed to grievously insult them.

It began when Mr. Turnbull lumbered up with Sasanoff to make introductions. In marked contrast to his doughy host, the actor was a small, slender man—no more than five and a quarter feet tall and whippet-lean. Perhaps to make up for his diminutive stature, however, Sasanoff was oversized in every other regard. He crossed one foot before the other, fluttered a hand over his head, and bowed so low he practically doubled himself up like a folded straight razor.

"At your service, Senator," Sasanoff intoned into the carpet. "I trust you enjoyed our humble fumblings upon the stage this evening?"

The Old Senator cocked a bushy gray eyebrow at me, probably wondering if such obsequiousness was the norm among the theater crowd. I had to wonder if this was the real reason Father had accepted the Turnbulls' invitation in the first place—so he could see for himself the sort of people I'd chosen to associate myself with. If so, he couldn't but be disappointed.

"It was a welcome diversion," he said dryly. He was wearing his best taciturn Yankee look, an expression that gives off all the warmth and cheer of a marble slab.

"And you?" Sasanoff said, as always with actors searching for a more receptive audience—in this case, in me. "What did you think of our little production?"

"Well…"

I smiled, taking a moment to chose my words carefully. The Old Senator, of course, has no use for "blarney" and no respect for those who employ it. For his sake, I would have to be honest…so far as I could.

"It was most spirited. I couldn't take my eyes off the stage."

It was, in retrospect, too transparent, as backhanded compliments go. Sasanoff squinted at me with slightly befuddled irritation, as if I were some mysterious, malfunctioning machine: a clock that sneezes when it should chime.

"The senator's son dabbles in acting himself," Mr. Turnbull said. "I'm sure he found your performance most educational."

"Yes. Quite," I said, hoping my seething wasn't as obvious as it felt. Four years as a utility player in companies across the country might not make me a star, but it's hardly the work of a "dabbler"!

"Ahhhhh," Sasanoff said in a way that implied this new bit of intelligence explained everything. "So tell me…what did you learn from us tonight?"

"It was instructive to see a work of this type brought to life with such remarkable vigor."

Sasanoff was ready for just such a feint.

"Oh? Do go on," he said with a hostile sort of chuckle, and I now recognized in him that most ubiquitous—and dangerous—of theater creatures: the thin-skinned Narcissus. If he sensed praise or scorn withheld, either one, he felt compelled to dig it out like a pig after truffles. "What made our 'vigor' so 'instructive,' in your opinion?"

"Well…the acting was so forceful throughout. In the time-honored tradition of the melodrama. Yet *Twelfth Night* is so light a confection."

"You're saying we overplayed it?" Sasanoff snarled, and around the room heads began to turn our way.

"I'm saying that a less…potent approach might have suited the material better."

"And if not potent," Sasanoff boomed, suddenly playing the scene like something out of *Richard III*, "then what else should a proper performance be?"

"Natural," I said quietly.

"*Natural?*"

Sasanoff threw his arms wide and swung back and forth on his hips, now addressing not just me but everyone within earshot—which must have included the entire population of Hartford, he bellowed so.

"Acting has nothing to do with appearing 'natural,' boy! Acting is about dynamism, vitality, dash, gusto. If you wanted to watch people being 'natural,' you wouldn't go to the theater. You could stand on any street corner and soon be bored to death by the 'naturalism' all around you! Audiences crave the magic of the stage. The grand gesture. The majestic pose. Heroes and villains, gods and goddesses. The *supra*natural. Or have they not taught you that in the great theaters of the American backwoods?"

"Hear, hear!" someone called out, and I turned to see that most of my "comrades" in our impromptu audience—my fellow thespians—were glaring at me with naked contempt.

"I disagree that acting is about so simple and easily shammed a thing as dash," I said to Sasanoff, and my training paid off this much, at least: I think I actually managed to sound calm and thoughtful rather than angry and humiliated. "I prefer to think it is about truth...something *bombast* quickly destroys."

Sasanoff leaned in so close I thought his forehead might bump my chest.

"I will not stand here and be called a hamfatter by some know-nothing pup," he stage-whispered, and he stepped back, bowed again to Father, and then whirled on his heel and swept away.

As much as I hated his acting, I had to give the man this much: He truly did have a knack for the "grand gesture." In the silent moment that followed, my biggest fear was that someone might actually applaud.

I was spared that indignity, at least. Eventually, the low buzz of conversation rose up again, followed by the clinking of glasses and the squeaking of chairs and the thousand other sounds one usually ignores at a soiree, but which I welcomed now with all my heart because it meant my scene with Sasanoff was truly over.

"*So* glad you could come," Mr. Turnbull said stiffly, and he stalked off toward Mrs. Turnbull, who'd been keeping watch over the party from a safehold by the punch bowl. The scowl she gave her husband—and then swung on me—would have had a charging tiger turning tail in terror.

"I'm sorry," I said to Father. "Perhaps we should go."

"Don't apologize," the Old Senator growled. But the glower upon his face was reserved—I was relieved to see—for Sasanoff alone. "You stood your ground before a fool. That's something to be proud of, not ashamed." He squirmed in his seat, as if suddenly finding himself atop a tack, then looked up at me. "Do you really believe what you told that gasbag about acting?"

"Every word."

Father nodded thoughtfully, and I was still waiting for whatever he might say next when someone came striding up and stopped beside me.

"Sir," I heard a man say—a man with an English accent. A member of Sasanoff's troupe, no doubt, eager to act as his master's second. I turned half-expecting the slap of a glove across my face.

Instead, I found our young Malvolio, William Escott...with his right arm stretched out toward me.

"May I shake your hand?"

"I should very much like to shake yours, if you're truly willing," I said as I clasped his hand warily. "You're the best actor in Sasanoff's company, Mr. Escott."

"Oh, no. Not the best." Escott flashed a wry smile. "Merely the most resistant to direction."

As our handshake ended—it had been firm yet decidedly friendly—Escott turned and offered his hand to Father.

"Senator," he said as they shook, "your son would make a fine critic."

"Perhaps he would," Father replied. "Only he believes he belongs onstage himself."

"I'll wager he belongs there a great deal more than certain others we could name."

"Mr. Escott," I said, shaking my head with amazement, "you're being incredibly polite to a man who just insulted your manager . . . perhaps your entire troupe. You're not in the least bit offended?"

Escott smiled again. "By no means! Intrigued is what I am."

Beyond him, on the other side of the sitting room, I could see Sasanoff huddling with his Viola and a few other cast mates, all of them scowling murderously at me—and at Escott.

I nodded ever so slightly toward Escott's colleagues. "You probably shouldn't be seen conversing with me so amiably."

Escott waved a dismissive hand at the other actors, his expression turning cold, almost scornful, with chilling speed.

"I've learned what I can from the likes of them. Of late, my thoughts have come more into alignment with yours, if what you said a moment ago is any indication. The classical style of acting does not offer a true reflection of humanity. It is a warped mirror, broadening that which is small, twisting and distorting that which is idiosyncratic. Unlike Sasanoff, *I* could stand on any street corner and find infinite cause for fascination, innumerable insights into the workings of man. Our company's grotesque caperings, on the other hand, are mere pantomime. Were anyone to emote and gesticulate and pop their eyes in public as we do on stage, they'd soon be sent to the madhouse!"

By the end of this soliloquy, Escott was emoting quite a bit himself, and his drawn cheeks and high forehead flushed pink with excitement. I was surprised by the passion with which he spoke—as was the Old Senator.

"Young man," Father said, "it sounds to me as if you're more interested in people than acting."

Escott nodded with what seemed to be rueful amusement.

"The proper study of man is man," he sighed. "Actually, that's what drew me to the stage in the first place. I've been working on the assumption that the study of acting *is* the study of man. But now I have my doubts."

"You were close," I said. "It's just that it's the other way around. The study of man is the study of acting."

Escott squinted and tilted his head slightly to one side, as if searching for a new angle to gaze upon something he couldn't quite pull into focus.

"Would you mind elaborating on that?"

"Not at all. Only..." I looked down at Father. I had so much to say, but was this the time to say it? "...I fear I'd put you both to sleep."

"I haven't felt so awake in weeks," the Old Senator said firmly, sitting up straighter in his chair.

"All right, then," I said, and it was my turn to soliloquize.

I spoke of things I'd never dared share with Father before, fearing he'd find it silly, devoting deep thought to such a trivial thing as playacting. I'd never even told him it was he who'd sparked my interest in acting in the first place, with his habit of inserting long, thoughtful, dramatic pauses into speeches I knew he knew by heart. I'd always assumed he wouldn't take it as a compliment.

Yet as I spooled out that and more—my ideas on verisimilitude of emotion and character and the importance of making each line not a pronouncement but a new, naturally occurring revelation—our father was just as engaged an audience as Escott. So freed did I feel by the Old Senator's attention, his actual interest in my thoughts, I even found myself revealing the researches

I've done in disguise, something I'd long assumed would scandalize our parents to the point of disinheritance.

"You set up practice as a doctor?" Escott marveled, looking both dismayed and deeply impressed.

"Only for a few days. While with a company in Cleveland. To see if I could pass as a medical man."

I turned to Father, who was finally wearing the frown I'd been expecting all along. Though only a small one, tinged with curiosity.

"Don't worry—I referred all my 'patients' to real physicians," I told him. "And after that, I kept to impersonations of a more harmless stripe. I've been a Hoosier blacksmith, an Irish railroad worker, a blind beggar—"

"And what did you learn from these little adventures?" Father asked gravely . . . though not necessarily disapprovingly.

"That successful acting—acting that creates *belief*—isn't about spectacle. It's about plausibility and honesty. Once an actor learns to focus, in his performance, on what is *real* and eliminate that which is not, what remains will be Truth."

"I see," Father said. Whether my words could make sense to anyone but another actor, though, I didn't know.

For his part, Escott had lapsed into silent reverie, nodding in such a distracted way it suggested not so much agreement with me as with some private notion of his own. If such was the case, private it was to remain, as Escott never got the chance to give it voice.

The curtain was rising on the evening's *real* drama.

"What?" someone roared from across the room. "Are you saying we've been *robbed*?"

We all turned—and by "all," I mean everyone in the house— toward the sound. Out in the foyer, I could see through the sitting room door, a red-faced, spittle-spewing Horace Turnbull was raving at the top of his lungs as his wife looked on in horror.

"A thief! A thief in my own home! I should've known this was how our hospitality would be repaid!"

And with that, Mr. Turnbull stomped off toward the master staircase, leaving Mrs. Turnbull behind. His wife stared after him a moment, then slowly turned a wide-eyed, open-mouthed gape on the guests all around her.

"Ummm," she said, attempting a smile that never quite took hold. Then she hurried off after her husband.

One might've thought her audience was a mere assemblage of particularly well-wrought topiary, for no one moved or spoke for a full half minute. When someone finally did spring into action, it was the person in the room least suited for springing . . . or stand- ing, for that matter.

"Help me up," the Old Senator said.

I took one arm, Escott stepped in and took the other. When we had Father on his feet, he began shuffling toward the door. Escott and I exchanged a puzzled glance, then dutifully followed after him.

As we moved out into the foyer, headed for the stairs, the Old Senator—as was so often the case in years past—began to collect followers. Several noble men of Hartford fell in behind us as if we were marching off to take Jerusalem.

When we reached the staircase, however, Father stopped and turned to face his little makeshift regiment.

"Thank you, gentlemen," he said. "But I suspect a dose of discretion is what's called for now. Please wait here. I'll send for you if help is needed."

The men nodded and murmured their assent, some looking disappointed to be denied a role as spear-carrier, others relieved to be left out of anything so plainly smelling of scandal.

Father started to go, but a face in the crowd stopped him in half-turn.

"Mr. Sasanoff," he said, "perhaps you should join us. I'm sure you'd like to see this matter resolved quickly."

"Indeed, I would, Senator. Thank you."

Sasanoff stepped forward with head high, back straight, and eyes abrim with bitter reproach for me and Escott both. Yet he wasn't a good enough actor to hide entirely the nervousness that lurked behind the indignant mask.

Once Escott and I had helped Father totter to the top of the stairs, it was easy enough to locate our host and hostess. Mr. Turnbull had launched into a tirade about sneak thieves and backstabbers, and we had but to follow the sound of his blusterings.

The Turnbulls were in a room at the end of the hall, and stepping in after them, we found ourselves (and here forgive the unsteadiness of my hand, for a shiver of dread has overtaken me) in the couple's boudoir. I will not describe it, lest it haunt your nightmares, except to say this: It was neat and orderly, with all things seeming to be in their proper place—except for the mahogany jewelry box atop a dresser in the corner. It was open, its every drawer pulled out, and Mr. Turnbull stomped up and down before it spewing abuse like a director berating a second-rate actor before the entire cast.

Father silenced him with a rap of his cane on the floor and one low but steely "*Turnbull.*"

The Turnbulls turned toward us looking too agitated to even be angry that we'd entered their sanctum uninvited.

"What's this all about?" Father asked.

"Burglary, that's what," Mr. Turnbull fumed, and he locked a smoldering glower on Sasanoff. "*Someone* has helped himself to my wife's jewelry."

I felt my face flush. Of course, Sasanoff or one of his company would be blamed. Who else could be so dishonorable, so ungrateful, so lacking in morals as a lowly *actor*?

"Take care with your implications, sir," Sasanoff bluffed weakly, voice cracking. The only grand gesture he seemed capable of now was jumping out the nearest window. "Slandering me and my players—" Here he acknowledged Escott with a sulky nod. "—won't bring back your wife's baubles."

"Slandering *you*? Ha!" Mr. Turnbull jeered. "I didn't think the likes of you had reputations to soil!"

"*Turnbull,*" Father growled again. "Close your mouth and collect your wits."

Mr. Turnbull whirled on the Old Senator, scowling. Yet even in his weakened state, Father can outglower any man alive. Mr. Turnbull realized what he was—a terrier barking at a lion—and forced himself to take a deep, calming breath.

"That's better," Father said. "Now . . . tell me what happened."

"There's nothing to tell. Eleanor came up here and found all her jewelry gone."

"Oh?" Escott said, and when I looked at him I found that his whole countenance had changed. His eyes were alight with a fervor and purpose his earlier sermon about acting had only hinted at. Far from being ill at ease to find himself in this scandalous scene, he seemed excited by it—even grateful for it. He looked for all the world like an eager actor waiting in the wings knowing his cue was coming soon.

"Surely not all the jewelry was gone," he said to Mrs. Turnbull.

"Whatever do you mean?" she asked, rousing herself from the appalled catatonia that had fallen over her the past few minutes.

"The pearl necklace you were wearing earlier this evening," Escott said. "It couldn't have been stolen, too."

I looked at the dangling wattles of Mrs. Turnbull's bullfrog throat—usually something I avoid gazing upon at all costs, you understand—and noted that the wrinkled flesh was bare. No necklace was there.

"The pearls are safe," Mrs. Turnbull said. "The clasp broke. That's why I came up here—and found my jewelry box like that."

"Exactly like that?" Escott pressed. "With the drawers pulled out?"

Mrs. Turnbull's upper lip curled ever so slightly into the hint of a sneer.

"No. Empty is what I meant. The jewelry box was closed."

"Ahhhh," Escott sighed, nodding with a satisfaction no one else there shared.

"Honestly, I don't know why we're wasting our time on all this blather." Mr. Turnbull jerked his head at Sasanoff so forcefully his considerable jowls didn't stop jiggling for what seemed like the next minute. "We all know who's to thank for this."

"Sir!" Sasanoff protested with a stomp of his little foot. "You go too far!"

I had to agree. Condescension toward actors I'd been able to weather—for I've had much practice. But the suggestion that a life on the stage somehow equates a life of crime was too much.

"You keep insisting your *guests* had something to do with this, Turnbull, yet you offer no proof," I snapped. "Did you see any of the actors in this part of the house? Or even on the stairs? Or are your accusations as empty as your—"

The Old Senator went into a sudden—and suspiciously well timed—coughing fit that blotted over my last words (which were, by the way, "big, fat head").

"No, I didn't see any of the actors on the second floor," Mr. Turnbull grated out once Father was through hacking into his fist. "I was too busy playing host."

His expression shifted then, going from sour to sly, almost triumphant.

"In fact, now that I think of it, everyone was distracted for a moment there," he said to me. "When you and Mr. Sasanoff had your little tiff. What a convenient opportunity for someone to slip upstairs and do some quick burgling."

A jolt ran through me, as from a shock of static electricity or a slap to the face, and I found myself stepping angrily toward Turnbull just as Sasanoff did the same.

"Outrageous!" the actor howled.

"If you're implying that I had something to do with this, Turnbull—!"

"My, there are a lot of moths in here," Escott said blandly.

The statement was so matter-of-fact yet so clearly apropos of nothing, it stopped me and Sasanoff in our tracks.

"What?" we said as one.

Escott nodded at the gaslights along the walls. Each one had at least three small, brown-gray shapes fluttering around it.

"So many moths," he said. He turned to the Turnbulls. "Are they a problem for you?"

"They get in sometimes, as one might expect," Mr. Turnbull replied warily, as if speaking to a bomb somehow set to explode should the wrong words leave his mouth. "I wouldn't call it a problem."

"I see."

Escott turned his attention to the nearest window. Outside were several more moths flapping against the glass, drawn by the light of the room's lamps.

Escott started for the door.

"I hope you'll excuse me. I have a ... theory I should like to test."

"See! See!" Mr. Turnbull cried out. "He's making his escape!"

Escott slowed, but the Old Senator waved him on.

" 'Making his escape'?" Father said once the actor was gone. "Really, Horace. Have you taken to reading penny dreadfuls? Now, tell me ... what is it you propose to do?"

"Why, throw the rascals out of my home, of course!"

"And which 'rascals' might you be referring to?" Sasanoff asked, putting clenched fists to his hips and opening his eyes wide. He was getting better at feigning effrontery, yet still I could sense his panic. Even a hint of scandal would stain his entire tour—probably his entire career.

"Assuming they are rascals ... and I don't make that assumption,"

Father said to Mr. Turnbull, beetling his formidable brow, "why would you throw them out when one of their number might have Eleanor's jewelry on his person?"

"Those actors, with their stage tricks…," Mr. Turnbull muttered. "They've probably already hidden the spoils where we'll never find them."

"I'm afraid I must disagree with you there," Escott said. "On more than one count."

And he stepped back into the room carrying a bulging white bag.

Only *not* a bag, I saw when he walked over and placed it on the bed. It was a nightcap tied shut.

Escott undid the knot, upended the cap… and dumped out rings, chokers, bracelets, brooches, and other assorted bangles.

"My jewelry!" Mrs. Turnbull exclaimed (more than a little needlessly), and she darted up next to Escott to hover joyfully over her trinkets. It almost looked like she wished to scoop them up and hug them to her breast like a mother reunited with a lost child. "Wherever did you find them?"

"They were but twenty feet away," Escott told her. "In the rosebushes below one of the bedroom windows."

I gaped at the man as if he were not an actor but the most accomplished magician I'd ever seen, for it felt as though he'd just conjured the missing treasure out of thin air.

"But how did you know to look for them there?"

"The moths, of course," Escott said, smiling primly at the irony of his own "of course." There was no "of course" about it for the rest of us, as was all too clear after a moment of dumbfounded silence.

"They came in when the thief opened the window?" I finally ventured.

Escott inclined his head, tilting it to one side in that way that says, "Just so."

"Hogwash!" Mr. Turnbull roared. "He knew they were in the bushes because he dropped them there himself!"

Escott's self-satisfied little smile never even wavered.

"But why should I—or anyone—do that?"

"So you could sneak back and collect the loot later, of course!"

Escott shook his head and clucked his tongue.

"No, no, no. There would be no need for that, so far as our burglar knew. Remember, the theft would not have been discovered for hours—after the reception was over and you were turning in for the night—if not for your wife's trouble with her pearls. Had the guilty party been one of the guests, he simply could have stuffed his pockets and strolled off with 'the loot,' as you so colorfully put it. There would be no need for him to complicate his plan with a risky return to the estate *after* his crime had been found out."

"But, then . . . I don't understand," I said. "If the thief wasn't one of the guests, then who—?"

The Old Senator cleared his throat.

"Your valuables have been recovered, that's the important thing," he said to Mrs. Turnbull. "And even if they hadn't been, I assume Horace took the precaution of having the entire collection insured."

"Why, yes. He finally broke down and purchased a policy . . ."

Mrs. Turnbull's eyes went wide as she—and we—at last realized who the culprit really was.

"...last month," she finished in a whisper.

"Right around the time Mr. Sasanoff's visit to Hartford was announced," I said. "How ironic."

"I don't think that's quite the word for it," Escott said dryly.

The word, from Mr. Turnbull's perspective, would have been "convenient," of course. Fate seemed to have delivered to him the perfect scapegoats for a swindle that would double the value of his wife's jewelry—once the insurance money was collected and the curios themselves were quietly sold off out of town.

We all turned to look at Mr. Turnbull—who couldn't meet our eyes, for he was staring straight down.

"Well, thank goodness there's no need to involve the insurance company—or the authorities—now," Father said. "No need for a scandal. Not if we all go downstairs and laugh off this little misunderstanding... right, Horace?"

"Quite right, quite right," Mr. Turnbull said, still addressing himself to the floorboards.

"Yes. A misunderstanding, that's all it was," Mrs. Turnbull added. And she gave her husband a look that made it quite plain he wouldn't be escaping justice of the harshest kind—that dealt out by an embarrassed and enraged wife.

Father turned to Mr. Sasanoff. "So we're all agreed, then? This matter is settled?"

"I shall not be indiscreet, if that's what you mean," the actor said, and he raised his chin, puffed out his chest, and assumed the noble, lordly bearing of his Orsino or Henry V. "For I am a man of honor."

The Old Senator didn't bother making the same inquiry of Escott—an indication, I'm sure you'll recognize, of how quickly the young Englishman had won his respect.

Instead, Father simply seemed to shrink in upon himself, like a ripe fruit that shrivels and wrinkles before one's very eyes.

"Fine," he said, his voice suddenly hoarse and weary. "Now I believe it is time for me to go."

Soon, we were all downstairs again, and with a few chuckles and winks the myth was born that has probably reached your ears already: that the Turnbulls, tipsy at their own affair, became convinced they'd been raided by gypsies... when, in fact, a maid had simply set aside the lady's favorite baubles for polishing. The story had spread throughout the house before Father and I even reached the front door.

Escott escorted us out, and as we waited for Jason to bring around the rockaway, he remained with us on the edge of the gravel drive.

"Well done, young man. Well done," Father told him. "Your application of logic was most impressive."

Escott offered us a bashful little bow.

"And yet I can't help thinking, Senator," he said, "that you somehow knew the truth of things even before the lady's valuables were recovered."

"I had my suspicions, yes. The way Horace reacted to news of the 'theft,' raging and stomping and generally making a fuss. It was as if he *wanted* a scandal." Father glanced over at me, and even in the dim light I could see his tired eyes take on a little sparkle. "It put me in mind of something a wise man once told me about

the fine art of acting. That a good, truthful performance empha-
sizes believability over bombast."

"So Turnbull's scheme was foiled because he overacted," I
said. "Watch out, Mr. Escott. Sasanoff may recruit him to be the
troupe's new Malvolio."

It was a weak jest intended to distract from the gleam in my
own eye—a shimmer of moisture that suddenly threatened to
pool there.

"Ah," I said, turning away. "Here comes our coach."

Father and Escott shook hands as the rockaway rumbled toward us.

"Good-bye, Mr. Escott. I have a feeling we'll be hearing your
name again one day."

"I doubt it, sir. Not 'William Escott,' at any rate. It's merely a
stage name—and one I don't think I'll have need of much longer,
whether Sasanoff sacks me or not." The Englishman offered me
his hand. "My name is Sherlock Holmes."

"It's been a pleasure meeting you, Mr. Holmes," I said.

"Likewise, sir. I have little doubt I'll be hearing your name
again one day."

"You're very kind," I said, thinking his words mere flattery at
first. Yet Holmes held my gaze so intently, even after our hands
unclasped, that I felt as though some sincere connection between
us lingered on—something Holmes would take with him from
Hartford.

He stayed to help Father up into the coach, and even as the
rockaway rolled off, he remained outside, alone, to watch us go.

"What an extraordinary man," I said.

Father had slumped into his seat, formless and slack, and for a moment I assumed he'd fallen asleep the second he was off his feet.

" 'Some are born great, some achieve greatness, and some have greatness thrust upon 'em,' " he said, quoting one of Escott/Holmes's own lines from the play that evening. "Our young friend there, I think, is very close to achieving his."

He stretched out a wavering hand and placed it on my shoulder.

"As are others."

My throat and chest tightened, and despite all my training, I found I couldn't speak a word. All I could do was put my hand over his and keep it there until he wearied and his arm dropped and he was asleep.

The next day, he seemed to wake from some years of slumber, for he was heartier and in higher spirits than he'd been in months. Yet it couldn't last. By nighttime, he looked haggard, and the next morning he did not leave his bed at all. The days that followed brought a steep decline.

If the excitement I exposed him to did damage to his fragile health, I must shoulder that blame. Yet I cannot regret that night—nor, I truly believe, would Father have me.

The Old Senator will be laid to rest soon, I know. And what's more, *he* knows. That the last vestiges of acrimony between us have been laid to rest first is a comfort we all share, Father and Mother and Eliza and I. I hope you will find some solace there, too, for surely my next communication to you will be infinitely shorter and sadder.

Until then, know this: Nothing save Death can split the Gillettes again, and even then the division will be—as it proved now—only temporary.

Your devoted brother,
William
September 27, 1879

Mr. Lovisi here offers an alternate theory as to how Holmes reached the United States. Here you will meet the model in whose image Sherlock Holmes was cast: Dr. Joseph Bell.

THE AMERICAN ADVENTURE
by
GARY LOVISI

PART I: *London, 1876*

He'll be here soon, so please do try to make a good impression," Mycroft Holmes said in warning to his younger brother, "at least for my sake. This is a great opportunity for you."

"Very well, then," Sherlock replied, as their guest was escorted into the Visitors' Room of the Diogenes Club.

Dr. Joseph Bell was a lean, tall man, with the sensitive fingers of a musician. His steel-gray eyes had a sharp focus to them; they could twinkle with mirth and good fellowship or become cold with stark shrewdness. Bell had an angular nose and a chin that matched. He was the type of man who commanded immediate respect.

"Mr. Holmes," Bell acknowledged Mycroft, though his eyes darted to the young man who stood nearby waiting to be introduced.

"This is my brother, Sherlock," Mycroft said, presenting the young man to the doctor for the first time. The two shook hands.

"It is good to meet you, Mr. Holmes. I have heard interesting things about you from Mycroft," Bell said pleasantly.

"And I about you, Dr. Bell," the younger Holmes replied.

"Well, now," Mycroft interjected, "I am afraid I must take my leave. Please excuse me, but feel free to remain in the room to discuss your business."

A moment later the two men stood face to face alone in the room.

Dr. Bell cleared his throat preparatory to speaking but it was the lad who spoke first.

"I have been led to believe that you require my services?"

"That is correct," Bell answered. "The mission however, is quite unofficial."

A thin, almost imperceptive smile came to Holmes's lips.

"Well now, Mr. Holmes . . . Sherlock," Bell began slowly, "I have a problem. Someone very dear to me is in trouble in a foreign land and I am the only person she can count on for help."

"Who is this person?"

"My sister, Diana Strickland. She is an actress, far away in America—in New York City, to be exact."

"And what do you require of me, Doctor?"

"Your assistance, your companionship in my journey to America," he said softly. "I need someone I can rely on, someone I can trust—not averse to action if necessary. Can you use a revolver?"

"I am adequate with a pistol."

Bell nodded slowly, "And as for my choosing yourself for this deed, you must know my first choice was your brother, Mycroft."

Holmes laughed now. "Who quite strenuously refused you!"

"Quite so," Bell admitted, somewhat taken aback. "However, he heartily recommended you, and now that I have met you in person, I admit I am not disappointed."

Holmes nodded, "All right then, Doctor, when do we start?"

"Arrangements have been made, we leave tomorrow from Liverpool…"

PART II: *Aboard the Oceanic, 1876*

"This is quite an impressive vessel," Holmes said, as he and Dr. Bell strolled the deck of the mighty steamship.

The *Oceanic* was a beautiful three-masted ocean liner built for the White Star Line in 1870 and the first ship to carry transatlantic passengers in luxury and grace.

Bell and Holmes strolled the promenade deck. The rough sea and rain of the previous two days had finally abated, giving them this first opportunity to enjoy the ship's sunny and peaceful deck.

Sherlock Holmes smiled and nudged Bell softly. "Well, there is certainly an unsavory character, if ever I have seen one," he said, as they passed a nefarious-looking fellow limping along the ship's rail.

"Oh, I don't believe so, Sherlock," Bell answered.

"What do you mean?"

"Well, the man's obviously a pensioned soldier," Bell said simply. "He was a sergeant by the looks of him, fought in India, no doubt wounded in the mutiny and has been sadly cast aside like too many of our heroic old veterans. He deserves our pity and favor, not scorn. Now he's seeking a new life in America, and I, for one, applaud his industry."

Holmes stopped and looked at the doctor squarely. "So you know the fellow?"

"Why, I never saw him before this moment."

"Upon your word?"

"Upon my word, Sherlock," Bell replied seriously.

Holmes shook his head slowly. "Then how do you explain all you have said about him? How can you know such things are correct by guessing?"

"I never guess!" Bell returned sharply, obviously offended.

"I meant no insult," Holmes quickly corrected. "I just want to understand."

"Well, it is all quite elementary," Bell replied as they continued walking.

"You are seeing the fellow with your emotions and most superficially, I might add. Doing so gives you a false picture of him. Rather, you must strip away all emotions and feelings and observe only facts. Observe the details. Only by gathering facts can you ever deduce truth. Feelings will betray you every time, my young friend. I see that, like many your age, you wallow in your feelings and emotions."

"The poets tell us to indulge our emotions and to trust our feelings," Holmes countered.

"The poets? Ah, yes," Bell said with a wry grin, "but the poets are wrong."

"How can you say that?"

"Feelings will betray you, mark my words," Bell said more forcefully.

"Well," Holmes said softly, "I'm afraid I do not agree."

Bell laughed indulgently. "As you enjoy the intoxicating scent of the rose, never fail to notice the stinging thorns."

Holmes nodded, then said eagerly, "Teach me your methods. Tell me about that soldier."

Bell smiled, happy to take on the role of teacher. "It is all quite simple, really. His clothing contains small articles of his past military uniform, I believe the Forty-sixth Regiment of Foot."

"Ah, yes, I see the badge now on his belt," Holmes said softly. "I did not notice it before, it is such a trifling thing."

"That's just it, Sherlock, you must always notice the little things."

The young man nodded, looking at his older companion in a new light. "Tell me more."

"Well, if I am not mistaken, the history of that regiment includes the fact that it served during the Indian Mutiny in 1857. Where, no doubt, our fellow received his wound. Note the limp in his right leg? The man appears almost twenty years past retirement age, so it is logical to assume he has been pensioned off since that time. Furthermore, he is apparently alone and without family."

"How do you know he has no family?"

"None aboard, certainly. Look at the fellow, his ragged clothing, his ill manner. No loving wife, dare I say it, no wife at all, would allow her husband to be seen in such condition. Do you see a wife anywhere? No, he is a lone fellow, long ago cast off," Bell said simply.

Holmes thought it over. "What about the fact that you said he was a sergeant?"

Bell laughed. "The right sleeve of his battered old jacket still contains the shadow of his stripes, long since removed."

Holmes suddenly walked over to the limping man and engaged him in conversation. When he returned his face was flushed with excitement. "You were correct in every instance!"

"So what do you think of my methods now?" Bell asked.

Holmes was about to answer when a man's shouts attracted their attention.

"Doctor Bell!" It was Thorson, the ship's purser, running down the wooden deck toward them, out of breath and obviously frantic.

"Here, Mr. Thorson," Bell shouted. "What is it?"

"You are needed at once!" he shouted. Then, lowering his voice, he carefully added, "There's been a terrible accident. A man is dead!"

"Lead the way, my good man," Bell said, as he rushed off with Holmes following quickly behind him.

When they reached the ship's upper level, they were greeted in the passageway by a grim Captain Charles Morrow. "Nasty business, and on my own ship. I thank you for coming, Doctor."

"What is it?" Bell asked.

"Over there, inside." Morrow pointed into a nearby stateroom. The door was open and Bell entered.

"His name is John Martin, a Yank returning to America. He has hanged himself."

Bell and Holmes walked into the room and carefully approached the body, where it dangled from a chandelier. Neither man touched anything, but each stood and observed the body intently, transfixed. A belt had been hooked to the chandelier and was wrapped around the man's neck. His body, slack, swayed gently with the rhythm of the ship.

"Jackson here found the man," Morrow explained, pointing to a steward, who stood nervously behind him.

Captain Morrow then motioned to the purser. "Cut him down, please, Mr. Thorson."

"No, wait!" Bell blurted suddenly. He took out a large magnifying glass and observed the corpse closely, then the floor and the rest of the room, and finally he stood on a chair and examined the belt around the dead man's neck. Holmes watched intently.

"Really, Dr. Bell!" Morrow exclaimed, his temper growing short. "This is all very unseemly."

"All right, Captain, you may cut him down now, but do so carefully, and have your men place the body upon the table here. I need to examine it more closely."

Captain Morrow gave the order, and John Martin's body was placed on the stateroom's short dining table.

Now Bell got to work, performing a minute medical examination upon the corpse.

"Sherlock, come here, look at this," Bell said.

When Holmes approached, Bell took the young man's hand and placed it under the dead man's head, just above the back of the neck. The area was covered with Martin's long black hair.

"Notice anything?" Bell asked.

Holmes nodded, his eyes open wide in surprise. "It's sticky— wet. Blood?"

"Yes, but not enough to notice without close examination,"

Sherlock Holmes looked at the doctor and then back to the body on the table.

Captain Morrow's face blazed and he quickly ordered his men from the room. When they were gone he closed the door and looked at Bell. "What is the meaning of this?" he demanded.

Bell just grunted, examined Martin's clothing, then stated, "This man was hit on the back of the head. It was such a powerful blow that it killed him instantly."

"That's impossible!" Captain Morrow shouted. "The man clearly hanged himself. He is a suicide and shall be listed as such in the log."

"The man was struck and died almost instantly," Bell insisted. "Then he was strung up to make it *look* like a suicide."

"Mr. Martin was clearly murdered," Sherlock Holmes stated.

"That's outrageous!" Morrow barked, aghast. "It's a suicide, I tell you."

"What is truly scandalous, Captain Morrow, is that you refuse to admit you have a murderer among your crew who needs to be brought to book for this crime before he kills again. Think about that," Bell said, his high-pitched voice exuding confidence.

Holmes looked at his companion curiously. "What makes you think the murderer is a crewman?"

"If the captain will call in Mr. Jackson then I shall demonstrate."

Captain Morrow fumed; he was already measuring the implications of such a scandal to his career with White Star.

"Call the man!" Bell demanded.

The captain reluctantly walked to the door, opened it, and called for his men to come back into the room.

When Jackson entered Bell called him over. "You say you found

Mr. Martin hanging here when you came to perform your attendant duties?"

"Aye," Jackson replied, stiff-lipped.

"And you say that he was dead when you entered the room?" Bell asked as he slowly walked around the man, his shrewd eyes examining the attendant minutely.

"Aye, I've plainly said as much," Jackson said nervously.

"Then where, may I ask, did you get *this*!" Bell thrust his hand into the man's jacket pocket and withdrew something bright and shiny.

"That's my watch!" Jackson said, and made a play to grab it back, but Bell was too fast for him and held it just out of reach.

Holmes remained silent but looked at the watch as if it had suddenly been conjured up by magic.

Jackson, shaking with fear, blanched white.

Bell handed the handsome and valuable timepiece to Captain Morrow. "I believe if you examine this you will find that it belonged to the murdered man."

Morrow looked over the watch, "Why, yes, it has Martin's name engraved right here on the back."

"No!" Jackson shouted.

"Mr. Thorson, place that man under arrest!" the captain ordered, and Jackson was soon held fast by the purser.

"How did you know?" Holmes asked the doctor.

"Once I determined that Martin had in fact been murdered, it was really quite easy for me to extrapolate a killer, based upon the facts," Bell said with a wink to young Holmes. "It is all about access. An American traveling alone, he knows no one aboard, so his personal steward would have to be a prime suspect."

"He promised me that watch as payment!" Jackson yelled from the doorway as he was taken away. "He was into me for over a hundred quid."

"Gambling?" Holmes asked.

"Precisely," Bell replied. "Well, captain, you have your man and a murder has been solved."

Captain Morrow nodded slowly, but he was none too happy.

"Well, Doctor," Holmes asked, "answer me this one question, then. How did you know about the watch?"

"It was a trifling thing, really," Bell answered. "When we looked over the body I could not find the man's watch, though a fob was clearly present. I thought that quite odd. I looked around the room, even on the floor, but could not find it. Nor could I find a timepiece among his clothing. So I knew it was missing because someone must have taken it. It just remained for me to find out who. Steward Jackson was the logical suspect and the bulge in the jacket pocket of his uniform told me he was our man."

PART III: *America, 1876*

Holmes had never seen such a vivacious creature before; she shone with absolute radiance and sensual energy.

"Oh, Joseph," she cried to her brother. "Is it really you? After so long."

"Yes, Diana, we came as soon as we could," Bell said, holding his sister in his arms.

Finally she looked more closely at her brother's companion and smiled warmly. "And who is this handsome young gentleman?"

"I am Sherlock Holmes."

"Sherlock has proved an invaluable assistant and traveling

companion, Diana," Bell explained. "We had the most amazing journey, which I shall tell you about later, but right now we want to hear about your own troubles and what we can do to help."

Diana shook her head in evident despair, taking a moment to collect her thoughts. "I'm afraid I've become embroiled in a disastrous situation that can only end badly."

"You can speak freely in front of Sherlock," Bell prompted. "I trust him implicitly."

"I don't quite know how to tell you," Diana began. "I know you and Mr. Holmes will think terribly of me and that perhaps I deserve all that an unkind fate has thrust upon me."

"Let us be the judge of that," Bell said softly.

"Why not begin at the beginning, Mrs. Strickland," Holmes offered.

Bell's sister nodded. "Of course, that would be best, Mr. Holmes. You just now called me Mrs. Strickland, and that is where all my problems originate. For I tell you, a dark shadow came over my life when first I met that man."

"That man?" Holmes asked. "Your husband?"

"Yes, my husband, Rupert Strickland. You see, he is very wealthy, from a quality family, and they all hate me with a passion. While Rupert adored me, soon after our marriage he changed; he suddenly demanded that I quit the stage. We fought furiously over it and it has been a bone of contention between us ever since."

"Well," Holmes offered, "you cannot blame the fellow for that. He merely wishes the woman who shares his name to be a proper wife."

"But, Mr. Holmes," Diana said sternly, "Rupert heartily approved of my career and was my biggest supporter. He never missed a performance, and one of the reasons I accepted his proposal of marriage was because he promised to allow me to continue my profession on the stage."

"Well, really, Diana!" Bell protested. "You cannot be serious. You are a married woman now and should follow your husband's wishes. You must be aware of the unsavory aspects of your profession? Why, these 'women of the stage' are often nothing more than common...prostitutes."

"Is that what you think of me, Joseph?"

"Of course not!" Bell blushed. The entire conversation was making him quite uncomfortable.

Holmes cleared his throat. "I believe what your brother means is that you have to admit your profession has a certain unsavory aspect to it in the mind of the public—who do not know any better."

Diana's anger softened. "Yes, Mr. Holmes, there are those unsavory people, but not all of us are like that, I can assure you."

"Of course not," Holmes said softly.

"Well, then," Bell continued, "what is this problem? Your telegram was most vague and lacked details."

"Tell us everything now," Holmes said. "Hold back nothing."

Diana nodded. "My life was never an easy one back home, Joseph will attest to that. I was ostracized and disowned by our father for my profession. After Mama died I came to America to make a new start. Here in New York I found what I had been looking for. I admit there is pressure put on some of the girls to entertain important men, but I never succumbed. Until I met Rupert. He is young and handsome and it did not hurt that he is wealthy. And best of all he was never bothered by my stage work—until recently."

"Well, what do you want us to do about this, Mrs. Strickland? We are hardly experts on marital relations," Holmes said.

"Perhaps if I talk to Rupert?" Bell offered.

"It has gone far beyond that now, dear brother," Diana said sadly. "You see, divorce is not an option for such a family, and now I fear…I *know* Rupert is trying to kill me."

There was complete silence in the room. Holmes and Bell looked at each other and then back at Diana.

"That is a serious accusation, Mrs. Strickland," Holmes said.

"Diana, how do you know that?" Bell asked.

"Events have moved quickly. Rupert has already been arrested but has since been released."

"Arrested?" Bell asked.

"Yes, a month ago a man came here to the theatre. He appeared at the stage door with flowers, as do many admirers of the actresses. After bribing one of the stagehands to gain admittance, he burst into my dressing room and tried to strangle me. If it weren't for a stagehand, he would have killed me. As it was, I escaped his attack and the man was caught and held for the police. I heard he later confessed after interrogation, admitting he had been hired by my husband to murder me."

"The beast!" Bell muttered in anger.

Holmes appeared less outwardly upset, but within, his emotions were raw with turmoil.

"Where do things stand now?" Bell asked finally.

"Of course Rupert denied it all, and his family came to his aid. They tried to buy me off with a rather paltry sum if I would drop all charges," Diana said, looking from her brother to Holmes. "You see, we are still married. The laws in this state, while quite liberal, still do not allow a woman many more rights than mere chattel. And married women can be most tightly bound by law and custom. I cannot testify against my husband. I cannot divorce him. I had no choice but to drop the charges and hope he would leave me in peace."

"This is very bad," Bell growled.

"But that's not the worst of it, I'm afraid, dear brother," Diana said softly. "You see, fearing for my life, I was forced to leave Rupert, and took a room at a boardinghouse. It is run by a Mrs. Shay, who keeps a clean house for proper young ladies. Two weeks ago, Rupert came to Mrs. Shay's and demanded I come home with him and be an obedient wife. I refused. He vowed then that if I did not come back to him he would rather see me dead. I'm afraid I have no one to turn to, no one to help me. The police view the problem as a private matter between a husband and his wife. They are loath to get involved until an actual crime has been committed."

"But what of the assassin your husband sent against you?" Holmes asked.

Diana smiled. "I knew you would focus upon him, Sherlock. May I call you Sherlock? The man recanted his confession. It would have been a terrible scandal for the theater, so I was forced to drop all charges. He was released by the police and that is where matters now stand."

"That is a ghastly injustice!" Holmes said.

"And now you know, Joseph, Sherlock. My life is in danger from my own husband and there is not one thing I can do to stop him. Until there is an actual crime committed, and an actual corpse—*my own*—the police will hear nothing of it. I do not want to wait until that fatal moment to be proven right."

There wasn't much to say after that. Bell and Holmes escorted Diana back to her room at Mrs. Shay's and proceeded to their rooms at the Union Square Hotel.

"Well, Sherlock?" Bell asked. "What do you think? What can we do to help her?"

Holmes looked up. "I'm not quite sure."

"Well, I for one am going to visit this husband of hers first thing tomorrow," Bell stated. "Diana gave me the address of his hotel."

Holmes nodded, "And what do you think about all that she has told us?"

"It's ghastly, Sherlock, ghastly that my own sweet sister should fall into the hands of such a monster," Bell said. "I take it you noticed the old bruises on her cheek and shoulder?"

Holmes nodded. "I thought it prudent not to mention them, since she did not."

"Yes, I thought the same, though it galled me mightily," Bell said in anger. "I noticed more as we embraced—I could feel what seemed to be welts upon her back. I tell you, Sherlock, my lovely sister has been ill-used by this brute and he shall be made to pay."

After visiting Rupert Strickland the two men arrived at the theater and went their separate ways, Bell to talk with the staff and workers, Holmes to Diana's dressing room.

He knocked lightly upon the closed door.

"Come in, Sherlock," a soft, feminine voice called to him.

A thin smile played upon Holmes's lips as he slowly opened the door and entered the dressing room to behold a vision of loveliness that fairly took his breath away.

"You expected me?" Holmes said incredulously.

"I am glad you are here without Joseph," Diana said. "I wanted to speak to you, to see you again, alone."

Holmes's eyes roved over Diana Strickland's face and form. She was seated at a dressing table before a large gilded mirror. She wore a white lace gown, her back toward him as she brushed her long red hair. She did it slowly and almost languidly, with long, sensual motions the young man found most alluring.

He was entranced. He took a deep breath as Diana slowly turned to face him. She allowed a smile to escape her pouty red lips, and the young man could not help but grin like an overexcited schoolboy. Diana was everything he had ever dreamed of in a woman. The young man stood there in awe, forgetting the reason he had come to see her.

"You and Joseph talked to Rupert?" she asked softly.

"Yes, not an hour ago."

"And I'm sure he told you all kinds of terrible lies about me, Sherlock."

"Actually, I found him to be a very angry man with violent tendencies. You are right to be afraid of him," Holmes said softly, marveling at Diana's alabaster skin, the swell of her breasts as she breathed, the bright allure of her deep blue eyes. A man could become lost in those eyes.

"Come here, Sherlock," she said, her voice light, her manner inviting. "Sit down, beside me, and tell me what Joseph thinks."

Holmes was only too happy to comply with her request and shared her settee in front of the dressing table. He felt his heart beat faster as the closeness of their bodies produced a heat that seemed to grow between them.

"Your brother is most upset by this situation," Holmes said, not knowing quite what to say, nor what was expected of him. "He fears for your safety … as do I."

"Oh, Sherlock, you are so sweet," she said. "So he believes my story?"

"Of course."

Diana turned to look at Holmes, her eyes gazing longingly into his own. "And you, Sherlock, do you believe me?"

"Is it important to you that I do?"

"More than you can ever know," she replied.

"Then yes, Diana, I believe you," Holmes said, amazed at the deep blueness of her eyes, reveling in her closeness. Diana elicited feelings that both delighted and terrified him. He was shocked at how easy it would be for him to throw off all strictures of gentlemanly decorum and wallow in wild abandon.

As if reading his thoughts, Diana suddenly stood up and moved away from him. "That's very nice to hear, Sherlock. But what do you and my brother intend to do about it all?"

Holmes's amorous plan evaporated as he watched her move away from him.

"Do about it?" he asked.

"To protect me from that beast," she said.

Holmes hadn't really thought things through that far ahead yet, and he cursed himself for a fool. He had to do something to meld Diana to him and so considered the question now. Apparently Strickland wouldn't try anything while he and Bell were here. However, once they left New York and went back to England, Diana would once again be in danger. So the solution was simple; Diana must go back to England with them. He told her this now.

Diana did not take it well. "I don't think so, Sherlock," she said adamantly. "I am not going back to England. Maybe some day, but not now."

"Well, you cannot stay in New York, it is much too dangerous for you," Holmes said. "And we cannot stay here and protect you indefinitely."

Diana looked at him with a deep smile. "Dear Sherlock, you do care about me, don't you?"

Holmes looked hurt. "Of course, Diana."

Diana walked over to him and slowly wrapped her arms around his neck as she brought her face down to his lips. The moment was everything Sherlock had ever dreamed it would be. They kissed long and passionately before she suddenly broke the connection.

"Oh, my," she giggled, "I don't know what made me do that. I'm so sorry..."

"I'm not..." Holmes replied quickly.

"Well, I just... oh, Sherlock, I do feel a bond between us. Don't you feel it also? It is so strong, like a power over me. We should not deny these feelings."

"Yes, Diana, I feel it too."

Then she suddenly moved away from him again. "Perhaps we should not become... involved? It may only complicate the situation."

"No, Diana, you said so yourself we should not deny our feelings," Holmes heard himself say.

Diana smiled. "Joseph will be here soon and I don't want him to see us like this. Come back later tonight, after my last show. Meet me in the alley by the stage door."

Holmes looked up, unable to hide his disappointment.

"Cheer up, Sherlock, dear," she said with a promising wink, "we shall have plenty of time together tonight. Remember, meet me at the stage door in the back alley, and bring flowers, Sherlock. A girl so does love to have a handsome beau bring her flowers. Now be gone, love."

Holmes walked out of Diana's dressing room in a delirious fog. Love and lust jousted within, and Diana was the prize. Forgotten was the fact that she was a married woman, and that she was his friend and mentor's sister. Forgotten also were the questions he had wanted to put to her.

Holmes looked for Bell but was told he had since left the theater, so the young man walked back to his hotel alone, his mind a whirlwind of emotions he'd never experienced before. Emotions he knew even less how to deal with. All he could do was count the hours until the end of Diana's show tonight, when he would see her again.

Bell wasn't in his room at the hotel when Holmes returned. The doctor came back a few hours later and the two men went out to Delmonico's for dinner and to compare notes.

The show later on was as delightful as Holmes had expected, and Diana was indeed a goddess onstage. After the final curtain Holmes and Bell said good-bye, and Holmes quickly exited the theater and walked into the side alley. At the end a stage door stood open, the light from inside illuminating the area.

Here he found a small group of well-dressed men, each, like himself, holding a bundle of flowers. Holmes watched as they greeted the young actresses who emerged, talking excitedly and dressed for a lively evening on the town. A moment later Holmes found himself alone.

"Hey, Johnny. Who you waiting 'round for?"

Holmes *thought* he had been alone, but now saw a skinny boy sitting on a crate, the stage-door boy, no doubt.

"What did you call me?" Holmes asked sharply, knowing very well he had been the butt of some unsavory American slang.

"I called you a Johnny," the youth replied boldly, with a derisive laugh. "Just another stage-door Johnny come to see the gals. They're all gone by now and I reckon you're plum outta luck. Well, who you waiting for?"

"Diana Strickland."

"Oh, the princess herself!" the boy laughed knowingly. "You'll not win the likes of her with just flowers..."

"Impertinent wretch!"

The youth only laughed, "She's long gone, mister, off with her professor friend."

Holmes looked at the boy. "She's... not here?"

"Gone a good ten minutes ago, saw her myself."

"I was to meet her here, we had an appointment after the show," Holmes said softly, more to himself than to the boy. Suddenly his face flushed and he felt like a fool. The red roses he held so proudly in his arms had now become a flag to that foolishness.

Before the boy could utter a word the bundle of flowers was thrust upon him and Holmes was gone.

That night Sherlock Holmes walked the streets of New York alone. His thoughts made for ill company indeed. His passion had been stoked and his feelings were hurt. Why had she done this to him? Arranged a meeting and then gone off with another man!

The analytical part of his mind was truly amazed at the amount of pain this caused him. He wished he could talk to Mycroft about it. Surely his more worldly older brother knew how to deal with such things.

"Where were you last night?" Bell asked when they met for breakfast the next morning. He knew his young assistant had been out almost all night. "You had me worried. This city can be quite dangerous after dark."

"I was out walking," Holmes replied guardedly.

"All night?"

"I was thinking," Holmes replied, and Bell could feel the pain in his young companion's voice and so did not press him.

"I also was doing some thinking, Sherlock," Bell admitted, changing the subject now. "In fact, I did quite a bit more. I went around to my sister's room at Mrs. Shay's early this morning to speak to her. You'll never guess what I saw there."

"The professor?" Holmes blurted.

"The professor? No, no professor, it was Strickland."

"Really?" Holmes said, surprised now in spite of his dark mood.

"For a couple whose relationship has been complicated by accusations of attempted murder, they seemed to be quite fond of each other. I watched as Diana kissed Rupert good-bye. I heard her tell him she loved him dearly."

A dark cloud covered the young man's face. He could not respond.

Bell noted his companion's dark look. "My feelings exactly," he stated. "Something is not right here."

115

Holmes nodded. "I think we need to speak to Strickland and get the truth out of him."

Bell was about to reply when there was a loud knock upon the door. He answered to find a hotel bellboy framed in the doorway and behind him another boy in working clothes. Holmes recognized the second boy at once as being from the Criterion.

The bellboy moved out of the way and the other boy spoke up, "Begging your pardon, sir, but are you Doctor Bell?"

"Yes, I am Bell," the doctor said impatiently.

"I was sent by Mr. Jacobs of the Criterion. He said to fetch you at once. There has been a killing."

Bell looked at Holmes frantically. Each feared to utter what was uppermost in his thoughts. "Do you know who it was?"

"No, sir," the boy replied nervously.

"Was it a woman?" Holmes asked sharply.

"Don't know, sir, I wasn't there. Mr. Jacobs told me to run and fetch you. All I know is that it happened in Mrs. Strickland's dressing room."

Bell let out a muffled curse. "My God, he's finally done it, Sherlock!"

Holmes said not one word, but his soul was drowning in a sea of desperation.

Bell and Holmes rushed to the Criterion, where they were met by Jacobs, the director, who quickly led them to Diana's dressing room.

They gasped in surprise when they saw Rupert Strickland lying on the floor, a bullet hole in his chest. He was obviously dead. Diana was crying at her dressing table, two detectives standing over her, their hands thrust in their pockets, the cigars in their mouths unlit, their faces noncommittal.

"What happened here?" Bell ran to his sister and they embraced. She was still sobbing when they parted. Then she saw Holmes and quickly embraced him as well. "Oh, Sherlock!"

"What happened, Diana?" Holmes asked.

"Oh, it was terrible," she cried.

One of the detectives said that he was satisfied with Diana's explanation of the events, and since the witnesses all backed up her story she was free to go.

"Thank you," Diana stammered as the police left the room.

"Tell me what happened here," Bell insisted.

Diana nodded and took a deep breath. "Rupert contacted me through a friend of his, a visiting professor, who convinced him that he should attempt to reconcile. It was the professor who came to see me last night and escorted me to Rupert. Sherlock, I know you were disappointed, but I had to take this last chance to save my marriage. The professor brought me to see Rupert and we met at a neutral location—Delmonico's."

Holmes felt a twinge somewhere deep inside him.

"You met Rupert alone? Was that wise?" Bell asked.

"Maybe not, but we talked and after a while it was like all the trouble between us had been set aside and ended. Finally, Joseph, things looked bright after so much darkness. Rupert came with me to my room. Mrs. Shay would never have allowed it had she known, but we were discreet. We are married, after all…and he stayed the night with me. It was like a…second honeymoon."

Bell nodded. Holmes remained quiet, outwardly stoic, but the knowledge was tearing him apart inside.

"I really thought all was finally well between us. I sent him off this morning with nothing but love in my heart," Diana added.

Bell turned to Holmes and caught his eye. Any suspicions he had were gone now that he understood what he had seen early in the morning outside Mrs. Shay's.

Diana began speaking again. "But Rupert's anger and violence could not be contained. He came here demanding I leave the theater again. I told him we could talk about it later, but he would hear nothing of it. We argued . . . he hit me."

Bell noticed new bruises on his sister's arms and neck.

"He hurt me, Joseph." The pain in her face was mirrored in the faces of Bell and Holmes. "Then he took out a gun and pointed it at me. He told me he'd rather see me dead than have to share me with other men when I was on the stage. Some of the stagehands rushed in, attracted by the shouting, no doubt. They pushed Rupert from behind, and he dropped the gun. It slid over to me and I picked it up and pointed it at him. I told him to stay away, pleaded with him to leave me alone, but he just kept walking toward me with that bestial look in his eyes. His arms reached out for my neck. He was going to kill me, strangle me right there, I was sure of it. I don't think he believed I could pull the trigger, neither did I, but when I looked into the cold blackness of his eyes I knew I had no choice. It all happened so quickly. I pulled the trigger and sent the bullet that killed him into his heart."

They were all quiet for a moment.

"Who are these witnesses?" Holmes asked carefully.

"Two stagehands, and the professor was here. They saw it all and back up my story," Diana said confidently.

There didn't seem to be much else to say. Holmes went to

speak to the stagehands and they corroborated Diana's story. He couldn't find the professor; the man had apparently left right after speaking to the police. However, since he also corroborated Diana's story, there seemed no pressing need to locate him.

The affair, as far as the police were concerned, was ended. Bell and Holmes prepared for their return trip to England.

The violin was played fast and furious in loud, frenzied improvisation; it spoke from behind the solid oak door with a fierce, burning passion. The sound stopped with his first knock, then she let him in.

"I knew you'd come," she said simply.

"I had no idea you played the violin," he began, watching her as she put the instrument down and then came over to him. "I have often thought of taking it up myself."

"You really should, Sherlock. I find it quite conducive to the thinking process, and it can be most relaxing," she said with a smile, taking his hand in hers. She led him to a settee in the corner of her room at Mrs. Shay's.

"We leave first thing tomorrow morning, and I had to see you one last time," he said softly.

They sat down. She offered him tea. He declined with a wave of his hand. She said nothing else, but just looked at him.

"What will happen now?" he asked.

"You and Joseph will go back home and I shall continue my stage career here in New York," she said simply.

"I don't mean that," he said. "I mean between us?"

"Sherlock, please don't make this more difficult for me than it is. I've been through so much with Rupert. I really do like you.

You're smart and handsome and any woman would be lucky to have you."

The words hurt him savagely.

He decided to try a different tack. "How much was Rupert Strickland worth?"

"I don't know for certain. Millions of dollars. He had substantial properties back home, gold mines in South Africa."

"Now it's all yours."

"Yes, Rupert was the sole heir," she explained. "As his wife I stand to inherit all holdings from his demise."

"Demise?" Holmes said curiously. "That's an odd way to put it. You killed him."

She bristled, recovered quickly, "I had no choice."

"I'm sorry, 'killed' was a poor choice of words on my part," Holmes said, and saw relief flicker in her eyes. "What I meant to say was that you murdered him."

Diana's eyes shot wide with anger, even rage, but there was no fear. Then her face softened and she looked longingly at him. "Oh, Sherlock, how can you be so cruel. Don't you want me to be happy after all I have been through?"

"Tell me about the professor."

"There's nothing to tell."

"What was his part in this?"

Diana's face clouded, her lips pursed for a moment, but she did not speak right away. Holmes knew she was deciding what to tell him, working it out in her mind, trying to gauge her response by determining just how much he knew. She laughed lightly, gaily. "I met him last year when he came here to lecture. Now he has returned and we have resumed our friendship."

"And you love him?"

She nodded, then boldly added, "Yes, I do love him, and he loves me. You have no idea of the power of his mind and personality. He is a brilliant man."

"I could be brilliant for you, Diana," Holmes heard himself say. "If you would only let me."

Diana smiled, apparently touched by the young man's words. And while Holmes saw not a hint of mockery in her response, he saw no love there for him either. Then she looked away, hiding her face from him. He could not tell if she was crying…or laughing.

Sherlock bowed his head in sadness.

"I'm afraid it's all done, Sherlock," she resumed. "Go back home with my brother. Learn from him. He is a brilliant man, in his own way. I do hope you find in your life all that you seek and truly desire."

"As long as your brother doesn't realize?" Holmes countered.

"Realize what?" she asked carefully.

Holmes smiled grimly. "You know."

"Sherlock, why do you doubt my word?"

"It bothers me that you claim there were three men who came into your dressing room when Rupert pulled the gun out. You said they knocked the gun from his hand, yet three men could not restrain him from attacking you? Come now! Tell me the truth."

Diana merely shrugged, then laughed gaily, "Well then, you do have an eye for detail. So you want the truth? You mean the truth of the plan to steal the Strickland millions? Oh, don't look so shocked, Sherlock, I have no worry about admitting it to *you. You're* nobody of consequence. I can tell you all, if I so desire. I know you suspected as much."

"Yes, but I simply could not believe it . . . *of you*," he said sadly.

She smiled, victorious. "That is because you did not *want* to believe it, Sherlock. And I counted on that."

He nodded, inwardly hurt but angry now with her—and himself.

"I can read you, Sherlock, I can read you like a book. It does not matter now. I can freely admit it before you, and there is nothing you or anyone else can do about it. If you bring it to the authorities, I shall deny everything. You have no proof, while I have witnesses. No one can change the outcome. Not now."

"Tell me the truth then. What happened in your dressing room?"

"Silly boy, I'm afraid I played poor Rupert from the very beginning. Rupert thought we were finally going to reconcile. We did. The professor and his men brought him to me, and I shot him dead. You should have seen the surprise on poor Rupert's face!" She laughed at the memory.

Holmes said nothing, his mind a cauldron of conflicting emotions.

"Oh, Sherlock, don't look so shocked. You really were out of your depth here. I played you and my brother just as I played poor Rupert. It is over now. Much like you, Joseph could never believe anything evil of me, the dear man. And you, Sherlock? You thought to win my affections." She laughed bitterly, and her harsh reaction cut him like a knife. "I have a far better man than you could ever be. A man who understands me completely unto the very depth of my soul."

"If you have one," Holmes countered.

"Oh, bitter boy! You are just like all men, wanting what you can never have, and angry when you cannot have it!" She laughed wildly. "You were used, Sherlock Holmes! Admit it, I played your emotions like I played that violin!"

Holmes was shocked by the length and breadth of her boldness, of her evil.

"And I know you will not say one word to anyone about it— especially my dear brother Joseph. I've seen the way you look at him, how you admire, even worship him." Diana's confidence overflowed. "Should you ever tell him the truth about me and what I have done, I am sure he would never believe you."

Holmes remained quiet, thoughtful. A small but growing part of him was analyzing her words carefully and finding the entire situation most instructive, even as he felt a pain and hurt the depths of which he had never experienced before.

"And if Joseph somehow did believe you," she added, "I can assure you the news would kill him as clearly as I killed poor Rupert."

Holmes let her words flow over him.

She smiled demurely, "You see, Joseph is a good and loving brother and I knew he would be all for me, and then welcome me when I came back home to claim my fortune."

"You plan to return to England?" Holmes asked, surprised now.

"Some day, the professor and I will return to take charge of the Strickland holdings," she said simply. "He has some ideas about developing a certain organization and the Strickland wealth will prove most useful in that endeavor."

"How could you, Diana!"

She laughed uncontrollably at his words. "Oh, callow youth, you are priceless! Now, Sherlock, you must take your leave of me. Hurry, please! For my own true love will be here soon and I do not want to keep him waiting. Do have a safe journey back to England."

PART IV: *Baker Street, October 1911*

"Well, Holmes?" Watson blurted impatiently. "You can't just stop there! What happened?"

"What do you think happened, old friend?"

Watson sat silent for a moment, thinking it through. "Oh my God, so you told him! You told Doctor Bell all about his sister and how she had planned the murder of her husband?"

"Yes," Holmes admitted. "I had to. We were companions, friends. I admired him greatly. I still do, John."

Watson cleared his throat nervously, "I imagine he did not take it well."

"You are correct," Holmes replied. "I told him that first night, when our ship left New York. He would not believe one word of it. He said it was all because I was infatuated with Diana, angry with her because she had spurned my advances."

Holmes gave a rueful smile as he took something out of the pocket of his dressing gown.

"I say, Holmes, what have you there? A letter?"

"Would you be a good fellow, John, and read it out loud."

Holmes passed the envelope to his friend, who took it in hand most carefully.

"I was given it by Mrs. Abernathy, the charwoman, when I went up north last week to close Dr. Bell's house. There I also saw to the doctor's burial and provided a proper headstone for his grave," Holmes explained. "I have held the letter unopened since then."

Watson looked astonished. "But how could you not read it immediately? If it were I, I should..."

Holmes nodded. "I know, but I feared what I might find written therein. Open it, Watson. It is time."

Watson nodded, slit open the envelope with Holmes's own dagger, and then withdrew the contents. There was just one sheet of bond writing paper, which he unfolded nervously.

"Well, read it," Holmes prompted impatiently.

"Of course," Watson replied. After clearing his throat, he began:

Dear Sherlock,

I am quite cross as I write this letter, though not with you, old friend, but with my own self. We have been at odds and loathe to speak these past forty years, the fault of which I put squarely upon my own shoulders. I acted abominably to you and I hope you can forgive me.

Emotions not only skew judgment, they can ruin friendships. I want you to know I have never held you far from my thoughts. The truth is I have followed your career, every case, all these many years with great interest and much satisfaction. I have rejoiced with your every success, particularly against that evil fellow who so deservedly went over the falls. My only regret in that matter, as I know you agree, was the result it inflicted upon my sister, Diana.

There, I have mentioned her name. No longer should her evil deeds be a barrier between us. I tell you now that you were correct about her all along. It is sometimes difficult for an old Scot to admit the errors of his ways. We tend to carry those mistakes with us too long in life and even to the grave. I pray this letter in some small way can set things right between us.

Sherlock, I am proud of the man you have become. I am proud to have known you and call you friend. I remember with great fondness our American adventure. I have followed your life and career, albeit from afar, and tell you now in all honesty and profound respect: well done, Sherlock Holmes! Very well done indeed!

Watson saw a great softness come to the face of Sherlock Holmes. One lone tear, then another, rolled down his cheek, but once he saw Holmes smile, the doctor knew they were not tears of sadness but tears of joy.

Watson wiped a tear from his own eye before he continued. "It is of course signed, 'I remain your most devoted servant, Dr. Joseph Bell, Edinburgh.'"

Holmes smiled brightly, looking much relieved. "How I feared what that letter might say."

The two men sat silent, each wrapped in his own thoughts.

Having exhausted the myriad delights of Hartford, Connecticut, Mr. Mallory moves Holmes on to the Baghdad of New England: Bridgeport. And introduces us to a true American original.

THE SACRED WHITE ELEPHANT OF MANDALAY

by

MICHAEL MALLORY

When my traveling companion arrived back at our tiny and rather dusty room at the New York boardinghouse, I could read nothing from his expression. "Well, Holmes, how did it go?" I asked.

"My E-flat did not soar as highly as I would have liked, but I did nothing to disgrace myself," he replied. "The fact that one of my adjudicators was positioning his head in such a way as to indicate he was slightly deaf in his right ear may work to my advantage."

I had by this time become accustomed to such pronouncements from Sherlock Holmes, who tended to observe people the way Babylonian astronomers observed the heavens, and then deliver astounding conclusions based upon what he saw. Although no more than three years above my own age of twenty-one, Holmes nonetheless managed to carry himself as though he had walked the earth for decades and had acquired the wisdom of the ages as a result.

He had come to New York at the invitation of the newly formed Symphony Society of New York, which, having been apprised of his virtuosity on the violin from his Austrian fiddle master back home (a man whose name I could not begin to pronounce), had asked him to audition. My presence on the trip was twofold: I was helping Holmes share the not inconsiderable expenses of an ocean voyage from England while at the same time satisfying my long-held curiosity about the biggest city in America.

Holmes set his violin case down on the room's one chair and rested himself on one of the beds, which groaned in protest. "This is the most taxing part of all, Stamford, doing nothing but waiting to hear their decision."

I knew from the experience of our sea voyage that boredom was anathema to my companion, and I did not savor the thought of seeing him through the waiting period. I attempted to think of some way to distract him during it, but as luck would have it, he found one on his own.

Holmes had gone out to purchase a local newspaper, leaving me in the room (for better or worse, I have never considered idleness an enemy). Upon his return, he fairly burst into the room, the newspaper held open in front of him. "Listen to this, Stamford," he said. "It says, 'A very rare white elephant will be placed on public display in Bridgeport the morning of Thursday, May ninth, at the Went Field site of Mr. P. T. Barnum's circus storage compound.'"

"*The* P. T. Barnum?" I asked.

"It is unlikely there is a surfeit of them," he said, then continued his reading:

> Mr. Barnum is taking the unusual step of publicly exhibiting the creature free of charge to the customer, between the hours of ten o'clock and eleven o'clock. The elephant, upon which the name "Xanthippe" has been bestowed, after the wife of Socrates, is a gift to the Sovereign of the Independent Kingdom of Upper Burma, and almost immediately after its display here it will be transported across the ocean to Mandalay. White elephants such as this one are extremely rare in nature, so much so that they are considered legendary and even sacred in many countries of the Orient.

Well, Stamford, what do you think of that?"

"Sounds like a white elephant, if you ask me," I told him.

Holmes did not laugh. "I think it sounds like something definitely worth investigating," he countered, "particularly since the public showing is tomorrow and we have nothing else on our social calendar."

"You mean you want to see this creature? Where is Bridgeville?"

"Bridge*port*. It is a town in Connecticut, and I believe it is easily accessible by train."

I knew that seeing such a rarity as a sacred white elephant is precisely the sort of thing in which Holmes reveled, so I acquiesced.

The next morning I found myself accompanying Sherlock Holmes on the early (*too* early, in my opinion) train for Bridgeport, Connecticut. Holmes spent the journey poring over more American newspapers, while I simply watched the scenery go by. I was particularly amused when the train stopped at a town called *Stamford* and fought the desire to leap off the train and engage a local photographer to take a picture of me standing under the station sign, which I could then send to my father as proof that I was, despite his worst fears, making my way in the world.

True to its name, Bridgeport was a seaport of sorts, situated along both a sound and a river, nowhere near as large and bustling as New York, but still an active town. My fondest wish as we detrained was that we could find a place that served breakfast, for I was quite famished, but after a quick glance at his watch, Holmes proclaimed there was not enough time. While he was querying the stationmaster as to the location of P. T. Barnum's compound and the elephant exhibition, however, I spotted a nearby small café with a quasi-Parisian atmosphere, where I was able to obtain a baguette and a piece of cheese.

I nibbled on the bread and cheese as we walked through the city, following the directions, and on the way I noticed that Holmes appeared unusually interested in the windows of the stores we passed. "Shopping?" I asked.

"Hardly," he replied, examining the window. "The goods on display are of little concern to me, unlike the man across who is reflected in the glass. When we walk, he walks. When we stop, he stops. Clearly, we are being followed. I am merely trying to ascertain why."

"Followed?"

"Do not look at him, Stamford," Holmes cautioned. "Whatever his game is, it is best that he not realize we are on to him. Let us continue walking."

We continued our trek to Went Field, which was on the outskirts of the town. It held a series of large, flat-roofed buildings that were certainly big enough to house an entire circus. An assembly of people was already gathering, directed to the largest of the buildings by a series of roughly painted signs that read, *This Way to the Sacred White Elephant.* We took our place in the line, but before we could actually enter the building, a voice behind us called: "Holmes!"

My companion spun around and I with him, and we now found ourselves in the company of a well-dressed man with a natural air of authority about him. The man said something that I did not fully catch but finished once more by addressing my companion by name.

"He recognizes you!" I gasped.

"And I him," Holmes said. "This is the man who was following us."

The fellow began to speak again, and now I understood his words to be in a different language. "I assure you, I understand English perfectly," Holmes told him.

"Good," the man replied. "You will come with me."

"We shall do no such thing!" I protested.

The man then opened his coat and revealed a pistol tucked inside his belt, which he deftly removed and pointed in our direction.

"It appears that we are to go with him," Holmes said. We were marched away from the building at gunpoint and to a waiting hackney cab and instructed to get inside, which we did, since it would have been folly to do otherwise. "Please don't try to jump out of the cab," the man said, stepping inside with us, and keeping his gun pointed in our direction. "You won't get far."

"Where are you taking us?" I demanded.

"Waldemere. Perhaps there we can put an end to this dirty business."

As it turned out, Waldemere was not far away, and while it sounded like another town, it was in reality the name of a fantastic mansion, an imposingly huge structure that was gabled like a manor house, but with a high tower at its center. It sat in the middle of a large open green that overlooked the water, and was criss-crossed with carriage drives and dotted with fountains. "Who lives here?" I asked, taking it in through the window of the cab.

"Really, Stamford, who else *would* live here?" Holmes said. "Obviously we are being invited, so to speak, to have a personal audience with Mr. P. T. Barnum." Turning to the man with the gun, he added: "Since we have accommodated you thus far, may I ask who you are?"

"My name's Weymouth," the man said. "I work for Mr. Barnum."

The cab pulled up in front of the house and stopped. Weymouth got out first and, keeping his pistol trained on us, instructed us to exit the vehicle. We were escorted inside the place, whose interior was just as impressive as its exterior, though much of the main entryway area was obscured by scaffolding and drop cloths. The smell of fresh plaster and paint permeated the area, and various workmen could be seen bustling about, at least one of whom wore a hat and kerchief over his face as protection against the dust. "A bit of remodeling?" Holmes asked, surveying the work.

"Mr. Barnum is never satisfied with the place," Weymouth

replied, "not that it's any of your concern. We're going this way." He walked us to one door in particular, but before he could open it we heard a woman's voice call out behind us: "Charles, is that you?"

"Yes, Mrs. Barnum," Weymouth called back, hiding his gun from view.

Upon hearing the name "Mrs. Barnum" I expected a matronly woman of somewhat advanced age. I was therefore surprised to see a comely dark-haired woman who appeared barely older than either Holmes or myself approach us.

"Are you gentlemen here to see my husband?" she asked us, pleasantly.

"So it would appear, madam," Holmes said.

"Is it about the problem in the drawing room?"

"No, not at all," Weymouth said, nervously. "Now, if you would please excuse us..."

Holmes faced the young woman. "What is the problem in the drawing room, madam?" he asked, and Weymouth fired him a look that could have etched glass. Even Mrs. Barnum seemed to notice it, for she replied: "Oh, well, perhaps I should not say."

She took her leave and Holmes and I were walked across the entryway to a door, upon which Weymouth rapped loudly. "Come in!" a voice boomed from the other side. Opening the door, we found ourselves entering a large oak-paneled library that was filled with bookshelves and decorated with glass cases containing stuffed birds. The centerpiece of the room was a large, heavy desk that was overburdened with papers and objects (one of which looked like a miniature head in a jar!). Seated behind the desk was a man on the far side of sixty who studied us for a minute before rising and stepping toward us. He was of medium height, heavily built, and clad in a long dressing gown, pantaloons, and bedroom slippers. A diamond stickpin adorned his shirt. His features were blunt to the point of being bulldoggish, and while his pewter-colored hair was quite sparse on top of his large head, the sides and back were ringed with a natural laurel of curly locks that gave him the appearance of a Roman bust come to life. "I am Phineas Barnum," he announced redundantly, in a voice that filled every cranny of the room.

"How do you do, sir?" Holmes said, giving him a respectful nod. "My name is—"

"You do not sound French," Barnum interrupted, "you sound English. Charles, why is this man not French?"

"I addressed him in French, Phineas, and he responded," Weymouth said. "I had been watching the train depot, as you suggested, and saw them arrive. Their clothes are European and they clearly acted like strangers to the city. I followed them to the compound and when I spoke, this one..." he jabbed a finger in my direction "... acknowledged that the other one had been spotted."

"I was startled that you called my companion by his name, is all," I protested.

"Name?" Weymouth said. "I used no name."

"I distinctly heard you say 'Holmes!'"

Holmes was now smiling. "I believe I can clear up at least this part of the little drama into which we have all been cast," he said. "While I am less than expert at the French tongue, I clearly heard Mr. Weymouth call '*Voux hommes?*,' which translates to 'You men.' What startled my friend was the use of the word *hommes*, which sounds nearly identical to my surname, Holmes, particularly when pronounced by someone even less expert in the language than I."

"So you are Holmes," Barnum said, then turned to me and demanded my identity as well.

"My name is Stamford, sir."

"Like the town down the road?"

"Quite."

"And neither one of you has ever sent me a letter?"

"I assure you, sir, that we have not."

Barnum scrutinized both of us and then turned his gaze to Weymouth, who appeared to flinch. "Phineas," he began, "I would have put money on one of them being our man."

"You know what they say about a fool and his money," Barnum fired back. Then, shaking his head, he said: "Mr. Holmes, Mr. Stamford, it appears I owe you an apology and so does Mr. Weymouth. I am not in the practice of inconveniencing visitors to such a degree. I am also, I fear, rather preoccupied, so please tell me how I might recompense you for the trouble we have put you through, and then be on your way."

"Well, I for one should very much like to see the white elephant," Holmes said. "Not the one on exhibition back in that animal storage building, which I assume to be a fake, but rather the real one you are concealing in your drawing room."

The mouths of both P. T. Barnum and Charles Weymouth dropped open. "How in blazes did you know about that?" the showman sputtered.

Holmes smiled. "The very fact that Stamford and I were brought to this house at gunpoint—"

"*Gunpoint*, Charles?" Barnum said.

"A precaution, Phineas."

"If I may continue," Holmes said. "We are here because you were clearly expecting someone in particular to arrive today, a Frenchman apparently. Why would he be coming today? To see the elephant, of course. But many people came today to see the elephant, we included. So the question stands, why were you waiting for this particular Frenchman, and why were you willing to abduct him when he arrived? The obvious inference is that he posed some sort of threat to the elephant. In fact, I would argue that the decision to exhibit the elephant was really an attempt to draw this man out into the open. That being the case, you would hardly be expected to risk the actual white elephant. I imagine that the creature on display is most likely a common elephant painted white for the occasion."

"It is covered in plaster dust, not painted," Barnum said, "but otherwise you are alarmingly correct."

"The rest is simplicity itself. Once we have established that the real elephant is not in the field building, the question remains, where is she? The agitation that Mr. Weymouth displayed when Mrs. Barnum began to speak of the 'problem' in the drawing room indicated that there was something in there that he wished us not to see. Given the rest of the facts, the obvious conclusion is that the so-called problem was Xanthippe herself, hidden from view in the last place anyone would expect to find an elephant."

"Lordamighty," Barnum said, clearly impressed by Holmes's deductions.

"May we see the elephant, then?" Holmes asked.

"Very well." He led the three of us out of his library and through the main entryway, where we dodged workmen carrying materials, to a set of large double doors, on which he gave a coded knock and shouted, "It's me, Davy." Once the doors were unlocked from the other side, we were ushered in.

The drawing room of Waldemere would not have been out of place in the doge's palace in Venice. One wall contained an enormous hearth and fireplace; the long wall perpendicular to it contained four large windows, all of which were heavily draped. An ornate crystal chandelier that hung from the center of a decorated ceiling, and the rest of the furnishings, which included a long table, at least a dozen chairs, and two large carpets that were now rolled up, had been shoved up against the far wall. All of this was to make room for a gigantic wooden crate with several round holes in its side that sat atop a large, thick canvas tarpaulin. A bale of hay rested near the crate, which, along with the noise that was emanating from inside it (not to mention the smell), clearly identified its inhabitant.

"These men would like to see her," Barnum told the man named Davy, who was small and possessed the largest ears I have ever seen on a human, which gave him a decidedly simian appearance. He walked back to the crate with a pronounced limp and thrust a large key into the lock that secured the front. Swinging open the door, Davy disappeared inside the crate momentarily and then emerged leading the most exquisite creature I have ever seen.

As elephants go, Xanthippe was not large, but she was of a startlingly white hue, with pink shading around her eyes and mouth. Her tusks, which actually appeared darker and more yellow by contrast, were quite small, indicating she must be young.

"The sovereign who is to receive her shall be delighted," Holmes said.

Barnum patted the elephant's trunk affectionately. "No doubt, though Xanthippe is going to him for reasons far beyond delight," he said. "All right, Davy, you can put her back in now. We are trying to get her used to staying inside the crate, which will be necessary for her long ocean voyage. Now you have seen her, gentlemen. I must take my leave."

"If you don't mind, Mr. Barnum," Holmes said, "I should like to hear the details of this problem you are experiencing."

"This is no business of yours," Weymouth snapped.

"I don't know, Charles," Barnum said. "Maybe having another brain working on this will help us, and this young fellow has certainly proven he has a brain. All right, let us go back to the library and I will tell you more."

"Phineas, I have some things to attend to," Weymouth said.

"Be about your business," Barnum said with a nod. On the way back to the library, Holmes asked him: "What exactly does Mr. Weymouth do for you?"

"It is Charles's responsibility to look after all of my holdings and properties here in town." He ushered us back into the book-filled room and closed the door. After motioning for us to sit down, he installed himself behind his massive desk. "Now then," he began, clasping his hands together, "what do you two know of the present political situation in Burma?"

For my part, I had never stopped to consider that Burma had a political situation, though Holmes, of course, responded immediately. "The British Empire controls the lower part of the nation," he said, "but that is not the part in question, is it?"

"No," Barnum said. "The part I'm concerned with is the upper part, which remains independent. King Mindon Min, who has ruled independent Burma for years, is gravely ill and there is no successor to the throne. No sooner does the king put forth a name than that man is assured of being assassinated by rivals. The situation has the potential to throw the nation into chaos."

"That is quite illuminating," Holmes said, "but how does it concern you directly?"

"Last year I received a letter from a representative of the Royal House of Independent Burma who was loyal to the king, virtually pleading for my help in finding a white elephant. My reputation for finding unusual animals has spread even to Asia, and they were willing to pay handsomely for my assistance."

"Why did they require a white elephant?" I asked.

"I believe I can answer that," Holmes said. "Burma is one of the places where creatures such as Xanthippe are genuinely considered sacred. The sudden appearance of one in the presence of a particular heir would be taken by the Burmese people as a sign that a successor had been chosen by a higher source. It would be an endorsement that even that candidate's rivals could not dismiss. Is that it?"

"In a nutshell, yes," Barnum confirmed. "The plan is to have the king's designee ride through the streets on its back as a kind of coronation ceremony, one aimed at ending the bloodshed and insurgency."

"As a plan, it is brilliant."

"Indeed. It is also risky, since there was no guarantee that I would actually be able to find such a creature. One may debate their sacredness, but there is no denying that white elephants are rare. However, my sources did locate one in India. When I was making preparations to retrieve her I received a letter from the

French Office of Oriental Affairs signed by a Pierre Carraveaux, informing me that the government of France would take a very dim view of my providing the elephant to the representatives of King Mindon. Why the government of France even cares about any of this is beyond me."

"I can hazard a guess," Holmes said. "If I am not mistaken, France is in control of the neighboring nation of Laos, and likely sees itself in competition with the empire for control of the remaining independent lands of Burma. It is possible that the government has negotiated directly with a rival heir for future allegiance in return for official backing."

For the second time today, P. T. Barnum stared at Holmes in amazement.

"You must forgive my friend, Mr. Barnum," I said. "He knows everything. It is quite annoying."

"Perhaps I should be exhibiting you as 'The Human Encyclopaedia,'" the showman said.

"You flatter me, Mr. Barnum," Holmes said, "but we are straying from the subject. This letter, did you reply to it?"

"Only to say that with me a business arrangement was inviolable, and I had every intention of honoring it. For a while I thought that had settled the matter, but after I had accepted delivery of Xanthippe another missive came, also from Carraveaux, and this one greatly disturbed me. He threatened to abduct the elephant and cause her great harm in order to prevent her from being transported to Burma. That was heinous enough, but the man managed to tighten the screws even further. He claimed he would publicize the torture and killing to damage my reputation."

"But surely you could not be found at fault," I said.

"Oh, my culpability or innocence has rarely mattered," Barnum said. "There are animal protectionists out there who delight in hounding me over the methods in which my menagerie is kept and presented. I assure you, I do nothing to harm my animals. Why would I? They are my livelihood! But were a rare elephant to die violently while in my custody, whether it was my fault or not, these groups would have me run out of town on a rail. That, though, would be nothing compared to the outrage that would come from the Orient upon learning a white elephant had been desecrated."

"So you believed that staging an exhibition would lure Monsieur Carraveaux all the way from France?" Holmes asked.

"That letter containing the threats was mailed from New York. Carraveaux is already here, somewhere. That is why Charles concocted this scheme to lure him out. Instead he netted you two."

"Why not simply turn this matter over to the police?" I asked.

Barnum smiled ruefully. "I recently served as mayor of Bridgeport. One of my civic crusades was to rid the police department of the corruption that ran rampant within it. The public applauded such a move, but many on the police force did not, and they still don't, so I cannot expect the police to help me. I am afraid I am quite alone in this matter."

"Not quite," Holmes said. "We shall be happy to help you."

"We shall?" I asked skeptically.

"We are not known here," Holmes explained. "We could watch for this man Carraveaux without being detected ourselves."

"Your argument has merit," Barnum said. "Very well, as of now you two are in my employ. Where are you staying?"

"Well, we have a boarding room back in New York," I said.

P. T. Barnum waved his hand impatiently. "Not good enough.

You shall stay here at Waldemere for as long as you need. The Lord knows we have enough available rooms. If there is anything you require, see Charles about it." The showman then bounded toward a circus poster on the wall behind him, which he swung away from the paneling to reveal a small wall safe. Deftly turning the knob, he opened the door and pulled out a thick stack of American currency. "Since you are working for me, you shall be paid," he said, counting off several notes and handing them to Holmes. "Will that be sufficient?"

"Eminently."

"Excellent. Now then, where will you begin?"

"First, I should like to send a telegram," Holmes said. "Could you direct me to the telegraph office?"

That office was, not surprisingly, located in the center of the bustling town, not far from the river's edge, which was a short cab ride away. Dashing inside, Holmes began to jot down the message he wanted sent and handed it to the telegrapher.

"London, England, huh?" the man said, appearing to have trouble reading it. "What's that word there?"

"Diogenes," Holmes replied. "Please make certain the recipient knows that we need a reply as soon as is possible."

As we left, I asked: "Holmes, what was so important about that telegram?"

"I am contacting my brother, Mycroft, in London, seeking information that may be of great import in this matter," he said. "Now then, since Mr. Barnum is generously paying for our stay here in Bridgeport, what do you say to a bite of lunch?"

That was the best idea I had heard that morning, though we passed by several suitable-looking establishments before Holmes arrived at the one that met his approval—the same Parisian café where I had purchased the baguette only hours before! "Why here?" I asked.

"The man we are tracking is a transplanted Frenchman," Holmes replied, as we entered. "This is precisely the sort of place that would attract such a man."

Over slices of quite excellent Quiche Alsacienne, Holmes peppered the waiter, an elderly man who spoke with a slight Continental accent, with questions as to whether a French national had frequented the place in recent weeks.

"No, monsieur," the man replied, "nor have many others."

I found that surprising, since the food was quite excellent, and said so, but the waiter merely shrugged and muttered something derogatory about the American palette.

The reply to Holmes's cable was awaiting us upon our return to the telegraph office. "I suspected as much," he said, reading the telegram with a knowing smile. After asking the telegrapher if he had received or sent any recent messages from or to Paris, and receiving a negative reply, we left.

"Don't leave me in suspense, Holmes," I said. "What did the message say?"

"Mycroft confirmed that our Monsieur Carraveaux is not who he purports to be. My brother is employed by Whitehall and as such has access to diplomatic information. Not only has he never heard of a French government official named Pierre Carraveaux, but he says there is no such agency as the Office of Oriental Affairs."

"Who is Mr. Barnum dealing with, then?"

"There is only one man who can shed light on that question. We must return to Waldemere."

Taking a cab wherever I wished to go was a luxury I could not afford back in London, but here I was becoming quite accustomed to it. As we sped up the carriage drive toward Waldemere, we had to maneuver past a supply wagon bringing still more construction materials. Seeing its masked driver, I vowed that whatever it was I decided to do with my life, it would not involve paint fumes, plaster, or sawdust.

Mr. Barnum was still in his library—though how he managed to get any work done, or even any reading, given the din of the construction work, was a mystery.

As we entered, Barnum looked up anxiously. "Have you learned anything?"

"Only that your Monsieur Carraveaux is a humbug," Holmes said, explaining that the French government was not involved.

"I suppose that's a relief, since I have no desire to be the cause of an international incident," Barnum said. "But then what is this man's game?"

"That is what we must discover," Holmes said. "Let us assume for the moment that the man's nationality is not part of a ruse, but that he is indeed French. Have you come into the acquaintance of another Frenchman in recent years who might bear you ill will?"

He furrowed his brows in thought, and then said: "Well, one perhaps, but it cannot be he. His name was Étienne Artaud. A number of years ago he showed up at my American Museum in Manhattan, presenting himself as a member of the French aristocracy. In truth he was nothing more than a confidence man. He claimed to have the remains of a genuine water horse, which he wanted to sell to me for the museum."

"A sea serpent?" I asked.

Barnum nodded. "I have issued a bounty for such a creature, but have yet to pay out, and frankly do not expect to. This one was a fake, of course, but more pertinently, it was so slipshod that the even dullest schoolboy would not have paid a penny to see it. But it turned out that Artaud cared little whether or not I bought the thing. He was only using the fabricated wonder as a means of gaining entrance to my museum to that he could burgle it, which he attempted to do, before he was caught. He was sent back to his homeland for trial and the last I heard he was in prison. Are you suggesting that he is free, and has come here to exact revenge?"

"The thought is worth considering," Holmes said.

"Lordamighty. I will not truly feel secure until I know that Xanthippe has safely set foot in Mandalay. I am hoping that within the week the special rail car that will take her to San Francisco will be fully prepared."

"And from there, she will take sea portage to Burma?" Holmes asked.

"Precisely. Until Xanthippe is on her way she must remain under constant guard. Whoever this blackguard turns out to be, if he emerges from hiding, he will not be able to get to her."

Mrs. Barnum then entered the library. "I am sorry to disturb you, Phineas, but you know it is your rest time."

"Nancy, really, I have far too much to do," the showman protested.

"I'll hear none of it," she replied, going to him and lifting him out of his chair. "You know what Dr. Shank's says."

"Very well," Barnum sighed. "Gentlemen, I must leave you for my medically imposed hour of rest. I would like you to stand guard in front of the drawing room door and see that no one goes in there. With Davy inside and you outside the room, I will feel better about leaving. I'll stop and let Davy know that you will be there on the way out."

I wanted to protest the assignment, but he was already out of the library. With a sinking feeling I watched Barnum trot across the entryway while his wife waited impatiently. From the doorway of the library I could see him pounding on the drawing room door and waiting for Davy to answer it. He then went inside and moments later reemerged and went up the staircase with his wife beside him. Casting a look across the way at me, Davy nodded and then slammed the door shut again.

"Holmes, I fear this is getting out of hand," I said, turning to him. "We are not guards!"

"Mr. Barnum has faith in you, and so do I," he said. "Now, if you would be so good as to take your post, I have work to do."

"What do you mean? We are both supposed to be standing watch."

"Yes, but now that our host is preoccupied I shall be able to investigate Waldemere a bit more thoroughly."

"Are you mad?" I cried, but to no avail. He was already beginning to search the papers on Mr. Barnum's desk. Since standing guard seemed a more desirable option to abetting someone while he upturned a private office, I made my way to the front of the drawing room and took my place, occupying myself by watching the various workmen bustle back and forth and listening to the sounds of sanding and sawing.

After three-quarters of an hour, during which time Holmes emerged from the library only to disappear again into another room of the house, the tedium was finally relieved by the reappearance of Mrs. Barnum.

"My husband is working tirelessly to build a hospital in this community," she said to me, "but I fear that he will become its inaugural patient. You are Mr. Stamford, I believe? I presume Phineas has told you what you are guarding?"

"Yes ma'am. We saw her earlier."

"I don't mind telling you that I will celebrate when that beast is gone and I can have my drawing room back. However, her presence here is important to Mr. Barnum, so there's an end. Just like all of this renovation of the house. It is important to him, so we endure. Frankly, Mr. Stamford, I would like to move to a smaller house. We are the only two people here, except for some servants, and it is simply too big for our needs. There are rooms here I have not entered in months."

As she continued to talk on all manner of subjects, it occurred to me that Mrs. Barnum must not have had many people her own age with whom to converse. I was rather enjoying chatting with the charming lady, which made it something of a pity that Holmes chose that moment to reappear, marching toward us holding up what looked to be a broadsheet. "Stamford, I have found something of interest," he said from behind it.

"What has that man got?" Mrs. Barnum asked.

Lowering the paper, Holmes regarded the wife of our host and employer with what I felt was a dismissive expression. "Oh, Mrs. Barnum, I did not realize you were here. I found this in the room at the end of the hall."

"I know you are a guest of my husband's, but that doesn't give you leave to loot the premises."

"My sincere apologies, madam," Holmes said, "but I found something in this poster that piqued my curiosity." He laid it down on the floor so we could see it. The banner announced Barnum's Grand Traveling Museum, Menagerie, Caravan and Hippodrome and it was illustrated with animals and performers all down the sides. Holmes pointed to one image in particular. "This is the one that interested me. Does this fellow look familiar?"

I knelt closer to look at the picture, which was headlined, "Davalos the Daredevil," and immediately saw what Holmes had noticed. It was a picture of a small man with enormous ears walking a plank that was balanced between two horses galloping around a ring—without a doubt Davy, the elephant keeper. "He is a performer?" I asked.

"*Was* a performer," Holmes said, "and a star one at that, apparently. But you have seen the way the man now limps. One could surmise that he met with an accident that ended his career as a trick rider and forced him into his present line of work, caring for an elephant." Turning to Mrs. Barnum, he asked: "What do you know about this man?"

"Nothing," she replied. "I do not get involved in the business of the circus. You would have to ask my husband or Charles."

"Or the man himself," Holmes said, rising and pounding loudly on the drawing room door and calling out to Davy. There was no reply. He pounded again, and turned the knobs. The door held fast. "I fear something is amiss," he cried. "We must get in there! Stamford, help me."

Much to Mrs. Barnum's distress, we threw our combined weight against the doors until they gave way. Racing inside, Holmes called for the keeper again, but the room appeared empty.

"The crate!" Holmes rushed to the enormous container that held Xanthippe and peered through one of the airholes. Then he ran to the room's huge fireplace and grabbed an iron poker, raced back to the crate, and attacked the lock with it. Within seconds, the heavy lock had snapped off. Holmes threw open the door to the crate. It was empty. The white elephant was gone.

"But…how could…Holmes, how could this happen?" I stammered. "Not one hour ago I saw them inside this room! No one has entered this room or left it. How could they have disappeared?"

"You actually saw Xanthippe?"

"Well, no, but I saw Mr. Barnum enter the room, and had the beast not been there, I believe we would have heard."

Holmes turned to Mrs. Barnum. "Is there any other way into or out of this room?"

"Well, I imagine a man could leave through the windows," she answered, "but hardly an elephant."

At that moment a booming voice rose from outside the drawing room: "Why are these doors hanging open?" We did not need to turn and look to identify the speaker. P. T. Barnum strode into the room and marched straight to the elephant crate, and his oath, upon finding it empty, caused Mrs. Barnum to blush and raise a hand to her mouth. "You two were supposed to guard this room! What have you done with her?"

"Please, sir, we are as shocked as you by this," I said.

"I doubt that! Where is Davy?"

"It seems he has disappeared as well," Holmes said.

"Men and elephants don't simply disappear!" Barnum roared. "They have been abducted! Are the two of you in cahoots against me after all?"

"Mr. Barnum, we are innocent!" I protested, not having the faintest notion what *cahoots* meant.

"Then I suppose Xanthippe and Davy just turned into smoke and went up the chimney, is that it?" the showman bellowed. "Or perhaps they shrunk to the size of General Tom Thumb and they're hiding in the curtains! Do not try to convince me of the impossible, Holmes, for if I've learned anything in my three-score-and-seven on this earth it is that the impossible exists only to be dismissed. Once you've done that, there remain only logical explanations, no matter how improbable. So I will ask you one more time... how did the elephant get out of this room. Holmes? Holmes, I am talking to you!"

But my companion was not listening, appearing instead to be completely lost in his own thoughts. "When you eliminate the impossible," he muttered, "whatever is left, no matter how improbable, has to be the truth... that is brilliance!"

"What are you babbling about now?" Barnum demanded.

"Mr. Barnum," Holmes said, "before you left, you came in here to speak with Davy, did you not?"

"Yes, what of it?"

"Did you actually see Xanthippe?"

"No, Davy told me she was resting, finally, inside that box, and I didn't want to disturb her."

"On the contrary, sir, I believe the elephant was already gone by that point," Holmes said.

"Rubbish!" Barnum cried. "Had she been gone, Davy would certainly have known it!"

"I fully agree."

Barnum's face paled. "Good God in heaven, man, are you trying to tell me *Davy* is the man we are looking for?"

"He used to be a performer for you, did he not?"

"He did a trick riding act in my circus until he fell and was trampled. Once he recovered, I kept him on the payroll to look after my menagerie."

"Did he ever demonstrate resentment over his reduced circumstances?"

"Never! This is preposterous! Even if Davy were involved, what did he do with the elephant? You claim she was gone when I came in here earlier, then tell me how she got out!"

"The only explanation that does not defy the realm of possibility, Mr. Barnum, is that this room contains another exit," Holmes said.

"Blast it, Holmes, I built this house!" Barnum roared. "I know every inch of it! I tell you there is one doorway to this room, *that* one." He pointed to the double doors.

Holmes fell silent at that. The only sounds to be heard in the room were P. T. Barnum's slightly labored breathing and the muffled din of the construction. Then Holmes's eyes caught fire. "Yes, of course! That explains it all!" he cried. "Mr. Barnum, there may have been only one way in or out when the house was built, but I will stake all I own that another one has been added, and very recently."

"What are you talking about?" the showman demanded.

"The workmen! Under the cover of your construction work, who knows what sort of unauthorized renovations might have been made?"

Barnum blinked at the thought. "You mean the workmen built a doorway in here without my knowledge?" He looked over every wall. "Show it to me, then. Produce the secret doorway large enough to accommodate an elephant."

Holmes's face was now glowing. "It is already here," he said. Rushing to the hearth, he kicked away the fire grate and stepped inside the cavernous fire pit. He pounded on the sooty walls of the fire pit, finally coming to the back, which echoed with a hollow thud. "Aha!" he cried, and with both hands, he pushed against it. To the utter amazement of the rest of us, the back wall of the fire pit began to move! With another mighty shove, he pushed it all the way through the wall and into the next room.

"Dear God in heaven!" Barnum cried, running through the passageway that had been created by removing the back the drawing room fire pit and hollowing through the wall. Mrs. Barnum and I quickly followed him into the adjoining room, which was much smaller and filled with the rubble of destroyed brick, plaster, and stone. The fireplace in this room, which shared a chimney with the one in the drawing room, had been completely dismantled.

The "wall" that Holmes had pushed through was not brick but rather a large wooden panel, braced in back and painted to look like brick. In the middle of the room, a wooden ramp had been constructed that led up to a picture window, from which the glass had been removed. Peering through the window, Holmes looked down at the ground. "As I suspected," he said, "wheel tracks. They must have backed a wagon up to the opening and loaded the elephant on, then driven off."

The showman buried his face in his hands. "I cannot believe Davy would do this to me."

"He cannot have done this alone," Holmes said. "The workmen had to be involved. Who oversees them?"

"Charles, of course, but... *damnation!*" P. T. Barnum then spun around and stormed through the opening between the rooms. Seconds later his bellowing cry "*Charles!*" echoed through the entire house, and continued until the man was found. Protesting vociferously, Charles Weymouth was literally dragged through the opening in the wall by his employer, who demanded: "Charles, what do you know of this?"

The sight of the room, the ramp, the open window, and the lack of an elephant rendered Weymouth speechless. He produced a handkerchief and used it to mop his forehead as he took in the room. "Phineas," he finally said, "I *swear* to you I knew nothing about this, nothing."

"I want to believe you, Charles."

"You must!" Weymouth held the cloth up to his mouth to cover his look of horror and silently shook his head. Then a shout burst from Holmes's lips, which caused all of us to jump.

"Why did I not see it before!" he declared. "Mr. Weymouth is not behind the abduction, though the act of raising his handkerchief to his face just now has suggested another. There is a workman here who is never seen without a mask over his face."

"I'm told he is sensitive to the dust," Weymouth said.

"Then why enter a trade where dust is a common factor?" Holmes rejoined.

"Yes, and I saw him earlier today, still wearing that mask while driving a supply lorry up to the house," I added. "There is no dust in the driver's seat of a lorry."

"What are you suggesting?" Barnum demanded.

"That the mask is not to protect him from dust at all," Holmes declared, "but to keep him from being recognized by his employer. Mr. Barnum, would you be able to recognize this man Artaud by sight?"

"Of course," Barnum said. "Are you suggesting that Étienne Artaud has been here in my house the whole time?"

"I fear so," Holmes said. "We have an advantage in that they probably were not expecting us to discover that the elephant was gone for quite some time, but we cannot squander it. Mr. Barnum, you more than anyone know how to transport animals. What would they do with her?"

"If they wanted to leave town they would go to winter quarters and put her on a train car," Barnum said. "But if they wanted to harm her, they could take her anywhere."

A thought suddenly occurred to me. "No, sir, not anywhere," I said. "If the goal is to cause you personal harm, whatever physical proof or evidence is to be offered has to reflect a place that is allied with you. If they plan to take a photograph of the elephant in some stage of danger or distress, it would have to be exposed against a backdrop that is both recognizably yours and a logical place for an elephant to be, or else the evidence would have little effect. Therefore Xanthippe must have been taken to your compound."

"Bravo, Stamford!" Holmes cried.

"Then we must get there as quickly as possible!" Barnum cried. "Come on!"

In turn, we dashed through the hole and back into the drawing room, and Holmes, Weymouth, and I followed P. T. Barnum—carpet slippers and all—out of the house and onto the estate's sprawling lawn. Even though the great showman was thrice my

Thank you for using
Bear Library
302-838-3300
Mon. - Wed. 10-9
Thurs. & Sat. 10-5
Sun. 1-5

User ID:
23910002050709

Date charged:
12/14/2017,13:04
Title: The sunshine
sisters
Item ID:
33910050746446
Date due: 1/4/2018,23:
59

Date charged:
12/14/2017,13:04
Title: Sleeping in the

Item ID:
3 3910050761973
Date due: 1/4/2018,23:
59

Date charged:
12/14/2017,13:04
Title: Come sundown
Item ID:
3 3910050745216
Date due: 1/4/2018,23:
59

Date charged:
12/14/2017,13:04
Title: Sherlock Holmes :
the American years
Item ID:
3 3910040355936
Date due: 1/4/2018,23:
59

Online access @
www.lib.de.us or
www.nccdelib.org
Like us on Facebook

THE SACRED WHITE ELEPHANT by MICHAEL MALLORY

age, I found myself lagging behind him as we sprinted to the carriage house. The phaeton that he had used to speed to his office in town was still liveried and ready to go, though I barely had both feet inside of it when Barnum whipped the steed into action and we took off. Even though I had every confidence that he knew the streets of the city and how to navigate them, I was forced to close my eyes as we took some of the turns on the way to Went Field. After careening around one at a dangerously high speed, we passed a police wagon. The officer shouted at Barnum to slow down, but he did not.

As we approached the field that housed Barnum's menagerie building, Holmes shouted: "Look!" The supply wagon we had seen earlier that day, its cargo platform now tented with canvas, was parked at a back building, behind the one that had housed the faux white elephant's exhibition. Barnum headed straight for it, making a sharp turn at the last moment and reining in his horse forcefully, so that the phaeton itself blocked the path of the wagon team. Leaping down, he charged inside the building as the rest of us followed.

There was faint illumination inside, but one area seemed brighter than the others, and that was the one to which we ran. Soon we made out the forms of two men: one was clearly Davy, while the other was dressed in a workman's smock and a straw hat, and still wore that mysterious kerchief over his face, as well as heavy gloves.

In between them, standing majestically, was Xanthippe.

"Cease at once!" Barnum shouted, startling both men.

"Aw, God, it's himself!" Davy cried. Rushing toward the showman as fast as his limping gait could take him, he threw himself onto his knees and wailed, "Honest, Mr. Barnum, this wasn't my idea. He made me do it, I didn't want to."

"Silence," Barnum ordered, pushing the man aside, and striding toward the masked figure, pointed at him dramatically. "The game is over, Artaud," he announced. "Yes, I know who you are, so you can remove that foolish disguise."

"Disguise?" the man said from behind the cloth. "You think this a disguise, *mon ami*?" The last two words were spoken with vicious bitterness. "You think you recognize Artaud, eh? We shall see." With gloved hands he removed his hat and pulled off the mask and revealed his face. I could not help but gasp.

The man's entire face was horribly disfigured; his nose, cheeks, mouth, and chin were runneled and covered with welts, and of a ghastly grayish-yellow pallor. Removing his gloves evinced that his hands had not spared by his affliction, either. "'Ere is a freak for your museum, Barnum, a living, talking monster!"

"Lordamighty," Barnum uttered. "What has happened to you?"

"*You*, that is what happened to me!"

"I . . . I did nothing to you that was not deserved." He strode toward the ghastly figure. "Explain yourself!"

"Mr. Barnum, do not move any closer!" Holmes commanded. "Do not touch that man. He is leprous."

"Dear God," Barnum said, stepping back.

"It was on your testimony, Barnum, that I was convicted and sentenced to a prison camp in French Guiana, where I endured the tortures of the damned," Artaud said. "And for what? What did I take from you? Baubles . . . nothing! Compare that to what I received!" He put his hands on his ravaged face. "Every day I spent on that stinking island I plotted to avenge myself for what you did to me. I planned my escape. What 'ad I to lose? I did escape. I stowed away on board a ship to New York. I came 'ere. I entered your employ. I even lived in your mansion."

"You did *what?*" Barnum shouted.

"So many empty rooms, no one discovered me," Artaud said. "I was in a position to learn everything that was 'appening. I wanted to ruin your life the way you ruined mine. When the elephant appeared, the chance to use one of your own beasts as the means of your destruction, the irony of it seemed too savory to ignore." He pointed toward the cringing Davy. "The *peu crapaud* there told me 'ow much you stood to lose if anything 'appened to the white elephant."

"He forced me to help him," Davy whined. "He made me put those letters in your mail and stay quiet while he tore out the fireplace. He said if I didn't play along, he'd give me his disease! It was bad enough losing my career, but I didn't want to end up like him."

Holmes spoke up: "I cannot make sense of why you attempted to implicate your own government in this scheme."

"Simply to repay a *kindness*," the villain said bitterly. "My government sent me to 'ell to die, all on the word of a *great man*."

No one said anything for at least a minute; we all stood in silent stillness. Even Xanthippe seemed reluctant to move. Then Holmes shattered the quiet. "You realize, Monsieur Artaud, that you have failed," he said. "There is no other recourse for you except to surrender."

"No other recourse, eh?" the man said. Then, almost as though by sorcery, a small pistol appeared in his hand, causing the rest of us to tense. "Anyone care to come and wrench this from my grasp?" he taunted. "No? Very well..." He slowly raised the gun and pointed it at Xanthippe's right eye.

"No!" Barnum cried. "Artaud, please do not harm her. I beg of you."

"I cannot 'ear you."

"I beg of you, Artaud, I beseech you!" The showman sank to the floor. "I am on my knees."

"The great P. T. Barnum beseeches me, eh? 'E 'umbles 'imself to me. I am touched, monsieur. Very well, Artaud will not 'arm the elephant." He lowered the gun. "For years I 'ave been dying. Now I shall die satisfied." Étienne Artaud smiled horribly, and before anyone could do anything, or even think to do anything, he placed the pistol to his temple and pulled the trigger.

Xanthippe trumpeted at the sudden noise, while her duplicitous keeper fell down in a dead faint.

"Charles," Barnum said, rising slowly, "please forgive me for doubting you."

"I do, Phineas," Weymouth replied in a cracked voice. "What do we do about the body?"

"I shall consult with Dr. Shanks as to how to deal with him. Lordamighty."

Once the unconscious Davy was brought to, Weymouth instructed him to help prepare a cage in the menagerie for Xanthippe, whose safety in the compound was now assured until she could be transported.

Holmes and I followed P. T. Barnum out of the building and

back into the phaeton. None of us uttered a word on the way back to Waldemere, and even when we reassembled inside Barnum's library, it was in silence. Finally the showman spoke. "Mr. Holmes, Mr. Stamford, I do not know what to say. What can I offer you. Name it."

"Dinner would be most acceptable," Holmes replied. "I am quite certain that my friend would agree."

That evening we dined in the finest restaurant in Bridgeport, overlooking the harbor, which was forested with masts and shadowed by the encroaching night. "As delighted as I am that Xanthippe is unhurt, I cannot help but feel like a fool," Barnum said, sipping a cup of steaming coffee (we had already learned that he never touched alcohol, more's the pity). "The Great Hoaxer, they call me... look at the hoax I fell for."

"Some might say, sir," I said, "that it was simply your minute to be born."

The sidelong glance he gave me did not communicate amusement. "You are somewhat less than comforting, young man. Besides, I never uttered that line about born suckers. It was attributed to me by another, but since it seemed good publicity, I never went out of my way to deny it."

"What is going to happen now to little Davy?" Holmes asked, effectively changing the subject.

Barnum sighed. "His life and livelihood was shattered once in my employ, and I cannot do it to him again. He will remain in the company, but I have instructed Charles to make certain that he nevermore sets foot in Waldemere."

We, on the other hand, were guests at Waldemere that evening, and a finer bed I had never slept in. The next morning, Mr. Barnum personally took us to the train station and saw us on our way back to New York.

"That was certainly sporting of him to allow us to keep the money he advanced us," I said to Holmes, as we pulled away from the platform. My companion did not immediately answer, instead fixing his gaze at a spot far off. "Holmes, are you all right?" I asked. "Oh, I see. Now that our adventure is over, you are worried about your tryout with the symphony."

"Quite the contrary, Stamford," he replied. "Even if the symphony beckons, I have no intention of joining their ranks."

"*What?* Why else did we brave the Atlantic?"

He looked at me with fire in his gray eyes. "Didn't you feel it, Stamford, the excitement of puzzling out that impossible situation and tracking down the one responsible? What if I could do that sort of thing all the time? I could return to London and open an office, and then advertise myself as a consulting detective, one to whom people could bring their problems, which I would solve for a fee."

"You would starve."

"Then I would need someone reliable to assist me, to keep me out of debtors' prison. You, for instance."

"*Me?*"

"Oh, come now, Stamford, it was your speculation that Artaud would take the elephant to a property of Barnum's and nowhere else that enabled us to find them in short order. You cannot deny that."

I leaned back in the seat. "What I truly cannot deny is that my father may be right after all," I said. "Perhaps it is time for me to settle down and pursue a career. The old man has been preaching medicine to me."

"Fine. You could still work with me while studying."

I sighed. How was I going to put Holmes off the idea of us working together as detectors for hire? Knowing of his persistence, I would simply have to find someone else more suited for the role when we returned to London.

Miss Carole Buggé here invokes the Bard, as Holmes
discovers that the earth hath bubbles as the water has,
and this is one of them.

THE CURSE OF
EDWIN BOOTH
by

CAROLE BUGGÉ

In the year 1880 all of New York knew my
name. I could hardly go into the streets without strangers murmuring to each other, "That's
Edwin Booth, the actor!" and then coming up to
me to ask for an autograph, a handshake, a lock
of my hair.

It was also in the spring of that same year
I became quite certain someone was trying to
kill me.

One Thursday night, as I emerged from the
theatre after what seemed an endless rehearsal
of our coming production of *Hamlet*, a shot rang
out from what appeared to be an empty street.
I felt a burning on my neck, and when I clapped
my hand to the spot, it came away wet with
fresh blood.

I had faced many situations that required keeping a cool head, so I did not panic, but stepped quickly back through the stage door. The wound on my neck was superficial, and I was soon able to stop the bleeding. I told no one what had happened; my concern for my own safety was tempered by the realization that I was a public figure, and adverse publicity could be ruinous for my theatre company. When I next emerged it was half an hour later, with two husky stagehands on either side of me. I had told them that I was feeling faint; they hustled me into a waiting carriage, the driver put the horses into a brisk trot, and I was home within minutes.

However, this time my feeling was one of dark terror—so dark, in fact, that I took a step I never would have imagined taking: I put an advertisement in the paper.

> WANTED: *Professional detective for private employment. Must be discreet, trustworthy. Experience with Pinkerton Agency or similar employment preferred. Assignment possibly dangerous; monetary reward considerable. Only serious applicants need apply. Reply to Post Box 28, City.*

The reference to Allan Pinkerton and his excellent agency was bitterly ironic, since he had foiled an assassination attempt on President Lincoln in 1861, only to watch helplessly with the rest of the nation as my brother John Wilkes gunned down the great man a few years later.

I took no one into my confidence save for my Negro servant, Hector, who had been with our family since my boyhood in Maryland. Since my father's death, he had become my constant attendant and companion; a more competent and considerate man of any race could not be found this side of the Atlantic.

The paper in which I had placed the advertisement had been at the newsstands and book stalls for just a few hours when there was a knock upon the front door of the Players Club. I was in the grill room having a late lunch, and as the doorman was also taking a late lunch, I sent Hector to answer it.

The Players Club is a three-story brownstone on Gramercy Park South. I had purchased and remodeled the building to serve as a meeting place for prominent men of the theatre, as well as other outstanding professionals. The first two floors included a pool room and a small theatre, as well as a grill room and bar; I occupied the third floor when I was in New York.

I have an actor's instinct for character, and as a theatre manager and director, I am used to sizing up people quickly. When Hector ushered our visitor into the grill room, I knew at once that here was a singular and extraordinary man.

His eyes were dark—so dark that they appeared black in the dim light, reminding me of the Indians I had known in my youthful days in California. He was taller than average; I would have guessed well over six feet—but then many men appear tall to me, as I am only five foot seven in my stocking feet. The Booth family may have had its share of talent, but it did not breed giants.

His face and figure were long and lean; I was reminded of Cassius in *Julius Caesar* (which we were doing in repertory with *Hamlet*), whom Shakespeare describes as having "a lean and hungry look." (Sadly, our current Cassius, Geoff Simmons, was overly fond of sausages and porter, and was anything but lean—in his green toga, he rather suggested a fat garden slug wrapped in a leaf.)

My visitor did not wear a hungry look but rather one of keen interest and curiosity. I had the impression that nothing much escaped those deep-set eyes; he seemed to take in everything around him at a glance. He wore a simple but expensive frock coat and vest, with perfectly pressed trousers and shining black boots.

"How do you do, Mr. Booth?" he said in a decidedly British accent. "I have arrived in answer to your advertisement."

"But the advertisement gave no address—only a post office box."

He waved away my objections as if they were an annoying insect. "A mere formality—I assure you it was not difficult to discover who you were."

I stared at him. "How on earth did you—"

"That you were well off was evident from the suggestion of considerable monetary reward."

As a child, I had suffered from a stutter, which I had conquered years ago. To my surprise, I felt it beginning to return now.

"Yes, b-but—"

"That you were well known was evident from the phrase regarding discretion."

"But how d-did you know it was *me*—this city is full of well-known people!"

"It was a simple matter to follow this gentleman from the post office," he said, indicating Hector, who had just brought me half a dozen letters on a silver tray. "I had my eye on Box Twenty-Eight and when he looked inside for the replies, I knew he would lead me to you. I had only to follow him here."

I felt the tension of the past twenty-four hours begin to drain away from my shoulders.

"Oh, so it was a bit of detective work after all! All you had to do was wait patiently at the post office for him to turn up, and then follow him. So all those deductions about my being well-known and wealthy were just—"

"Oh, no—I had already deduced those facts before seeing your servant."

"I see."

"So when I followed him here, I was quite certain I had the right man."

I looked around the grill room. The bartender was busily polishing glasses, and several actors were congregated in the back of the room, laughing and talking among themselves. They did not pay particular attention to my visitor; however, I thought privacy was called for, so I summoned Hector, who stepped soundlessly into the room.

"Hector, would you show my visitor up to the second floor lounge?" I said. "And bring us up a bottle of brandy and two glasses, please."

The lounge was a small room on the east side of the building, mostly used for playing cards, and was unlikely to be occupied in the middle of the afternoon.

I settled my tab in the grill room and headed up the stairs after them. When I entered the lounge, my visitor had folded his long body comfortably into a leather burgundy armchair.

"I am perhaps not what you expected," he commented as I took the chair opposite him.

"I must admit I was expecting a somewhat…rougher type of man."

"Rest assured that I am the man you seek," he replied smoothly. "My name is Holmes—Sherlock Holmes."

"Holmes, is it? What a curious thing indeed."

"What is curious?"

"My dear first wife Mary's maternal family name was Holmes."

"Her mother, then, was a Holmes?"

"Yes."

"It is not an uncommon name."

"True…this will sound hopelessly superstitious, but we actors are superstitious folk, so forgive me. But it feels almost as if your coming here was an act of providence—as if my dear Mary were somehow looking after me from beyond the grave…"

"I am very sorry to hear that your wife has passed away."

"Thank you."

"And yet you are remarried," he commented, indicating the ring on my left hand.

"Yes…my current wife's name is Mary also. She suffers from brain seizures and now lives with her parents. She hardly knows who I am—or who anyone is, for that matter." I sighed deeply. "But on to the matter at hand," I said, doing my best to shake off my black mood.

"Yes indeed," he replied. "Now, then, what can I do for you?"

I realized at that moment *he* had been interviewing *me*, rather than the other way around, and was now operating under the assumption that the job was his. I felt a bit put out by this, and wanted to protest, but something in me silenced the words.

Instead, I blurted out, "I'm afraid someone is trying to kill me."

He nodded, as if completely unsurprised by this. "I see. In that case, I may be of some assistance."

"You have experience in these matters, then, Mr. Holmes?"

"I can provide references, should you require them."

"Somehow I don't think that will be necessary," I replied.

"Good. Now then, please tell me everything, being careful to omit no detail."

He was the kind of man who immediately inspires confidence; the mere fact of his presence was mysteriously calming.

"Well, the first incident seemed innocent enough at the time: a hanging flat in the theatre swung down during a performance, and I ducked—just in time to prevent being decapitated."

"I see. Was the cause of the accident ever determined?"

"It seems someone had forgotten to tie up the rope holding it in place—or tied it so loosely that it came undone. No one came forward to confess to having tied the rope badly."

Holmes nodded gravely. "And the second incident?"

"A trap door on the stage collapsed during rehearsal. When I stepped on it, it gave way and I nearly fell twenty feet into the building's basement."

"And did you ascertain the reason for this odd occurrence?"

"The bolts holding the hinges on had been removed, so that when I stepped on it, the entire thing gave way. Fortunately, an alert stagehand who happened to be standing next to me grabbed my arm and prevented me from falling. I am not an alarmist, Mr. Holmes, but it quite unnerved me."

Holmes leaned back in his chair and placed his long fingers together.

"Who else knows about this?"

"Well, everyone saw the incidents take place, so my entire company, I suppose."

"Was any innocent explanation for this possible?"

"It just so happened that some workmen had been installing

some new floorboards the day before, so everyone blamed them. I felt differently, of course."

"Have you told anyone else about your suspicions?"

"No. I kept them to myself—except for the anonymous advertisement in the paper which you answered."

He smiled grimly. "That is good—that is very good. Be certain that you continue to keep your own counsel. It is essential that we preserve as much secrecy as possible."

"I agree."

"Good." He leaned forward to sip his coffee, the lamplight shining on his thick black hair, which he wore combed back from his high forehead. "And the third incident?"

"You're quite right, Mr. Holmes—there *was* a third incident." I paused and took a sip of brandy, which burned my throat with a comforting familiarity. "A few days ago someone tried to shoot me."

Holmes raised a single eyebrow. "I assume you failed to get a look at your assailant?"

I nodded. "I'm afraid I didn't see him at all. It was dark, and—"

He waved a long hand impatiently. "Tell me what happened. Omit no details, no matter how trifling."

"I had just finished a rehearsal, and I was leaving the theatre after lingering to talk to the stage manager about the following day's rehearsal. As I turned the corner out into the street from the alley leading to the stage door, I heard the report of a gun."

"You are quite certain that it was a gunshot?"

I took a deep breath; I was not pleased to dwell on the sound of gunshots in theaters. "Yes, quite certain. I immediately heard a whistling in my ear, then felt a burning sensation on the side of my neck."

I opened my collar and showed him the thin red slash across my neck. Holmes examined it, frowning, then leaned back in his chair. "That is indeed a bullet crease. You didn't by any chance recover the bullet in question?"

I shook my head. "I was too shaken to even think to look for it. That corner is very dark late at night. The lights in front of the theatre had long since been turned off."

"I see. Were there any other people about?"

"No; as I said, it was quite late by then. The street looked deserted."

"I'm sorry to say that your fears seem to be quite justified, Mr. Booth. Not only is someone trying to kill you, but I am very much afraid it may be someone known to you—perhaps even a member of your company."

He now accepted my offer of a glass of brandy, and I poured myself some more as well, my hand shaking a little as I grasped the crystal decanter. Alcohol is my only true vice, as it was my father's before me. I have struggled all my life to control my drinking, but now I felt that I might be forgiven for indulging in a glass of brandy.

"What do you propose I do?" I asked Holmes. "I cannot simply refuse to go out in public—I am an actor, for God's sake!"

"What about using an understudy? Surely you must—"

Now it was my turn to dismiss him impatiently. I rose and began to pace the room distractedly. "If I put on an understudy in my place, people will demand their money back. I say this in all humility, Mr. Holmes: people come to the theatre to see *me* as Hamlet, as Brutus, as Iago. They do not come to see an understudy."

"I quite understand. But is not disappointing your public worth paying for with your life?"

"It is not that simple, Mr. Holmes. Scores of people depend upon me for their livelihood. I can't cancel performances indefinitely—the theatre and its employees would lose hundreds of dollars every night."

I gazed out of the window, where cold gusts were whipping the tree branches along Gramercy Park. It was May, but a chill wind had overtaken the city in the last few days. People passing by drew their cloaks close around them as dried leaves scattered by the gusts circled them like miniature tornados; the wind seemed to be bent on knocking them from their feet. I looked back at Holmes, who sat still as a sphinx, his profile sharp in the dim light.

An idea suddenly seized me. "Have you done any acting, Mr. Holmes?"

"As a matter of fact, I have."

"I *knew* it! You can always tell a man who has been upon the stage—the way he uses his voice, the way he holds himself. I have recently lost my Horatio. I was about to hold auditions for the role, but now it occurs to me ... have you ever done Shakespeare?"

"I confess I have—a little."

"Would you be so kind as to take over the role?"

He paused for a moment. "I think I perceive where you are headed with this. Being a member of the cast would give me unparalleled access to the people who surround you profession-ally."

"Exactly! Well—what do you say? I'll pay you a salary of twenty dollars a week—in addition to your fee, of course."

He smiled, softening the angular planes of his long face, like the sun breaking through the clouds on a gloomy day.

"Why not? I don't see what we have to lose, and we may have much to gain."

"Capital! I shall introduce you to our stage manager tonight at rehearsal. Where are you staying while in New York?"

"At the Hotel Washington."

"You must stay here as my guest—there is a spare bedroom on the third floor, just down the hall from my own. I will see that Hector lays out all the necessary items for your comfort."

"Thank you. That will enable me to watch out for your safety more effectively."

"And now, if you don't mind, I think I shall perhaps try to catch a few hours' sleep, as it promises to be a long evening."

"Certainly."

I went upstairs and lay down in my bed, but I could not sleep. Why would someone in my own company want to kill me? Including stagehands, actors, and theatre staff, the list of suspects numbered well over sixty—just for our current production alone. Eventually I must have fallen into a fitful sleep, because I dreamed that my father was standing in the corner of my room, his face sad and mournful. I tried to speak to him, but no words would come. He raised an arm toward me, as though he wished to beckon me to him—or perhaps it was in warning; I couldn't tell.

Then the chimes on the grandfather clock in the hall struck five, and a moment later Hector appeared at the door with a cup of coffee.

Dressing quickly, I went downstairs to find Holmes waiting with his overcoat on his arm. We walked briskly to the theatre, which was in Union Square, only about half a mile from the Players.

When we arrived, I introduced Holmes to the assembled company with a story about knowing him from my youthful days in California. Everyone appeared quite pleased that we had a new Horatio so soon—except for Geoffrey Simmons, our Polonius, who frowned and pulled at his beard. Geoffrey was a fine actor but an odd fellow. He was short and round, so corpulent that he appeared almost as wide as he was tall. His skin was pink and smooth as a baby's, and with his small, bright blue eyes and mane of white hair, he rather resembled a cherubic Santa Claus. He was a moody and private man, and did not socialize much with the rest of the company; no one could claim to know him very well. But he was a great favorite with audiences; his Polonius was both a comical bumbler and an oddly touching father figure to Laertes and Ophelia.

The rehearsal went smoothly; Holmes was an even better Horatio than I had imagined—noble, resolute, and sensitive, all the qualities the character should have. He also possessed a darkness that contrasted wonderfully with the upright, steadfast Horatio. He was very effective in his closing speech at the end of the play. Several of the actors congratulated him on it—but Geoff Simmons continued to scowl and pull at his beard.

However, our Laertes, young Nate Carlisle, seemed much taken with him. He watched Holmes with great interest during his scenes, and made a point of talking to him during breaks. Nate was a lively, nervous young man with golden curls and intense, deep-set eyes of the palest blue. His Laertes was fiery and passionate, and he was an excellent swordsman, equally skilled with the epée and the rapier. I am no mean swordsman myself, but the final duel scene with him was a challenge that kept me on my toes. I had never acted with him before; he had come to me with a recommendation from a theatre manager in Savannah.

He reminded me of my younger self—energetic, eager, and athletic, full of desire to light the world on fire. By the time rehearsals began he had his lines completely memorized. I watched him during rehearsals somewhat wistfully, knowing that those days were behind me.

But though age has much to tell youth, remembering too well what it was to be young, youth has little interest in listening, because it does not believe it will ever be old. But I knew that one day he would look back, as I have, and wonder where it had all gone—the promise, the adventure, the glamour of a life just beginning, a career on the verge of glory. The sweetest moment of all is the one just before the doing—the breath taken before the fulfillment of a long-sought dream. The savoring afterwards is always tinged with sadness, with a bitter aftertaste, and is never as sweet.

At our first break Nate stood in the wings, conversing with Holmes, his face eager and flushed with the excitement of youth.

"Have you acted in London?" he asked Holmes.

"Only at university, when I was in school—and not very much; I was more interested in other things," Holmes replied.

"I would love to go to England—I want to see how the English do Shakespeare!" Nate exclaimed as Geoff Simmons sauntered up to them.

"It's highly overrated, my boy," Simmons remarked, never taking his eyes off Holmes.

"I quite agree," Holmes replied, turning a level gaze upon Simmons. "Your Polonius is as good as any I've seen in England."

Simmons was utterly flustered by this, and before he could respond, the bell rang to resume rehearsal.

To my distress, I was finding it difficult to concentrate on the play. I was now in the uncomfortable position of watching everyone around me, studying them and wondering what grudge they might possibly hold against me, what the content of our last exchange was, had I ever slighted them, and so on, as my thoughts circled through the past hunting for any motive one of them might have for taking my life.

During the break Holmes and I sat in my dressing room talking quietly, and Holmes remarked that we had better keep an eye on Simmons.

"Do you know him from elsewhere?"

"I have never laid eyes on him before," Holmes replied calmly, lighting a cheroot. He seemed to smoke as much as I did—my doctor had warned me about it, but I found it even more difficult to give up than alcohol.

"He doesn't appear to have taken a shine to you," I observed.

"Yes, I noticed that."

I rose from my chair and began to pace the dressing room. It was a nervous habit I inherited from my father, who would often pace when he was ill at ease. I had spent my childhood years following him from town to town, trying to soothe his restless spirit with my banjo playing or storytelling—anything to keep him away from the bottle. Most people regarded him as the greatest American actor of his generation, but even as a young boy I saw that the gift of genius could exact a terrible price.

"Well, Holmes, have you seen anyone whom you suspect?"

He shook his head. "It is early yet. Is there anyone who would benefit monetarily from your death?"

"Not especially. I am worth much more alive; as I said, there are a great many people who depend upon me for their livelihood."

He blew a smoke ring into the air above his head; it curled and dissipated into a thin gray mist. "If we rule out money as an explanation, then we are left with more personal motives."

"But who would hate me so much that they want to kill me?"

"Oh, it is not at all necessary that they should hate you personally in order to want to kill you—only that they hate someone or something."

"What do you mean?"

"The mind is a curious thing," he replied slowly. "Once a diseased thought has taken hold, the symptoms may present in a variety of ways. In that respect it is not unlike the body, actually, in which the same disease may present with radically different symptoms in different people."

"That's true," I said. "When my brother John and I got chicken pox as children, all I had were a few spots and a mild fever, whereas Johnny nearly died…" I fell into silence, suddenly struck by the disturbing thought that it might have been better for the world if he had died.

"Exactly," Holmes replied. "And there are even more bizarre cases than that in the medical literature—which is why diagnosis of disease is so much more of an art than a science. Likewise, the diagnosis of crime has its challenges… in this case, for example, several things present themselves to me. Firstly, the would-be killer is very patient. Secondly, he or she is equally determined. That would most probably rule out a crime of passion—though not necessarily. Are there any ladies in your company who are especially smitten with you?"

I sighed. "Unfortunately, yes." (Some have described me as handsome; I do not agree with them. It is true that I have my father's dark eyes—critics are fond of using such words as "luminous" and "lustrous" to describe them—but I think my nose is too prominent and my lips too thin to rank me as truly handsome. I would reserve that description for my brother John, whose high forehead, strong jaw, and noble profile made him a great favorite with the ladies.)

"Do you have a particular admirer in mind?" Holmes inquired.

I sighed again. "Her name is Kitty, and she is a perfectly nice young woman, but not much of an actress, I'm afraid. I also suspect that her admiration is not for my person so much as my position, to be quite honest."

Just then there was rapid, lively knock on the door; and, as if responding to a cue, Kitty's voice sounded in the hallway.

"Edwin!" she sang out in her high, bell-like voice. "May I come in?"

"That's her now," I whispered to Holmes. "Should I—?"

He nodded, and I rose to open the door.

Kitty was standing in the hall, dressed as a lady-in-waiting in the Danish court. It pleased the gentlemen of New York when I sprinkled the stage with comely young women, and I had no objection to bringing in more audience members, even if they were not there to admire Shakespeare's verse.

"Hello!" Kitty said brightly. Her blond hair bounced in tight ringlets around her face, and her blue eyes were cheerful as spring daisies. "Oh," she said, peering around my shoulder to spot Holmes. "I'm sorry—I didn't realize you had company!"

"Not at all," I said. "Please come in."

"Hello, Mr. Helms," Kitty said.

"Holmes," I corrected.

"Yes, yes—I am sorry, Mr. Holmes!" Kitty corrected herself, blushing prettily.

"This is Kitty Trimble," I said to Holmes.

"Pleased to meet you," he said graciously.

She gave a little curtsy in response; she came from the slums of the Lower East Side, and was forever at pains to behave like a lady. As she entered the room, her fluffy white terrier, Prince, trailed behind her, his sharp little eyes just visible under the shaggy fur on his head. When he saw Holmes, he gave a high, piercing bark, wagging his stub of a tail.

"Stop it, Princey!" Kitty cried, picking him up and cradling him in her plump white arms.

"Your dog does not appear to like me," Holmes commented.

"Oh, no—he *does*!" Kitty protested. "He only barks at people he likes."

"Curious," said Holmes. "He wouldn't be much use as a watchdog."

Kitty erupted in peals of silvery laughter. "He's not a watchdog, silly! Did you hear that, Princey? Mr. Holmes thinks you're a watchdog."

She hugged the dog close to her lilac-scented bosom and fluttered her eyelashes at us. I mused that she would be more attractive if she didn't overplay her hand; as for Holmes, he seemed immune to her charms.

"What can I do for you, Kitty?" I asked.

"I was just wondering if perhaps it might be a good idea to have more of the members of the court onstage for the final scene," she said, putting the dog back down and twirling a lock of golden hair between her dainty fingers. "It would heighten the tension to have more spectators onstage."

I smiled. Kitty was always anxious to spend more time onstage.

"You may be right," I replied, and her already pink cheeks reddened even more.

"Thank you for the idea," I continued, ushering her to the door.

"You're welcome," she said with a charming smile. "Good-bye," she called to Holmes. "Welcome to the company!"

"Thank you very much," he replied.

With a rustle of skirts and a flash of yellow hair, she turned, leaving behind a trail of lilac perfume, her little dog trotting obediently after her.

"A very cheerful young woman," Holmes remarked dryly when she had gone. "And a very ambitious one."

I stared at him. "You don't suspect—"

He smiled grimly. "My dear Booth, I suspect everyone."

"But surely—" I began, reddening.

"Your gallantry toward the fairer sex does you credit, but one of the most charming women I ever knew drowned all three of her children in a bathtub."

I shuddered.

"Really, Holmes, I am not sure I would care to have your perspective on humanity."

"I can quite understand that," he replied evenly. "However, if

THE CURSE OF EDWIN BOOTH by CAROLE BUGGÉ

one wants to engage in solving crimes, one must not shy away from the truth."

I was just about to turn my attention to a platter of cold roast beef that had been delivered to my dressing room when the bell rang to resume rehearsal. Disappointed, I gazed longingly at the beef for a moment before we hurried off to the stage.

We were approaching the gravediggers scene when I realized I had left Yorick's skull in my dressing room. I hurried back to retrieve it, hoping to grab a piece of roast beef before returning.

The door was ajar, and when I opened it, I saw Kitty's little dog Prince lying on the floor, unnaturally still. I knelt beside him; he did not appear to be breathing. I felt for a pulse but could find none. There was white foam clinging to the corner of his mouth. I also saw that a chunk had been bitten from the thick slice of roast beef on the table.

My head began to spin and my knees suddenly went weak. I realized immediately what had happened: the poisoned meat was meant for me. Taking several deep breaths in an attempt to steady my nerves, I leaned against the dressing room wall and ran a hand across my clammy forehead; I had broken out into a cold sweat.

There was a quick, light knock at the door. I hesitated for a moment.

"Who is it?"

"Holmes."

Relief flooding my veins, I opened the door to admit him to the room. He took one look at the poor dog and grasped the situation immediately.

"Dear me," he said, frowning. "This is very bad indeed."

"What should we do?"

"We must remove the dog from here immediately—the killer must not know we are on to him."

"Poor Kitty," I said as we lifted the small, lifeless body.

"Yes; it will go hard with her when she discovers him in her dressing room."

"But shouldn't we tell her—"

Holmes shook his head. "It is most regrettable, but also vital that the dog appear to have died of natural causes."

We took the poor creature down the hall to the dressing room Kitty shared with the other ladies-in-waiting, and left him next to her chair. I felt my throat thicken as we closed the door behind us, and my forehead burned with shame at the ruse we were perpetrating on poor Kitty.

"And now?" I said.

"Now we return to rehearsal as though nothing happened."

And so we did.

We had just begun Act II when a bloodcurdling wail came from the direction of the dressing rooms. Everyone stopped what they were doing and listened, horrified. It was a woman's voice, and the chilling sound made my skin prick out all over in goose bumps.

Of course, I knew only too well who it was, and why she was crying. Moments later one of the other young actresses, Carolyn Maloney, rushed into the room, tears streaming down her face.

"It's Kitty!" she wailed. "Her poor little Prince is dead!"

Moments later Kitty appeared, carrying the inert body of her pet dog, her pretty face swollen from crying. I admit my own eyes did not remain entirely dry—the sight was so piteous that I doubt if any of us were unmoved by it.

Kitty was petted and hugged and made much fuss over, but she was inconsolable. No one was more solicitous than young Nate Carlisle, who took her hand in his and, with a trembling voice, expressed his sincere regret. When Kitty wouldn't stop crying, he looked beseechingly at the rest of us.

"You can always get another dog," he suggested hopefully.

"I don't *want* another dog!" she wailed. "I want my Princey!"

Poor Nate looked miserable, as if he was about to cry himself, and I decided to save him by calling everyone back to rehearsal. It would have been nice to take the rest of the day off, but we were scheduled to open in a week.

Kitty struggled bravely through rehearsal, but it was clear that the death of her beloved Prince had devastated her. The shock of grief was stamped on her face—her lower lip trembled during the queen's speech about Ophelia's death, and she shed real tears during my death scene at the end of the play. If she were only able to summon up such real emotion consistently onstage, she might have been a principal player instead of a lady-in-waiting.

Finally rehearsal was over, and I was waiting in the lobby for Holmes to join me when I saw Joseph Jefferson hurrying toward me. I had known Joe since my days in California. He had agreed to play the small but key role of the First Gravedigger in our production. It was a role he had played many times before, and he was always an audience favorite. The repartee between Hamlet and the First Gravedigger is some of Shakespeare's wittiest; one mark of his genius is his ability to relieve the mounting tension of the tragedy with this brief comic scene.

"I say, wait up for a moment!" Jefferson panted, running after me on spindly, storklike legs. A long black greatcoat hung off his lean, slightly bowed back, and with his coarse black hair and piercing dark eyes, he reminded me of a bird of prey—a crow, perhaps, or a raven.

"Edmund, my boy," he said, catching up with me, "I have something for you." It was one of his little jokes to call me Edmund, which was the name of the evil bastard son in King Lear.

He fished a slip of paper from his pocket and thrust it at me. "Geoff Simmons gave this to me to give to you."

"Very well—thank you, Joseph," I replied, putting the note in my pocket.

"Don't mention it." He began to leave, then turned back to me, his black eyebrows furrowed. "I say, old man, is everything all right?"

"Yes, perfectly—why do you ask?"

"Oh, no reason, I suppose…it's just that you look a bit—well, forgive me, but distracted, I suppose." He leaned closer to me, and I could see the yellow in his eyes. "I say, it's not your wife, is it? Taken a turn for the worse, has she?"

It was Joe Jefferson who had first introduced me to Mary Devlin, my beloved first wife, and I always thought he found my current wife a poor substitute.

"No, no—she's much the same," I answered.

"Poor thing," he clucked, his eyes crinkling sympathetically. "Madness runs in that family," he added, with a conspiratorial nod.

"Yes, well, I must be off," I said, buttoning my coat.

"Do take care, won't you?" he said earnestly.

"Yes," I replied, thinking his comment somewhat odd.

"Right, then, old man—see you tomorrow."

With that he loped off into the night, his greatcoat flapping around his ankles like the wings of a giant black bird.

As I stood watching him, I was suddenly aware that someone was behind me. I turned to see Holmes standing there silently, arms folded, looking after Jefferson.

"Curious man," he said when I turned around.

"How do you mean?" I was both fascinated and irritated with Holmes's ability to pluck observations out of thin air. "What do you know of him?"

"Oh, nothing much," he answered airily, "other than he owns a Springer spaniel of advanced years, is overly fond of coffee, and is quite the amateur gardener. He is keen on roses in particular, I should think."

I stared at him.

"Really, Holmes, how on earth—?"

"Do not distress yourself, my dear Booth," he replied. "That he owns a dog is evident from the short, curly hairs clinging to his trousers. That it is a medium-sized dog is evident from the fact that the hairs are found only as far up as his knees. As the hairs are both black and gray and curly, the most obvious choice would be a spaniel, probably a Springer, which is a very popular breed just now."

"But the age of the dog—"

He smiled. "There I confess I was surmising. A man his age does not get a young dog—in fact, if he has a dog at all, it is likely to be as advanced in years as he is. That and a preponderance of the gray hairs led to my conclusion."

"And the rest of your conclusions? The coffee drinking, for example?"

"My dear Booth, one of the first things I noticed was the color of his teeth—and few things except tobacco can stain the teeth quite that shade of gray. However, as he has not a whiff of smoke about his clothing or his person, I discounted that conclusion and surmised that he is overly fond of coffee."

"And the gardening?"

"Again, simple observation. He is impeccably groomed, and yet his fingernails are ragged and somewhat dirty. That and the ruddy glow of his cheeks leads me to believe he spends time among his flowers—and the scratches on his hands lead me to the conclusion that he is particularly fond of roses, which, as poets have oft noted, are not without their thorns. Are you satisfied now?"

"Oh, very well!" I said. I'm afraid I sounded a bit exasperated, which was not my intent, but I couldn't help myself. "I'm satisfied, but you have to admit it's a bit . . . well, irritating."

He smiled. "Perhaps. But just as a man who wishes to improve his bodily strength must do his exercises, so I must exercise my brain. May I ask what you were conversing about just now?"

"He had a note to give me from Geoff Simmons."

"Oh? May I inquire what was in it?"

"I haven't read it yet," I said, fishing it out of my pocket. I glanced at it quickly—it was written on the back of one of our programs for *Hamlet*. I handed it to Holmes, who read it aloud.

" 'My dear Edwin, would you kindly meet me tomorrow after rehearsal in the grill room of the Players? I may have something of import to tell you. Geoff Simmons.' "

"What do you make of it?" I asked.

"It's very curious," he murmured, handing it back to me. "Observe the wording: I *may* have something of import to tell you—it suggests that he does not yet know whether he will or not."

"Yes, I noticed that."

"Furthermore, it is written hurriedly, on the back of a program—almost as though he did not plan to write it, but suddenly had the need, and grabbed whatever was to hand at the time."

"Yes, I see what you mean."

"Also, why not request a meeting with you tonight instead of tomorrow?"

"Presumably because of his appointment."

"Indeed. The whole thing is very mysterious, and I don't like it."

We left the theatre, heading northeast toward the Players, starting up Fifth Avenue, then winding east through side streets, past stalls of booksellers and greengrocers. We walked for a while in silence, breathing in the early spring air; the cold snap of the previous week had lifted, and the air was suddenly heavy with the smell of cherry blossoms. We wandered uptown through the gaily decorated theatre district as carriages careened past us, bouncing briskly down Broadway.

It was late when we arrived at the Players, and the grill room was about to close. However, an exception was made for me. We ordered lamb chops and roast potatoes, and though I normally am very fond of lamb, I didn't have much appetite. I was silent all throughout dinner, and only when Hector brought us our coffee and brandy in front of the fire did I finally give voice to the thoughts I had been nursing all night.

"Do you believe in fate, Mr. Holmes?"

"It depends upon what you mean by fate."

"Do you have a brother?"

"Yes, I do."

"And what is he like?"

"Completely unlike me in certain ways, but in others very much like me indeed."

"How so?"

A faint smile flickered across his thin lips.

"We are both of an intellectual turn of mind ... in fact, his intellect is probably superior to mine."

"Really? He must be quite impressive. And how are you different?"

Holmes's dark eyes searched my face for a moment, then he lowered them and shook his head.

"Except for a certain ... aversion to our fellow man, our temperaments could not be more distinct. Whereas I am all nervous energy, kinetic and restless, my brother is a sloth of a man. You may perhaps have remarked upon my rather pronounced leanness."

It was my turn to smile. "That would be difficult not to notice."

"Well, my brother is my exact physical opposite. If you saw the two of us together you would not believe we were related— except perhaps for a certain resemblance around the eyes. I am convinced that nothing would please him more than to live the rest of his life seated in his armchair at his club, moving only to turn the pages of a newspaper or order another brandy."

I nodded. "Yes, it is quite astonishing how far apples can fall from the same tree."

Holmes nodded but did not reply. A silence fell between us, heavy with the unasked question.

"And your brother, Mr. Booth?" Holmes said at last, his voice gentle.

"My brother," I began slowly, as if by delaying the words I could somehow delay the thought of those terrible days, "my brother John was very like me in some ways—and completely different in others."

"He was a gifted actor, I hear."

"Oh, yes—and handsome too. All the ladies were in love with him."

"It is hard to imagine one whom Nature has provided with so much being driven to such desperate extremes," Holmes replied, then his voice softened. "This must be difficult for you. My apologies if you feel I am prying into matters you would rather not discuss."

I shook my head and lit a cigar. "Thank you for your concern, Mr. Holmes, but my sister Asia insists it does me good to talk about it."

"Perhaps," Holmes murmured. "There are more things in heaven and earth..."

"My poor brother bore within him a darkness—a hunger, if you will—that was never completely satisfied by what other men would have deemed profuse blessings. Youth, talent, beauty of form and face, a family name of honor and renown... all of these gifts were bestowed upon young Johnny, and yet he was possessed of a dissatisfaction with life the rest of us could never understand. He identified always with the South, even though everyone else in our family considered ourselves Northerners. None of us fought in the war, but Johnny seemed determined to rail against the North whenever the chance arose. Then, when victory came to the Union forces, he seemed to come apart in some way. But upon my soul, Mr. Holmes, I will never to this day understand what evil force propelled him into such a desperate and despicable act!"

"Can you not, Mr. Booth?" he replied softly. "You yourself have been considered the preeminent actor in this country for most of your career, the sole inheritor of your father's mantle of greatness."

"Perhaps, but Johnny was—"

"Your younger brother, never destined to reach your heights— or so he must have believed."

"But he had fame, and the adoration of women wherever he went."

"But *you* had the respect and adulation of your peers, the press, and everyone who truly mattered in his eyes. I believe your brother realized he would never be the great tragedian that you are—and having come of age in your shadow, he craved attention more than virtue or honor."

I laughed—a short, bitter exhalation of air. "I find it ironic that you say this, because I swear to you I would exchange all of my renown for a return to the simple pleasures of married life once again. To sit by the fire with my dear Mary once again! That, to me, is real bliss—not dashing madly about from town to town, sleeping in a different bed night after night, eating indifferent food in dull company. To be an actor, Mr. Holmes, is to feel that one's life is never truly one's own."

"Perhaps it is the human condition to be in a state of continual longing—to yearn for what we cannot have."

"Perhaps."

We talked on into the night. I lost track of time, until I became aware of the slow, steady clip-clop of the milk horse as it plodded down the cobblestone street, and realized that we had stayed up all night.

I yawned, feeling suddenly how tired I was. My weary body cried out for sweet sleep; I longed to sink into blissful oblivion.

"I hope you don't mind if I leave to retire for the night," I said, "or rather, to sleep away the rest of the morning."

"Not at all," Holmes replied. "By all means—you must get your rest."

"Good night, then."

"Good night."

I turned and went up the stairs, but could not resist a glance back as I did. My last glimpse was of him sitting, shrouded in pipe smoke, peering into the half light of the coming dawn, as if the rising sun itself held the answer to the secrets plaguing us both.

I fell into my bed, but still I could not sleep. I tossed and thrashed about for over an hour, and finally, when sleep did come, I drifted in and out of heavy dreams, in which my brother John always seemed to be lurking in the background.

I awoke to a terrific clap of thunder. Shortly afterward, the skies opened up and the rain pelted down with a sharp, percussive sound, like handfuls of pebbles being tossed at the window panes. I watched as the drops hit the glass; defeated in their attack and drained of their energy, they slid harmlessly down the windows. If only my assailant were so easy to overcome—if only I could put up an invisible barrier between us! A deep strain of melancholy threaded through the Booth family like an evil, creeping vine—perhaps it was the price we had to pay for the genius bestowed upon us. As I gazed out at the furious storm, I couldn't help but think of my poor brother. In him the melancholy grew, rampant and untended, into a madness that burst forth in terrible fullness on that fateful night at Ford's Theatre.

Finally I dragged myself out of bed, bathed, and dressed. Rehearsal had been called for two o'clock in the afternoon, so after a hasty breakfast, Holmes and I took a cab to the theatre.

That day we were scheduled to rehearse the scene in which Hamlet visits his mother, Gertrude, in her bedroom. During the course of the scene he mistakes the busybody Polonius, eavesdropping behind a screen, for his Uncle Claudius, the man who murdered Hamlet's father. Gertrude calls out for help, and, in a panic, the foolish Polonius echoes her cries. Hamlet hears him and stabs Polonius through the screen, thinking he is stabbing the murderous Claudius. In one of the play's many sad ironies, poor Polonius is rewarded for his meddling with an ignominious death, and Hamlet incurs the wrath of the old man's son, Laertes, while Claudius remains free.

We used a prop sword with a collapsing blade—a simple enough device—so that when I "stabbed" Geoff Simmons, the blade retreated into itself, giving the illusion of sinking into his flesh. The effect was very realistic, even seen from close up, and audiences invariably gasped when the sword "penetrated" his body.

The scene between Hamlet and his mother was going well. Elizabeth Zare, the veteran actress playing Gertrude, was wonderful—and when the moment arrived for the stabbing, I was charged with emotion. I spoke Hamlet's lines as he hears Polonius:

> How now? a rat?
> Dead for a ducat, dead!

As I said the lines, I seized the sword from Gertrude's bedside table. As I did, a small voice inside of me sounded faintly: *This is not the right sword.* It did not feel like the usual prop sword that we used—it was heavier, and the handle felt different. But the moment was fleeting, and I was so hot with emotion that I ignored that faint voice and continued with the scene.

I will never forgive myself for what happened next.

I grasped the sword and plunged it into the curtain Polonius was hiding behind. But instead of the metallic click of the collapsing blade, there was the sickening sound of steel ripping into flesh. Stunned, I pulled my hand back, the sword still clutched in it. It was wet with blood—not stage blood, but real blood. I staggered backward as Geoffrey Simmons stumbled out from behind the screen, his face white, clutching his stomach. With a groan, he sank to his knees. He looked up at me with the most pitiful expression of disbelief, hurt, and accusation. I tried to speak but could not utter a word. I knelt beside him and caught him in my arms; I was vaguely aware of a woman screaming behind me. And then all was blackness; it was as though someone had pulled a shade over my eyes, and I lost consciousness.

The next thing I knew I was lying on the divan in my dressing room, Holmes bending over me.

Squinting in an attempt to focus my eyes, I tried to sit up.

"Easy, now," Holmes said. "Don't try to stand just yet. You've had a shock—we all have."

"Geoffrey!" I cried. "Is he——?"

"He has been taken to hospital," Holmes replied. "Everyone believes it was an accident."

"It was no accident," I said grimly.

"Yes, I know. Someone put that sword there on purpose."

"But why kill poor Geoffrey?" I lamented.

"Clearly he knows something. That is no doubt why he left the note asking to speak with you." He began pacing the room, his face dark. "This is really getting to be too much—we must act decisively, and soon."

It struck me that we were caught in the same dilemma as Shakespeare's famous character: to act or not to act—and when?

When I had recovered from my shock I made a brief appearance in front of the rest of the company to announce that rehearsal was canceled indefinitely—at least until we found a new Polonius. A report arrived from the hospital that Geoff Simmons was alive, but for how long he would remain thus they could not say. Following that news, I sent the actors home. I was careful to call the event a "horrible accident," and cautioned everyone to check his or her props carefully from now on. Perhaps others also suspected this was no accident, but if so, they did not tell me.

Holmes hailed a cab and I sat in moody silence as it rattled through the streets. I now was in a moral quandary, and had to seriously consider canceling the entire production. I had thought up until now that I was the only one in danger, but clearly I was mistaken.

No sooner had we seated ourselves in the grill room when Hector handed me my mail. In it was a bill from the theatre owner for our monthly rent, which made my decision even more painful. If I did not present *Hamlet,* the bill would go unpaid and my entire company would be out of work. I sighed deeply and tossed the envelope on the table next to me.

"What is it?" Holmes asked.

"A bill from our landlord," I replied. "Each year he threatens to sell the building, and each year I find a way to dissuade him. He claims if he turned it into a store it would be much more profitable."

"No doubt he is right," Holmes answered. "I wonder why he continues to operate it as a theatre."

"I don't know—I suspect prestige has something to do with it."

"Of course," Holmes said with a nod. "He can boast at parties that he is Edwin Booth's landlord . . . that makes me wonder."

"Wonder what?"

"Well, I had previously discarded money as a motive, but perhaps I should revise my thinking. There may be an unseen player in this affair after all."

I was about to respond, but at that moment the door opened and in strode Lawrence Barrett.

Barrett and I had known each other for many years, since my earliest days in New York. He was an intense and gifted actor, but a difficult and demanding man. We had had many ups and downs over the years—after one quarrel we didn't speak for months. I had refused to cast him in a lead I felt he was unsuited for, and he refused to forgive me. He was as covetous of fame as I was weary of it. His Cassius in *Julius Caesar* was renowned—he was suited to the part as few actors are, being himself not only lean but possessed of a truly ambitious and "hungry" nature. Though a critically acclaimed actor, he never drew large audiences as I did, which rankled him terribly.

He swung into the grill room on his long legs, wearing a forest green wool cape and shiny black riding boots. He looked around the room, no doubt hoping to be recognized by some young actor who might ask him for an autograph. No one paid him any attention, though, and he flicked his cape over his shoulder, much as a cat flicks its tail when irritated. Spying me, he stalked stiff-legged to our table; a frown passed across his face when he saw Holmes.

"Hello, Larry," I said, smiling up at him.

"Good day, Edwin," he replied, still looking at Holmes.

"Allow me to present Mr. Sherlock Holmes," I said. "He is our Horatio for this production. Holmes, this is Lawrence—"

"Lawrence Barrett," Holmes interrupted smoothly. "One of our greatest living actors. I had the honor of seeing your Cassius once—I found it to be the definitive interpretation of the role."

"You flatter me, sir," Barrett replied, coloring. He had a broad Irish face, with a Cupid's bow mouth, rosy cheeks, and a fair complexion that betrayed his emotions. (It was rumored that his father's name was Brannigan, but that he changed it for his stage career.)

"I think not," Holmes answered, "though your modesty becomes you."

I was forced to hold my tongue—Barrett was many things, but modest was not one of them.

"In any case," Holmes continued, "the honor is all mine."

"Thank you, sir," Barrett replied, somewhat placated, but I still sensed an uneasiness on his part.

"Won't you join us?" I said.

"No, thank you—I have urgent business to attend to; however, I heard of your terrible accident, and I wished to offer you my services as Polonius."

(Barrett was five years younger than I—and, as my critics liked to point out, I was long in the tooth for the role of Hamlet, but I continued to draw more crowds in that role than in any other.)

"Why, what a capital idea," I replied.

"I have just ended an out-of-town engagement, as it happens, and am quite free at the moment," Barrett said, all the while flicking his cape nervously. It occurred to me that possibly there was no "out-of-town engagement," and that Larry was in fact in need of a job. But I knew the man too well to puncture his pride needlessly, so I nodded seriously.

"How kind of you to think of me," I said. "Can you start immediately?"

"Indeed I can," he replied.

"Tomorrow at noon, then?"

"That will be fine. And now if you'll excuse me, I have some business to attend to. It was a pleasure meeting you," he added, addressing Holmes.

"The pleasure was all mine," Holmes replied.

"Until tomorrow, then," Barrett said, bowing slightly.

"Yes—and thank you, Larry," I answered.

His mouth curled upwards in a smile, and again I was reminded of a cat—precise, wary, watchful. "Always a pleasure to help out a friend."

"He does indeed have a lean and hungry look," Holmes remarked when Barrett had gone.

"Yes," I answered. "He was born to play Cassius."

"How long was he in the military?"

By now I had become so used to Holmes's ways that I didn't even bother to show my astonishment.

"About four years, I believe, during the Rebellion," I replied casually.

"An officer—a captain, perhaps, or major," Holmes said.

"Captain."

He looked at me as if expecting the usual questions and pronouncements of amazement, but I refused to play along.

"Now then," I said, enjoying the faint expression of disappointment that crossed his face, "what are you going to order for dinner?"

But we were both exhausted, emotionally and physically, and neither of us ate much dinner. By the time we were ready to retire I was yawning uncontrollably. I settled into my comfortable four-poster bed and closed my eyes, but before I drifted off to sleep, two unwelcome thoughts occurred to me: that as a cavalry officer, Barrett was presumably a very good shot, and furthermore, perhaps not all was forgiven after all.

My mood was not improved when I arrived at my dressing room the next day to find a piece of paper nailed to the door. Trembling, I plucked it off and read it, instantly recognizing Richard's Act III speech from *Richard II*:

> For God's sake, let us sit upon the ground
> And tell sad stories of the death of kings;
> How some have been deposed; some slain in war,
> Some haunted by the ghosts they have deposed;

> Some poisoned by their wives: some sleeping killed;
> All murdered.

I turned to see Holmes coming toward me, and handed him the note without speaking. He glanced at it, then shook his head.

"Someone is toying with you."

"Maybe it is time to admit defeat and cancel the production," I said.

"If you can grant me one more day," Holmes said, "I think I can flush out your assailant. However, should you decide to give up, I can certainly understand—"

"Very well," I interrupted him. "At the end of today, though, I must make the decision."

The bell rang for rehearsal, and we headed off down the corridor toward the stage. Today we were to rehearse the final duel scene, but I was not sure I was up to the task.

All good actors must learn to immerse themselves in the emotional life of their character, all the while keeping a part of their brain detached, so that they may remember their lines, as well as execute any necessary blocking and stage business. This "double life" extends to their attitude toward their fellow actors: Othello, for example, must experience all the torment of jealous passion toward poor Desdemona, at the same time taking care not to actually strangle her during their final scene. Of course, these lines have been crossed—I myself have more than once had to restrain my impulse to actually choke another actor onstage, and have come away with bruises more than once from a fight scene that got out of hand.

Nowhere is a combination of control and restraint more

necessary than in the final scene of *Hamlet*. During the duel between Laertes and Hamlet in front of the entire Danish court, each man is required to give and receive a nick of the sword, which must appear to pierce the skin. Laertes's sword has been dipped in a deadly poison, something Hamlet is unaware of, and when he receives what he thinks is a tiny scratch, he has in fact been fatally poisoned. Later in the duel, when Hamlet seizes Laertes's sword—still unaware it is coated with poison—he inflicts a minor cut upon his friend, not knowing he has fatally wounded him.

It has always been my desire to create as much realism as possible, so I always provide myself and Laertes with a small pouch of stage blood to be held in the left hand during the sword play—then, at the proper time, the pouch is clapped on the area of the "wound," creating a very realistic effect for the audience. I have heard gasps from the gallery during these moments—a sound that is music to the ears of any actor/manager.

Given Nate Carlisle's superior swordsmanship, I was on my guard, though my duel with him had been carefully staged. As we squared off for the fight, I thought I saw a gleam in his eyes I had not noticed before—or perhaps it was a trick of the light, the glare of the hot gas lamps catching his face just so.

We crossed swords and began our duel. The actors playing members of the Danish court were onstage with us, including Gertrude and Claudius. From where I stood, I could see the rest of the company standing in the wings, watching—including Lawrence Barrett, who was observing us with a keen expression on his face. He had come to the theatre, even though his scenes were not scheduled for rehearsal.

It was not unusual for other actors to watch the duel scene, but

I felt a shiver trickle down my spine as I touched swords with Nate.

At first the scene ran exactly as we had rehearsed it—but when the moment came for the first "touch," when Laertes nicks Hamlet with what turns out to be a fatal wound, to my surprise, Nate seemed to lose his balance, and his sword actually raked across my face.

My left cheek stinging, I brought my hand to my face. There was a murmur from the wings, and several of the women gasped.

"Sorry!" Nate panted. "I lost my balance. Are you all right?"

"I'm fine," I replied, wiping away a trickle of blood from my cheek.

"Shall we stop?"

"No, no," I said. "Let's continue."

I glanced at Holmes, who, as Horatio, was standing to one side of the other Danish courtiers. I thought I saw him nod almost imperceptibly, but perhaps I was mistaken. I returned to the duel.

It seemed to me that Nate was fighting with even more vigor than usual—he huffed and sweated and leapt from side to side, and more than once I had to dodge an unusually vigorous swipe of his sword. I had an impulse to stop and ask what had gotten into him, but something prevented me—a desire to not lose face in front of the rest of the company, maybe; or perhaps it was a darker, more self-destructive impulse.

When the moment came for Hamlet and Laertes to exchange swords—thus giving Hamlet the poisoned sword—he suddenly changed the blocking and lunged at me. Reacting completely on instinct, I dodged out of the way, dropped to the floor, and rolled to the other side of the stage. When I stood up I saw he was still charging toward me.

"Nate!" I panted. "For God's sake, what are you *doing?*"

But he just roared with rage and kept coming at me. I rolled in the other direction, then suddenly realized I had dropped my sword and was defenseless. Backed up against the wall, I was cornered. I saw the glint of his steel blade headed toward my face, and closed my eyes, expecting the blow.

But it did not come.

When I opened my eyes, I saw that Holmes had taken up my sword and was fighting with Nate.

"Holmes!" I cried.

"Stay clear, Edwin!" he yelled back.

I had no choice but to obey. The blades were flashing silver in the stage lights, and to come anywhere near them was to risk serious injury. Though Holmes was clearly a skilled swordsman, Nate's rage had turned him into a madman, and he sliced and jabbed with the fury of a man fighting to the death. It was all Holmes could do to stave off his vicious attack, parrying each thrust with an alert desperation. The rest of the company hovered in the wings, cowed by Nate's rage. I grabbed a theatre page and drew him close to me.

"Run and fetch the police!" I hissed.

The boy nodded at me, his eyes wide with terror.

"Now!" I bellowed. "*Run!*"

He took off, scampering down the stairs and out through the back door. I turned back to the stage, where to my horror I watched Nate back Holmes into the opposite corner of the stage.

"Now," he panted, lifting his sword over his head, "you will die too!"

Hardly aware of what I was doing, I sprang to my feet and hurled my body through the air, landing on Nate with a thud, knocking him to the ground. He writhed and fought like a rabid beast, clawing and kicking at me. But Holmes snatched his sword, and three or four other members of the cast—including Larry Barrett—threw themselves upon him, helping to subdue him. We wrestled him to his feet—he continued to struggle, but he was outnumbered now, and we managed to hold him.

"Are you all right, Edwin?" Barrett asked, true concern in his voice.

"Yes, Larry—quite all right, thank you," I said.

Nate Carlisle strained against his captors, trying vainly to wrest himself free. "Damn you, Edwin Booth—why aren't you dead?" he panted. To my surprise, his accent was different—it was now decidedly Southern.

"I took the liberty of removing your sword from backstage and replacing it with another one," Holmes said to him.

Nate turned his gaze on Holmes. "Damn you!" he gasped, still quite out of breath.

I stared at Holmes, confused.

"He had poisoned it," Holmes told me. "So when he cut your face, he expected you to die—and when you didn't, his plan was thrown off."

I heard a collective gasp from the rest of the company.

"He hoped it would look like just another unfortunate accident," Holmes explained.

Nate glared at Holmes and struggled, but his fellow actors held him firmly. "You—you—what *are* you, a wizard?"

"No; merely one who observes," Holmes responded.

"I don't understand, Nate," I said. "Why would you want to kill me?"

"My dear Booth," Holmes began, laying a hand on my shoulder.

"No, no—I want to hear," I said, pulling away from him and facing Nate. "What I have I ever done to you?"

He wrenched a hand free and pulled a locket from his neck, throwing it at my feet. "This is my sister Daisy—the poor unfortunate girl your brother ruined. The day she died I vowed a Booth would die to avenge her!"

"But why? What have I to do with any of this?"

"Your wretched brother discarded her like he did so many other women," he replied, in a voice choked with rage. "She never recovered, and when he shot Lincoln, she went mad from grief."

"How is this my f-fault?" I stammered, my childhood affliction once again returning.

"Do you have *any* notion what it is like to endure the humiliation of Reconstruction? 'Reconstruction'—ha! What a bitter joke!" He spat out the words, his eyes blazing with fury. "Lincoln was a tyrant, but when your brother killed him, the North took revenge upon us by humiliating us—if your cursed brother had not murdered that mountebank, things might have gone differently. And now my poor, sainted mother is dead—she died of grief and hardship! She never recovered from my sister's madness—I watched her steady decline, until at last she died of a broken heart."

"But I could not have prevented my brother's—"

"Why not? If you had not been so absorbed in your own career, your *fame*, you might have noticed what he was planning! You were as blind to your own kin as a cart horse!"

"B-but I—" Once again I began to stutter painfully.

Holmes stepped forward and laid a hand on my arm.

"There is nothing more to be learned from this man," he said in a low voice. "His mind is addled."

I knew he was right, and yet I could not take my eyes from Nate's face, red and twisted with fury. I felt that I was somehow looking at my own brother Johnny's face. I was aware of Holmes's hand on my arm, gently pulling me away, as half a dozen uniformed policemen strode purposefully down the aisles of the theater. The assembled company stood watching in silence as they climbed the stairs to the stage. It was as if we were the stunned spectators of a tragic play, waiting passively to see what would happen next.

"This is your man," Holmes said to a burly, redheaded sergeant, indicating Carlisle.

The sergeant nodded and turned to his men, who quickly and expertly cuffed Carlisle's hands behind his back and began to lead him away. He wrenched himself free for a moment and pivoted unsteadily back toward us.

"A curse on you and your family, Edwin Booth!" he managed to cry before the policemen set upon him again and dragged him away.

The red-haired sergeant approached me and coughed delicately.

"When you have a moment, we'd like to take a statement from you, Mr. Booth," he said respectfully.

"Of course," I replied, feeling light-leaded, with the unreal sensation that I was adrift in a horrible dream.

The sergeant turned to leave, but then turned back again.

"Uh, I—that is, well, sir, I want to say how much I enjoyed your Brutus in *Julius Caesar* last week. My wife, she... well, I wonder, sir, if you would mind—perhaps this isn't the time, but…" He fumbled in his pocket and extracted a small black notebook. On the cover, "NYPD" was embossed in gold lettering. "If you could just—it's for my wife, you understand, sir."

The sergeant's face was a deep crimson, and he was sweating at the collar of his tight wool uniform.

"Of course, Sergeant," I said, touched by his affection. Though both of my Marys had been taken from me—the first by death, the second by madness—how well I knew the bliss of having a wife to come home to.

I signed the paper and pressed it into the sergeant's perspiring palms.

"Love her well," I said. "Love her and care for her with all your heart."

He looked at me, transparent pearls of sweat gathering on his broad forehead.

"I will, sir—th-thank you, sir," he stammered, running a hand through his bristle of red hair. He grasped my hand and shook it vigorously. "Best of luck, sir—all the best to you."

With that, he turned and hurried off after his officers. The company members stood in silence for a few more moments, then a low murmur began among them. They all seemed to be in shock, understandably, and I called off rehearsal for the rest of the day. They were quiet at first, still stunned by the sudden violence, but by the time everyone had their coats on, they were bursting with questions and demands for explanations. Some of them were making plans to head off for Tom's Tavern, a favorite watering hole for theatre folks—run by an old former actor named, improbably enough, Thomas Lawless. Several of them importuned Holmes and myself to join them. As is true of all actors, they thrived on drama no less than the sound of their own voices. Now that the danger had passed, they could savor the aftermath of the excitement in endless discussions, digressions, and dissections—and, best of all, countless drafts of whatever Tom happened to be serving.

However, I wanted nothing more than to sit and stare into the fireplace at the Players, a glass of brandy in my hand, the ever faithful Hector at my side.

Holmes and I hailed a cab and made our way back to the club. I said very little during the ride, being preoccupied with my own thoughts. Perhaps sensing my need for silence, Holmes stared out the window into the darkening streets.

When we were settled in front of the fire, I spoke at last.

"I want to thank you for everything you have done, Holmes—not only did you you save my life, but also—"

He silenced me with a wave of his hand. "I do not feel I was successful at all; after all, a man almost died because of my inability to anticipate the deviousness of this killer."

The latest report on poor Geoffrey was that he would survive—thank God—but I took Holmes's point.

"What made you think that Nate had poisoned his sword?"

"After the first disaster with poor Geoffrey, I kept a very close eye on all the props—especially the swords. And I took the liberty of following Nate Carlisle after rehearsal yesterday and noted that he paid a visit to a pharmacy."

"So you think he bought the poison then?"

"I went in afterwards myself on the pretext of needing some valerian root, and managed to have a look at the receipt when the chemist's back was turned. It was a curare derivative—very rare and very deadly. A paralytic agent which, shortly after entering the bloodstream, causes paralysis and death. There is no known antidote. This was an example of life imitating art—a very deadly example."

A thin, cold shiver slithered down my spine as I realized the truth of his statement, and I suddenly felt the full impact of my narrow escape.

"How did you know he would use the poison on the sword?"

"I didn't know for certain—that's why I had to find out what would happen if I switched the swords. It wasn't enough that he bought the poison—that in itself is no crime, and he could always claim that he purchased it to poison rats or some other vermin. No, he had to be caught red-handed, as it were."

"What made you suspect him in the first place?"

"In some ways it was a process of elimination. But one or two things he said or did led me to think he was the most likely culprit."

"Such as—?"

"For one, his pronounced grief at the death of Kitty's dog, and his attempt to console her, struck me as unusual—unless he was somehow responsible."

"What else?"

"His background was shadowy. You said he came to you on recommendation from a theatre company in Savannah."

"Yes. He presented me with a letter."

"How well do you know that city?"

"Not well. I traveled there once with my father."

"Well, I sent a telegram to the address on that letter, and there is no such theatre."

"Good heavens—my poor Mary always said I was too trusting of people."

"You are a very busy man. Savannah is far enough away that he assumed you would be unlikely to check on the reference."

"True; I often hire actors on a single recommendation. I can always fire them if they are inadequate to the task."

"That is precisely what young Carlisle was counting on—which is why he came with his part perfectly learned. As you pointed out, he is quite a good actor, so you were not likely to fire him. And, I suspect, faking a recommendation is perhaps not unusual in the theatrical community."

I sighed ruefully. "You're quite right—even had I found out the letter was false, I still probably would have chalked it up to the eagerness of a young actor to find employment."

Holmes smiled. "There was one more thing."

"What was that?"

"As I just remarked, he is a gifted actor."

"Yes, that's true. But what—?"

"And he did a credible job of pretending to be a Northerner."

"Yes, his accent was quite convincing."

"I agree—except for one small thing."

"What's that?"

"He made one small slip. When the cast was ordering breakfast the other day, he asked for 'a egg.' Not 'an egg,' but 'a egg.'"

"How odd. But I don't see what that—"

"In certain parts of the South, that is a very common usage. However, it is virtually unknown in the North, which made me suspect he was not all he claimed to be."

I shook my head. "But that's such a small detail, Holmes."

"My dear Booth, details may be small, but they are often anything but insignificant. They can indeed be the difference between—well, as in this case, between life and death."

Holmes left New York soon after our production closed, and some months later I received a postcard from him, sent from Chicago. After that I heard nothing—until I began following his exploits in London some years later.

As for me, I went back to my life as an actor without further incident. My part in the ongoing life and adventures of the great detective was over... the rest is silence.

Now we find Holmes in the Midwest in Peter
Tremayne's study of the lesser-known history of the
Irish in Civil War America.

THE CASE OF THE
RELUCTANT ASSASSIN

by

PETER TREMAYNE

*H*ow very singular!"
    *The exclamation came from my estimable
friend, the consulting detective Mr. Sherlock Holmes, as
we sat sipping brandy one evening in front of the fire in
our rooms in Baker Street. Holmes was going through a
pile of old newspapers, cutting out the occasional item
for the scrapbooks that he kept. These items were usually confined to matters of arcane and peculiar events,
in which Holmes delighted to indulge. He would spend
hours in pursuit of solutions to the mysteries that they
often contained.*

    *I glanced across to the yellowing newspaper that
he was peering at and found it was an old edition of
the* New York Times. *Some friend or acquaintance
of Holmes's in New York, knowing of his penchant*

211

for scouring old newspapers in search of such matters, had recently sent him a pile of that paper.

"Singular, Holmes?" I said. "Pray, what is it that you find singular?"

Holmes put the newspaper on his knee and tapped at it with a lean fore-finger.

"There is an item here that informs me that Holt City, in Holt County, Nebraska, is being renamed O'Neill. Not that the place was ever a city in the way we might interpret it. It was only a small collection of homesteads when I passed through it. And, to be sure, it is singular that they choose to name it after a distinguished Irish rebel."

I was puzzled.

"You say that you have been there, Holmes?" I was astonished, as I had not realized he had ever traveled across the Atlantic.

"I was in that very town just over ten years ago. I had the fortune to discover the would-be assassin of General O'Neill."

"General O'Neill?" I said truculently. "I thought that you just said that he was an Irish rebel?"

Holmes leaned back in his chair and smiled curiously. He took his pipe from the side table and spent a few moments igniting the noxious mixture with which he had filled it.

"My dear Watson, I shall tell you a story, but it is one that I strictly forbid you to turn into one of those penny-dreadful accounts that you turn out for the popular magazines . . . at least, not until I have shuffled off this mortal coil."

He paused a moment or two in order to gather his thoughts and then continued:

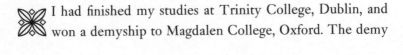 I had finished my studies at Trinity College, Dublin, and won a demyship to Magdalen College, Oxford. The demy

is derived from *demi-socii*, half-fellows, and it is a scholarship that my acquaintance Oscar Wilde had previously won from Trinity. Before starting my course at Oxford, I had some leisure and, with money and little concern, I resolved to visit some members of my family in the United States. One of my cousins was then residing in Holt City. He was Toorish Sherlock, after whose branch of my family I was named. I believe that I have already confided to you that the Sherlocks were one of the most important families established in Ireland after the Anglo-Norman invasion. They became thoroughly Hibernized, unlike my branch, the Holmeses of Galway.

Toorish Sherlock had graduated from the Royal College of Physicians in Dublin and left for America. Thus he found himself one of a few medical men in Holt City in that year of 1877. The designation of "city" was a misnomer, for I found it no more than a hamlet of several wooden houses sprawled over quite a distance on the Great Plains of the Midwest. Indeed, it was in a vast area that had recently been designated the State of Nebraska, which, I was informed, was from the native Chiwere word meaning a place of "flat water."

I had arrived by an exhausting method of a steam locomotive and a journey by a very uncomfortable mail coach. Rather weary, I had just reached my ultimate destination, the house of my cousin, when the door flew open and he came out bearing his physician's bag and evidently in a great hurry. There was a pony and trap outside the house with an elderly servant holding the horse's head.

"Holmes!" he cried on seeing me, and halted abruptly and in some consternation. "I was expecting you any day, but you have arrived at an inopportune moment. I am called away urgently. A case of suspected poisoning. The general, no less. I am not sure how long I shall be."

Indeed, for a moment I was put out by this cavalier greeting after so long and tedious a journey. Then my curiosity got the better of me. Even as young as I was, I was still then consumed by a fascination for poisons and mysteries, and the mere mention of such quickened my blood and awoke all my senses.

"A general has been poisoned, you say?"

"I do say. His manservant has just come posthaste by horse. He rode off as soon as he secured my word I would follow him this minute," replied Toorish solemnly. "He says the general is at death's door."

"Have the police been informed?"

"Police? Holmes, this is a small settlement in Nebraska. It's hardly fifteen years since the Homestead Act. People have not been settled here long enough to acquire the services of a police force. There is a sheriff here who goes about with a large pistol at his waist. It is not like towns that you know of. Besides, there is no word as to whether this matter is an accident or not."

"Then let me dump my bags here and come with you," I suggested with enthusiasm, all thought of fatigue vanished from my mind. Indeed, it is my nature that conundrums and the oddities of life keep my brain from ossifying. Physical exhaustion seemed to vanish as well. "Perhaps I can be of some help?"

Toorish gave me a wry look.

"I doubt it," he said, for honesty was his forte. "You have no medical training, although I am told that you are studying chemistry, among other things. Besides..." He hesitated.

"Besides, what?" I demanded.

"It is a known fact that your brother, Mycroft, is now working in Dublin Castle."

Dublin Castle was the seat of the British administration in Ireland, and Mycroft, my elder brother, had entered the Imperial Civil Service.

"What has that to do with the matter?"

Toorish hesitated again.

"The general... well..." He shrugged.

"We are wasting time," I snapped. "Your patient may be dead or dying. You can tell me what you mean on the way."

Toorish signaled to the man who had been holding the horse's head and instructed him to remove my bags into the house. Then he motioned me to climb into the trap. He threw his bag behind the seat and climbed in. I gathered the general's house lay in its own grounds on the far side of town. We trotted along at a fast rate.

"Now," I said, "tell me how Mycroft's work in Dublin Castle comes into this story?"

Toorish glanced at me grimly.

"The general that we are going to see is John O'Neill."

The sight of my blank expression disappointed him.

"You have not heard of him?" he asked in astonishment.

"I am not interested in military matters," I declared. "Nor political ones, come to that."

"Then let me explain. O'Neill came to this country from Drumgallon, in County Monaghan. At the age of twenty-three he joined the army. During the Civil War he rose to the rank of colonel, commanding the Seventh Michigan Cavalry on the Union side. He had a distinguished career and he was wounded during the battle for Nashville in December of eighteen sixty-four."

He paused a moment and then went on: "Like most Irishmen here, he never forgot the homeland and the struggle to make Ireland an independent nation again. He joined the Irish Republican Brotherhood and so, when the Civil War ended, he was given command of the Thirteenth Regiment, as it was designated, of the Irish Army of Liberation."

I must have smiled.

"It was no joke," admonished Toorish. "Irish veterans of both the Union and Confederate armies joined by the tens of thousands. In June of eighteen sixty-four, the leaders of the IRB had realized that they could not transport an army of twenty-five thousand veteran soldiers from America to Ireland with the ships of the Royal Navy to block them. They decided that the best way to free Ireland was to invade the provinces of British North America. The idea was to head into the French-speaking areas, like Montreal, where the French, such as the Parti Rouge, also wanted to be free from the British. They would seize the saltwater seaports along the St. Lawrence and then negotiate with Britain. A quid pro quo. Leave Ireland and the Irish would leave British North America."

I was still smiling. "A capital idea, but it needs men and experienced soldiers not a bunch of idealists."

Toorish regarded me with a pitying expression.

"Have I not just told you that these were veterans of one of the fiercest wars ever fought? And twenty-five thousand of them with the latest weapons, cannons, even Gatling guns and three warships that they had bought surplus from the U.S. Navy."

"It is hard to believe," I said, shaking my head.

"But it is true. They were commanded by Major General 'Fighting Tom' Sweeney from Cork, who lost his arm in the Mexican

War, and in the Civil War commanded a division under Sherman. As I say, there was no joke about it when these Irish veterans, in regiments and brigades, gathered along the border with the British provinces and launched a three-pronged attack. One division was to go from Chicago and Milwaukee across the lakes to make a feint against Toronto. A central division was to make another feint from Buffalo along the Niagara Peninsula. But the main attack would move from St. Albans and Vermont toward Montreal with some sixteen thousand men and a brigade of cavalry to capture the salt-water seaports along the St. Lawrence. Once secured, they would provide a base for the three rebel Irish warships."

"And it was your general who led this?"

"No, that main attack was commanded by Brigadier Sam Spear."

"So how does this general fit into the picture?"

"Come the day of the attack, and in Buffalo things were not going according to plan. Not all the division due to make the feint from Buffalo had mustered, and even the commander, Brigadier William Lynch, had not arrived to take command. O'Neill found himself the only senior officer at the rendezvous. Knowing how much was reliant on the feints to deflect the British elsewhere while Spear began his main attack, O'Neill decided to lead the crossing to Fort Erie with what men he had. Only six hundred men, instead of the designated five thousand, crossed with him. British troops were already moving to face him. He managed to set up positions beyond Fort Erie at Ridgeway. The British Queen's Own regiment arrived and were promptly sent flying from the field. But O'Neill had intelligence that more troops were on the way, so he moved back to Fort Erie, where he won another skirmish before he withdrew his men."

I was surprised at hearing this news, for, frankly, it was an event totally unknown to me. Subsequently, I checked this in the local newspapers of the day and found that every word of what Toorish said was true.

"Good luck favored the British," went on my cousin. "Although Spear began his crossing, and won a few skirmishes against the British advance guards, President Johnson concluded a deal with the British ambassador, Lord Monck. Britain agreed to pay many millions of pounds in compensation and reparation for supporting the Confederate army during the war. Britain also agreed to give up some of their claims to western territories. The president then sent General Grant to cut off the Irish supplies and prevent rein-forcements crossing. The invasion collapsed.

"The British have represented the crossing as a bunch of drunken Irishmen wandering over the border. The story hid the reality. In fact, the following year, the provinces of British North America united as the Dominion of Canada. So Canada has the Irish invasion to thank for its existence."

"And what of this General O'Neill, as you call him?"

"O'Neill, as the victor over the British at Ridgeway and Fort Erie, became the hero of the conflict. He didn't give up the idea easily and wanted to make a second attempt to invade British ter-ritory in pursuit of Irish independence. He became president of the Irish Republican movement in the United States and eventu-ally settled here in Holt City."

"And now you say he has been poisoned?"

"So it seems. And, as you say see, from his history, he is a man who has made powerful enemies."

"And your fear about it being known that Mycroft works at

Dublin Castle, together with my arrival at this time, is that this might be construed as an attempt to eliminate O'Neill by the Castle authorities?"

Toorish shrugged.

"It is not the first time that assassination has been used as a political tool. The general does have a small staff around him who are very protective."

"You sound as though you support him."

Toorish looked sharply at me.

"I admire the man and I agree that Ireland should have its own government again. However, I would give my support to Mr. Butt and his Irish Home Rule League. I am no Fenian."

"In view of what you say, does that not make your role as doctor to General O'Neill somewhat questionable?"

"Not at all. We both agree on the end to be achieved but not the method to achieve it. We have a mutual respect." Toorish suddenly gave a wry smile, "Besides, I am the only Irish doctor in this town at the moment."

We had driven some way beyond the main section of homesteads and buildings. The general's house was a grand wooden structure that had been fairly recently erected. The grounds seemed large, with a river running nearby and an orchard spreading along its banks. Two men patrolled the gates leading to the house. They both carried carbines, and I noticed that they wore green jackets with insignia on them, and that one had a sergeant's chevrons sewn on his sleeve. It was as if they were soldiers guarding the place. In fact, that was exactly what they were, but of this Irish Army of Liberation. They recognized Toorish but regarded me with suspicion.

"Who's he, Doc?" demanded the man with sergeant chevrons. His Dublin accent was unmistakable.

"My cousin recently arrived from Ireland," responded Toorish. On this intelligence we were waved through the gates toward the house.

I noticed that a flag was flying over the porch, a tricolor of green, white, and orange. I had no memory for such symbols, but Toorish told me it was the flag presented by the French to the Young Ireland movement of the 1840s and was now used by the Fenians.

A young woman was on the porch, wringing her hands, eyes red with weeping. Pretty, with pale skin and red hair, she was nearly disfigured by her tears. Beside her was a young man who seemed to have been speaking earnestly to her. He wore rough working clothes and only a shirt. On our arrival, he said something quickly to the girl and disappeared around the side of the veranda, or what is called the stoop in these parts. The girl came to the top of the steps as Toorish drew up.

"Oh, Doctor, thank God you have come. It is painful to watch the general so."

"He still lives?" demanded Toorish, leaping down and taking his bag.

"Barely, sir," she replied.

Toorish entered the house preceded by the young girl, who I understood must be one of the servants. Inside the hallway stood another of those green-jacketed men, with a revolver in his belt. Toorish muttered something in an aside to the man, which I think was by way of identifying me, and went directly up the stairs, the girl leading the way. I followed closely on their heels.

The general, a handsome, mustachioed man much diminished

by his poor health, was lying, fully clothed, twisting and turning on the bed. His cheeks sunken, he was pale, sweating, and in a state of unconsciousness. There appeared to be a spasmodic rigidity to his body. Toorish bent over him and began his examination. A few minutes of it confirmed his estimation of poison.

"You can do nothing, Holmes," he said to me. "I must try to present an antidote to this. That he has not died so far is proof of a strong constitution."

"You have identified the poison?"

"The muscular convulsions are an indication. Strychnine."

"But if he had taken it in any quantity he would be already dead," I pointed out, knowing that much about chemistry.

"Strychnine has a bitter taste. Perhaps after the first sip he was warned? It would take ten to twenty minutes to start the convulsions. Death would come in two to three hours, depending on how much he swallowed. Now, let me do what I can. If you want to make yourself useful, find out how the general managed to imbibe this poison."

He waved both the maid and myself out of the room.

I looked at the red-eyed girl, who was in a state of great distress.

"Come downstairs and tell me how this happened," I suggested.

She led the way down to what appeared to be the general's library. It was filled mostly with books of Irish and American history and items of a military nature.

"Begin by telling me your name," I said, leaning against a large oak desk.

"Kitty, sir. Kitty McKenny."

"I judge that you are from Monaghan by your accent."

"Indeed, I am."

"How long have you been in service to the general?"

"Since I came to this country. My family knew the general's family in Monaghan. That was five years ago."

"And in what capacity do you serve here?"

"I am both maid and cook, sir. In truth, sir, the general has no other domestic servants, only myself and Kevin, who serves as aide and valet to him. At the moment, Mrs O'Neill and her children are in Omaha visiting some relatives."

"No other servants here? I thought I saw several men about the place."

"Oh, indeed you will. There are half a dozen of the general's soldiers who serve as guards and help out about the grounds."

"Why would the general need guards?"

"You are not Irish then, sir."

"Dr. Sherlock is my cousin," I pointed out, but I feared she meant that I was not of her ilk of Irish.

"Then you should know that the general is an enemy to the British government and his activities brought him into conflict with those who run affairs in Washington. Only a few years ago he was arrested by a United States marshal at the Canadian border."

"I can understand the British seeking his arrest, but why Washington? Was he not a hero of the late war between the states?"

"He is more of a hero to the Irish people, sir. In disturbing the settlement between Washington and London, he is regarded with deep hatred in many quarters on both sides of the Atlantic. There have been several threats on his life. That is why he needs a bodyguard."

"And do you know how this accident happened?"

"Accident, sir?"

"How did the general come to imbibe the poison?"

The girl sniffed.

"I do not know. It happened after the midday meal, scarcely two hours ago."

"Well, tell me the circumstances leading to your sending for Doctor Sherlock."

"I had poured a glass of whiskey for the general while he sat in this very study. It was his habit to take a glass in midafternoon while working at his desk there."

"You handed him the glass of whiskey?"

"I placed it on the desk beside him. Look, it is still there."

I glanced to where she pointed and saw a glass tumbler half filled with whiskey on the desk.

"Then what?" I asked.

"Then I left the room. After a moment I thought that I heard him call. I came back and found him standing by the cabinet over there, where the drinks are stored. He had a bottle in his hand, peering at it. "Did you want another glass?" I asked him. He glanced up at me and shook his head. "It was bitter," was all he said. I saw that the glass on his desk had barely been touched."

"You poured the whiskey while at this cabinet?" I interrupted.

"I did."

"From a decanter?"

"From a bottle, sir. The general has cases of it shipped from John Power's distillery in Dublin. He refuses to drink anything else."

"What then?"

"I withdrew from the room and had barely stepped into the

hallway when I heard a thud from the study. I returned and found the general on the floor having a fit. I called Kevin and we managed to get him to his bedroom. But with the condition worsening, Kevin took to his horse and rode for Doctor Sherlock."

"You were alarmed at the condition. Yet why was Kevin able to report to the doctor that the general had been poisoned?"

She frowned as she considered the question.

"There were flecks of spittle around his mouth and the convulsions. I supposed that alerted him."

"Do you know that such symptoms meant poison, then?"

She shook her head.

"It was Kevin who said so, sir. That's why he rode off immediately."

I glanced back to the glass tumbler of whiskey on the desk.

"Nothing has been touched since you poured the whiskey?"

"It seems so, sir."

I bent over it to sniff its aroma. It had no other smell than whiskey. So I dipped my forefinger in it and carefully tasted it with the tip of my tongue. There seemed nothing out of the ordinary about it. It was good, plain Irish whiskey. There was certainly nothing bitter about it. I noticed there was an oily thumbprint on the glass.

"Was the general engaged in oiling some implement at this desk? Perhaps a pocket watch?" I asked.

The girl seemed to think me mad.

"The general, sir? He was writing some letters."

"Show me the bottle you poured from. Was it the same that the general was inspecting when you saw him?"

"There was only one bottle newly opened, sir. It is in the cabinet."

I went to look for myself. There was, as she had told me, one bottle of Power's whiskey that had been opened, and, by my judgment, about a half-tumbler full had been poured from it. Once again, I sniffed at the bottle. And then gingerly tasted some of it on my fingertip. There was no bitter effect. It seemed that however the general had imbibed the strychnine it was not through the means of its being disguised in Mr. Power's distillation. Once again, I noticed a few drops of oil adhering to the bottle.

Yet, and here the logic of deduction was quite clear, if the general had imbibed nothing before the whiskey and nothing afterwards, and within ten minutes of taking the whiskey fell prey to the symptoms, then it must have been through this means that the poison was introduced into his body. But there was no other glass or open bottle within the room.

"Has this man Kevin returned to the house yet?" I asked.

"He has, sir. He came back before you did. He felt that his place was at the general's side."

"Ah, was he the young man I saw with you on the porch?"

"Indeed it was not, sir. That was Billy McCartan, one of the men..."

There was a high color in her cheeks, which told a story.

"Your fiancé?" I hazarded.

"We have walked out together. But he has not been here long. He's from County Down."

"So he is not one of the general's veterans?"

"He's hardly older than me," asserted the girl. "He tends the

225

gardens. He got into trouble at home and had to take passage here. He joined the republicans in New York and then made his way here by their recommendation. The general took pity on him and gave him a job. He wants to make something of himself and..."

She paused, blushing even further.

"Well, let us continue," I said. "Ask this Kevin to come in here. We will see how he diagnosed poison so quickly."

The man whom Kitty showed into the study was the man who had been standing in the hallway when we arrived. He was clean-shaven and had obviously been in military service, judging from the way he carried himself and almost stood at attention before me. He wore that green jacket, and now I could see that he had a lieutenant's insignia on the shoulders. I was also aware of the revolver he carried in the holster at his belt, whose military flap, I noticed, was open.

"Your name?" I asked.

"Kevin Mullan, sir. Lieutenant of the Irish Army of Liberation. The Thirteenth Regiment."

"You have been employed by the general for how long?"

"I fought at his side at Ridgeway and at the skirmish at Fort Erie. I was in his command under General Sherman in the war between the states. I have been his aide since we withdrew across the Niagara."

"So you were always a soldier?"

"I came to this country just as the war between the states started and immediately enlisted in the cavalry in Michigan. The general commanded the unit. However, in Ireland, I had been a student, sir."

"Where and what was your subject?"

"I was at Queen's College in Galway and I studied botany."

"Botany? From botanist to soldier, a curious change."

"Not so curious, sir. But you have surely not come to waste time on my life story. I thought you were a doctor, a relative of Dr. Sherlock."

"My cousin has asked me to discover how the general came to take strychnine. Do not worry," I added, "my cousin is even now fighting to save your general's life."

The man who had continued to stand at attention seemed visibly to relax, but not entirely, for there was a certain tension in his body.

"How did you know that the general had taken poison?" I demanded suddenly. "When you came to my cousin's house, you told him that fact."

"That's easy. I had seen animals display similar symptoms when poisoned."

"You must explain that to me."

The man pointed to the window.

"You will observe, sir, that we are close to a river. This building was much troubled by rodents when it was first erected. The general ordered that these creatures be poisoned to keep their numbers down."

"And what poison was used?"

"A concoction was distilled from the seeds of *Nux vomica.*"

As I said, even at that early stage I had made some study of chemistry and poisons. I knew that strychnine was a colorless crystalline alkaloid that, according to books, could be used to put down rodents. But it was not common to Europe and neither to

America. It had to come from the seeds of the *Nux vomica* tree native to the East Indies. I said so.

Kevin Mullan smiled.

"You are well informed, Mister Holmes. You will find, near the rives bank, three examples of *Nux vomica*—those medium-sized trees that you see. Some years ago a Captain O'Bannion, who claimed this land back in 1862 when this country was opened to settlement, brought some species here from Hawaii, where the trees were growing. There used to be six, but conditions have caused their decline."

"It is a long way from growing *Nux vomica* trees to creating a strychnine sulfate," I suggested.

"You seem to know your chemistry well, sir," he replied indulgently. "It was a simple procedure. I prepared the mixture and we used it to good effect to keep down the rodents."

"And you still have some of this mixture?" I demanded.

"Indeed. But do not worry. It is in a cupboard in the cellar of this house. It is kept strictly under lock and key."

"Show me," I demanded.

I had a feeling of excitement as I followed him down into the darkened cellar. There was a cupboard with a padlock in one corner. Mullan had to light a lantern, for there was no access to light down here. He went to a board concealed behind the stairway, where there were several hooks with keys hanging from them. He reached up and then hesitated and moved his hand along to pick down a key. He wiped something from it, and for a moment he examined it before moving to the cupboard.

On opening the door, two bottles of colorless liquid were

revealed on the top shelf. The bottles had labels with crudely drawn skulls and crossbones and the warning "Poison—Beware."

"Who else knows of this?" I asked. "Would anyone else have access apart from yourself?"

"Only if they knew which key to choose. The general and I know where to find the key, and that poison was kept in this cupboard."

"Are you sure? What of Miss Kitty?"

He shook his head.

"I don't think it was a matter for her to know."

"You do not often open this cupboard?"

"What makes you say so?"

"You hesitated when reaching for the key from the hooks, as if you were not sure which one."

"I hesitated only because the key was not where I expected to find it. The last person to open the cupboard put the key back on another hook."

"The last person being?"

"I presume it was the general. A moment of forgetfulness."

I took the key from the cupboard and felt it between my fingers for a moment, then handed it to him.

Back in the study I dismissed Mullan, sat down behind the general's desk, and stared at the full glass of whiskey. Had there been strychnine in it, the matter would have been simple. An idea occurred to me, and I rang the bell rope for Kitty. She came racing in and then realized it was only I. Perhaps she thought it was the general recovered and calling. I did not apologize.

"Is there an inventory kept of the bottles of whiskey bought and consumed by this house?" I demanded.

She blinked and seemed puzzled by my question.

"The question is simple. Who does the catering and ordering for this house?"

"Mrs. O'Neill when she is in residence, sir. Failing that, I do." Her chin came up defiantly.

"Then surely you have an answer to the question?"

"The whiskey is ordered every three months from an importer who resides in Lincoln."

I knew this to be a major town in the state, named such after the president who had been assassinated.

"And is a count kept of the bottles used?"

"No, sir. Not by me. If I notice we are running out, I remind the general and order more."

Her answer was disappointing, to say the least.

I sat drumming my fingers for a moment.

"Where is the liquor kept before you bring it to that cabinet? I see you bring only one bottle here at a time."

"It is kept in the cellar, sir."

"Did you say that the drink you poured was from a bottle that had to be newly opened?"

She frowned and nodded nervously.

"So this was a new bottle that you fetched to place in the cabinet?"

"It was."

I rose and went to the cabinet again and opened it.

"Tell me, Kitty. Do you wash your hands before serving drinks?"

"Sir!" The girl stared at me in outrage.

"I mean, if you have been engaged in some task—oiling

something, say—and are called to serve drinks to the general, would you clean your hands before doing so?"

"Of course." Her voice was scornful. "The general and Mrs. O'Neill are most particular."

"Come," I said abruptly. "Show me where this whiskey is kept."

Once again, I headed down into the cellar. On the far side, away from the locked poison cabinet, was a stack of bottles laid on their sides. Many were wines, but there was a selection of Mr. Power's famous distillation. She pointed to them, and then I saw a frown cross her face.

"There is something singular about them?" I pressed.

"It... it is nothing," she said hesitantly. "Just that I thought that I had taken the bottle from the end of the row... where that empty space is."

"Well? It is empty, so why does it disturb you?"

"But the next one is also empty. I take the bottles up in an order, working from that right-hand space along the row. There seems a bottle unaccounted for."

I picked up one of the bottles, as I had noticed a damp area under them. I put my finger on the dampness and sniffed. It was whiskey.

"These corks are easily removable," I observed. "Tell me, Kitty, do you remove them down here or when you get up to the study?"

"I take the bottle directly to the cabinet, and when the drink is needed I remove the cork, pour the drink, and always replace the cork."

"So there is no need for spillage here?"

She shook her head.

"There aren't many places around this estate to—walk out?" I suddenly remarked, changing the subject.

Her head came round sharply.

"What do you mean?" she demanded.

"Do you ever come down here with young Billy?"

The crimson on her face showed me my question had found its mark.

"We do not come down here and steal the general's whiskey, sir!" she protested.

"I did not suggest that you do," I placated her. "But perhaps you have brought Billy down here for some privacy. Where do he and the other men stay? I presume you and the general's aide have rooms in this house even when the general's wife and family are in residence?"

"There is a bunkhouse behind the house. That is where all the other men stay."

"Would I find Billy in this bunkhouse if I went to find him now?"

She frowned and then nodded slowly.

"Very well. Ask Kevin to join me in the general's study in twenty minutes."

An hour later, my cousin Toorish came down the stairs as I stood waiting in the hallway.

"Well?" I asked. "How fares your patient?"

"If he survives the next twenty-four hours, then we have good reason to hope for a full recovery."

"Yet it was strychnine poisoning and there is no known antidote. How did you manage to perform this miracle to keep him alive thus far?"

"There were several means," confided Toorish, and not without a touch of vanity. But then it seemed he had good reason to be well pleased with himself. "It was luck that he took no more than a sip or two of the poison. I needed to absorb the poison from the digestive tract, and so infusions of active charcoal and then some tannic acid were the next steps. I keep a bottle of tannic acid with me, distilled from oak and walnut, which is good. Then, to stop the muscular convulsions, I gave the patient an inhalation of Guthrie's chloroform. It is a better way of inducing relaxation and sleep than Long's ether preparation. It anaesthetizes the system. So, if he relaxes this way, as I say, and is alive tomorrow, he will be on the road to recovery." Toorish regarded me with curiosity. "And what have you been doing? Did you discover the means whereby he took this noxious brew?"

"Not only that," I answered, with equal pride in my achievement—for remember, I was still very young. "I know who administered it and for what purposes."

I asked Kevin to call everyone into the hall and stood on the stairway a few steps up from the floor to address them.

There was Kitty and her amour, Billy McCartan, and Kevin Mullan and the half dozen or so men who worked as guards and on the small estate.

"There has been an attempt to poison General O'Neill," I began without preamble. "An assassination attempt or, in other words, attempted murder."

There came a gasp from the assembly as if in one breath.

"The assassin remains among you," I added, as the sound died.

This caused an even greater gasp and a little shriek of terror from Kitty.

"Are you going to tell us how it was done?" Toorish demanded in some irritation at my theatrics.

"It was simply done," I replied. "The poison was administered in the general's afternoon drink, through his favorite glass of whiskey."

Another scream came from Kitty. One or two of the men looked at her suspiciously.

"For heaven's sake, Holmes, go on," muttered Toorish.

"Kitty had brought up a new bottle of whiskey from the cellar. She opened it and poured the customary afternoon glass of whiskey. This was placed on the general's desk as he was working. Then she left him in the study. The general took a sip or two and noticed the bitter taste and uttered an exclamation of disgust. Curious, he rose from his desk, walked to the cabinet, and took out the bottle to examine it. Kitty thought his exclamation was a call and returned. She saw him by the cabinet and thought he was helping himself to another glass. She then left and a moment later the general had collapsed.

"She and Kevin Mullan carried him to his bedroom and Kevin, diagnosing poison, rode to get help from Dr. Sherlock here, leaving Kitty to tend to the general as best she could in the bedroom."

"So who was responsible?" inquired Toorish sharply.

"The bottle of whiskey had already been doctored in the cellar when Kitty went to fetch it," I replied. "Someone had gone down there, removed the cork, and probably swallowed enough of the whiskey to make room for the strychnine. He spilled a little where the bottles were stashed. Then he went to get the key for the poison cupboard, took a bottle of the poison, and poured it into the whiskey bottle so that the colorless liquid had little visible effect on it. He then put the cork back, replaced the bottle as the next one to be taken, replaced the poison, and hung the key back on the hook."

"But you said there was nothing wrong with the whiskey in the study," protested a tearful Kitty.

"Neither was there," I replied. "We are faced with a very cunning murderer. He had tried to make Kitty the reluctant assassin. As soon as the deed was done, with the general writhing in agony on the bed, he went back into the study, removed the bottle and the tumbler, and placed a noncontaminated bottle there. He even poured a similar measure in the glass and left it on the desk. He then took the poisoned bottle and tumbler to his bedroom."

Kevin Mullan stepped forward with a grim expression.

"It is the truth, men. And thanks to young Mister Holmes's direction, I found them—the bottle and the tumbler."

There were more expressions of amazement from the assembly.

"Where, lieutenant?" demanded the man with the sergeant's chevrons. "Who is the assassin?"

Mullan smiled as he turned suddenly.

"I found them under the bunk of Billy McCartan."

There was a louder shriek from Kitty and the men moved forward to grab the young man.

"Wait a moment," I shouted. "Perhaps Lieutenant Mullan will tell us why that bottle was not under McCartan's bunk when I went to see him a short while ago?"

Mullan hesitated and turned to me, puzzled. His mind seemed to be working fast.

"But you told me that you suspected Billy. You told me to go and search his bunk."

"I did indeed. It was elementary. I had worked out the method and knew the suspect. You seemed to be the only one to know about the properties of strychnine and where it was stored, and you had access to it. I knew that you must have hidden the poisoned bottle and needed to find it. I first went to find Billy, and he was quite willing to let me search his bunk area to prove his innocence. A short time later I met with you and told you that I suspected Billy. I presented you with the ideal opportunity to incriminate him by planting your hidden poisoned whiskey under his bunk. I asked you to search and not disturb anything but to report to me, then telling you that after this meeting we would go in a group to Billy's bunk and uncover it. So it is there now, where you placed it. Indeed, Billy and I waited until you had been to the bunkhouse and left. Then we made another search and, lo—a miracle—the poisoned whiskey and tumbler had appeared as if by magic."

"It's a lie!" shouted Mullan. "Someone else did it. They didn't even hang the key to the poison cupboard back on the right hook. I showed you."

"A good piece of theatrics, indeed," I agreed. "Several hooks were on the board and you were at pains to show me that you knew the right hook for it to be placed on. Also, to muddy the waters, you showed me it was on the wrong hook. But you yourself had placed it on the wrong hook to throw me off the scent. There is also one other thing that gave you away..."

I smiled and pointed to his revolver that hung in the holster at his side.

"You are proud of that weapon, lieutenant, aren't you?"

He frowned.

"I noticed it was one of the new Colt Single Action Army handguns. They only started to be issued three or four years ago. Highly prized. You are so proud that you use a lot of oil on it to keep it in good order. Personally, I dislike firearms, although I keep myself up-to-date and know the latest models. I do not know whether over-oiling is a good thing or bad. One thing I did notice was an oily thumbprint on the replacement tumbler of whiskey in the study. There were oily marks on the neck of the bottle of whiskey in the cabinet. And, when you took down the key to the poison cabinet, I noticed that you had to wipe the oil away from it. I still felt the residue of the oil when I took it from the cabinet to hand to you..."

I had barely finished when Mullan stepped back and drew the revolver.

"Very clever, Mr Holmes. Stand back! All of you. I am going to finish the job, but not with poison."

He brushed by me and began to rapidly ascend the stairs toward the general's bedroom.

There was a single crack. Mullan dropped his gun and staggered, missed his footing, and fell backwards down the stairs.

Young Billy stood holding a smoking revolver in his hand.

I bent over Mullan.

"Why?" I demanded, seeing the light fading from his eyes.

"A...a pardon...money...Ireland."

Then he was dead.

Cousin Toorish was successful in his treatment. The general survived the twenty-four hours and recovered, although I cannot say that he recovered entirely. It was in January of the following year that he died. I suspect that the poisoning helped contribute to his demise; he was only forty-four years old. I never spoke to the man, for I left Holt City a few days later. I did not bother to find out how the body of Mullan was disposed of. There was no law in the country to speak of, so I presume it was quietly buried or even left up in a tree for the vultures to consume, which I was told was a Chiwere custom.

Holmes sat back after concluding his narrative and, without a glance at me, started to refill his pipe. His scrapbook and the newspaper from which he had cut the item had slid to the floor.

"Well, Holmes, it makes a good tale, but I'll respect your wishes not to write it."

"Capital of you, my dear fellow," he said, languidly lighting his pipe.

"One thing I don't understand."

"Only one?" Holmes smiled skeptically.

"Mullan had served O'Neill for twelve years or so. Fought with the fellow in the American Civil War and then in this nonsensical invasion business."

"Nonsensical?" Holmes said. "It was a plan that could have succeeded. It's one of those 'if only' matters."

"It was treason. Treason never succeeds."

"Ah, dear Watson. 'Treason never prospers; why, what's the reason? For if it prospers, none dare call it treason.'"

"Come, Holmes, you know what I mean. Anyway, what I meant to say is why did the fellow wait all that time before he tried to assassinate O'Neill?"

"He explained in his last words, I imagine. He was offered a pardon and money and a return to Ireland to enjoy the rest of his life in return for eliminating an enemy of the state."

"*But that would mean that Dublin Castle had hired a paid assassin?*" I protested.

"*Or London,*" admitted Holmes cheerfully.

"*It's outrageous!*" I declared. "*It's not British.*"

Holmes chuckled cynically.

"*Poor Watson. I would have thought that you have been long enough in this vale of tears to realize that governments are capable of anything... whatever their nationality.*"

Sherlock Holmes travels out west in Rhys Bowen's tale, and learns a bit about the art of detecting from a Native American.

CUTTING FOR SIGN

by

RHYS BOWEN

A nd how about you, young man? You are surely not from these parts. From back east, are you?" The speaker was a woman with a severe-looking, angular face and pointed chin. She was dressed from bonnet to boots in black, giving the impression of being a witch.

Ever since the stagecoach had rumbled out of Albuquerque she had taken it upon herself to be the grand inquisitor of the other passengers, never allowing the conversation to lag. The young man she now addressed was tall and slim, with long, elegant hands and a slightly effete manner. His countenance was striking, with a hawklike nose and intelligent gray eyes. His clothes proclaimed him to be a city dweller, as did his pale countenance. No trace of buckskin or ten-gallon hat for him; rather, he wore a stiff white collar over a long black jacket and black waistcoat, with a tasteful silver watch chain. On his feet were black highly polished shoes, their laces hidden by spats. His skin was rather pale in contrast to the weather-beaten faces around him, and he flushed a little at being the center of attention. "You are correct about the first part, madam. As you wisely note, I am not from these parts. But not from back east either. I am an Englishman."

"I thought as much," the woman said, with a flash of triumph in her eyes. "See, Henry, what did I tell you? An Englishman."

"May I ask your name, sir?" The speaker was a man of the cloth, seated opposite.

"My name is Holmes. Sherlock Holmes," the young man replied, as if it vexed him to give out this information to complete strangers who were not of his class.

"Delighted to make your acquaintance, Mr. Holmes." The man leaned across with outstretched hand. "I am the Reverend Claybourne Williams and this is my good wife, Dorothy. We are traveling west to bring the Lord to the heathen."

"So you plan to work among the Indians, do you? I admire your bravery. I understand some of the tribes are known for their ferocity," the young Mr. Holmes said.

"There are plenty of white unbelievers in these parts, Mr. Holmes," Mrs. Williams replied sharply. "And our duty is to them first. Would you believe that there are towns with ten saloons, with houses of ill repute and not one house of worship? The Reverend Williams and I shall have many souls to save."

"Then I wish you good fortune," Sherlock Holmes said. He opened the book he was carrying, hoping that this would give a hint that he had no wish to converse further. In truth, the constant

242

jolting and lurching of the stage was making him feel rather queasy, and the constant chattering had reached the point of being annoying. He was used to English reticence, and the ready familiarity of Americans made him uneasy. He glanced around the carriage. Apart from the missionaries, there was a big-boned man with weathered skin and the unmistakable uniform of a westerner: buckskin trousers and waistcoat and an enormous hat with curled brim. His face was now half hidden, as he had tipped the hat forward and was attempting to sleep—probably trying to escape from the chattering Mrs. Williams, Holmes decided.

Across from him was a younger man, also in western garb. A cowboy, Holmes deduced, because his clothes were imbued with the smell of horse. He had answered the questions Mrs. Williams peppered at him with no more than a "yes, ma'am" or "no, ma'am," but from these monosyllables Holmes understood that he worked on a ranch outside Tucson, where the stage was bound, and had returned to Texas for the funeral of his father. The final passenger was a young woman, simply dressed in calico, who had revealed herself under Mrs. Williams's questioning to be a Miss Buckley from Ohio, traveling west to take up the position of schoolteacher in a hamlet called Phoenix. She had a pleasant, innocent face and Holmes studied her with interest. Not a bad little ankle peeping out from under those skirts, either.

"And what brings you to America, Mr. Holmes?" Mrs. Williams's strident voice brought him back from his contemplation. "And to this part of America in particular? Out to make your fortune prospecting for gold, are you?"

"No, indeed, madam." The young man smiled. "I gather that I'm a little too late for the gold rush in California, although I

SHERLOCK HOLMES: THE AMERICAN YEARS

understand there are still fortunes to be made in the mountains of Nevada. But I do not see myself up to my thighs in icy water, swinging a pickax in the hope of finding a few grams of gold. In truth, I am here to broaden my experience of the world. I am recently come down from Oxford University and have yet to decide upon a profession."

"Have you an inclination as to where your talents lie?" the clergyman asked.

Holmes shook his head. "I have been studying the sciences and am much drawn to chemistry. My father has been trying to push me into medicine, but I do not think I have the patience to minister to the sick. And frankly I have no wish to spend my days in a dingy research laboratory."

"A man of action then, are you?" the clergyman asked, grabbing onto the strap as the coach bounced over a particularly rough part of the track.

"I rather see myself as a true Renaissance man, sir, with no wish to be bound to one thing. Frankly I enjoy opera as much as science. Sometimes playing my violin brings me more pleasure than staring at a petri dish. But I have little love for social formalities. I have been staying with family friends in Boston and had a great desire to see more of your magnificent country before I returned home, especially the so-called Wild West."

"You'll find it wild enough, I'll warrant." The big man pushed his hat back upon his head and sat up. "From here onward it may be officially part of the United States, but don't count on any law or order. The order of the gun rules out here. The order of the strongest. And then there's the Indian tribes. None of them can be trusted an inch. So my advice to you, young man, is to watch your back, and buy yourself a Colt."

"Thank you for the advice," Holmes said uneasily. "But my plan is just to pass through this territory, make my way to California, and then take the train back to the East Coast. I don't anticipate too much excitement along the way. In fact the biggest challenge may well be not to bite my tongue as I try to speak through the confounded lurching of this coach."

"It is terrible, isn't it?" the young schoolteacher said, then blushed shyly as the passengers looked at her. "The coach seems to be traveling awfully fast."

"It has many miles to cover before dark," the big man said, "and this is all Indian territory. Not a place to linger."

"Do you think we are in danger of being attacked?" the young woman asked, her eyes open very wide.

"I doubt it. They know the Wells Fargo coach is no threat to them."

"God willing, we'll be in Tucson by tomorrow night," Mrs. Williams said.

Conversation lapsed. It grew stuffy inside the compartment, but the copious dust made it impossible to open the windows. The young woman had her handkerchief up to her mouth. Holmes stared out of the window at a rocky, featureless landscape. In the distance there were occasional glimpses of far-off mountain ranges, but nearby all was dreary and desolate, with just an occasional low shrub breaking the monotony of the rocky surface. No sign of birds or animals. No end in sight.

They stopped along the way at trading posts and occasional

hamlets to change horses and allow the passengers to stretch their stiff limbs. Each stop revealed a landscape more dreary than the last, and Holmes began to have serious misgivings about his decision to take this route. Why had he thought that the West would be dramatic and in some way glamorous? Even the Indians he glimpsed, hanging around the trading posts, were dirty, dispirited creatures, far from the image Holmes had conjured of proud, bronzed warriors on horseback.

"So what will Tucson be like?" he asked as they set off again after one of these brief halts.

"Tucson's a nice enough little oasis," the big man said. "Ranching community, green meadows, streams. Better than this, anyway. Of course it's the territorial capital now, but don't expect too much of it. Just a small presidio and a few stores and saloons. You won't find anything fancy this side of the West Coast, and then you'll have to travel all the way up to San Francisco before you come to a real city."

"Now there's a true den of vice—San Francisco," Mrs. Williams said, nodding sagely to her husband. "From what I hear there is depravity on every corner. Opium dens, houses of ill repute—shocking." She shuddered as if a physical chill had passed through her.

"Don't distress yourself, my dear," the Reverend Williams said. "I shall not be subjecting you to the horrors of San Francisco."

Passengers overnighted in a one-horse town called Lordsburg and set off again next morning. Spirits were considerably lighter as they knew that they'd be in Tucson by nightfall, with, they hoped, a civilized hostelry, clean bed, and good food awaiting them. In midafternoon a sandstorm blew up, causing the drivers to rein in the horses and proceed slowly. When the coach lurched to a stop, the travelers thought at first that nothing was amiss. Then they heard the sound of a gunshot and the door was wrenched roughly open. A tall man was standing there, his hat pulled well down over his eyes and the rest of his face covered by a red bandana.

"Everybody out. Jump to it!" He waved a gun in their direction. "Come on. We haven't got all day." His voice was deep and rumbling, with a rough edge to it.

One by one they climbed down stiffly into the swirling dust. Through the murk they could make out that they were in the midst of a circle of horsemen, with guns aimed in their direction. Their faces were covered by similar neckerchiefs and their hats shielded their eyes. The drivers had already climbed down and were standing with their hands in the air and worried looks on their faces.

"I tell ya, we ain't carrying nothing worth having," one of the drivers was saying. "We don't have no money on board. Just the mail and some goods to be delivered."

"Get them down and let's take a look then," one of the men on horseback said. "And it will be a sorry day for you if you've been lying to us."

Holmes noted that his speech was more refined than the first man's. He spoke with what almost might have been an English accent. The terrified drivers complied, climbing up to the roof of the coach and wrestling with the ropes that lashed down the baggage. The group of passengers huddled together, coughing and holding up hands to fight off the biting sand.

"And you guys. Hand over your valuables and money," the first man barked.

The big westerner shifted uneasily. "As you can see, we are only poor folk. We don't have much in the way of valuables. I've a few dollars in my pocket and you're welcome to those." He came forward, hand full of silver dollars. The masked man took them, then grabbed around the westerner's wrist. "And your gun, friend. You don't think we're stupid enough to let you keep that?" He reached down and pulled a pistol with a mother-of-pearl handle from a holster at the man's hip, then dropped it on the ground beside the pile of goods that was now being flung down from the roof. "And I'll wager there's a fine pocket watch in that vest of yours." He reached inside and crowed with glee as he produced a shiny watch. "No valuables, huh? We'll be takin' a close look at your bags, you can bet your bottom dollar."

Two other men had now descended from their horses and slit open bundles and packages with fierce-looking knives. Out came calico and coffee, books and beans, spilling in a horrible mixture onto the dry earth.

Mrs. Williams leaped forward with a cry. "Those are our Bibles for the heathen. You have no right to destroy them. God will surely punish you if you do."

Holmes had to admire her brave if foolhardy action.

The leader on foot approached her in a threatening manner. "You shut your mouth, ma'am, and keep it shut if you know what's good for you." He pointed the gun deliberately at her face and she stepped back with a cry of horror.

"Come now, sir. You are speaking to the wife of a missionary," her husband attempted to say.

"And you too, ya old windbag." The first man prodded

Reverend Williams in his ample belly with his gun. "Just hand over your trinkets and you'll be all right."

"But we are poor missionaries. We have no worldly goods," Rev. Williams whined, but to no avail. Rough hands were already delving into his pockets. The first man had moved on to the schoolteacher from Ohio. "Well, what have we here? A little beauty, with a trim little waist. We might just carry her off for ourselves, eh, boys?"

She let out a whimper of fear. Holmes could stand it no longer. He stepped forward. "Take your hands off her this instant."

The man turned toward him and a deep chuckle emanated from under the bandana. "And you're going to make me, are ya? A dandy from back east?"

"If you care to fight me fair and square, I am competent in the martial arts," Holmes said, "and I would fight for the honor of a lady, as would any man of breeding."

"Would you listen to him?" the man chuckled again, and Holmes heard another of the men laughing, a high "hee hee" sound. Holmes glanced around and saw a glimpse of red hair under the man's hat, and an arm covered in so many freckles that it looked almost orange. I won't forget you in a hurry, Holmes thought.

The leader came toward Holmes. "Wanna fight, do ya? Well, this is how I fight, boy." And he brought the butt of his pistol crashing down on the side of Holmes's head. Holmes fell to the ground and knew no more.

He awoke to darkness and silence. His mouth was encrusted with sand, and when he tried to open his eyes, they too were caked together with sand. He sat up and the world swung around alarmingly. A wave of nausea overcame him. Where the devil was he? Then it came to him—the coach, the robbery, and that blow descending. At least he wasn't dead, he decided. They had spared his life. He got to his feet and looked around him. Complete darkness. The only pinpricks of light came from stars that hung, unnaturally large and bright, in the heavens. He realized then that it had been no act of mercy to spare his life, but rather the reverse. He had been left in the middle of nowhere to die slowly.

For a moment he fought with despair. Then resolve triumphed. He was going to make it out of here alive. He was going to bring those men to justice. It was imperative that he cover as much ground as possible while it was still dark, because he would have to seek refuge during the blistering heat of the day. He stared up at the sky until he located the North Star. Tucson, he reasoned, was due west. He turned to face what he decided was the right direction and set out. It was not easy going. The ground underfoot was a horrible mixture of rocks and sand, dotted with sharp, scrubby bushes and the occasional cactus. He blundered forward, cursing when he met cactus spines or tripped on a loose rock. In this manner he kept going for some time, fighting waves of nausea. His head throbbed like the devil and sometimes lights danced before his eyes in the blackness.

At last he could go on no longer. He sank to the ground, intending to rest for only a short while, but instead fell into a sound sleep. He woke with the first rays of the morning sun shining straight into his face His mouth was parched and dry and his tongue felt like an alien object. He staggered to his feet, pain shooting through his head. The landscape had changed. It was no longer flat and featureless. Rugged purple mountain chains rose up ahead of him. There was no sign of human habitation. Just more rock, more cactus. If anything, it looked more hostile and forbidding than the day before. Those mountains obviously stood between him and the green valley of Tucson. How would he find the strength to climb them without water?

He wondered what time it was and reached for his pocket watch. It wasn't there. They had taken it, and all his money. Anger welled up inside him, propelling him forward. He set off, lurching rather than walking, a grotesque figure covered in yellow dust moving jerkily like a puppet. As the sun came up, the desert flamed with orange light. Even in his current pain and despair, Holmes stood for a moment, appreciating the savage beauty of it. Then on again, rugged mile after mile.

As the sun rose in the sky, the heat on the back of his neck was intense. He realized then that he wore no hat. Of course it still resided on the luggage rack of the coach. No point in wasting energy thinking about it. By noon the mirages appeared—sheets of water hanging improbably on mountainsides, always just out of reach. The desert shimmered with heat. Nothing moved, except for a snake that slithered across his path and under a rock. He wondered how one killed a snake and whether they could be eaten. He put his hand into his pocket. They had even taken his pipe and tinder box.

Water. He must find water or die. But every depression and hollow was dry. He could see where streams had cut through the sandstone on their way down from mountains, but only in a rainy season, if there ever was one in this accursed place. He thought of home—misty days, green grass, the sound of a cricket ball against a bat, rain pattering on windows, afternoon tea on the lawn—and wondered if he'd ever see it again. At last he could go on no longer. He dropped to his knees and crawled under the shade of a prickly bush, where he fell into a half sleep.

He awoke with a start. Someone was squatting over him. A hand reached to touch him. He raised his head to look and saw the bronzed, naked torso, the red-brown face, the long black braids of an Indian brave. Rumors of savagery flashed through his mind— victims scalped and other unmentionable tortures. He tried to get to his feet, realizing he had no weapon and was defenseless.

The Indian must have seen the panic in his eyes. "Be still. I wish you no harm," he said in a deep, guttural voice. "I come to help."

"How did you find me?" Holmes asked.

"I see vultures circling. They know when a creature is about to die."

Holmes glanced up in horror.

"How did white man come to be so far from his brothers? Where is his horse?"

Holmes explained the stagecoach and the robbery. "I've been trying to walk to the settlement in Tucson. Do you know it? Am I far away?"

The Indian pointed toward what looked like the north. "Beyond those hills. Two days' march for a man in good health."

"So far? I don't understand."

"You are to the south of the white man's houses. You have almost crossed the boundary to the land they call Mexico."

"How did I get here? I tried to walk due west. I should have followed the track."

"It is easy to go astray in the desert," the Indian said. "You are thirsty. You need to drink."

"Do you have any water?" Holmes asked, wondering where on his person it could be stored, seeing that he wore little more than a loincloth.

The Indian had already turned away and approached a giant cactus. He studied it, then produced a hatchet and lopped off a branch, nodding in satisfaction. "Watch for spines," he warned, then demonstrated, reaching into the cactus and scooping out liquid. Holmes drank greedily, then washed his face.

"I'm much obliged to you," he said. "You've undoubtedly saved my life. May name is Holmes. May I know yours?"

"You can call me Shadow Wolf," the man said.

"Do your people live nearby?" Holmes asked, studying the desert scenery.

"Not near. Now they are camped a day away, on the other side of the white man's border. I have been sent to the town to trade."

"What do you trade?" Again Holmes looked at the almost naked man.

"I bring precious stones and animal skins. I will return with tobacco and cloth and wool for weaving blankets." He opened a little pouch he carried tied to his waist and Holmes saw the glint of unpolished stones. "The skins are over there. By that bush."

He went to retrieve the tightly wrapped bundle. "Can you walk? I do not think you can walk all the way to the white man's town. I will take you to the nearest of their ranches. Come."

He motioned for Holmes to follow him and set off mercifully slowly.

"How do you know your way?" Holmes asked. "I see no kind of trail."

Shadow Wolf smiled. "I read the signs. My people call it 'cutting for sign.' To me the desert is like a story, waiting to be read." He paused. "See here?" He bent down and pointed to a low shrub. "A rabbit passed this way." Holmes noticed a tiny shred of white fur caught on a spine. "And here, where the sand is soft, we can see his trail. The footmarks are fresh. Yesterday the wind blew the sand, so I know that he passed this way since last night. But his trail does not continue here, so what happened? A drama. I will show you. Specks of blood on the rock, here. But no other animal tracks. How can that be? I will tell you. A great bird came down and took him. An eagle maybe. See here where the wing tip brushed the sand?"

He nodded at Holmes with satisfaction. "Even the smallest of signs tells me a story. I can tell you who walked here and how long ago, whether they were carrying burdens or walking lightly."

"Fascinating." Holmes was still staring at the tiny specks of blood on the rock. "Can you teach me to read the signs?"

Shadow Wolf smiled again. "It takes a lifetime of practice. Maybe a man has to be born to it. But I can show you how I cut for sign."

"And how do you find your way in this featureless place?"

"In this place there is no problem. We must cross those mountains. The water takes the easiest path downward after rain, so we will follow the path of the river." He indicated the dry wash and motioned Holmes to follow. Holmes struggled after him. All afternoon they climbed steadily. At last the sun sank behind the hills, speckling the vast sky with pink, like an archipelago of islands in a blue ocean.

"We make camp," Shadow Wolf said. "You must eat and rest."

He found an area of soft sand. Holmes sank down gratefully. His head no longer throbbed dangerously, but his feet were blistered and his tongue felt so swollen that his lips wouldn't close around it.

"Do we have any food?"

"I will find food for us." He moved off. Holmes was disappointed to see him returning empty-handed. "I have found the road of the pouched rat," he said. "I have set traps. We will wait. But until then..." He climbed effortlessly up to where a spreading cactus bush spilled over a rock, and lopped off some green tips. "Your people call this prickly pear," he said. "When I have taken off the spikes, it is good to eat."

With his hatchet he skillfully removed the outer layer and handed the segment to Holmes, who crunched on it greedily. It was full of moisture, almost like a fruit. The Indian then set about building a fire, taking a piece of flint from a small leather pouch and striking it against the side of his hatchet. Sparks fell upon a small heap of dried moss, which he carefully blew on, and he soon had a blaze going. "There are wolves in these mountains," he said, "and coyotes and even puma. They will not harm us unless they are very hungry. But they may be very hungry. We must be prepared."

They sat on opposite sides of the fire. The red man's face glowed in the firelight. Slowly a young moon rose over the horizon. The Indian stood up. "We will see if the traps have brought us dinner yet."

Holmes followed him, trying to walk as silently as the Indian but somehow managing to step on dry twigs and kick loose pebbles, much to his embarrassment. Shadow Wolf did not look back at him, but proceeded at a steady pace, staring down at an invisible trail with interest. At last he held up his hand for Holmes to stop. Holmes could see that some kind of trap had been rigged between two rocks—a thin sapling bent back, bait beneath, and a rock poised to drop at the right moment.

It had not yet been triggered. The Indian shook his head and motioned for Holmes to step around the trap. They went on and then the Indian trotted forward to another trap. This one had been sprung. A small mammal lay beneath a rock, quite dead. It was hardly enough to feed two men, but the Indian seemed satisfied as they made their way back to camp. He produced a small knife from his pouch and skillfully skinned the little carcass before spitting it over the blaze. It provided little more than a nibble, but Holmes was able to fall asleep feeling reasonably content.

Shadow Wolf woke them at first light. He had visited the rest of his traps and had cooked another of the pouched rats, as well as a porcupine he had apparently killed with his small knife. He demonstrated to Holmes how he had removed the spines by burying the animal in the embers of the fire. They ate, then set off. As they climbed steadily, Shadow Wolf pointed out the smallest of clues that Holmes would not have noticed—a bee flying toward a nest in a dead paloverde stump, the tracks of a coyote stalking a jackrabbit. Holmes wished he had his notebook with him and tried to memorize everything the other man said.

They reached the crest and made their way down the other side of the mountains. At last, after many miles of traveling, they came upon a white man's fence, then the first cattle, and by afternoon they saw the ranch house, low and sprawling and made of adobe brick the color of the landscape. Shadow Wolf indicated that Holmes should go on.

"Will you not come with me?" he asked. "Let me at least provide you with a good meal, and I should like to reward you in some way, if I could."

Shadow Wolf shook his head. "The white man sees the red man as his enemy. Sometimes this is true. Sometimes it is not. But the white man expects the worst. I have no wish to meet the white man's bullet." He held out his hand to Holmes. "Walk safely, my friend. Everywhere you go, may you have good luck."

"And you too, my friend," Holmes replied. There was a lump in his throat as the tall, bronzed figure moved swiftly away. Holmes walked toward the ranch. Soon he heard the barking of dogs and ranch hands came out to meet him. He was brought into the delightful cool of the ranch house and began spilling out his tale to the rancher and his wife over a cup of coffee and a slice of pie.

"So you see, I am at your mercy, sir," Holmes said. "I have been robbed of all my possessions and my money. If you could somehow help me into the nearest town, then maybe I can persuade the local bank manager that I am a man of honor and that funds from my bank in London will be transferred with all speed."

"You're not going anywhere for a while, young man," Mrs. Tucker, the rancher's wife, said. "You looked as if you were about to expire when you staggered up to our door. You stay with us for a few days while I get some nourishing food into you, and then you can ride with Mr. Tucker when he goes into Tucson to collect the mail on Friday."

"I'm much obliged to you, ma'am."

"And as for money," Mr. Tucker said, "I can see that you are a gentleman, and I was raised to believe that a gentleman's word is his bond. I'll advance you what you need to take you back to civilization."

"I'm am truly grateful, sir," Holmes replied,

"We have to make amends for those varmints who robbed the stage, don't we?" Tucker chuckled. "Otherwise you'd believe nothing good about the Wild West. There are more hardworking and honest men out here than bandits, I can assure you."

"Just as there are more kind and trustworthy Indians than hostile ones, I expect," Holmes said, and noticed the instant coldness.

"I wouldn't be about to say that," Mrs. Tucker said. "We live in constant fear out here so far from town, and Mr. Tucker will tell you that the rogues are always trying to rustle our cattle."

Holmes thought it wise not to pursue this topic. So he remained at the Tucker homestead, allowing himself to be spoiled by Mrs. Tucker's ample meals and constant ministrations. He also showed considerable interest in the running of the ranch and begged Mr. Tucker to teach him as many western skills as possible. On his last day a steer was butchered. Mr. Tucker, wearing a large canvas apron, did most of the butchering himself while Holmes watched and made notes.

"Damned flies." Mr. Tucker waved them away.

"I'm surprised at the number of flies," Holmes said. "We've scarcely seen one or two before now."

"Danged creatures can smell blood from a mile off," Tucker said. "They make straight for it. Smallest drop of blood and they'll find it out, mark my words."

He went back to butchering.

That night there was an outdoor ox roast in Holmes's honor, and next morning they left in the buckboard for Tucson. It was five hours bumping over a rutted and rocky track before the township appeared before them, lying in a green valley with a small stream meandering through it. They passed between wooden shacks and adobe buildings before coming to a halt in the one dusty main street. Shop fronts lurked in deep shadow behind deep porches. Wooden sidewalks kept dust and mud off boots and ladies' hems. As Holmes and Mr. Tucker stepped down from the buckboard, a young man came out of one of the saloons. He had bright red hair and his forearms were covered with orange freckles. As he came out, he turned back to say something, then let out a loud "hee hee hee."

Holmes froze. "That man," he whispered to Mr. Tucker. "He was one of the ones who robbed me, I'm sure of it."

Tucker frowned. "I thought you said they wore masks."

"But I'd recognize his forearm and his laugh anywhere."

"Then if I were you, I'd keep quiet about it, if you know what's good for you," Tucker replied. "That boy is Willard Jensen. His daddy owns half this town. His daddy hires the sheriff."

Holmes thought he saw the young man stare for a second as he passed, but he hurried on to join a group of men standing outside the jail. A loud buzz of conversation was coming from the group and then a voice boomed loudly, "I say we string him up right now. Ain't no sense in waiting around. He's as guilty as sin."

"Come on now, boys." This speaker was an older man, portly and well dressed in western manner. A heavy gold chain was strung across his chest and he wore a large white hat. "Everything has to be done properly, according to the law. You know that. We got us a representative of the federal government in town at the moment and you wouldn't want him to go home and report that folks on the frontier act like savages, would you?"

"Whatever you say, Mr. Jensen. Okay, first we try him, then we string him up," someone said and got a general laugh.

"What's going on, Hank?" Mr. Tucker asked a storekeeper who had come out of his general store to observe.

"Why, they brought in an injun who killed Ronald Fletcher. You know, that Englishman who's been working for Tyler Jensen. Educated type of fellah."

"How do they know the Indian killed him?" Holmes asked.

Hank appraised the newcomer. "You a relative?" he asked. "He sounded like you."

Holmes shook his head.

"Anyway, they caught this injun actually bending over the body. We got us a guy from Washington in town so it looks like there will have to be a trial."

At that moment there was a commotion further down the street, the crowd parted, and a procession emerged from the jail. Gun-toting deputies walked ahead, clearing the throng of onlookers who had come out of nearby businesses. And in the middle, handcuffed and shoved roughly between two burly guards, was Holmes's Indian companion, Shadow Wolf.

"String him up, the no-good rat. We don't need no trial. Kill him." The words echoed through the crowd.

Shadow Wolf raised his eyes for a second and Holmes saw the flash of recognition before he lowered them again.

"I know that man," Holmes whispered excitedly to Mr. Tucker. "He saved my life. I should do something."

"I'd stay well out of it if I were you, son," Tucker said. "This isn't justice like you're used to, and folks around here have little love for Indians. Isn't much you can do."

"I'm sorry, but I can't stand by and do nothing. It may be futile, but I have to try." Holmes stepped into the tide of people, allowed himself to be swept along into the courthouse, and took his place on one of the back benches. The room buzzed with excited anticipation. Tyler Jensen and a tall man in black took their places at the front.

The presiding judge was announced, a wiry little man with spiky white hair. He brought his hammer crashing down. "Court's now in session," he said. "We have before us the injun who killed Robert Fletcher—fine, upstanding man who managed the ranch for Tyler Jensen. Don't think this should take too long. We've got witnesses who caught him in the act."

Holmes took a deep breath and stepped forward. "May I ask who is representing the defendant?" he asked.

"Don't need no attorney. Open-and-shut case," the judge said. "The injun has pretty much pleaded guilty."

"According to the law of this land, I believe that every person is entitled to a fair trial with representation, is that not correct?" Holmes asked.

The man in black rose to his feet. "I am Carter Cleveland, and I have been sent to observe our newest territory. Since Arizona is now officially part of the United States, then the law of the United States must be observed. Every man is entitled to representation."

"Then I should like to volunteer to represent this man," Holmes said.

"You a bona fide attorney, son?" the judge asked.

"In England, where I come from, I am considered an educated man," Holmes said stiffly. "And I suspect you have no other volunteers to represent the Indian in the courthouse."

The judge looked at him for a moment, then nodded. "Go ahead. Can't do no harm. Won't do no good."

"Then I should like to confer with my client," Holmes said.

A titter of laughter, mixed with catcalls, echoed through the courthouse.

"Ten minutes, then," the judge agreed.

Holmes went up to the Indian. "Don't waste your breath, my friend," Shadow Wolf said. "They have already prepared the gallows for me."

"But you didn't do it."

"No. I did not kill that man."

"Then tell me what happened, for God's sake," Holmes implored.

Shadow Wolf stared out beyond him. "I was walking alone in the darkness last night. I did not go near the bright lights of the streets because I did not wish to pass the saloons. Men full of liquor have been known to become violent when they see one of my people. I heard noise—raised voices, men shouting—in the alleyway ahead of me. I heard a voice say, "No more. This has gone on long enough." Then a few more words. Then departing feet, and silence. I continued on my way until I saw something lying in shadow. It was a man. I bent over him to see if he was still alive. Suddenly hands grab me and they drag me away. They are shouting that I am the killer. I tell them I am innocent, but they don't listen to me."

"Do you have any idea who the men were you heard quarreling? Or what they were quarreling about?"

The Indian shook his head. "As to their words, I only heard the words I have told you. One has a deep voice, rumbles like mountain thunder."

Another of the men who robbed me, Holmes thought. Clearly the whole gang is in town, and this could have been a falling-out among thieves. The man with the refined English voice wanted no more of it, so they killed him. But how to prove this?

"Where did this happen?" Holmes asked.

"Behind the tavern there are stables. Behind those stables there is a way through to the road out of town. I have been sleeping in safety away from the houses of the white men."

"But why are you still here?" Holmes asked. "Surely your business must have been concluded long ago?"

The Indian shook his head. "The man who would buy my stones has been away. They told me he would return yesterday. So I waited. But he did not return."

"And your stones?"

"Safely hidden."

"Okay, you've had your confab," came the judge's voice. "Let's get on with it."

"One more thing," Holmes said to the judge. "I should like to see the scene of the crime for myself."

"Ain't necessary. Nothing to see there."

"All the same, it is only right that I view the site for myself," Holmes said.

"Shut him up." "Let's get on with it." "Let's get on with the hanging." The voices echoed from the dark stuffiness of the courtroom.

The tall man in black rose to his feet. "As an outsider I can only advise, but this does not seem an unreasonable request. The defending attorney needs to see the scene of the crime."

"Oh, very well. Have it your way," the judge snapped. "Court adjourned for fifteen minutes. Maybe if we hurry we'll have time for a quick visit to the tavern to fortify ourselves."

Holmes waited not a moment longer. He ran out of the courtroom, found the stables and then the little-used walkway between the back of the stables and the fence of a private dwelling. He stared at the ground. Think, he told himself. Remember what he taught you. The land tells a story. He looked down at the sandy soil. The first thing he noticed were some flies on a black tarry area that Holmes deduced was dried blood. He dropped to his knees and examined the ground for prints. Several sets of boot prints, and then he picked out one set of the soft-soled shoes that the Indian wore. He studied the ground carefully. The Indian had come that way, as he said. The prints did not proceed beyond the spot with the blood. He also noted that one pair of boots had an interesting, almost heart-shaped metal tip to the toe and the heel. It came down the alleyway before the Indian, as the latter's print was over it, and then continued on. Could have been coincidence, or he could be looking at the boot print of one of the killers. From the width of the stride and the depth of the print, Holmes could deduce that the man was running.

Reluctantly he returned to the courtroom. He noticed from the raised volume of noise that many of the occupants had indeed fortified themselves at the tavern while he had been gone. Their rowdiness was now bordering on belligerence.

The trial began. The first witness was called. He gave his name as Chuck Hawkins. He told how he had heard a ruckus the night before, gone into the alleyway, and seen the Indian bending over a body. The body was still warm. He and some other men had grabbed the Indian and dragged him to the jail.

"Don't seem no need to go any further," the judge said. "Open-and-shut case, like I said."

"One moment, please." Holmes got to his feet amid groans and catcalls. "First I would like to speak to the character of the defendant. He is no killer. Only last week he saved my life when I had been robbed and left for dead in the desert." He let his gaze move deliberately around the courtroom. "It may surprise honest men among you to know that a gang of stage robbers actually resides in this town and are here among you today."

Murmurs rumbled through the crowd.

"But this is not the business at hand. We are speaking of the life of a man, a human being, no matter what the color of his skin. Like any other man here, he is innocent until proven guilty. I should first like to call the doctor who examined the body. I presume a doctor did examine the body."

"Most certainly did," the judge said. "It was me, son. He died instantly, stabbed through the heart."

"Interesting," Holmes said. "Stabbed from the front, you mean? Now I have just examined that alleyway and note that the Indian's footprints go no further than where the man fell. So I can only deduce that he came upon the body, as he said, and bent to examine it from behind. Now, if he had just stabbed the man, he would have been standing in front of him, wouldn't he? But there is no sign of his footprints beyond where the man fell. On the contrary, I could see two pairs of rather distinctive boots, running away, by the size of their strides. White man's boots, mark you, not Indian moccasins."

"Footprints don't prove nothin'," someone near the front shouted. "Those prints could have been there for days. And the injun could have snuck up from behind, spun the poor fellah around, and then stabbed him."

There was growled agreement to this.

Holmes took a deep breath. He could see they'd have an answer to almost any kind of evidence he produced. They wanted the Indian to be guilty and they were going to make sure he was.

"Doctor," he said. "You examined the body. What size would you say the wound was?"

The judge thought for a moment. "About two inches, I'd say. Nasty, vicious wound. Went straight into the heart."

"And who took the Indian's weapons from him when he was arrested?"

"I did," a voice called from the back. "They're locked up now, in the jail."

"Can you please produce them as evidence?" Holmes demanded.

They waited. A few seconds later an out-of-breath deputy placed the hatchet and the knife in front of the judge.

"This is correct," Holmes said. "During the time I was with this man he was carrying only these two weapons. The hatchet could not have been used for stabbing. It wouldn't make a cut deep enough to kill. Now, let us examine the knife. It is a throwing knife, you will note. Light, designed with a teardrop shape for flying swiftly and easily through the air. But at its widest the blade is only—what would you say, Doctor—one inch wide?"

The judge leaned forward to examine the blade. "Yep. About that."

"So it could not have been the blade that killed Mr. Fletcher, could it?"

Another rumble went through the crowd. "And what's more," Holmes went on, emboldened, "I believe I can prove which knife in this room did kill him. If you'll follow me outside..." They complied, jostling for position.

Holmes walked behind them, checking their footprints in the soft sand of the street. "Would you step forward, sir?" He went around touching shoulders apparently randomly. "And would you place your knives on the bed of this buckboard?"

He had summoned ten men. He recognized two of them.

The knives were placed. Holmes waited.

"What you goin' to do, a magic trick? Goin' to make the dead man appear and point to his killer?" Tyler Jensen demanded, and got a general laugh, although not from the men standing in that line.

"While we wait," Holmes said, "let me fill you in on a little background so that you understand better. Last week I was in a stagecoach that was robbed in the desert. I tried to protect a young woman and was knocked unconscious. I was left for dead. I should surely have died if this Indian had not found me and brought me to safety. Imagine my surprise when I came into town and saw the men who robbed me. It is true that they were masked, but they each had something about them that gave them away—a peculiarly deep, rumbling voice, for example, or bright orange freckles on a forearm and a high-pitched laugh. One of them had a smooth, English-sounding accent. I surmise that he is Mr. Robert Fletcher, who now lies in your morgue. I also surmise there was a falling-out among thieves. Mr. Fletcher was overheard to say, 'No more. This has gone on long enough.' I suspect his conscience was getting the better of him and he wanted out. But he could not be allowed to leave the gang, in case he betrayed his fellow bandits. So they killed him. It was purely fortuitous that the person who happened to stumble upon the body was an Indian. An obvious scapegoat, wouldn't you say?"

"Utter rubbish," one of the men standing in that line said. "Come on, Judge. This has gone on long enough. What's the fellah think he can prove? He's just making things up to protect his Indian pal. I say we string 'em up, both of 'em."

Holmes held up his hand. "Only one more minute of your time, I promise you. The proof has arrived. While I was staying with Mr. Tucker, he taught me a good deal of things, including that flies will always home in on blood. The killer thought that he wiped his knife clean, but not clean enough. The flies still smelled the traces of blood on it. If you will turn your attention to the knives, you will now see which knife killed Robert Fletcher."

There was a gasp from the crowd. One knife now had five or six flies on it. The others did not.

"Would the other men now retrieve their knives?" Holmes instructed.

He looked at the young redheaded man. His face was ashen. "Willard Jensen, is it not?" Holmes said, "And if I'm not mistaken, your boots have distinctive metal tips. I saw your prints as you ran away from the scene of the crime."

As hands went to grab him, Jensen whipped out a gun. "He

made me do it," he shouted, waving the pistol at the big man in the red shirt. "He said we had to make sure Robert didn't talk."

"What nonsense is this?" Tyler Jensen stepped forward. "Accusing my boy? That's a mighty stupid thing to do, stranger. You've been nothing but trouble since you came into town. And if you men know what's good for you, you won't listen to a word he says."

"On the contrary." The federal agent pushed his way to the front of the crowd. "I believe he has put his case extremely well. I for one am satisfied that he has arrived at the truth. If you wish to deal with him, you will have to deal with me first. And I can assure you that my colleagues in Washington would have the cavalry here in a minute flat and would take over the running of this town if anything happened to me."

He moved to stand beside Holmes. "Judge," he said. "I think it behooves you to release this Indian."

The judge shot an anxious glance at Tyler Jensen. "Oh, very well. Bring out the Indian. But you guys better get him out of town pretty danged fast, or I'll not be responsible for what happens to him, or to any of you."

"As it happens, I planned to leave today anyway," the man in black said. "Would you care to join me, Mr. Holmes? I am on my way to Phoenix and then to the West Coast."

"My dear sir, I'd be delighted," Holmes said, "if we can give my good friend Shadow Wolf a ride to safely."

"We most certainly can," Mr. Cleveland replied.

"Before I go," Holmes said, turning back to the crowd. "I should like to retrieve my pocket watch. I don't know what happened to the rest of my belongings, but that watch was dear to me." He walked up to the big man in red and held out his hand. "I noticed it in court," he said.

"Hey, I bought this watch fair and square from a trader," the man snapped. "Ain't no way you can prove it's yours."

"I think that the inscription inside the back cover might convince some people that it is mine," Holmes said. "To my dear brother Sherlock on his twenty-first birthday. It is signed Mycroft."

Hands removed the watch and opened it, and a murmur of recognition went through the crowd. The watch was handed to Holmes.

"Now take it and get out while you're still alive," Mr. Jensen barked.

Shadow Wolf was brought out and climbed into the buckboard. Holmes and the federal agent climbed up beside him.

"I fear that justice will not be served in that place," Holmes said.

"We have done the best we can do without reinforcements," Mr. Cleveland said. "You should be glad the outcome was so positive. Had I not been there, I rather fear that both of you would be swinging from a noose at this moment. I will report the case to my superiors in Washington, but I doubt that much can be done. We shall have to wait until more women come out west. They are always a civilizing influence."

The buckboard started off. As they swung to take the road out of town, Tyler Jensen ran forward and drew his pistol. "Take that, ya damned meddler," he yelled. A gunshot reverberated in the clear air.

Then a surprised look came over his face and he slumped to the ground. An equally surprised smile spread over Holmes's face as he replaced his smoking pistol into its holster.

"One of the things Mr. Tucker taught me during the time of my recuperation was how to shoot one of these things. I must have mastered it remarkably quickly."

The horses picked up speed as the town fell away behind them.

Marta Randall writes with passion and fire and her usual
grace of the Mexico of 150 years ago and what Sherlock
Holmes found there.

THE ENGLISH SEÑOR
by
MARTA RANDALL

I had long ago lost patience with the young
man who shared the carriage with me. It did
not matter that my son-in-law Teobaldo had
begged me to take him safely out of Mexico
City, it did not matter that he was not quite the
age of my youngest grandson, it did not matter
that he was ill and barely fit for travel, and it
mattered less and less that if he were discovered
his life was forfeit, as was that of Teobaldo, and
quite possibly my own. If they strung this young
English señor from a lamp standard, it was only
what he deserved.

Because he was here, with his long nose
sticking out of his nest of blankets like the beak
of a particularly annoying bird, I was missing the
only performance of Ludwig van Beethoven's
sublime Ninth Symphony, the culmination of

the cycle conducted by the famed Hungarian conductor Arthur Nikisch. It had been a triumphant season, our classically trained musicians rising to meet the challenge of the impressively mustachioed Nikisch so that a three-way partnership burst forth, conductor and musicians and chorus filling the grand concert hall with music as sublime as—but I digress...

I had agreed to forgo Sr. Beethoven's crowning creation only because Teobaldo had quite literally fallen to his knees, taken my hands in his, and wept over them. My son-in-law was known for his melodrama, but how could I refuse him? He was the family's bulwark against the political storms that continue to buffet our poor country: revolutions, dictators, invasions, the shameful occupation by the hated French, and the monarchy of the pretty boy Maximilian and his poor, crazy wife, Carlota.

Teobaldo had fought at the side of Benito Juarez, a true hero, and helped drive the French from the country, but the memory of the invasion still rankled. An English army had landed together with the French, a fact not lost on Mexicans, and so periodically the English were booted out of the country. Apparently the English trade delegation had trodden on the delicate sensibilities of the mayor of Mexico City and his pocket army, led by *el maldito* General Tomás Pulgón de Coliflór. The mayor had vowed that if the Ingléses were not out of Mexico within a week, any lingering member would be shot, or hanged, or perhaps both. He was a powerful man and known for such outbursts, which usually passed within a year, *mas o menos*. Unfortunately until they subsided, General Pulgón was happy to hang, or shoot, or possibly both, any putative offenders. This one, who undoubtedly deserved it, had been too sick to travel and his brother had begged that Teobaldo save the boy's life. The boy was newly out of school, accompanying his older brother as an adventure, to see the New World, innocent of all evil intent, just a child, worthy of salvation. What was he to do, my son-in-law asked me as he watered my hands with his tears. It was a matter of honor. Honor! And so here I sat, while this young jackanapes muttered into his blankets and wiped at his beak with my best linen handkerchief.

All of this was bad enough, but he himself added to my fury. Why? I will let him tell you himself, in his tweetery English. Mind you, when he said all this we were barely out of the heart of the city and he had no idea that I spoke his language.

"Señora, I am tremendously grateful (sniff) that your most kindly relative (snuffle) has taken it upon himself (sneeze) at great peril to himself (snort) to come forward in my hour of need (cough) and arrange for you to transport me (gag) to safety, saving me from the grasp (sniffle) of that great barbarian (cough) who runs this poor, benighted (snort), and miserable country."

Poor, benighted, miserable country! He could only say this because he did not think himself understood by the poor, benighted, miserable woman who was saving his life. In addition, he thanked Teobaldo, but did he thank me, Ana Magdalena Coraje Montalvo de Conejo? He did not, and yet my peril was almost as great as this child's, and probably greater than Teobaldo's, who was a consummate politician and could wheedle his way out of any number of sticky situations. But I was just the widow of a *hacendado* from the north of Jalisco, owner of a small but wealthy *rancho* well apart from the worldliness of Mexico City. My lands were fruitful, my herds fat and tempting to those in the capital who would be glad of any excuse to declare them forfeit. Teobaldo would survive but I,

I would be incarcerated at best and shot at worst, and it did not matter that the soldiers would take care to shoot me below the neck, so as not to damage a lady's face.

It added to my annoyance that we traveled not north toward my hacienda, but east toward Veracruz, in the footsteps of the fleeing Englishmen. Have you been to Veracruz? It is the antechamber to *el infierno*, hot and sticky and pestilential, and the air so studded with obnoxious insects that one cannot breathe without snuffling up a kilo of them. I would rather spend a month in, oh, *por ejemplo*, the wretched village of Pénjamo than spend an hour in Veracruz.

I told him all of this in furious whispers, in Spanish, while he coughed and blew his nose and stared at me, for if he could not understand my words he certainly understood my tone. The carriage rattled over the cobblestones. Eduardo, my majordomo, sat atop and drove the carriage, his son Heriberto rode alongside, and Maria, my maid, sat beside me and covered her mouth, giggling silently, as I finished my tirade. All of these people carried my life, and the boy's, in their hands, but I trusted them implicitly. We had been together for a long, long time.

The boy pulled the blankets around his ears and I turned away, trying to settle myself by remembering the melody of the great chorale from Sr. Beethoven's final symphony. My music master had taught it to me when I was just a girl, and I had never heard it given full throat by a professional chorus. Now I never would. I hummed the melody under my breath, furious.

Suddenly the boy sat up, alarmed. "Something is happening ahead," he said, suppressing a sneeze with such ferocity that his face turned crimson. "Ahead!" He pointed and made wild gestures with his hands. Eduardo rapped on the carriage roof and slid back the little window behind him.

"Doña Ana, I fear the road is blocked—there are carts backed up ahead of us."

"Damn!" I said in English, at which the boy's eyes opened wide. "¡Maria, *mi bolsa!*" Maria snatched up my valise. I snapped it open and grabbed at the clothes within it. "And damn Teobaldo for making us leave so hurriedly." I thrust an armload of petticoats to-ward the boy. "Quickly, take your clothes off and put these on."

"You, you speak English," he said. His nose was even more red than his face.

"And you won't speak it again if you know what's best," I re-torted. "Go on, you have nothing that Maria and I have not seen before. They are searching the wagons ahead, you don't have much time." I pushed the clothes into his arms. "Now, unless you want to die!"

At this he became greatly animated under the blankets. Maria giggled again and I tapped her shoulder, hard.

"Listen, young man," I whispered. "You are my niece Cande-laria and you are gravely ill, and I am trying to get you home be-fore you die. I think you have, um, what do you have? Cholera? No, nor typhus, they are both too smelly. Ah! You have the swellings in your armpits. You must carry your arms like this." I illustrated, holding my elbows up and away from my body. "Maria, *una man-tilla.* You must keep your hands covered under your blankets, they are most inelegant, you have bitten the nails to the quick." I took my powders from the valise. "Close your eyes," I commanded, and powdered him until his face looked ghastly.

Maria folded his discarded clothes and stuffed them under the cushions. We sat on them and he half reclined on the opposite seat, his preposterously long legs doubled up under the blankets and the dress and the petticoats, his head under a thick flannel, and a mantilla over all. I myself was convinced that this would not work and could picture him swinging from a tree, his long red nose still dripping, while the comandante kindly instructed his men not to shoot me in the face. I rapped on the carriage roof, and when Eduardo slid open the window I said, "the plague." He nodded and closed the window again, and the carriage bumped to a halt.

"And you are mute!" I added in a hiss. The flannel and mantilla shook as the boy nodded. A moment later the carriage door opened. A young lieutenant thrust his head in and executed the sketchiest of bows.

"What does this mean?" I demanded before he could speak. "I do not have time to play these little games, there is a sick woman in this carriage and I must get her home immediately!"

The lieutenant raised an eyebrow. "Señora, we are searching for a dangerous criminal, an Inglés, known to be an agent of his government intent upon discovering secrets of the most high type and using them against our beloved country. A small matter of illness cannot stand in the way of our national security."

The English señor produced a treble groan and, under the blankets, raised his elbows away from his body. The lieutenant leaned back, looking surprised.

"*La peste bubónica,*" I whispered. "Do not say it to her—she does not know she is dying." I produced a tear. "Such a tragedy, she is so young."

But I said this to nothing. The door had snapped closed and, after a brief interlude of shouting, we were on our way again.

Eduardo threaded the carriage through the waiting carts and wagons. News of our pestilential cargo must have preceded us; beyond the window I saw the carters make haste to move out of our way, squeezing up against each other and holding their clothes against their noses and mouths. The young señor sat up.

"Candelaria, lie down," I said in Spanish. "You are gravely ill."

"Someone touched the carriage," he said, his eyes wild. "There is something on the back of the carriage."

Feverish again, I decided, and touched his forehead. He jerked back but I felt the heat against my fingertips.

"Lie down," I said again in Spanish, pushing his shoulder. "You are dangerously ill."

If he didn't understand my words at least he understood my gestures, and lay back. After what seemed like an eternity, we were out of the city and on the open road. I breathed a sigh of relief but did not let him sit up until the city had fallen behind us and the farmlands gradually faded back into pastures and then into the rough flanks of the mountains. By the time I thought we might be clear of problems, at least for the time being, the boy was sound asleep, and I left him so.

I am, as I have said, Ana Magdalena Coraje Montalvo de Conejo. I married when I was very young, as my parents and his had arranged. When Armando Regiberto Conejo de Platas y Zanahória first took me so very far to the north, I was convinced that I would die away from the cosmopolitan atmosphere of the capital. I had been raised amid statesmen and artists and had attended schools in Madrid and London, so what possible interest could a ranch hold for me? And indeed in the first years I suffered much misery, hiding it as well as I could from Armando. It was not a happy marriage.

I felt continuously out of place, out of time, and out of life. He died just before the marriage of our oldest daughter, falling from his horse while overseeing herds far from our hacienda. I could not return to the capital then, for the Army of the United States had invaded and my family thought I and my children would be safer hidden away in the north.

By the time it was safe to travel, I had fallen in love with my home, with the wild barrancas and far vistas, the bright hot cleanliness of the skies and the voices of my Indios as they worked the land. These clean, free expanses welcomed me, now that I too was free. More, I had entered into a grand experiment and could no more leave it than I could cut off my own hand.

I had read the books of *el obispo* Vasco de Quiroga, the bishop of Michoacán three hundred years ago, who was a believer in Sir Thomas More's Utopia and created, around Lake Pátzcuaro, a series of self-governing villages based on different crafts, which supplied the area with needed goods and the villages with income. Armando thought it all nonsense and called me a little fool, but I kept the books hidden away in my own room and did not forget them.

After Armando's death, barred from returning to the capital and bored with the long, quiet days, I met with the village leaders and began applying Tata Vasco's teachings to our hacienda. We were fortunate to have good deposits of clay and many of the minerals needed for the glazes; the riverbanks provided an abundance of tules and willow for making baskets and wickerwork; for the first few years I paid to import copper from *la tierra caliente*, until my copper-working village could afford to purchase its own raw materials. Expeditions to the Sierra Madre brought the wood needed to make furniture. As soon as possible, in each case, I withdrew myself so that the people themselves developed their businesses, took their profits, and governed their pueblos. I maintained a hospital on the grounds of my hacienda, as Tata Vasco had maintained hospitals near his cathedral in Pátzcuaro. Did I say that I trusted my Indio companions implicitly? It is because I, in turn, had earned their trust.

Any widow with a good portion is a source of constant interest, and I had had my share of suitors and proposals. I turned them all away. Why should I trade my freedom for a coddled life as another man's little fool? But I was nonetheless an object of some interest, even now that I was stout and gray, even as a great-grandmother, and thus must act with some circumspection. Indeed, I had come to Mexico City circumspectly, for the season of music and fiestas but, far more importantly, to order supplies for the steam-powered mill we were building. The gears and wheels were on their way north, a source of great satisfaction to this little fool. Miserable and benighted, indeed!

The English señor muttered and thrashed, and I pulled the flannel away from his face. His forehead burned. We needed to get him into a bed, and quickly. I rapped on the roof.

Eduardo found a pueblito with a shaded well where we filled our water bags. Maria and I stripped the young man down to his small clothes but I kept the petticoats and dress close by—we had barely entered the mountains around the capital's basin, still far too close to General Pulgón for my peace of mind. Eduardo handed up water bags, then touched my hand.

"*Mira, Doña Ana*," he murmured, and held up his fist to show me a red cloth. "It was stuck behind one of the nails on the back of the carriage."

I took it, remembering the boy's earlier panic. It was a cavalry-man's bandana, ironed and starched, obviously the property of an officer. The young lieutenant, I thought, marking our carriage to make it easier to follow. I thanked Eduardo and tucked the bandana away, angry with myself for not paying more attention.

Maria and I sponged the boy down while he muttered and shouted in English, his limbs thrashing about until Maria tied him up in his petticoats. Heriberto watched for a little while, then snorted with disgust and mounted his horse. He was still a young man and, like all young men, had little patience for anything he thought *sin machismo*. We followed him up the mountain along roads that, for all the traffic they had borne over the centuries, were miserable, rutted punishments better suited to purgatory than to a God-fearing and progressive country like Mexico.

An hour passed as the boy slept uneasily; another hour passed but he could not be said to be awake. In midafternoon I rapped for Eduardo and we spoke again. We waited in the shade of some pines while his son spurred away, and came back with word that a monastery lay off the road ahead and that they would take us in for charity's sake. Eduardo took us off the road to Veracruz and guided us along a narrow, rocky track while the sun sat lower and lower in the sky behind us.

We had entered the shadows of evening when we came around a final bend and saw, just above us, the monastery, its lanterns lit to guide us in. As we grew closer, I saw that only a few windows were lit; the bulk of the monastery was dark. The monks lost no time in lifting the young Englishman and carrying him gently into their infirmary, and just as gently turned me toward the guest quarters, where I could wash and compose myself before the evening meal.

The monastery was an old one, probably built during the Spanish conquest. We were high in the mountains and the cold crept in through the thick walls and up from the stone floors. I splashed water on my face and arms. Maria gave me a clean shawl and mantilla, and a minute later a monk came to show me to dinner.

Of course it is not seemly that a woman join the monks, so the abbot had arranged to share a meal with me privately. He was a tall, spare man, younger than I, but then most people are younger than I. He introduced himself as Father Bernardo del Caldo. I remembered his parents, good people with an estancia near Cuernavaca, and I told him that. His older brother had, of course, inherited everything, but Bernardo would have grown up knowing that, and knowing that he was destined for the priesthood. It was an honorable disposition for a younger son, and this one carried it well.

By tradition the evening meal is a light one, but when the abbot learned that I had been on the road since before sunrise and had not stopped for the midday meal, he sent his steward for cold meats and some cheeses. I tucked my hands into my sleeves and regarded the plate.

"My people," I said, "have also not eaten since before sunrise."

The abbot smiled at this, the first full and open smile he had given me. "I have already instructed them to be fed, Doña Ana. With your kind permission."

I smiled at him in return, and reached for the meats.

The food was good but simple and very plainly cooked, and the wine tasted new and harsh. Father Bernardo probed for news from the capital. I temporized, wondering how much I could tell him. Since the days of the expulsion of the Jesuits, Mexico's formal relationship with the Catholic Church had been uneasy; often our various governments had expropriated church lands. What the government, any government, takes, is unlikely to be returned. Was this priest therefore in favor of Benito Juárez or against him? Juárez was no enemy of the church, but he had raised money by selling confiscated church lands to *hacendados*. It made things complicated both for the clerics and for ordinary citizens.

So we talked about matters of culture. The discussion came around to Sr. Beethoven, who had written at least one Mass of which the priest approved, although he said he himself preferred Bach. Our discussion was cordial and careful on both our parts. I told him that the young señor was, and I tried to blush as I said this, the illegitimate son of my nephew from a visit he had made to the United States, and that I had promised to put him on a boat to New Orleans but he had fallen ill on the road.

The abbot smiled at me. "Fallen ill on the road to Damascus?"

"Hardly, Father, and Veracruz does not qualify as a holy city."

"Had you arrived earlier, I would have sent you on to the hacienda in the valley below us. It is far more comfortable, and General Pulgón's hospitality has been praised."

I raised an eyebrow. "*¿De veras?* By whom?"

The abbot smiled into his wine glass. "He is most generous with us, and we in turn pray for his soul." He sipped. "The general has mentioned you to me, Doña Ana."

My shoulders stiffened. This could not be good.

"He has told me of your villages in the north, of the aid you have given to the Indios. He mentioned schools, I believe, and a hospital?"

I nodded, my lips pressed together.

"And some scheme having to do with *el obispo* Quiroga?"

We looked at each other in silence for a moment. He leaned forward to refill my wine glass. "The valley below was once, of course, a part of our holdings. The general bought it ten years ago. His ways are…different from ours."

I had my own reasons to despise Pulgón, but the monks probably ate only through the general's charity. I did not care to speculate where the abbot's heart lay, and only murmured and kept my thoughts to myself, and sent a small prayer to the Virgin.

After the meal I asked to visit the infirmary, which was in a small building of its own, and the abbot brought me there himself. A welcome fire burned in a brazier. I hastened to it, for I had been freezing since we entered the monastery. Two cots were drawn near the fire. In one, a very old monk lay partially propped up, gumming at a piece of bread. My young Englishman lay on the other, thrashing against the blankets, his fever not yet broken. The infirmarian eyed me suspiciously as I touched the boy's forehead. I picked up a cup of watered wine and held it to the boy's lips. He managed a few sips.

I asked after herbs. Soon the infirmarian and I were deep in a discussion of worts and balms and reducers of fever. Into this civilized discourse came a tremendous banging at the monastery gates. The abbot and I looked at each other in alarm: Who could it be, this much past sunset? We heard the gate creak open and the clatter of hooves, and shortly after that the gatekeeper came into the infirmary, almost running.

"It is General Tomás Pulgón, he seeks an English assassin who has escaped from the capital!"

The abbot looked at me. I shook my head but held my breath. He carried our lives in his hands: Englishman, me, and my people. The lantern hissed and the gatekeeper shuffled from one foot to another, fingers twisting together. At last the abbot nodded.

"Fra Pedro, take the general to my room and see that he has a glass of brandy. His trip must have been very arduous and I am sure he is thirsty. Quarter his men in the old wing. Tell him I will be with him soon."

The gatekeeper's sandals slapped against the stones as he hurried out.

"Pulgón will search," I began.

"And will find two sick monks in the infirmary," the abbot said. "Fra Hortensio, I believe you keep a small supply of walnut juice on the shelves. Bring it to me, and more blankets. Señora, you know what to do?"

I nodded, already working the boy free of his clothes. We stripped him and dyed his face, hands, and feet with the walnut juice, dragged a brown cassock over him, and wrapped him in the blankets. He woke and began shouting in English, and the abbot took up a rag and stoppered his mouth with it.

"He is blaspheming," the abbot said gravely. Fra Hortensio nodded. The boy tried to claw the gag out, so we tightened the blankets around him until he could not move.

By then I was panting, my hair in disarray and my clothing pulled out of order. This would never do: I could not let the general know that I had been anywhere near the infirmary. I did not feel content to leave the boy with the monk, so frowned at him a moment and decided that, all in all, threats were probably best. The abbot took his leave to attend to the general, and I took the infirmarian aside.

"You know that your abbot wants this young man's identity hidden," I said to the monk, who nodded. "Are you under a vow of silence?" He shook his head. "Very well then, I believe that your abbot has put you under one as—as a penance, yes. Do you understand?"

He opened his lips. I held up one admonitory finger, and he closed his mouth and nodded until his head bobbed. There are times when it is very good to be a stern grandmother. I lifted my hem and swept from the infirmary.

I came into the cloister and wrapped my shawl against the shock of the cold mountain air. It was very dark, save for a pale wash of light near my rooms. As I approached I saw a silhouette against the light; a shape with a cap and sword. I shrank back into the shadows. How to explain my presence? The privies were nowhere nearby, so I could not use them as an excuse. What to do?

I felt a hand on my shoulder and jumped only a little, then saw in the dimness that it was yet another monk. He tugged at my arm and I followed him through dark, empty rooms. We passed into the church, a cold space scented with incense. A curtain rustled as we went through it, then the monk led me along a narrow, lightless hallway. After what seemed an eternity, he ushered me through a doorway into a dark room and disappeared. I had no idea where I was until I heard Maria's voice, muttering a prayer in the next room. Filled with relief, I entered and collapsed into a chair.

I wanted nothing more than to go to bed; a grandmother should not be subjected to such tiring events. But there was still more to come, for Maria told me that the general had sent a man to take me to the abbot's rooms. She had put him off as long as she could, but she thought that in another five minutes, he would break into the room. So, sighing with exasperation, I helped her drag off my outer dress and lace me into another one, identically black but less crumpled. She dressed my hair and wrapped my thickest woolen shawl around my shoulders. Then, satisfied that I once again looked like a dignified matron, she opened the door and I swept out, glared at the soldier, and demanded that he lead the way.

As I entered the room, Pulgón rose with insulting slowness and made a sweeping bow, displaying all of his teeth in what was most emphatically not a friendly smile. The years had not improved him: He still looked like a coyote.

"Ah, Doña Ana," he said. "What a pleasure it is to meet you again, after such a very long time. How long is it, señora? Fifteen years?"

He knew how long it was as well as I did: Fourteen years ago, when he had been a colonel in a ragtag Conservative army fighting in one of our many revolutions, he had caused my most productive village to be burned to the ground. His claim that we harbored enemies of the state was a transparent lie: He burned down my village because I had refused to give him my hand in marriage. To my great relief, God came to my aid by providing a bloody battle to the south, which sent Pulgón galloping toward Michoacán to see what extortion and misery he could create there. His rise to a position of power in Juárez's liberal government must have been the result of deep corruption, lamentably nothing new in the history of our poor country.

"General Pulgón," I said, and pressed my lips together. He was, in truth, no better than a chief of police, but he controlled Mexico City and hence the heart of our country. A cockroach, but a very powerful one.

Father Bernardo offered me a seat far from the window. This room, like all the rooms in the monastery except for the infirmary and the kitchen, had no fireplace. The life of a monk, after all, is dedicated to God and not to the flesh. I drew my shawl more closely around myself as I sat, wishing that the good Father was just a little more worldly and a little less strict.

Pulgón didn't seem to mind the cold. He strode up and down the room, his hands tucked behind his back, shooting stern glances at me. I waited in silence. Finally he stopped and rocked back and forth, hands still behind his back.

"You know, señora, the peril our country faces from foreign enemies. Even your esteemed son-in-law is alive to the menace of foreign spies and agents of chaos intent upon the overthrow of our revolutionary government and the return of the despicable French, and their English companions."

This was nonsense, but of course I said nothing. The English and the French trusted each other in the way coyotes trust each other when they desire the same patch of desert. If Pulgón and his Conservative cohorts wanted to use the French to demonize the English, it was only what I would expect of them.

"You would be fond of the French, I believe, since you and their revolutionaries share the same beliefs about the peasantry. Equality and fraternity, indeed. This is dangerous nonsense, señora, as you well know." He paused and resumed pacing, then rounded on me. "Your actions in the north are known to us, Doña Ana. We were unable to touch you during the shameful monarchy of that known liberal Maximilian, but those days are past. You would do well to think of your future, and that of your family."

I seethed inwardly but kept my tone calm as I said, "With respect, General, the days of true and honest liberals are still very much with us."

Someone rapped at the door. The young lieutenant, the one who had stopped us in the city, entered and saluted. Then he glanced at me and grinned. "Ah, Doña Montalvo." He bowed so low that the insult was obvious. "How is your poor sick niece Candelaria? We know she is still with you, for your carriage did not stop at any great house along the way. And we know, of course, that you only stop at great houses. Or monasteries."

I said nothing. The lieutenant chuckled and turned away from me. "We have found him, *mi general*. He was masquerading as a monk in the infirmary. Shall we shoot him?"

Pulgón grinned like a shark. "Eventually, but not immediately, I think. I believe this lady must have had a hand in bringing him here, yes? Disguised, perhaps, as her plague-infected niece?"

I raised my chin. "You make dangerous allegations, General. Benito Juárez is an old family friend. It would not go well with you if we were impeded. Or harmed."

He gestured this aside, impatient. "Enough. Families more important than yours have proved to be traitors." He turned toward his aide. "You have rounded up her servants? Very well. You may tell me, señora, precisely what his plans are, and yours. Or I will have your people shot. One by one."

The abbot's back stiffened. "My son, take care not to perform violence, or even to offer such, in the Lord's house. God listens."

"Then perhaps He will learn something," Pulgón retorted. "Well, señora? Which is it to be?"

"How can I tell you that which does not exist?" I said. "There is no spy, as you well know. There is no vast English conspiracy, as you well know. I doubt that you act on behalf of any legitimate government. I will tell you nothing, Pulgón. If you intend to shoot my people, you can start with me." I gave him the same look that caused my grandchildren to quail; not that I expected him to flinch, but how else was I to respond to this dangerous, stupid nonsense? The lieutenant came forward as if to lay hands on me. Father Bernardo's chair scraped back against the stone floor. I stood, gathering my shawl around my shoulders.

"Tomás Pulgón, you are a snake and your mother would weep tears of blood to see what you have become. Thank the blessed Virgin that she is safely in Her keeping." Father Bernardo crossed himself, but Pulgón sneered. The lieutenant reached for my arm. I shook him away, leaving my mantilla in his grasp. He dropped it. The abbot picked it up as I walked, my back straight, out of the room. All in all, I thought as Pulgón's men surrounded me, I was fairly pleased with myself. I had called him a coyote, a cockroach, a shark, and a snake, even if just in my own mind. Surely the Virgin would not allow me to come to harm at the hands of such a menagerie of pests.

They put us into a disused wine cellar. The English boy lay against one of the dank walls, his eyes barely open. His fever had broken, but the cold and damp would surely kill him if we could not flee this room.

Escape seemed impossible. The wine cellar was dug well into

the mountainside, in what must originally have been a cave. The ceiling soared well above the light of the two miserable candles we were allowed. Three heavy doors lay between us and the rest of the monastery; I had listened to the bolts clang in each of them as I was escorted into the cellar, then pushed inside. I had turned, demanding bedding and our coats, but the lieutenant just grinned at me and slammed the door in my face. His footsteps diminished, punctuated by the bolts slamming home in the other two doors.

The shelves were cobwebbed, dirty, and bare. It seemed that this room had not been used in a very long time, and I wondered how General Pulgón had known about it. I felt a tiny draft. Eduardo followed it, sheltering a candle behind his palm, and came back to report that the cavern ended in a smooth, inward-leaning wall with a tiny, inaccessible opening at the very top, through which came the wisp of air. Other than that and the locked doors, there were no openings in the room. I sighed and sank down to sit beside the English boy, who opened his eyes a little.

"I am sorry I have put you in this horrible position," he whispered.

I shrugged. "I am, to be truthful, more sorry about missing Sr. Beethoven's symphony."

He closed his eyes again. "What will happen to us?"

"Oh, I suspect that General Pulgón would like to shoot us all, but apparently I have frightened him a little by talking about my son-in-law's lofty connection to President Juárez. He will need to come up with an alternative plan, but he is not a very smart man so it will take him some time."

The boy was silent for a little, then said, "But the abbot, he is a smart man, is he not?"

I sighed. "I think so, yes. I wish I knew where his heart lies in all this. Men of God have not always behaved well."

"This monastery was larger," he said. "There are so many empty rooms. Even the infirmary—the monk told me we were in the small room that used to be the apothecary's drying room."

"Yes?"

"Someone, at some time, made the monastery smaller. Recently, I think. The apothecary's dried herbs still hang in the corners."

"Ah." I looked at him, his features almost indistinguishable in the dim light. "And what do you conclude from this?"

"That perhaps the abbot is still angry at the taking of the monastery lands, señora. Was it President Juárez who ordered the taking?"

"I do not know. The relationship between the church and the government has been very changeable over the years. It could have been anyone."

"And so we cannot rely on the abbot to be friendly." He shivered a little. I covered him with my shawl, despite his protests.

"And your own people?" I said.

"How can they know where I am? And if they do come here, the general could simply tell them that we came and went again. Who will contradict him?" He curled in on himself.

The cold increased. We huddled together, I and the boy and my family of servants, not talking. I had pinched out one of the candles, to make our light last longer. I thought about what I had said to the young man: It was true that Pulgón would not shoot me, but that did not mean that my life was safe. What story would he tell about the death of Teobaldo's dear mother-in-law? There are so, so many ways for someone to die, especially here in the tall, cold mountains, where the air is thin and warmth is only a distant memory. I shook myself away from these gloomy thoughts and instead remembered the long, hot days on my hacienda, the song of the cicadas under the rhythmic pulse of the looms, the way the copper shone in the hands of my skilled workmen, the sound of children reciting lessons. I did not want to die, but if I did at least I was happy with my legacy. I did not imagine that Pulgón could say the same. Heriberto licked his lips. I sympathized: We were all hungry and thirsty, despite the abbot's earlier hospitality.

Bolts banged and hinges screamed as the door opened. Light streamed in from bright lanterns. Two monks entered, one holding two lanterns and the second a large, steaming pot. The scent of mulled wine filled the room; I could not keep my mouth dry. The monk placed the pot on the floor and laid a ladle in it, the second monk put one of the lanterns beside it, and they both retreated, still in silence, locking the door behind them.

"Well," Eduardo said, "at least we will not die of cold for a little longer."

He reached for the ladle just as the Inglés cried out, lurched to his feet, and staggered toward the pot. Thinking that he meant to thrust his face into it, or at least his hands, I leaped up and reached for him but he drew back one long leg and kicked the pot hard. It tumbled end over end, emptying itself on the dry dirt. Within seconds not a drop of the hot wine remained.

"You stupid fool," Heriberto said, raising his fist, but the boy collapsed.

I knelt beside him, cursing in English. He coughed from the bottom of his lungs and grabbed my hand.

"Bunions," he said in English, and fainted.

What sort of incredible nonsense was this? The boy had obviously gone mad, stark mad, from the fever or the ill treatment or both. I shook my head and we stretched him out again, and I covered him with my shawl. At least he had not destroyed the lantern. It gave off a small amount of heat and we held our hands out to it, pretending that it was warm. Then Eduardo prodded his son and nodded toward the bare shelves, and in a moment Heriberto was breaking the dry planks over his knee and piling up the fuel for a fire. Eduardo shaved kindling with the knife he kept hidden near his skin. He piled the kindling and lit it from the lantern. The flame hesitated, then caught. We sighed and smiled at each other, and held out our hands.

Bunions. Whatever had the boy meant? I puzzled over it for a while, then gestured for Maria to pass the pot to me. I put my face into it and sniffed it, and touched the bottom where a drop of the wine remained. My tongue went numb where I touched the wine to it. I scrubbed it out of my mouth with my sleeve. Maria, seeing me, raised her eyebrows.

"I think this wine was poisoned," I said. "Eduardo, can you smell anything? Your nose is younger than mine."

Eduardo smelled it and raised his eyebrows. "It is possible, Doña Ana," he said. "But how would he know that?"

"He is in league with them," Heriberto said.

I thought for a moment, and smiled. "No. Just before he became unconscious, he said *juanetes*, 'bunions' in English. Who has bunions? People who keep their feet inside cheap boots. Do monks have boots? No, they do not, and so they have no bunions. And because that monk did, our young friend understood that he was not, in fact,

a monk, but one of General Pulgón's soldiers. Pulgón has no reason
to give us wine or any helpful thing. And therefore—"

"The wine was poisoned," Maria said. She looked at the young
Inglés with respect. "He has saved our lives."

We all gazed at the boy thoughtfully.

"So what else does he know?" Eduardo said.

"Wake him up and make him talk," Heriberto said with relish.

I thought about that for a moment. The boy was still sick, but
lying in this place would not make him any better. I patted his
cheek. The beaky nose wrinkled and he turned his head away. I
patted him again, with more force.

"Hit him a good one, Doña," Heriberto said.

"Don't be foolish, that will just knock him out even more."

"Well, do *something*," Eduardo said, so I boxed the boy's ear. He
came awake, howling.

"The wine was poisoned?" I said to him.

"Of course," he retorted, and closed his eyes again.

"No sleep," I said firmly. "Listen, *joven*, what else do you know?
Can we escape? What else can you notice, besides the condition
of feet?" I helped him sit closer to the fire. "Twice you have noticed things, small things, that have been greatly important. With
God's grace, perhaps you will notice another small thing again."

After a moment he nodded, then tipped his head back and
closed his eyes. Heriberto urged violence in a whisper and I hissed
at him to be quiet.

The boy's nose quivered. After a moment it quivered again. We
held our breaths. He opened his eyes and looked at us, then gestured toward Heriberto.

"Tell him to pick up that board," he said, nodding toward the fire. One of the broken boards poked out of the fire, its other end smoldering. "And him, tell him to help me up."

I translated. In a moment the Englishman was on his feet. The three of them made a circuit of the walls, keeping about a meter back from them, and all the time the Inglés kept his eyes not on the wall, but on the smoldering board.

"Stop," he said abruptly. He stared at the board for a long minute. So did I, but saw nothing remarkable. Heriberto held the cold end. The other end glowed while tendrils of smoke trailed toward the wall.

The boy looked down and gestured my men forward while he mumbled a little under his breath. Heriberto looked back at me and rolled his eyes. The English boy leaned forward against Eduardo's arms and brushed his hand down the wall, clearing away dust and cobwebs.

"Here," he said. "Door."

We settled him near the fire again before we all scrubbed at the wall with our palms. A rectangular outline appeared against the stones, the shape of a small door but without handle or hinges.

Heriberto muttered a curse and his father cuffed him. "This is useless," he said. "Perhaps you should hit him again."

"No, wait." Shadows danced over the stones, but soon my fingers touched what my eyes had barely seen—a tiny circular indentation that gave a little under my fingers. I pushed and a stone plug tilted and disappeared. I heard stone striking stone as it fell. I put my finger through the hole. It barely fit, but I felt something cold and flat, like a latch. My finger wasn't long enough to move it.

"Eduardo, give me your knife," I said. The blade was far too wide to fit into the hole, but I didn't expect it to. I handed the knife to Maria and turned my back to her. "Mari, cut a stay from my corset."

"Doña Ana!" she said, scandalized.

"Quickly! They will not wait too long to make sure that their poison worked."

The whalebone stay was soon free. I slid it through the hole, praying to the Virgin as I teased it under the latch. When I pushed down on the near end of the stay, it bent and the latch slipped off. I breathed deeply and tried again. The third time, the latch moved a little. I held my breath and let it inch up, and up, and up, before it fell abruptly back into place. I tried again and this time the Virgin heard my prayers. The latch quivered, then leaped up and swung away. I staggered back into Maria's arms, dizzy from holding my breath.

"Push!" I said. Eduardo and his son put their backs into it, and the door scraped opened.

We didn't wait for it to open all the way. We took up the Inglés and the candles, but left the lantern. "It will confuse them," I said and we pushed the door closed behind us. I found the stone plug and fitted it back into the hole, then Eduardo replaced the latch and, for good measure, jammed it tight with a stone. We crept down the inky tunnel, our little candles almost useless against the dark.

I would have sworn on the soul of my sainted mother that at least twelve hours had passed since I was thrown into the wine cellar, but when we finally emerged it was into the cold, pale light of dawn. We found ourselves in a small pine woods. Three horses were tied up nearby, our two carriage horses and one other. Their saddlebags bulged. From one hung a scrap of black lace—my mantilla, last seen in the hands of the abbot. I will never know how the abbot knew what might happen, or if he had the horses and supplies left in the hopes of a miracle, but it made no difference. Within five minutes we were mounted and headed down the mountain. Maria rode behind me, and Heriberto cradled the Inglés as though the boy was his own son.

A few days later, thanks to the kindness of Don Alejandro Hormigas del Santo, we were safely in his house in Puebla, on the road to Veracruz. Teobaldo had sent to ask him to expect us, and when we did not arrive he took to the road himself to find us, and find us he had. We must have been a pretty sight, tired and dirty, our clothes torn from the journey through the dark tunnel. When I recognized him I wept with delight. Don Alejandro had telegraphed to Veracruz, so that a few days after our arrival four men arrived in a closed carriage and were rushed into the house. My young Inglés's health had improved, but when he saw the plumpest of the men he cried, "Mycroft!" and fell into the man's arms.

He recovered in time to share a hurried meal, which was interrupted by our host. Don Alejandro came into the dining room, shaking his head.

"It is a great mystery," he said. "Apparently General Tomás Pulgón pursued a spy to a monastery in the mountains, but the general has entirely disappeared! His men say that he and his lieutenant traced the spy to a wine cellar. The two brave men followed, but a week has passed and neither of them has been seen since." Alejandro paused. "Doña Ana, do you know anything of this?"

I looked up from my plate. "Don Alejandro, I am an old grand-mother and I do not concern myself with these political matters. I believe your guests are ready to leave."

Alejandro looked at me a moment longer, his eyes bright, before turning away.

I walked with the young Englishman toward the carriage. I had previously seen him sitting, lying, or being carried, and had not truly comprehended just what a tall, gangly young man he was. I had a fine view of his Adam's apple, which made a consid-erable bump in his skinny neck.

"Before you leave, you must tell me something," I said, putting my hand on his arm to stop him. "How did you know there would be a hidden door in the wine cellar?"

He smiled. Really, once his nose had stopped dripping he was a good-looking young man. "I watched the smoke. Had there been no other opening, the smoke would have blown away from that small chink in the wall, but luckily the larger vent on the exterior wall pushed air in, so the smoke was sucked into the little latch hole and not away from it. I saw footprints on the dusty floor there. The prints of sandals, to be precise, and so I knew that the abbot had expected that someone would need to escape—perhaps he himself." The boy looked tremendously smug.

"There you are wrong, my arrogant young friend," I said. He raised his eyebrows. "You saw the care with which the abbot treated you, and I saw the care with which he treated his monks, and the care with which he touched the walls of his domain. He would no more desert his people than I would desert mine."

We arrived at his carriage. I put my hand out to stop him. "There is one further thing undone, *joven*."

300

At this he frowned. "I, I do not think so, señora."

"Think again. Put yourself outside yourself, if you can, and think again."

He was painfully bewildered, and at last I felt some small mercy toward him. "You have yet to thank me, or my people, for saving your pitiful English life." I tilted my head back and, I think, did a respectable job of looking down my nose at him. "And so I will leave you with this final piece of advice, Inglés. You may have a gift for the details, my friend, but you will never amount to anything until you achieve a similar gift for noting the details of the human heart."

He opened his mouth, either in protest or to thank me, but I raised an admonitory finger to him, turned, and swept away into my own life.

Yes, sometimes it is very good to be a stern grandmother.

Ms. Robertson gives us a story of stage coach banditry and bawdy houses as seen through the eyes of a keen observer of the customs and characters of the old west.

THE STAGECOACH DETECTIVE:
A Tale of the Golden West
by
LINDA ROBERTSON

... we are here in a land of stage-drivers and highwaymen: a land, in that sense, like England a hundred years ago.

> *Robert Louis Stevenson,*
> *The Silverado Squatters*

The Royal Family of Silverado, as I called us that summer, were as raffish a dynasty as ever disgraced the most dubious Balkan principality—an invalid literary man (myself), Fanny, my raven-haired American bride, and my stepson Sam, then a crown prince of eleven years.

On a bright day late in July we were making

our daily progress from our camp on the mountainside to the little hotel on the toll road where the mail coaches stopped. Rounding the last turn in our path, we saw the Lakeport stage stopped before the hotel, earlier than usual and empty of passengers. The dust from the coach's passage stood in a chalky cloud above the road.

In the yard, a group of men stood talking urgently among themselves. I saw Corwin, the landlord, dark and hollow-chested, and McConnell, the stagecoach driver, the tallest and broadest of them, glowering and turning his big blond head from side to side, like a caged bear. The landlord's wife was shepherding a couple of women passengers down the veranda to the hotel door. "Mr. McConnell," she called out, "can you wait for a bit before going on? I think the ladies could use a little rest and a chance to calm down."

McConnell turned and fixed his bearlike gaze on her. "I ain't goin' anywhere, Mrs. C.," he answered resentfully. "Gotta wait for the sheriff." He turned away and spat on the ground. "I guess we'll have to spend the night here. Be hell to pay in Lakeport," he added, shaking his head.

Trailed by Sam, I walked to the edge of the group to hear more, while Fanny joined Mrs. Corwin in the hotel.

"Who's gonna ride to Calistoga and tell the sheriff?" one of the men asked.

"My boy Tom," said Corwin. "I've sent José back to saddle up one of our ponies."

"We need to put together a posse—go out and hunt him down," another man said. "Mr. Corwin, how many horses do you have?"

"Not enough," the innkeeper said. "Besides, the fella's got a good hour's start. We'll need a tracker and bloodhounds, and they're in Calistoga." He caught Tom's eye and pointed over his shoulder to where José, the stableman, was walking up with a saddled horse. Tom ran over, took the reins, swung lightly into the saddle in true western style, and started at a gallop down the toll road.

"Sweet Jesus, Tommy, don't kill the pony!" Corwin shouted after him, as horse and boy disappeared into the woods. He looked around the bare, dusty yard at the little crowd of passengers, hotel guests, workers, and idlers, and announced, "Come inside and have a beer—it's on the house. Been a rough morning."

As we passed down the veranda, I saw one of the hotel residents leaning back in a rocking chair, a newspaper in his lap, watching the happenings in the yard with half-closed eyes. He looked up at us as we walked across the creaking boards.

"Your Majesty. Your Highness," he said, sitting straighter and tipping his battered straw hat.

"Interesting morning, Joe," I said. "What's going on out there?"

"Stagecoach was robbed again."

"Wow!" Sam said beside me.

"Again?" I asked.

"Twice in the last two months."

The last few men were clumping across the worn boards of the veranda and through the door of the saloon. "Free beer," I said to Joe as we turned to follow them. Folding his paper in half, he rose, casually, onto storklike legs and drifted after us.

The barroom was cooler than outdoors. A couple of opened windows at the back brought in a little air and the purling of water in the creek behind the hotel. The reek of old whisky and stale beer rose like mist on a marsh from the sanded floorboards and the varnished bar, stained with the rings of countless glasses. A few flies moved sluggishly through the warm air, as if biding their time until dinner. Corwin and Hoddy, the barman, drew pints of beer and slapped them down on the bar.

"It's a bad business," Hoddy said. "Second time this year. McConnell thinks this one was done by the same fellow did the last. Ain't that right, McConnell?"

"He sure looked the same."

"What did he look like?"

"Hard to tell much," broke in a mustachioed man in a new miner's outfit. "He was wearing a bandana, blue one, tied across his face."

"I thought it was red," said a red-faced, balding man in a rumpled gray suit.

"And a broad-brimmed hat," the first man added.

"Some kind of serape over his clothes."

"Looked to me like one of them green army blankets."

"How tall was he?" Corwin asked.

"Tall—a big fellow," said a stout man in a linen jacket.

McConnell disagreed. "He wasn't that big—kind of skinny, I thought. Couldn't really tell much, though, under that blanket."

All of them remembered he had a large-caliber pistol. "Silver-colored," said the stout man, and another agreed.

"No—gun-metal, with wood grips," McConnell said with conviction.

Near me, another man spoke up, in the familiar accent of an Englishman. "He was about five feet six inches in height, dark eyes, reddish hair, very nervous. Brown wideawake hat, with a broad brim, blue bandana, blue work shirt under a serape made from an army blanket, denim pants, black boots. He wore black riding gloves, and the gun was a .45-caliber Colt Firearms Manufacturing Company cavalry model, blue metal with darkened wooden grips—nice observation, Mr. McConnell."

We all looked at him blankly.

"And how do you know all that?" the miner asked, with the exaggerated suspicion of a fool. "You a friend of his or something?"

The Englishman turned and fixed him with a look of polite scorn. "I looked."

The miner was undaunted. "Well, shee-it," he shot back with what I assumed he thought was wit, then turned and spat on the floor. A couple of the other men shifted uncomfortably. Corwin broke the tension. "Come on, everyone, get your beer and settle down."

As the men moved toward the bar, the Englishman stayed where he was, watching them. I turned to him, introduced myself, and made some observation about being far from home. He shook my proffered hand. "Sherlock Holmes," he said. "You're from Edinburgh, I take it?"

"Not hard to tell that, I suppose," I answered.

He was young—under thirty, I'd say—tall and lanky as a Kentuckian, and thin in the face, with a long, sharp jaw, rather narrow-set eyes, and a high-bridged, aquiline nose that gave his expression the aloof inquisitiveness of a bird of prey. His hair, a nondescript brown, was combed back from his high forehead and parted high on one side. His suit was of a light wool, and his tie carefully knotted. There was an indescribable Englishness about his whole person—something in the cut and cloth of his jacket, the set of his shoulders, and the supercilious way he looked down his long English nose at the crowd of men at the bar.

I asked him what brought him so far from home, and he said he'd been working and traveling in America. He paused and studied me for a few seconds, then said, "I could ask the same of you. I see that you write a lot, but you don't appear to be employed, and you're short of money. I'd guess you to be a literary man, but not at this point a particularly successful one."

The remark was so unexpected and impertinent, coming from someone to whom I'd introduced myself only a moment ago, that I was left momentarily without a rejoinder. "What makes you think that?" I asked, a little hotly.

He gave me a thin smile. "Your right hand and shirt cuff are ink-stained," he answered, with a glance toward the offending article, "and the cuff is worn and frayed where it would have rested against a writing-desk. Your clothes are threadbare, your belt is old and too large for you, and your jacket and pants haven't been pressed or brushed for weeks. Your boots show that you haven't been staying at the hotel. No hotel guest who could get his boots polished while he slept would let them get into such a state. Your face and hands are brown, but you are not in good health, so your color isn't likely to have come from working in the sun, which leads me to surmise that you've been living outdoors. And," he said finally, "there are bits of straw in your hair."

His dissection of my appearance and finances made me flush with shame and irritation. "I apologize if I offended you, sir," he said, in a tone that suggested that I was not the first person he had affronted with his observations. "I was simply answering your question."

With some difficulty, I resolved to keep an open mind about my new acquaintance, if only because he was a fellow countryman.

"It's all right, really," I said, with more lightness than I felt. "I've been mistaken for a hobo or a peddler before, but you've drawn me to the life—a poor literary fellow, camping here on the mountain for his health—though I confess I didn't know about the straw."

"Ah," Holmes said, clearly pleased with himself. He paused, listening, excused himself, and walked to the bar. Corwin was saying to McConnell, "Why don't we take a couple of men now and ride down to where it happened? Meet the sheriff on his way and maybe help track the fellow. I have fresh horses for four of us." Corwin called to his younger son, "Jake, go help José saddle up Eddy, Duke, Pancho, and Red."

Holmes had reached the counter where Corwin stood, collecting beer glasses. "May I ride there with you?" he asked.

Corwin thought for a second. "I guess so—seems like you could tell the sheriff a good deal more than some of these yokels. You can take Duke." Holmes thanked him and disappeared out the door.

Corwin turned to me. "Would you like to come see how we handle these things, Mr. Stevenson?"

"But aren't you out of horses?"

"True," he said, and thought for a second or two. "You don't mind riding a mule, do you? Won't be as fast, but you'll get there in time to see the fun. I shouldn't think you'd want to join the posse anyway."

"I don't think my wife would stand for it," I said.

Corwin nodded knowingly. "Women," he said.

Hoddy and Corwin had just cleared the last of the beer mugs from the bar when Jake exploded into the saloon, shouting that the horses were in the yard. Corwin put down the towel he was using to wipe the bar and started for the door. McConnell downed the rest of his beer in one long swallow and followed. From the doorway, Corwin called back, "Tell José I said to saddle one of the mules for you, and we'll see you there."

The mule I was given was named Jasper. He was the size of a horse, with a horse's bay coat, but with a head like an anvil and a most unhorselike self-possession and confidence in his own decisions. José explained, perhaps to reassure me, that he was kept by the hotel to carry ladies and invalids.

I was just as glad to be alone as I rode down the toll road, because I hardly cut a dashing figure on my steed. Jasper's fastest gait appeared to be a matter-of-fact walk. If I tried to spur him with a kick of my heels in his flanks, he shook his head slightly, in a fatherly way, declining my pleas to enlist him in such recklessness. During our short journey, the stage to Calistoga hurtled past us in a chaos of dust, pounding hoofs, clattering wheels, and shouts. Jasper edged carefully to the side of the road and gazed reproachfully at the receding coach before resuming his dutiful progress.

The scene of the robbery was a ford, where a small creek crossed the road. It had washed out part of the downhill side, and the coach would have slowed to cross it. Tall pines and oaks overhung the road, and vines, bushes, and saplings grew together in a tangled mass beneath them. Its lushness and shade were ominous, as if created for an ambush—the sort of place a solitary walker might pass through with a quickening of heart and pace and a glance or two over his shoulder.

Corwin, McConnell, and one of the men from the hotel were standing with the horses on the near side of the ford. Near them lay the express box from the stage, its lid open. Among the trees to the right of the road, I saw something moving. Looking toward it, I saw Holmes.

Alone in a small clearing, where the stream formed a pool before continuing in its course across the road, he crossed slowly back and forth, like a tracker searching for signs marking the passage of his quarry. From time to time he knelt and studied the ground as though committing it to memory, and then jotted something in a small notebook he carried. Several times, he made measurements with a measuring tape and wrote the numbers down in his notebook. Along the way, he picked up a couple of small objects and placed them in a leather wallet he drew from a pocket of his jacket, or carefully untangled something from a branch and wrapped it in a bit of paper before adding it to the wallet. Sometimes a questioning frown shadowed his thin face, but most of the time his posture and expression held the concentrated energy of a man intent on dissecting a particularly interesting and challenging problem. A little later, he crossed to the downhill side, where he climbed for some distance down the stream bank until he was no longer in sight. He reappeared a few minutes afterward, walking back toward us on the toll road. As he approached, I heard hoofbeats and the clatter of wagon wheels in the distance, followed by the baying of a dog. Corwin looked up. "Sheriff and Sorensen, with the bloodhounds," he said.

In a minute we saw, rounding a curve, a half dozen men on horseback, followed by a farm wagon driven by a stocky old man in a straw hat. Two red-brown bloodhounds stood at the wagon rail, wriggling with excitement and baying their peculiar note, between a bark and a howl, from somewhere within their drooping dewlaps.

Holmes walked to the wagon and said to the driver, as it stopped, "You can try the bloodhounds, but they may not be able to get a scent."

Sorensen looked dubious. "And why would that be?"

"The robber doused the area with cayenne pepper."

Sorensen leaned forward in the seat of his wagon and looked at Holmes from under the brim of his hat. "You're kidding me," he said.

"No, I'm not. You can try the hounds, but I don't hold out much hope."

"May's well, since we've come this far," Sorensen said. He jumped from the seat, walked around to the back of the wagon, and pulled down the gate. The dogs jumped to the ground and shook themselves in a liquid flow of loose skin. Sorensen tied a length of rope to each dog's leather collar. "Hero, Rex. Come on, boys."

Holmes led them to the clearing. "The robber seems to have hidden in here beforehand, and then ridden on the road itself toward Calistoga," he told Sorensen.

"That was pretty brazen," said one of the sheriff's men.

"The whole damn thing was brazen," McConnell huffed. "We weren't even five miles from town."

Sorensen led the dogs to the clearing and gave them a command. They began eagerly sniffing the ground, but after a minute or two they stopped and stood shaking their heads and bringing forth a series of snorts and sneezes that rippled the loose skin up and down their bodies. Sorensen pulled them back toward him. "Aw, jeez," he said. "Come here, you two." He led the dogs, or, more rightly, was hauled by them, to the edge of the creek, where he pulled a handkerchief from his pants pocket and proceeded to sponge their muzzles with the water flowing between the rocks. The dogs drank, shook their dewlaps some more, and licked his hands and face. "Cayenne." He shook his head. "Who'd have thought of such a thing?"

"I've heard of it," Holmes said. "It's a clever trick, nonetheless."

One of the men in the posse said, "So there's no way to track him down?"

"Not with horses and hounds, at least," said Holmes. "And probably not with trackers. His tracks on the toll road have been covered over by now—by the Calistoga stage and, regrettably," he said, with a glance at the posse, "others." He turned to Corwin. "Perhaps we should go back to the hotel, so the sheriff can speak with the passengers."

Jasper, even energized by the prospect of home and food, was soon outpaced by the men on horses, and I was left to ponder the eccentric Holmes. Despite his irritating candor, I felt sympathy for him as a fellow countryman far from home. Then, too, I'd never seen anything like his scrutiny of the robbery scene, and I was curious to know what he'd found.

At the hotel, I mentioned meeting Holmes to Fanny (leaving out his references to my clothes and poverty). "I'm thinking of inviting him to visit our camp," I said. "Would you mind?"

She gave me a worried look. "Are you sure? We'll have to give him fry bread and bacon for dinner. I've been down here all afternoon instead of cooking."

"I don't think you need to worry," I said. "He doesn't look like a man who concerns himself much with food."

I found Holmes at a table in the saloon, in conversation with the sheriff and Corwin. Most of the men from the stagecoach had whiled away the afternoon drinking, and were sitting in the bar grumbling and cursing the sheriff, whom they seemed to blame even more than the robber for their predicament. I caught Holmes's eye, and he excused himself and walked over to me. With a glance past his shoulder at the scene of discontent, I said, "Our camp is up the hill in the old Silverado mining town—or what's left of it. If you don't mind the walk up the trail, you're welcome to come back with us and see the old mine. I have some good local wine keeping cool in the mine shaft." Holmes asked if we could wait until he had finished his business with the sheriff. A quarter of an hour later, he joined us on the veranda.

He seemed in good spirits on our walk up the trail. Catching his breath after the final climb up a hill of mine tailings, he appraised the platform, with its rusting machinery and looming ruin of a bunkhouse, that made up our kingdom. The mining equipment, the tumbledown scaffolding, and the physical design of the operation seemed to interest him, and I wondered if he was perhaps an engineer.

We climbed up to the mine shaft, where I filled a few bottles of wine from our improvised cellar in the mountain. Afterward, I nursed a fire to health in the ruined forge, and the four of us, Holmes, Fanny, Sam, and I, ate our simple supper *en plein air* as the sun sank behind the mountain. In the fading twilight, Holmes lit a pipe, and Fanny and I our cigarettes, and we shared a local Chasselas and then a Bordeaux. Holmes, who seemed fairly knowledgeable about wine, expressed his approval of both.

Fanny was unusually subdued. I had seen her thus before around strangers; in some company, she was painfully conscious of our cheap way of life in our mountain camp and the all-too-recent scandal of her divorce in San Francisco. As for myself, in an out-pouring of sentiment fueled by wine and the warmth of new acquaintance, I soon confided to Holmes the story of how we had come to our mountain home. "It's a poor man's spa," I concluded, "where I've spent the summer basking in the mountain air and seeking to recover my health. My wife—a woman of the frontier, and not to be trifled with" (I looked at Fanny out of the corner of my eye and saw that she was looking intently at her hands clasped in her lap), "stared Death down across my sickbed—and after that, did me the honor of marrying the little that was left of me. If it weren't for her—Fanny, my love, you know it's all true—I'd have been buried out here, in exile."

Fanny gave me a look as if she might take issue whether I were worth the trouble. Holmes, to my relief, turned to her with a sober nod of respect, in which I saw not a trace of irony. "Your husband is a fortunate man," he said.

The evening passed, more easily than I had feared, in wine and talk. Even touched by the mellowing influence of the grape, Holmes was a young man of almost reptilian reserve. But what he lacked in lightness and humor, he made up for in the breadth of his knowledge and thinking. He seemed free of the social prejudices so pervasive among the English, and spoke with a rare candor of observation, an honest willingness to acknowledge what he saw in things instead of what convention expected him to see. Even Fanny soon warmed to him and joined in the talk.

Our discussions ranged widely, touching on European and American politics, history, literature, architecture, engineering, and the sciences. The last particularly interested Holmes: He leaned toward us, and his eyes glittered in the firelight as he explained his ideas about how the methods and findings of modern science could be adapted to the solving of crimes and civil disputes. "I considered reading law at one point," he said, "but there is so much more the application of scientific methods can do to improve the methods of the police and the law courts. To a trained mind with an understanding of chemistry, physics, and the science of human motivation, I believe the scene of a crime can be a book in which one can read all that happened there, and see the criminal himself."

I had studied law and practiced, albeit for a short time, as an advocate, and I agreed with him about the need for better methods. The policeman's truncheon, paid informers, surmise, and the vagaries of trial juries are a poor set of instruments to separate the innocent from the guilty. I asked him if he had had many opportunities to test his theories.

"A few," he said. "I worked for awhile with the coroner in Chicago, from which I learned a great deal about the mechanisms of homicide. While there, I helped a colleague snare a blackmailer through the paper and ink in his letters, and thus obtained a reference to a banker trying to catch forgers. And that, in turn, has led to other work, most recently here in California. Also," he continued, "I have been teaching myself to observe people scientifically, that is to say methodically and as objectively as possible, deducing facts about them from the physical marks left by their lives and occupations."

I allowed that he had read me pretty well that afternoon. Fanny asked what I meant, and I told her what Holmes had drawn from a moment's look at me, like a magician drawing scarves from a hat.

Holmes managed a smile. "I have to confess," he said, "that I'd heard your name before. Your accent and the evidence of your shirtsleeve led me to consider the possibility that you might be the writer of essays—though I couldn't account for your being so far from home. The rest was merely deduction from your physical appearance."

I had almost forgotten my curiosity about Holmes's peregrinations at the robbery scene, but Sam, who had been falling asleep at his mother's knee, sat up and asked, "What did you see when you looked around this afternoon? Did you figure out who the robber was?"

"Not yet."

"Are you going to keep looking for him?" Sam asked.

"I think I will," Holmes said.

"What will you do next?" I asked.

"Probably visit the manager of the bank that sent the payroll money."

"Ben Ingram," I said. "I know him fairly well, if you need an introduction."

Holmes looked interested. "Thank you. Would you mind riding there with me in the morning?"

I turned to Fanny. "Can you spare me?"

She looked at me earnestly. "We'll manage—but promise me you won't let yourself get too tired."

"I'll take good care of myself," I said.

She looked dubious but didn't protest. "Go, then. Sam and I can work on the packing."

I explained to Holmes that we were breaking up our camp and would soon be going back to San Francisco and thence to

Edinburgh—such is the perversity of the homesick Scot, to gladly abandon an earthly paradise for the cold gray hills of home.

Early the next morning, I made my way again to the hotel. Abashed by Holmes's comments on my dress, Fanny and I had polished my boots and combed the straw from my hair, and I was garbed like a gillie at his wedding in my one decent jacket and my least frayed shirt. Holmes was waiting, with two horses already saddled, and we followed the toll road down the mountainside to the plain where Calistoga lay steaming among its sulphur springs.

After the quiet of the mountain, the town seemed a clash and clatter of wagon wheels and shouted voices. Holmes stopped at both general stores and asked whether anyone had bought a large quantity of cayenne pepper recently, but no one recalled any such purchase. Among promenading carriages and wagons of dry goods we made our way to the bank and, once there, were directed to Ben Ingram's office.

Ingram greeted us, adorned with a businessman's smile. The man looked made for the part of a banker—sleek, pink-cheeked, and freshly shaved. His light brown hair flowed back from a smooth forehead, and his hearty mustache was neatly combed and trimmed. His starched and gleaming shirt front had not yet begun to wilt in the heat, and his pants still kept their press. The heavy gold chain that looped from his watch pocket to the buttonhole of his gray jacket murmured reassuringly of success and prosperity.

He shook hands with me. "Mr. Stevenson, good to see you again. How are the plans going for your trip to Scotland?" he asked cordially—the friendship of bankers being one of the advantages conferred on the struggling author by a sizable cheque from home.

"Well enough, I think. We'll be leaving for San Francisco in a few days. I'm going to miss the mountain air."

"You're looking the better for it, I'd say. This is a healthy climate," Ingram said proudly, turning to Holmes. "It'll build you up like no place else I know."

I introduced Holmes to him. "Mr. Holmes was a passenger on the stage that was held up yesterday."

Ingram's smile faltered, and he looked at Holmes a little suspiciously. "You didn't lose anything, I hope."

"No," Holmes said. "The gentleman took only the express box. I asked Mr. Stevenson to introduce me to you because I believe I may be able to help you catch the robber."

Ingram's eyes narrowed. "Why talk to me? Why not the sheriff?"

"Because I'll need certain information from you to follow up on the clues I've found."

"You know I can't give you any information about the bank's customers," Ingram warned.

"I do; I'm not looking for anything of that sort."

Ingram shrugged and said, "All right. Come into my office."

He showed us to two chairs in front of his desk and closed the door behind him, then pulled out his own chair and sank heavily into it. He leaned back, folded his hands across his vest at about the level of his watch chain, and appraised Holmes with narrowed eyes. "So—why do you think you can help us?"

Holmes began, with his usual coolness, "The sheriff told me that the last two robberies of the Lakeport stage both happened when it was carrying the Cinnabar Flats mine payroll."

"Yes," Ingram answered. "I'm aware of that."

"I assume you've considered the possibility that it was what the police would call an inside job."

Ingram looked less than surprised. "The second one only happened yesterday, so I haven't had much time to think about it, but yes, the thought has crossed my mind."

"Do you suspect anyone?"

Ingram thought for a moment. "Not yet. I think I know my clerks pretty well."

"Who knows when the payroll is shipped?"

"All of us, I guess."

"Has anyone quit recently?"

"No." He thought for a second, and added, "And all of us were here yesterday."

"Ah," Holmes said. "Could someone have told an outsider about the shipments?"

"You mean someone here might have been in cahoots with the robber? It's a possibility, I suppose, but I'd be surprised. All my men are honest, upright fellows." Another pause. "As far as telling someone by accident, everyone here knows we don't discuss bank business with outsiders—and that would go double with something like a payroll shipment. But why are you asking me all this, anyway?"

Holmes explained. "I have some professional experience investigating crime. This one happened right before my eyes, and"—he paused for a second as if choosing his words—"there are some details about it that interest me."

"So," Ingram asked, "are you trying to get me to hire you?"

"No," Holmes answered. "I assume the standard reward will be offered. I'm not asking you to pay me, just provide me some information."

"Perhaps," Ingram said. "It depends on what you're asking for."

"I'd like to talk with the bank employees individually, if that would be all right."

"They have work to do—" Ingram started to say, but changed his mind, possibly deciding that the offer of free help solving the robbery was worth the sacrifice of a few minutes of work time. "But I guess we could spare them for a bit."

Ingram had his secretary show us to a small room near the vault. "Stay here with me," Holmes said to me. "It's useful to have a witness, and if you don't mind, you can take notes."

One by one we called the men in, and Holmes questioned them. All of them seemed honest in their insistence that they had said nothing to anyone about the payroll shipment.

The last bank worker to be questioned was Ingram's secretary, Frank Leiden. We waited a few minutes, and when he did not come in, I went to find him. "Oh, he left awhile ago," one of the clerks told me. "Said he was feeling poorly."

Holmes went to Ingram's office and knocked on the door. Ingram was surprised to see us. "Where's Frank?" he asked.

"He left before we could question him," Holmes responded. "Can you tell us where he lives?" Ingram directed us to a clerk who looked up Leiden's address—a boardinghouse in town—in a ledger book.

The house was a few blocks south of the main street. Leiden's landlady told us she hadn't seen him since he left for work that morning, and his key was still on its hook in the hall. "If you don't mind, we'll wait for him," Holmes said.

We sat in the parlor, Holmes leaning back in his chair with his eyes closed but opening them whenever anyone came or went, like a cat sitting outside a mouse hole. Lacking his patience, I strolled out every couple of hours to look around town for Leiden.

I found him a little after sunset, in a dim, weather-beaten saloon next to the railroad depot. He was sitting at the far end of the bar, staring straight ahead, with an empty whiskey glass in front of him. He gave a start when I put my hand on his shoulder and turned to me with a look of haggard despair. I told him Mr. Holmes was waiting for him at his boardinghouse, and he sighed and rose a little unsteadily to his feet.

Leiden was about my height, not a bad-looking man, but a little soft and beginning to run to fat. His hair, dark brown and lank, had been combed back and parted in the center but was now falling forward onto his forehead; he pushed it back now and again with an almost unconscious gesture. He had a thick, dark mustache, but no beard; his face was sallow, with heavy-lidded black eyes, a sensual mouth, and the beginnings of a double chin. On the walk back to the boardinghouse, he swayed and occasionally stumbled against me with a mumbled apology. When we came through the door, he looked at Holmes and, with a groan and a heavy shake of his head, fetched his key and led us upstairs to his room.

Leiden offered us the only two chairs and sat slumped on the bed, with his head bent over his knees. "Oh, God, I'm in trouble," he said to no one in particular.

"Why is that?" Holmes asked, the even tone of his voice conveying no accusation.

Leiden looked up at us despairingly. "You know—that's why you're here. I'm the one who told about the mine payroll. I'm going to lose my job over it, maybe go to jail."

"Why did you do it?" Holmes asked.

Leiden looked at him, alarmed. "Look, I didn't have anything to do with the robberies," he said. "I talked to a damned whore, that was all. It was pure stupidity, I was drunk and running my mouth. She must have had a beau. I can't believe she'd do this to me." He slumped forward, shook his head, and gave a long, tremulous sigh.

"Whom did you tell?" Holmes asked.

Leiden looked darkly across the room at nothing in particular for a second or two, then back at Holmes. "Her name is Russian Annie—Antonia. She's one of the girls at Mrs. Bannerman's house in St. Helena." He lumbered to his feet and made his way to a small desk, where he took something from a drawer. Handing it to Holmes, he slumped down again on the bed. "That's her picture."

It was a pasteboard photograph of a pretty young woman with long, languid eyes. She was looking over her shoulder in a co-quettish pose and wearing a dress that showed a bit more of white shoulder and trim little ankle than propriety might allow.

"When was the last time you saw her?' Holmes asked.

"Last Saturday night."

"Do you see her often?"

"Couple of times a month—about as much as I can afford to. I kind of liked her, and I thought she felt a little something for me. Am I in trouble with the law over this?"

"Not if you're telling the truth," Holmes said. "And I suppose we'll know that when we talk to her."

"I'm in a hell of a mess, whatever happens," Leiden said bitterly. "Damn fool girl. I hope you find the son of a bitch that did it." He slumped forward again, muttering curses to his shoes.

Leaving Leiden to the examination of his conscience, we found rooms at Cheeseborough's Hotel. Before retiring, Holmes asked me if I was free to ride with him to St. Helena. I was too caught up in the chase to turn him down, so the next morning, I left a note to be sent to Fanny by the Lakeport stage, to let her know I had survived the night and would be spending the day in the valley.

In St. Helena, we found Mrs. Bannerman's house by asking the barman at the first saloon we saw in town. "I'm afraid you gentlemen will be disappointed," he said. "Mrs. Bannerman's ain't open for business this early in the day." We declined his kind offer to direct us to a lady whose hours might better suit ours, and he wished us good hunting. "You just come back here if she don't give you what you want."

Mrs. Bannerman's was a respectable-looking gabled house on a lane just outside the town. A dark-skinned maid answered the door and led us into a parlor adorned with red velvet drapes, a thick flowered carpet, and a piano whose dark wood was polished to a high shine.

I'd expected that the lady we had come to see would be middle-aged, but Mrs. Bannerman didn't look much past thirty. Her chestnut hair was elaborately dressed, and she wore a yellow silk dress whose tight contours showed a fine figure, but her face was powdered and rouged, and behind her graceful manner and pleasant smile her gray eyes were watchful and calculating. As she held out a kid-gloved hand and said, "How may I help you gentlemen?" her eyes were sizing up what we might want and what she could get out of us. Fanny would have called her "a tough customer."

Holmes did the talking, and I tried to do my part by looking grave and nodding at appropriate points. He suggested, without actually saying, that we were bank detectives looking for Miss Antonia to ask her some questions about one of her gentleman callers. When Mrs. Bannerman asked what it was about, he hemmed and hawed unctuously about the need for discretion and the protection of the confidences of bank customers. "Surely, Mrs. Bannerman, as a woman of business, you know how it is to be entrusted with, ah, sensitive information about one's clients," he intoned.

Mrs. Bannerman graciously smiled and said she was willing to help if she could. "We keep a nice establishment here, and I wouldn't want trouble. I'm afraid I can't introduce you to Annie, though. She left two days ago, all of a sudden. She said she was going to San Francisco. She and another girl who used to work here, Josette."

"Did she tell you where she would be staying?" Holmes asked.

"I'm afraid not," Mrs. Bannerman answered.

"Do you know why she was going there?"

"She didn't say, but my guess would be to find a doctor for Josette."

"So her friend is ill?"

"Yes."

"She just left without giving any notice? That must be difficult for you," Holmes said sympathetically.

"Oh, you have no idea," Mrs. Bannerman sighed. "This whole business has been a trial. Annie can't think of anything but Jo. She was too distracted; the men notice. She kept talking about getting Jo to some sanitarium Dr. Jenkins—he's the doctor I send my girls to—told her about up in Colorado. She was saving money for it; she asked me once to lend her the rest, but I said no. I'm not a rich woman, and these girls are so flighty—who knows if I'd ever get it back?" She unfurled a lacy fan, fluttered it a few times, and gave Holmes a look that assumed that of course he would understand. Then her expression changed, as if she'd thought of something, and she asked Holmes, "Do you think they ran off with the man you're looking for?"

"We don't know at this point," Holmes said. "Did she have a— uh—gentleman friend?"

"A fancy man, do you mean? No, not Annie. She never stepped out with anyone, so far as I know."

"Do you know how they were traveling?" Holmes asked.

"These days, everybody takes the train. But I hear Jo is at death's door, and if that's so, I don't know how they're even going to get to San Francisco."

We asked what Jo's illness was, and Mrs. Bannerman said, "Consumption." She formed her face into an expression of sympathy. "Poor girl."

"Indeed," Holmes said with the proper touch of gravity. "A pity." He paused for a second of appropriate silence, and then returned, as if reluctantly, to the business at hand. "Can you tell us what they look like?"

"Well," Mrs. Bannerman answered, "Annie is a bit taller than I am, and I'm five feet five inches. She has auburn hair, thick and straight, fair skin, gray eyes, a bit of a foreign accent—some of the men call her Russian Annie. Jo's a Creole from New Orleans, dainty as a little doll, with wavy brown hair and big, dark eyes. Before she got so sick, she was so pretty, the men just loved her."

"What are their full names?" Holmes asked.

Mrs. Bannerman gave an artificial laugh and looked at us under her eyelashes. "I can tell you what they told me, but, you know, these girls almost never tell the truth about their pasts. Oh, my—let's see—Annie goes by the name Antonia Greenwood. She told me once what her real name was—something foreign, I don't remember what. Jo called herself Josette Duverger."

"Do you know anything else about them?"

"Not really. They showed up here, together, oh, six months ago—Annie said they'd been working in a house in Sacramento, but came up here for Jo's health."

"You said Miss Duverger wasn't working here?" Holmes asked. "Where was she staying?"

She gave him another sly look. "You gentlemen seem real interested in them. How big a deal is this? Is there a reward?"

Holmes ignored her question and asked if she'd mind if we took a look around Annie's room. Mrs. Bannerman, obviously hoping to catch a crumb or two of information, offered to show us upstairs herself and led us up a stairway with carpeted treads and polished banisters.

A maid was in the room, cleaning it. The window was open, and the sun shining through white curtains gave the place a poignant air of innocence. In the wardrobe hung a wrapper of silk and lace and a couple of evening dresses. Some satin slippers had been left on the floor beneath them. Little else remained of the girl who had worn them, except a box of dusting powder and a worn hairbrush on the dressing table. Holmes picked up the hairbrush and examined it and looked into the drawers of the table and dresser. Mrs. Bannerman followed after him, peering over his shoulder. When he had finished, he turned to her and thanked her with a positively courtly bow. "If you should hear from Miss Greenwood, or learn anything about where she might be, please, by all means, send word to Mr. Ingram at the Bank of Calistoga."

As we walked downstairs, Mrs. Bannerman gave Holmes directions to the boardinghouse where Jo lived and to Dr. Jenkins's office. She showed us to the door herself, and as we left, said again that she would certainly help if she could. "I really don't want trouble here. I just hope they're all right," she said sweetly, looking deeply into Holmes's eyes. "You will tell me, won't you?"

"But of course," Holmes said, with a bow.

Dr. Jenkins's office was on the way to the boardinghouse. He was seeing a patient in his surgery, but when he finished, he showed us into his study and offered us a glass of sherry. He was a spare, graying man, with steel-rimmed spectacles and a weary air of having seen enough sickness and death to have despaired of finding any divine plan in it. When I mentioned Miss Duverger, he shook his head. "A hopeless case," he said. "There's nothing left to do for her."

Holmes told him what Mrs. Bannerman had said. "Oh, God," he sighed, and closed his eyes. "That Annie. I tried again and again to tell her, but she wouldn't—couldn't—accept that it was the end. I've seen mothers like that with children; they just can't stop fighting."

He remembered mentioning a sanitarium in the Colorado mountains. "Run by an old friend of mine, Harvey McKinnon, so I know the place is on the up and up. No one but quacks promise anything with this disease, but mountain air seems to help in some cases. Not Josette, she's too far gone. But Annie wouldn't listen; she had to have some hope, even a false one. So I gave her the name. Not that she could afford it; a woman in the life doesn't make that kind of money. So I told her about a specialist I know in San Francisco, Silbermann. That was awhile ago, though. At this point, Jo probably couldn't make the trip."

He was surprised and saddened when Holmes told him the two women had left St. Helena. "Honestly, she was too sick to travel; I saw her just the other day. It would have been kinder to let her die in her own bed."

After thanking the doctor, we rode to the boardinghouse, where the landlady, a gray sparrow of a woman, told us, with much fluttering, that Miss Duverger and her friend had left that morning. "She was too weak to walk; the porter had to carry her to the carriage." She was puzzled when Holmes said we were trying to find the women and asked to look in Miss Duverger's room. "I haven't cleaned it yet," she apologized.

"Better yet," Holmes said.

The room was small and plain. Nothing of Miss Duverger's was left in it except a couple of dog-eared novels, a jar of flowers and an empty medicine bottle on a table next to the bed. Holmes looked through the room and from under the bed pulled a small pasteboard trunk. In it, wrapped in an army blanket, were a pair of men's pants, a blue shirt, a hat, and a blue bandana. "She must have forgotten that," the landlady said. "But I can't imagine why she'd have those clothes. No man ever came to see her except Dr. Jenkins."

Holmes closed the trunk and asked her to keep it until he could send a man from the sheriff's office for it. Her eyes widened in alarm. "The sheriff? What have they done? They seemed like such quiet girls." Shaking her head, she said, "I should have listened to my sister. She told me not to let to women like that."

As we walked from the house to the street, I asked Holmes whether those were the clothes the robber had worn. He nodded.

"So she did give someone the information about the payroll. Is he still here, do you think, or is he meeting them in San Francisco?"

"Neither, I suspect," Holmes said, but when I asked him to explain what he meant, he shook his head. "I don't know enough yet."

I wasn't surprised when Holmes told me he intended to start for San Francisco on the next day's train. "I would go sooner, if it were possible. The trail is already getting cold," he said. "If Miss Duverger dies, it will be that much harder to find Miss Greenwood; she'll be free to move almost anywhere and far less conspicuous without her invalid companion."

I gave him the address where we'd be staying in San Francisco, and of my parents' home in Edinburgh. "Please," I asked him, "let me know whether you find the robber. I feel like a reader forced to lay down a book just as the story becomes exciting."

But the days that followed were so filled with breaking up our camp, moving our possessions to San Francisco, and setting up our temporary household there that I thought of the stagecoach robbery only in passing, to wonder idly whether I would ever learn the end of the tale.

We had been in San Francisco only a day or two when Sam answered a knock on the door, and I heard a familiar voice ask for me. Fanny was in the kitchen, but the damp air had played havoc with my lungs, and I was coughing the afternoon away before the fire in the sitting room. Sam, all excitement, brought Holmes into the room. When Holmes saw me, he stopped and apologized. "Mr. Stevenson—you're ill, I see. I'm sorry if I've disturbed you."

I stood up to greet him. "I'm not all that sick," I said with more valor than I felt. "It's good to see you again. Come, sit down."

"Not now, I'm afraid," he said, "I've come on urgent business."

"Really!" I replied, welcoming a distraction from my personal ills. "What is it?"

He looked around. "Is Mrs. Stevenson here?"

A little surprised, I answered, "Yes, she's—" A movement caught my eye and, looking toward it, I saw Fanny in the doorway, smoothing her apron. "Fanny," I called to her, "it's Mr. Holmes."

Fanny hurried in. "Mr. Holmes, how good to see you," she said warmly, and turned to me with a stern look. "Louis, you should be resting."

"I know—it's you Mr. Holmes has come to see," I told her.

A little flustered, Fanny turned back to Holmes, who seemed unsure how to begin. "It's about the stagecoach robbery," he said.

We both stared at him, Fanny as curious as I was to find out where she fit into the case.

"We've tracked down the robber, and we're at the point of making an arrest."

"Really! That's good news," I said. "How did you find him?"

"I'll tell you. But at the moment, the situation is rather difficult. You remember that one of the women was gravely ill."

"Yes—Miss Duverger."

"You have a good memory. She is still alive, though at death's door, from what I understand. But we are about to arrest her companion, Miss Greenwood."

Fanny's eyes widened, and her hand went to her lips. I started to speak, to ask further about the robber, but Holmes continued before I could get a word out.

"Miss Greenwood is quite desperate on her friend's account. I think it will go more easily if we have someone with us—a woman—who can care for Miss Duverger." He turned to Fanny. "I remembered that Mr. Stevenson praised your skill as a nurse, though I fear there will be little even you can do for her. The purpose of having you there is to reassure Miss Greenwood that her friend will be cared for in her last hours. It's a lot to ask, but do you think you could help?"

Fanny didn't hesitate. "Why not? Where is she?"

"Wait," I said, with an upwelling of husbandly protectiveness. "Is my wife going to be in danger?"

Holmes didn't hesitate. "No. There are only the two women."

"So where is the robber?"

"Quite safe."

"You've arrested him, then?"

"Not yet, but we will shortly."

I didn't feel much mollified, but Fanny had already left to gather her things. I pulled my jacket and hat off the coat rack and put them on. In a moment, Fanny was back, in shawl and bonnet, and carrying a small satchel. She looked at me in alarm and frank disapproval, and I answered her before she could speak. "I'm not letting you go there by yourself."

Had we been alone, she would have quite overpowered me, but with Mr. Holmes present she felt constrained from quarreling. "Louis, you're crazy," she sighed, with a dark look and a shake of her head. She turned to Holmes. "I'm ready," she said.

A four-wheeler was waiting outside for us, and Holmes directed it to an address I didn't recognize. On the journey there, he was his usual uncommunicative self. His silence was catching, and Fanny and I said hardly a word, though I kept her little hand wrapped tightly in mine. As the cab climbed hills and turned down one street after another, I lost track of its route, and when it finally stopped we were in a part of the city unknown to me, on a block of tall, funereal houses set close together like black cypress trees in a windbreak. The hills and the sea fog cut off any long view, and the street and houses seemed confined in a small space, like a stone castle in a fishbowl.

As Holmes was paying the cab driver, a man in a tweed suit appeared, seemingly out of nowhere, on the sidewalk beside us. He nodded a curt greeting and spoke to Holmes in a low voice. "Nothing new since you left, sir. Shall I stay out here?"

"No," Holmes said. "Come inside. Mrs. Stevenson is here, and I think it's time to speak to Miss Rostov."

"Holmes!" I whispered, caught up in the general trend toward *sotto-voce* speech. "What do you mean, Miss Rostov? Where is the robber?"

Holmes looked at me almost pityingly. "Miss Rostov is Miss Greenwood. Mrs. Stevenson is in no danger, I assure you."

Fanny placed her hand on my arm. "Louis, calm down. Don't you think I can take care of myself?"

"With an armed road-agent?"

"I'd say you've got him pretty well outnumbered," she answered, with a glance that took in the three of us.

Not at all comforted, I collected myself and followed Holmes and the rest up the steps.

A servant girl answered the door. "May we come in, Mary," Holmes said, "and would you please fetch Mrs. Paxton for us?"

Mary stepped aside, and we walked into the entrance hall, on the left side of which a carpeted staircase rose to the upper floors. Holmes directed us, with the exception of Fanny, to a parlor to the right of the hall. The tweed-suited man took up a position where he could not be seen from the staircase and left me to sit on a chair near the parlor door from which I had a view of the hall and stairs. "By the way," he said, "I'm Alva Weston, with the Pinkerton Agency." I introduced myself, and we settled back to waiting.

Mary went silently to the back of the house and returned a minute later, followed by Mrs. Paxton.

Mrs. Paxton was a stout woman, plainly dressed, with her brown hair pulled back into a bun. She was clearly in on the story, and as she introduced herself to Fanny and spoke quietly with Holmes, she seemed entirely self-possessed despite the knowledge that the mistress of a stagecoach bandit was hiding out in her upstairs rooms. At a word from her, Mary climbed the carpeted stairs and disappeared, descending soundlessly a few minutes later. "She says she'll be right down, ma'am," she said to Mrs. Paxton, and backed away into the rear of the hallway, to watch, wide-eyed, what might happen next.

No one spoke, and the little noises of the day seemed to fall like raindrops into a lake of silence. I could hear my own breathing, and I stifled a cough. I thought I heard a door close upstairs, and a moment later, without the sound of a footstep, a young woman appeared on the stairs. It was the girl in the photograph, with the same long, dark eyes. She was tall, straight, and slender, and her face had a slightly foreign look, with wide, high cheekbones and pale skin that seemed luminous in the half light of the stairway. Her auburn hair was gathered in a coil at her neck, and the plain dark dress she wore hung loosely on her. She descended slowly and stopped, halfway down, on seeing Holmes with Fanny and Mrs. Paxton.

"Who are you?" she asked.

"Sherlock Holmes, from the Bank of Calistoga."

"Oh." She didn't seem particularly surprised, but her eyes closed for a moment, and she seemed to grasp the banister more tightly with her left hand.

Weston had moved from his place of concealment to a spot between the stairway and the front door. He and Holmes held pistols concealed at their sides.

Holmes spoke again, in a calm voice. "Miss Rostov, please hand your gun to Mr. Weston, there."

She walked a few steps farther down the stairs toward Weston, removed her right hand from the folds of her skirt, and handed him a revolver. "It doesn't matter anyway," she said softly.

She turned back to face Holmes, steadying herself this time with both hands. "My friend is upstairs. Someone needs to take care of her; she's real sick. You can go see for yourself. It's no trick, I promise." Her words, though weighted by a slight foreign inflection, flew with the headlong earnestness of youth. For all her experience of men and their vices, I thought, she's still just a girl.

"I know," Holmes said. "I've brought someone to care for her," he said, with a nod to Fanny. The young woman paused for a second, looking at them, then turned toward the top of the stairs.

From the landing we followed her down a hallway to the right, where she unlocked a door, opened it wide, and stepped into a room. Holmes and Weston followed, and after a moment, Fanny and I joined them.

The room was, in fact, a pair of rooms, a sitting room with

chairs, a table, a small sofa under a bay window, and a bedroom behind it. Miss Rostov had gone directly into the bedroom and was leaning over the bed. Fanny followed her there, and I followed Fanny as far as the door.

A young woman lay in the bed, tucked in like a child under a patchwork quilt and propped up a little with pillows. So thin was she that the coverlet scarcely showed where her small body lay beneath it. Her face was colorless, wasted and haunting, delicate in its outline, with a small, pale mouth and shadowed eyes. Her dark hair was loosely braided, but a few tendrils, damp with perspiration, curled on her forehead. As I watched, her eyes opened and she looked up at Miss Rostov as if trying to see who she was. "Annie?" she asked in a voice hardly more than a sigh.

"Yes, *petite*," Miss Rostov said, putting a gentle hand on the invalid's brow and smoothing the damp hair from her forehead. The girl's lips moved in the hint of a smile, and she closed her eyes as if exhausted by the effort.

Miss Rostov returned to us closing the bedroom door behind her. "Are you going to arrest me now?"

Fanny looked at her and then at Holmes. "I hope not," she said. "I need to speak with you." Fanny pulled two chairs together at the table in the sitting room, sat in one, and motioned Miss Rostov into the other.

With Holmes's permission, Weston left the room to wait downstairs. Holmes established himself in the window seat somewhat apart from the rest of us. Unwilling to leave, I took a seat on a straight-backed chair from which I could see the door to the hallway.

Fanny spoke to Miss Rostov. "I don't even know your names," she began apologetically. "No one has gotten round to telling me."

The girl gave her a look as if she was trying to decide how far to trust her. "I am Annie—Antonia Davidovna Rostov. My friend," she continued, with a slight hesitation before the word, "is Josette—Josephine—LaFreniere."

"I'm Fanny Stevenson, and these two men are my husband, Louis, and Mr. Sherlock Holmes—whom you've met. Now, Antonia," she went on, gently, "I understand that a doctor has seen Josette."

Antonia answered in a low voice, "Yes."

"And has he told you what's wrong with her?"

"I knew that already—consumption."

Fanny leaned toward her. "And has he told you how serious her condition is?"

Antonia nodded. "Yes," she said. She hunched forward in her chair, her hands covering her face, and drew in a long, sobbing breath. "Damn—oh, damn!" she whispered. "I don't want to cry so loud, she might hear me." She looked at Fanny, suddenly contrite. "I'm sorry, ma'am."

"It's all right," Fanny said. "Nothing I haven't heard before."

"I tried so hard, you see," Antonia said. "I did all of it to save her—just to end up here." She gave another shuddering sigh. Her eyes welled with tears, and her hands, now in her lap, grasped each other, their knuckles white. "I killed her, didn't I? Bringing her here. I made her worse."

Fanny laid her hand on Antonia's arm. "No, you didn't." she said, firmly. "You tried to help, but there wasn't anything left to do."

The girl seemed to relax a little. "That's what the doctor said, too," she answered, almost reassured, it seemed, to hear Fanny confirm his verdict.

A hollow cough from the bedroom made both their heads turn toward it. "Come," Fanny said, and Antonia followed her to the room. The door closed behind them.

I moved near Holmes and asked him, in a low voice, "So where is the stage robber?"

Holmes gave a nod toward the bedroom door. "In there."

It took a second for the meaning of what he had said to reach me. "You don't mean Miss Rostov?"

"Yes," he said.

"That girl? Are you sure?"

He turned back to face me. "Yes. You've heard her; she has all but confessed."

I was still skeptical. "Holmes," I said, "I'm prepared to believe you that she and her friend are here alone. But how do you know the robber hasn't just deserted them?"

"By the accumulation of evidence."

"What evidence?"

"There were clues practically from the beginning," he said, "at the scene of the robbery itself. A tangle of long hairs on a bush. The prints of a small-sized boot in the mud where she had led her horse to drink in the stream. Evidence—broken twigs, tufts of wool from the blanket, a ribbon bow clearly torn from a dress—that she changed her clothing in the clearing."

"How did you know she wasn't just there with the robber?'

"The signs indicated that only one person, with one horse, was waiting in that spot," Holmes answered. "I saw nothing that suggested the presence of a second person, and neither did the other stage passengers. What Mrs. Bannerman told us also suggested that Miss Rostov wasn't passing information to a man. And there were the clothes under the bed—on which, on examination, I found another couple of long reddish hairs. And finally, there was her accent—which I noticed at the time, though no one else did.

"Once I was convinced that Miss Rostov was the robber, I was equally sure that she had no male confederate. What man would send a woman out alone to commit a highway robbery?"

"What you're saying makes sense—but it seems so unlikely."

"Perhaps, but it's true. We've been watching Miss Rostov for several days. She didn't know she was being pursued, so it was easy to find her here. She had, as Dr. Jenkins thought, consulted with Dr. Silbermann, who has been coming to look in on Miss Duverger—or, rather, LaFreniere—and told us where they were staying. With the help of the Pinkertons—hired by the bank—and Mrs. Paxton, we have watched them at all hours, and no man has visited Miss Rostov except the doctor.

"I also had Mr. Ingram send a man to St. Helena to make some inquiries. He learned that a young woman resembling Miss Rostov bought a quantity of cayenne pepper from a grocer there and that a similar woman, heavily veiled, hired a horse from a livery stable on the morning of the robbery. Does that put you more at ease?"

I acknowledged that it did, and Holmes fell silent, leaving me to consider what he had revealed and to wonder at the desperate, hopeless courage of the girl in the next room.

It was some time before Fanny came from the bedroom, alone. The gray daylight outside the windows was starting to fade, and a chill draft, borne by the fog, seeped through the window and played shiveringly, like the touch of a ghost, through the shadowed room. "She had a hemorrhage," she said to Holmes and me, "but the crisis is past, for now. Annie is asleep, too. She's exhausted; I don't think she's slept in days."

Holmes, who had been reading a book, looked up. "What is Miss LaFreniere's condition otherwise?"

Fanny lowered her voice. "It won't be much longer, I suspect. I'll be surprised if she lasts the night. Can't you let Annie stay with her until the end? It seems so cruel to leave that poor child to die among strangers."

Holmes said nothing, but signaled his assent with a nod and went back to his reading.

Time seemed to settle in the room like the fog itself. I read absentmindedly in a lady's novel that had been sitting on the table. A maid brought coffee and sandwiches and wine, lit the lamps, and laid a fire in the sitting room, and soon after that, Dr. Silberman arrived to examine Miss LaFreniere. He emerged from the bedroom, trailed by Fanny and Antonia and looking sober. "It's the end," he told them. "With luck, she won't wake up, but if she does and is in pain, give her some laudanum. God bless you both," he said, and was gone—home to wife and children, perhaps, or to dinner and good wine with his friends.

At Fanny's urging, Antonia sipped at some coffee and picked apart, rather than ate, a sandwich, and then returned to her chair in the bedroom. Fanny remained in the sitting room, but near enough to the bedroom door that she would hear any change in Jo's breathing. Revived by meat and drink and the warmth of the fire, I decided to escape the oppressive atmosphere of the sickroom and, with a whispered word to Fanny, left to wait downstairs.

Almost imperceptibly, the evening turned into night. Mrs. Paxton came into the parlor and said good night, trimmed the lamp, and retired to her apartment in the back of the house. The coal fire in the grate burned low. I grew tired, but could not sleep for coughing and thoughts of the scene upstairs. I felt that if I walked out into the street I would see Death beneath the low clouds, brooding over the house and enfolding it, and all of us, in its dark, sheltering wings.

Every hour or so, restless, I lit a candle and climbed the stairs, to look in on Fanny and Holmes. I could hear poor Josette's harsh breathing and see Antonia seated next to the bed, her bent head silhouetted in the light of the bedside lamp. Fanny looked steadfast and tired, and Holmes looked inscrutable.

The twilight of morning was starting to fill the rooms of the house with a dim underwater light when Fanny came quietly downstairs and whispered that the ordeal was over at last. We waked Weston, who had fallen asleep on the parlor sofa, and Fanny said to him, "Mr. Holmes said to send for the police van."

I followed Fanny back upstairs to the rooms. Through the bedroom door I could see Josette's body, as still as a sculpture on a tomb. She was laid out in a fresh dress of some light color, her hair carefully arranged. Antonia, pale and red-eyed, was in the outer room, sitting at the table with Holmes. "There was no one else," I heard her say to him, "just me. Even Jo didn't know where I got the money."

"Where is the money?"

"In the valise in the bedroom." Her face was without expression, her voice lifeless. "Everything's there except what I spent. None of it matters now." She looked around at Fanny and me, and then again at Holmes, and asked, "Is it time to go?"

"When the van comes, yes," Holmes said.

"We'll call the undertaker," Fanny said. "Everything will be taken care of."

Antonia nodded. "Thank you," she said. "May I sit with her until we have to leave?"

Holmes nodded, and Antonia walked into the bedroom, bent down and kissed Jo's forehead, and took her seat in the chair next to the bed.

In a half hour or so, Mary knocked on the door and told Holmes that the van was waiting. Antonia appeared at the bedroom door, in a hat and shawl. She stood a little straighter and squared her shoulders. "All right, I'm ready."

She left the room with Holmes, and a minute later Weston came in and took the valise. Fanny and I went downstairs and asked Mrs. Paxton to send for the undertakers and a cab, and retreated to the parlor to wait. The morning sun, though it shone bright outside, had not yet taken the chill from the room. Fanny curled against me and shivered slightly. "Are you all right?" I asked her.

"Yes, just tired."

I put my arm around her and held her close and, as I did, remembered again the long, cold weeks, so far from home, when Fanny had held me as I coughed blood, or hurried to my bedside as I wakened from a fevered sleep, her anxious eyes looking into mine. I thought how tired and despairing she must have felt then, when it seemed more than I could do to keep on with life at all.

The newspapers quickly caught wind of the case, and for the next few days, the *Call* and the *Bulletin* carried front-page stories of "Russian Annie, The Fair Desperado" and the "Parlor House Road

Agent," with lurid engravings depicting the robbery of the stage and Antonia's arrest. Holmes was mentioned as a private detective whose fortuitous presence on the stagecoach had brought him into the case and led to the apprehension of the "beautiful bandita."

With Mrs. Paxton's help, Fanny made arrangements for Jo to be buried in one of the cemeteries at the edge of town. On the day of her funeral, I was too ill to go out, but Fanny and Mrs. Paxton rode behind the hearse and paid their last respects, with a small crowd of onlookers, as the girl was laid to rest.

When I was recovered enough to see visitors again, Mr. Holmes came by to wish us farewell. Fanny had been fretful and peevish that morning, worrying about my health, the journey, and the fateful meeting with my parents. I had dismissed her fears. She had called me heartless; we had quarreled; and when Holmes arrived, we were sorting books in wounded silence. With an effort, we put on company faces, offered him the sofa, and seated ourselves on a couple of chairs.

He told us Antonia had pled guilty to the robberies and would probably be sentenced to several years in the women's prison. "Most of the stolen money was accounted for," he said, "though I understand that Miss LaFreniere had quite an elegant funeral." He turned to Fanny, who met his look unflinchingly.

After he had left, I asked Fanny what Holmes had meant by his remark. "Did she give you money?"

She paused over the box of books she was packing. "Yes. She paid for the funeral, and for a plot in the cemetery and a headstone, so Jo wouldn't have to be buried in the potter's field."

"With money from the robberies?" I asked, knowing what the answer was.

She turned on me a look like the sighting of a pistol. "Do you care?" she asked. Her anger receded as quickly as it had risen, and a shadow of sadness darkened her face. She looked at the book in her hand, as if retrieving a memory, and then said quietly, "They were all alone, so far away from home—somebody had to do something."

ABOUT THE AUTHORS

RHYS BOWEN (*"Cutting for Sign"*)
Creator of the highly enjoyable Constable Evans and Molly Murphy novels, Bowen had her first play, *Dandelion Hours*, produced by the BBC in London. Since then she has been the author of award-winning children's books, young adult books, historical romances, and mysteries.

CAROL BUGGÉ (*"The Curse of Edwin Booth"*)
The author of five novels and numerous short stories, Buggé has received awards and glowing reviews for her poetry, her plays, and her fiction. She has been awarded a fellowship for a residency at the International Retreat for Writers at Hawthornden, just outside Edinburgh, Scotland, and her next novel will be published by Kensington Press later this year.

DARRYL BROCK (*"My Silk Umbrella"*)
The author of the best-selling novel *If I Never Get Back*, Brock writes regularly on subjects dealing with baseball, Mark Twain, and the American past.

STEVE HOCKENSMITH (*"The Old Senator"*)
Hockensmith is the author of the Edgar-nominated *Holmes on the Range* and, so far, two sequels featuring the "deducifying" Amlingmeyer brothers. He writes regularly for *Ellery Queen's Mystery Magazine.*

LESLIE S. KLINGER (*Foreword*)
The editor of the Edgar-winning *The New Annotated Sherlock Holmes: The Complete Short Stories, The New Annotated Sherlock Holmes: The Novels,* and *The New Annotated Dracula,* Klinger is one of the world's foremost authorities on Sherlock Holmes.

MICHAEL KURLAND (*the editor*)
Kurland has edited two previous Sherlock Holmes anthologies. His fifth novel featuring Professor Moriarty, *Who Thinks Evil* will be published shortly. Previous books in the series have been nominated for both the Edgar and the American Book Award.

GARY LOVISI (*"The American Adventure"*)
Lovisi's Holmes pastiche "The Adventure of the Missing Detective" was nominated by the Mystery Writers of America as one of the best short stories of 2005. His latest books include *The Secret Adventures of Sherlock Holmes* and *Sherlock Holmes: The Great Detective in Paperback & Pastiche.*

RICHARD A. LUPOFF (*"Inga Sigerson Weds"*)
Lupoff is the author of numerous science fiction, fantasy, horror, and mystery novels and short stories, as well as nonfiction books on subjects ranging from Edgar Rice Burroughs to the workings of the human mind. His story "The Incident of the Impecunious Chevalier," first published in *My Sherlock Holmes,* was picked for a Best Mystery Stories of the Year anthology.

MICHAEL MALLORY (*"The Sacred White Elephant of Mandalay"*)

Mallory is the author of the Amelia Watson mystery series, including the collection *The Exploits of the Second Mrs. Watson* and the novel *Murder in the Bath*, as well as nearly 100 short stories. His story "The Beast of Guangming Peak" (from *Sherlock Holmes: The Hidden Years*) was named a Distinguished Mystery Story of 2004 in the 2005 edition of *The Best American Mystery Stories*.

MARTA RANDALL (*"The English Señor"*)

The author of seven novels, among them the mystery *Growing Light* (as Martha Conley), Randall has written bunches of short stories, has edited original anthologies, and teaches writing in various venues.

LINDA ROBERTSON (*"The Stagecoach Detective"*)

An attorney for a nonprofit California law firm, Robertson has been published in the online magazine *Salon*, and has had both fiction and nonfiction published in newspapers and magazines. Two previous Sherlock Holmes pastiches have been published in the anthologies *My Sherlock Holmes* and *Sherlock Holmes: The Hidden Years*.

PETER TREMAYNE (*"The Case of the Reluctant Assassin"*)

Best known for his best-selling Sister Fidelma mysteries, featuring as his sleuth a seventh-century Irish religieuse, Tremayne has also published many fantasies using Celtic myths and legends as background. In 1981 he published *The Return of Raffles*, a pastiche about the "gentleman thief."